$\mathscr{S}$LUMBER

D1520954

05/19

Map of Phaedra

Index of Terms

The Rada – The Council
The Dravilec – Healers
The Glava – Psychics
The Azyl – Seekers
The Dyzvati – Evokers

Terms of Royalty and Nobility
Kral – King
Kralovna – Queen
Prince – Prince
Princezna – Princess
Vojvoda – Duke
Vojvodkyna – Duchess
Markiz – Marquess
Markiza – Marchioness
Grof – Earl
Grofka – Countess
Vikomt – Viscount
Vikomtesa – Vicountess
Baron – Baron

Might there come a time
When we stand over a grave
And mourn ourselves;
Mourn the past, a previous life?
Shall we weep for the passing of time?
Shall we grieve for unfulfilled dreams?
In my naivety; in my belief
In immortal youth,
I sleep walk through life.
Someone... wake me up.
Please.
Wake me up.
Slumber – Haydyn Dyzvati

TO MUM AND DAD
THE MOST SUPPORTIVE KRAL AND KRALOVNA THIS PRINCEZNA
COULD EVER ASK FOR.

Prologue

When I was a child the world smelled of summer.

The heady perfume of the dancing wildflowers would hug my senses every time the breeze rattled their song and took them with it on its journey to soothe my cheeks from the heat of the afternoon sun. I loved the relieving scent of the damp soil when the sun had pushed the sky too far and it wept rain for days on end. Then there was the refreshing aroma of lemons in the thick air of the house, mixing with my mother's baking as she prepared our afternoon repast of bitter lemonade and thick warm bread, slathered with creamy butter made cold from the sheltering shade of the larder.

The most comforting of all scents was my father's pipe. The sweet odor of tobacco would tickle my nose as he held me close and whispered the stories of our Salvation and the mighty Kral who lived in the grandest palace in all the land with his beautiful daughter the Princezna. Father would tell me of how kind and gentle they were— that they were the reason my private world was one of innocence and endless summer.

My memories of that life never leave me. I can still hear the sound of my brother's laughter carrying back to my young, happy ears as we ran through the fields of purple and gold, racing over the farm to the brook that ran behind our land. The gentle trickle of that stream drew us each day— my brother for the rope swing he had looped around the strongest tree, the one with the trunk that seemed to bend towards the water, as if thirsty for a taste of its pure relief. For me I was drawn to its coolness on my skin, its moisture in my dry mouth, its familiar smell, like damp metal and wet grass.

Sometimes I hear my mother calling our names in my dreams.

There was no warning to summer's end. Its end began like any other day. I lay with my brother beneath the shadow of an oak by the brook's edge, my young voice barely heard above the babbling water as I recounted the story my father had told me over and over, to my little brother. I could hear my father's rich voice in my head, had memorized every word, and as I recited it, I remembered to speak in the hushed, awed tones my father used to make a story sound as magical as this one really was.

"Eons and eons ago, our people were the most blessed of mankind. Powerful and beautiful we could tap into Mother Nature and draw from her powers. We were magical beings, spiritual and wondrous to behold. But mankind grew envious of us, and wise as we were we knew mankind, with so many wars already brewing between its people, could not withstand a war with us. The wisest of us persuaded everyone it was time to fade from mankind's earth, to fade as one into a world of our own making. We drew from the earth and imagined a paradise. Mankind began to melt around us as we fell deep, deep into the fade. When our people awakened it was to find themselves here in the Phade, in a new born land; a sky, a moon, a sun, trees, plants, water, and all animals familiar to them awaiting them— awaiting them to begin the new world in peace. Fearful of our emotions betraying us as they had to mankind it was decided that the Dyzvati, a clan of magical evokers, with the ability to lull the people and the land with peace, would reign as the royal family. The Dyzvati named our land Phaedra, splitting it into our six provinces, giving a province to the clans with the most powerful magic. Sabithia in the south was taken by the Dyzvati, and they built a beautiful palace in the capital city of Silvera, where the shores of the Silver Sea edge its coast with its vibrant silver surf. To the Clan Glava— the largest and most powerful of the mage with their many psychic abilities—was given Javinia to the east of Sabithia and also Daeronia in the northeast."

I turned my head to smile at my brother who gazed at me enraptured by the story. "And our own slice of haven, Vasterya, was given to the Clan Azyl—seekers: mage with the ability to seek whatever their hearts desired. Eventually, the Azyl became servants of the Dyzvati, using their abilities to seek whatever the royal family wished, helping the upkeep of the peace in Phaedra. Many centuries onwards and the Azyl's magic had evolved with their position. They were no longer able to seek that which they wished for themselves, only what others wanted sought."

"That's a little unfair." My brother frowned and I nodded in agreement. I thought so.

"The province of Daeronia, beyond the northern borders of Sabithia, was given to Clan Dravilec, the healers, to keep them close to the Dyzvati." I thought on how much a fairytale this sounded now, a many millennia on from the beginning of Phaedra. "Now there are so few mage left. Papa says there are none left in Vasterya at all. And now only the Kral and Princezna Haydyn remain of the Dyzvati."

My brother was no longer listening to me or my woe over our people's sad evolution. "What about Alvernia?" He asked instead in a hushed voice.

I shivered at the thought of Alvernia, at the thought of the stories I'd heard of the rough, uncivilized, northern mountain people; terrifying tales of their macabre misdeeds and unsettling lifestyle.

And all because the power of the Dyzvati waned towards the middle of their province.

"It was given to those of middling magical abilities. And as there were so many Glava, a few of them set themselves up in the southern most point, in the city of Arrana."

"Where the Vojvoda lives?"

"Where the Vojvoda lives."

"I wish I was a Vojvoda. Or a Markiza. Or a Vikomt!" He cried excitedly, pushing himself up into a sitting position. "I'd have horses. Lots of horses. And gold! We could play treasure hunt!"

I laughed and pushed him playfully. "All those titles and you didn't choose the best."

"What?!" He pouted.

I stood up, bracing my small hands against my youthful hips, legs astride, chin defiant. "Why… Kral of course!"

"Yeah!" He jumped to his feet now, mimicking my stance. "I am Kral of Vasterya!"

"And me?"

"My servant."

I growled in mock outrage. "Servant indeed."

I still remember the sounds of his beautiful laughter as I chased him for his teasing.

At the grumbling of our bellies, my younger brother and I reluctantly ceased playing and began walking back towards the house. I remember holding his hand as we wove our way through the fields. I remember the gust of wind that shook the gold and purple and blew my hair back from my face, sending shivers of warning down my spine. My feet moved faster then, tugging on my brother each time my heart beat a little quicker.

I remember the expression on my father's face when we appeared out of the fields. Pale and slack, his eyes bleak as they drank me in. My mother clung to his arm, as tiny as my favorite doll, her eyes just as glassy. At the sound of a horse's nicker I turned to see who stood outside our home. Four men. All dressed in livery that matched those of their horses. My eyes were drawn to the emerald and silver heraldic badges with the silver dove crest in the middle. Our symbol of peace.

They were from the palace.

I do not know why but I was scared. I remember trembling so hard I thought I must be shaking the very ground beneath my feet. Whatever reasons unknown my instincts had me pulling my brother behind my back, out from the view of the men looming ominously over our parents.

One of them descended from his beast. He did not wear the livery.

He came towards me like a serpent slithering on the ground, his purple cloak hissing in the breeze. His eyes were the deepest black and probing, so fixated on me I shivered in revulsion as if he had actually touched me.

"This is the one."

"You're sure?" The soldier who towered above my parents asked gruffly.

The serpent smiled at me, ready to strike his killing blow. "She is the one."

"No!" My father bellowed as my mother whimpered at his side. "Run, Rogan! Run!"

But I was frozen in place by their panic. An ice sculpture who watched two soldiers hold my father while he struggled in their arms as a third pulled a dagger from his belt and plunged it into father's heart. He twitched and stiffened in their hold, a horrifying, gurgling noise making its way up through his chest to spurt a thick, bloody fluid out of his mouth and down his chin. My mother's screams played the soundtrack to this memory before the dagger-wielding soldier strolled towards her crumpled figure, his black gloved fingers stroking comfortingly over her hair. They slid like leeches down to her throat and back up to her cheeks.

And then he twisted her head between his hands with a jerk that sent an echoing crack around my world.

At that moment I felt a tug on my hand and remembered my brother. With a thousand screams stuck in my throat I whirled with him and began to run, dragging him with me into the cover of the fields, my father's last shouts reverberating in my ears. I drowned out the sounds of my shallow, panicked breaths, the hiccupping cries of my brother as I practically hauled him with me, and the hollering and thundering behind us that made me race harder.

When the thundering eased I knew I had lost them in the fields. We were small and knew the land as well as we knew each tiny scar and line upon our palms. I headed east, picking up my brother when he tripped, and shushing him when I was no longer sure we were alone. At last we reached the cave my father had punished us for hiding in only a year before. *Bears*, he had warned. But now I feared the soldiers from the palace more than the bears. The soldiers wanted me. Why? I did not know. But they had slaughtered my parents to have me. Would they murder me too? My brother? At the thought I burrowed him against me in the dank cave, and felt his tears soak my dress.

"I'm sorry," he had whispered.

I wanted to tell him he need not apologize for crying, for grieving, but I feared if I spoke all my screams would burst forth with terrifying consequences.

"I didn't mean to."

At that, I pressed him back until a shaft of light filtered over his face. He looked so lost my young heart broke over and over again. He clutched his trousers, turning away from me, and it was then the smell hit my nostrils. I began to cry. I did not want him to be ashamed of his fear. He was so little.

"It's okay," I whispered and made to reach for him, but his shirt slipped through my hands as he was whipped out of sight. I think I yelled before I stumbled blindly after him back into a day that had suddenly turned gray. Back into a day that had once blazed in a beautiful fire of heat and life. Now it was gone. And as my gaze found my brother, I realized even the last sparks of the embers had been snuffed out, leaving only the fire's funeral shroud of smoke.

My brother's small body lay at the feet of the cave, the dagger edged in blood from his neck slipping back into its place on the soldier's belt.

The serpent stepped over my brother's body and knelt before me.

"Say goodbye to your family, Rogan. A new one awaits you."

Chapter One

I ached. I had never felt such pain before. But I had never been on a horse for so long, nor trapped in the embrace of the man who rode the horse. I was so stiff from keeping my body as far from his as possible, a difficult task with his long arms encircling me in order to hold the reins.

I didn't know where we were. It was dark and even muggier here. We had moved south. I twisted my neck to look at Kir, who rode trapped between the Captain of the Guard and the reins of his horse, Destroyer. Such a fitting name. He had helped the despicable mage behind me, Vikomt Syracen Stovia, a Glava, destroy my life as well as Kir's.

The Kral was dead.

Only Haydyn Dyzvati, Princezna of Phaedra, remained of the evokers. Kir told me Stovia was collecting those left with rare magic to help protect and reinforce the sovereignty, until Haydyn came of age and produced more children of the Dyzvati.

Kir was one of the Glava— a telekinetic.

"The Dyzvati power has waned," Kir had whispered to me, his eyes flickering to our guard not too far from us. That had been only two nights after the murder of my family. Kir had been with the Guard for a week. The other soldiers ate and talked quietly around the campfire. "Syracen has taken advantage of it. The way he talks…

as if the violence of his crimes is justified. He's protecting the sovereign and the peace of Phaedra. With blood and cruelty. With the selfish pursuit for the last of the mage."

"But I'm not a mage," I had whispered in shock.

We were sitting together offside of the fire. Strangers. But the wiry boy, a few years my senior, shared the haunted look in my eyes. They had destroyed his family too.

Kir had shrugged. "You must be."

But I wasn't. Was I?

I caught Kir's eyes now as we moved swiftly and quietly into the small village. His face was taut, his eyes narrowed. Something was happening.

The horses drew to a stop, not even a snort, so obedient to their masters will. An unpleasant shock went through me at the feel of Stovia's hand in my hair.

"Now, little one," he whispered in my ear. "Time to see how well that magic of yours works."

I shifted away from him. "I have no magic."

He chuckled. "You're one of the Azyl, child."

One of the Azyl? No. He was mistaken.

"I'm not." I looked to Kir for help. He could only look on.

With a growl, Stovia dismounted from the horse and none-too-gently ripped me from the saddle. My feet hadn't even hit the ground and he was shaking me, my eyes rolling back in my head with the force of it. "Stop pretending!" He hissed as he let me go. I stumbled and he lowered his body so his austere face was level with my own. Those wickedly black eyes burrowed through me. "In this village is one of the Dravilec. I want you to seek out my healer, Azyl. Now."

At the command I felt a wave crash through me, my whole body humming with tingling vibrancy. A mind of its own, my body turned to face the village. And I could feel her. The Dravilec. Six years old. Valena of Daeronia. We were in Daeronia. Thought so. We were growing closer to Sabithia. To Silvera. To the Princezna.

Wait.

I am an Azyl.

I swayed at the thought. All the time my father had told me the stories. All this time my brother and I had been desperate for a little piece of magic in our lives. And I was a mage. I wanted to cry. I wanted to be with my family.

What would Stovia do to Valena's family? Would he murder them in cold blood if they refused to hand her over? I knew, even without my help, that he would find Valena. He was a powerful Glava. Could sense magic. But that didn't mean I had to aid in the destruction of another family.

"No," I whispered.

"What?" Syracen growled.

I spun around, defiant, hatred blazing out of my eyes. I wished I was Glava with the ability to summon the elements. I'd set him on fire and watch him burn for what he had done to me. To Kir. For what he would do to Valena.

"I said... no."

His hand cracked against my face with such force I hit the ground. The breath whooshed out of me at the agonizing blow to my ribs as I made impact with the hard dirt. My eyes watered at the painful heat across the left side of my face, and I felt something warm trickle from my mouth. Hissing at the pain, I tasted copper where my lip had been split.

I heard Kir cry out my name.

But Syracen wasn't done. He grabbed me by the clasp on my cloak and held me so he could slap me across the right side of my face. The world rang in my ears. But I refused to cry.

"Find me the healer, girl, or you'll wish you were dead."

"No!" Kir yelled and I could hear the sounds of a struggle.

"Shut him up," Syracen hissed.

I heard the sound of flesh hitting flesh, of Kir grunting. No.

"No," I groaned, lolling limply in Stovia's grasp. "Stop."

"Will you find the Dravilec."

I couldn't. "No."

"Lash the boy to the nearest tree. He's going to pay for Rogan's disobedience."

My heart lurched in my chest and I shrugged around Stovia to watch through blurred vision as they dragged a bleeding, crying Kir to the nearest tree trunk. They ripped at his shirt. One of them produced a horse whip and Kir whimpered in terror. I felt vomit rush up my throat but I willed the acidic show of weakness down.

"Stop," I murmured weakly. "Stop. Don't hurt him. I'll do it."

I looked to Stovia. He watched me closely. Seeming fascinated. Then he nodded at his men and they quickly drew Kir's cloak over him and dragged him back to the horses. His right eye was already swelling shut and I imagined my left eye was much the same.

"Tut tut, Rogan," Syracen whispered, bending down to gaze at me face to face. "You've just shown me your weakness. I imagine I could have battered you into an oblivion of agony and you would not have given in. But you won't let someone else be hurt because of you. Interesting. And useful. Now find me the Dravilec."

I was gripped with nauseating shame as I took the guards through the winding, quaint, peaceful village. By now, we had made enough noise to rouse people from their homes, and they gathered on their doorsteps nervously as their eyes took in the Royal Guard and the two beaten children with them. I came to a stop at the doorstep of a shop. An apothecary.

"Here."

Syracen smiled at me, his eyes brimming with pride. I hated him. "Yes, it is. Thank you, Rogan."

He pulled the rope by the door and a brass bell rang loudly. We heard hurried footsteps and then the door was thrust open by an older man, tall and imposing.

"Can I help?" He queried, warily.

"I am Vikomt Syracen Stovia of the Rada. May I come in, Mr. Rosonia?"

Rosonia's eyes widened but he nodded, his oil lamp casting his profile against the shadows of the wall. Syracen turned back and nodded at two guards who strode forward to follow at his back. Sadistically, he pushed me past the threshold of the door. He wanted me to witness this.

Once inside Rosonia stood with a stout, middle-aged woman who appeared frightened, clutching her robes tightly around her. Two girls stood behind them. One was a tall, attractive girl, possibly in her early teens. Clutching her hand was Valena. Small and frightened, her large dark eyes too big for her face.

"I come bearing sad news." Syracen stood before them, intimidating and powerful. "The Kral is dead."

The Rosonias gasped at the news.

"Yes. I am afraid it is true. Princezna Haydyn is now alone in the world, the weight of carrying the load of Dyzvati too great for her young shoulders. As the only mage upon the Rada I feel it is my duty to seek whatever her highness needs to aid her in her mighty responsibilities."

"What can we do to help, My Lord?" Valena's father asked eagerly, his eyes full of genuine sadness for the Kral.

"There is very little magic left in our world. But I've been collecting the strongest of the magic. Here," he put his deadly hand upon my shoulder and I fought not to shudder, "Is one of the Azyl, thought to be extinct. But she found you well enough."

I saw how Mr. Rosonia and his wife gasped at my appearance. "What happened to the child?"

"One of my soldiers. He has been dealt with," Syracen lied smoothly. "But you have in your keeping someone who could help my little Rogan."

"Mama." The elder girl looked frightened now, drawing Valena closer. "Don't."

They knew why he was here.

"Valena." Mr. Rosonia exhaled heavily. "She is one of the Dravilec then?"

"You had your suspicions?" Syracen asked.

Valena's father merely nodded.

"She is needed. Your daughter is needed by her people."

"You want to take her?" The mother now spoke up, her voice trembling.

Syracen smiled. "She will be well cared for at the palace. And you may visit. She will be taught by the Royal Dravilec how to use her power. She is strong. I could taste her energy from Sabithia it was so strong."

The Rosonias stood in silence for a moment, mother and father questioning one another with their eyes. Finally, Valenia's father turned to Syracen and nodded. "You may take her, my lord."

I gasped in outrage. My parents had died rather than see me in the hands of this slithering beast of a man, and I wasn't the only one outraged. The elder girl shrieked and grabbed Valena to her, refusing to let her go. Valena screamed and cried— terrified and confused she did not know what was happening. Mr. Rosonia managed to wrench Valena free. He let his wife take her upstairs.

She returned quickly, Valena dressed snug and warm, but still crying. Her mother hugged her, quiet tears rolling down her cheeks as her daughter clung to her. Her husband came over and pulled Valena away, ignoring his elder daughter, who sobbed in a ball on the ground. He kissed Valena's cheeks, choking back his own tears as he promised her he would see her soon. Seconds later he handed her into the arms of Syracen Stovia. Immediately, sensing what only children could, she began shrieking and beating at him to let her go. Careful to hide his disgust, Syracen reached down and thrust the squalling six year old in my arms. I pressed her close, ashamed for my part in all this. Valena stopped struggling, and instead looped her little arms around my neck, her legs around my waist, and bawled into my shoulder. A memory of my little brother doing the same not too many weeks ago when he had fallen from a tree and cut his leg flashed through my mind and I squeezed the girl closer, as if I alone could protect her.

Stovia hurried us out of the house and we walked a distance away to the bridge that would take us out of the village.

"Lieutenant Sandstone," Stovia called quietly, and the soldier trotted forward on his horse, "Take Valena. I can't carry the two on my horse."

Sandstone dismounted and tried to pry Valena from me. The girl began to shriek, her tiny hands gripping my cloak, my hair, refusing to budge. And even though I winced at her tight hold, I refused to hand her over.

"That's enough," Syracen grunted. He pushed Sandstone out of the way and gripped a hold of Valena, bruising her small arms as he ripped her from me. I cried out as his arm swooped down, his hand cracking across her face. I rushed at him in a rage, beating and pushing at him until I was pulled off by the soldier. Syracen, to spite me, hit Valena one more time. Sobbing, furious, I fought against the soldier only to be beaten by the pummeling fists of the Captain of the Guard. The next thing I knew Kir was in the fray, hitting and punching at those who tried to hurt us. I no longer felt pain though. I was too angry— too immersed in my fury to feel anything else.

Finally, I was pinned to the ground by the Captain and as he stared down at me I noticed his eyes for the first time. They were blank. Empty.

"Captain... After we leave the village, I want you to take two of your men and burn the apothecary to the ground. With the Rosonias inside," Syracen demanded from somewhere to my left.

The Captain nodded robotically, and it was then I knew. With the evocation of the Dyzvati weakened by Princezna Haydyn's grief and age, Syracen's magic was able to penetrate it. He was compelling the soldiers to do his awful deeds.

I was lifted to my feet, my heart heavy and despairing.

Syracen appeared before me, holding Valena close, her little cheeks red from his slaps. "Now you can live with the fact that you just had Valena's family killed."

My despair must have translated to my face for Syracen laughed gleefully.

"Don't, Rogan." Kir struggled against a soldier, his young face mottled with anger. *"He was going to have them killed anyway. Don't let him make you think you did it."*

Syracen curled his lip in disgust. *"I've had enough of you. Sandstone!"*

The whip appeared in the soldiers hand and Kir was pushed into the dirt.

"NO!" I screamed, my heart lodged somewhere in my throat. *"NO!"*

"NO!" I bolted upright in bed. The sheets twisted around my body, my skin clammy, my hair stuck to my neck. Immediately, I sensed I wasn't alone. Turning slowly, I saw her sitting in an armchair by my bed.

"You were having a nightmare again." Her soft, gentle eyes were sad. "More memories?"

I nodded, feeling choked, the nightmare still keeping me in its hold. "More memories."

Haydyn sighed and slowly drew to her feet. I watched her float across my large bedroom suite and pull the heavy brocade curtains back from my windows. I winced as sunlight streamed in, too bright, too adamant, willing my bad memories away whilst I steadfastly anchored myself to them.

"I told you I'd speak to Raj to see if he had a tonic to help you sleep without the dreams."

Raj was the Royal Dravilec, and Valena was his apprentice. I shook my head. "I told you no."

"You're the only one who ever says no to me." Haydyn sauntered back to sit on my bed. Her pale hair shone almost silver in the sunlight, her beautiful face teasing and serene. "I wonder why I let you."

"Because you love me," I responded matter-of-factly as I pushed back the covers to get washed and dressed for the day.

"Yes, I do."

The statement was so melancholy I spun around to scrutinize her. It was then I saw it. That gloom in the back of her eyes, and the slight, dark purpling underneath them. The gloom had been appearing more and more over the last few weeks and I didn't like it. "Something's the matter."

Haydyn shook her head. "Just tired is all."

"Perhaps we should speak to Raj about a tonic for *you*."

She didn't look convinced but as always, to appease me, she nodded. "Perhaps."

I grimaced when I realized she was fully dressed for the day. Most times when Haydyn came into my suite it was still so early she was in her nightclothes. "I overslept?"

Haydyn grinned. "Haven forbid, but you did."

I rolled my eyes at her teasing. "You know I hate oversleeping. It muddles up my entire day."

"I know. That's why I let you sleep." She grinned unrepentantly. Sometimes she really was like an annoying younger sister. "You need a little ruffling up now and then, Rogan."

Making a face at her suggestion I was too straight-laced (which we both knew to be as far from the truth as possible), I pulled on the servant's bell to let them know I was ready for my morning bath. They would attend to me as quickly as they would attend Haydyn. After all I was her best friend, her family. I had been ever since I had been brought to the palace eight years ago by Syracen Stovia. I was only eleven years old at the time. Haydyn was nine. At my arrival, Valena was quickly ripped from me and given to Raj. Kir was taken to live with Syracen and his family. And I was left at the palace with Haydyn.

Both grieving for the families we'd lost it hadn't taken long for us to find solace in one another.

Haydyn's mother had died in childbirth, leaving Haydyn alone with her father. The Rada had pushed and pushed him to take another wife, to have more children, but he had loved Haydyn's mother too dearly. He couldn't bear the thought of making someone else his Kralovna. That left only the Kral and his baby daughter. Two peas in a pod they were, Haydyn told me. Inseparable. She had depended on her father for everything in life. Love, comfort, affection, friendship, advice, security. With him gone she was adrift. And I happened to be the float she grasped on to in his passing. She demanded I be put in the suite next to hers, where I had roomed ever

since. I was to be given the run of the palace as if I were royalty.
And I was. In return she looked to me for love, comfort, affection,
friendship, advice and security. I feared my presence was hindering
Haydyn to become the truly independent leader Phaedra needed, but
I gave her my strength because she was the only family I had left.
Moreover, I owed her. After a number of years of begging me to tell
her why I screamed in my sleep, I told her what Syracen Stovia had
done to my family, Kir's and Valena's. There was only my word
against his. By then I had been at the palace for four years. Kir had
run away only a year after our arrival and Haydyn had grown strong
enough that Syracen didn't chase him for fear of disrupting the
peace. As for Valena, she couldn't remember anything before being
brought here. Of course Syracen hadn't done anything violent or
untoward since Haydyn's evocation returned and overpowered him.

But she believed me and she made the Rada listen to me. She
ordered that all twelve members of the Rada travel to Silvera to
judge Vikomt Syracen Stovia for his crimes. Even if the Captain of
the Guard had not come forward and confessed what he remembered
doing under the compulsion of Syracen, I knew Haydyn would not
have stopped until he was punished. She was only thirteen. But I was
her family. And I was not to be hurt.

I pledged my everlasting loyalty to Haydyn that day.

The Rada *were* disgusted by Syracen's methods and ordered him
imprisoned in Silvera Jail – a lone prisoner. He didn't take the news
well. I remember the sweat beading on his forehead and the
nosebleed he sustained as he fought to break through Haydyn's

evocation. Powerful as he was, he was strong enough to reach for Haydyn to use her as a shield in order to escape. The Captain of the Guard did his duty, however, and killed the threat to the Princezna's life. His death didn't ease my grief. But I felt freer than I had since the death of my family.

The servants arrived and Haydyn took her leave while I helped the girls fill the bath with the hot water. Like every morning they swatted at me to stop.

"The Handmaiden of Phaedra shouldn't be doing servant work."

I grunted at the nickname I had been given many years ago. It made me sound like something I wasn't.

After they were gone, I let myself wake up as I soaked in the tub, and as I did I became irritated at myself for oversleeping. I hurried out of the bath, toweling my long hair dry and plaiting it. It hung heavy and damp down my back, the end brushing the bottom of my spine. Dressing quickly, choosing my dress with no thought. All my clothing was chosen by Haydyn anyway. Haydyn loved clothes and jewelry. I put up with it because appearances within the palace had to be upheld.

"Ah good, you're dressed." Haydyn barged into my room without knocking. Lord Matai, second lieutenant of the Guard and a young Vikomt of good family, was Haydyn's newest bodyguard. He hovered over her protectively even when it was just me and her.

My welcoming smile faltered as I observed the slight strain on her face. "What's happened?"

"Nothing. I think." She shrugged elegantly. "Jarvis and Ava have requested me in the Chambers of the Rada."

I hid the instant worry that caused me. His Grace, Vojvoda Jarvis Rada, was the highest ranking member of the nobility of Sabithia and the Chairman of the Rada, as well as the Keeper of the Archives. Her ladyship, Grofka Ava Rada, was a widow and the only other member of the Rada who lived in Sabithia. They were both good people, and they loved Haydyn dearly. But Haydyn relied too heavily upon their opinion, and oftentimes they forgot that Haydyn even had a voice. Particularly Jarvis, whose responsibilities and position— especially that of Keeper of the Archives, the very exclusive control over mage history (meaning no one but he was allowed entrance into the archives until his demise, and then only his appointed successor would have the privilege)—had given him an inflated sense of self.

It nettled me. But it wasn't my place to speak for her. Like a frustrated parent I wanted her to become aware of her own voice and independence by herself.

"Well then." I threw both Haydyn and Matai a blasé smile. "We best go and see what they want."

Chapter Two

"Ah, Princezna." Vojvoda Jarvis stood to his feet, Lady Ava at his side. He bowed deeply whilst Ava dipped as low as she could into a curtsey. "Looking beautiful as always." Like a doting grandfather, Jarvis smiled kindly at Haydyn. His eyes flicked to me and he gave me an expressionless nod. Jarvis and Ava were always uncomfortable around me. I knew it was because they were ashamed of what Syracen had managed to do to my family under their watch.

Ours was a strained relationship.

"Your Grace." Haydyn gave a shallow curtsey. "My lady. I trust you are both well."

"As well as can be, Princezna. We do not have good news, I'm afraid."

Haydyn and I shared a worried look and I followed her as she took her seat at the head of long Chambers table. I sat on her left, facing Ava. Jarvis took the seat next to the Grofka.

"What's wrong?" Haydyn asked quietly, afraid of the answer. I watched that gloom creep into her eyes again, and I could have sworn she swayed in her chair. I was just about to reach out for her when she seemed to shake herself awake. I withdrew my hand.

Jarvis cleared his throat, his expression grave. "I must ask first of all, Princezna, whether you are feeling well? Are you in good health?"

Like Haydyn I was surprised by his question. She stammered out, "Of course."

My eyes narrowed on her. I could have sworn she was lying. "Why?" I asked, even though it wasn't my place to question.

Ava's eyes were wide with anxiety. "Because it seems as if the evocation may be weakened somehow."

Haydyn gasped. "Weakened? Weakened how? It can't be. I'm projecting the evocation at full, as always."

"We've been receiving reports over the last few weeks from the rest of the Rada. The most anxious of them being Vojvoda Andrei Rada, Keeper of Alvernia. The province is worsening; the uncivilized loutish behavior of the mountain people grows steadily closer to his city in the south. He fears the people of Arrana may become contaminated by the aggression of the northerners and grows agitated by Silvera's 'negligence', as he calls it."

Haydyn threw me a concerned look. "I had no idea things were so bad."

"There is more," Ava told her.

"Yes," Jarvis continued. "I've had word from Pharya. A rookery has sprung up on the border of Vasterya in the towns near the glass works. Gangs of thieves and smugglers are disrupting import and exportation."

Dear havens, I had never heard the like. "Thieves? Gangs? A rookery? In Phaedra?" I was aghast. We all were. My eyes swung to Haydyn, questioning, pinning her to her seat.

She squirmed uncomfortably, her emerald eyes fearful. "Don't look at me like that, Rogan. I don't know what to tell you. I don't feel a change in my magic."

Jarvis coughed. "Lastly—"

"There's more?" I interrupted, in shock.

He threw me a look of admonishment but I was too upset to apologize. "There's more," he acknowledged finally. "Markiza Raven Rada has her guard dealing with gypsies—"

"The Caels?" Haydyn interrupted now, frowning. "But the Caels have lived in Northern Javinia for decades. It's their home."

"Not the Caels, Princezna. The Iavii. These Alvernian gypsies are not looking for peace. They've already begun taking land from the Caels, and now they've started in on the Javinians. It's causing tension between Javinians and the Caels, who are being held as accountable as the Iavii."

"That's not fair!" Haydyn cried. "The Caels are a peaceful clan."

"They are. *Were.* Nothing in Javinia is peaceful. The Javinian guards are busy dealing with disputes and protecting Markiza Raven in Novia. She calls for aid."

The magnitude of the news silenced the both of us. How quickly our beautiful world seemed to have turned in on itself.

"You're sure you're well, Princezna?" Ava queried again.

"Positive," Haydyn snapped, jolting out of her seat. I watched on, as wide-eyed as Jarvis and Ava. Haydyn never spoke harshly to anyone. "I will not be questioned again."

"Of course, Princezna. We meant no disrespect."

Haydyn nodded, relaxing a little. "Now, what is to be done?"

You tell *them, Haydyn*, I wanted to say. But I didn't. She already looked so lost and afraid.

Jarvis sighed wearily. "Well, I think before we panic, we should discover the realities of the situation for ourselves. I say we send some of the Guard to Alvernia, Vasterya and Javinia to report back their findings, before we decide upon action."

Haydyn exhaled, seeming relieved by his suggestion. She turned to look at Matai, who stood on guard at the door. "Lord Matai, please have one of the footman fetch Captain Stovia."

I flinched at her command and bit my lip, my heart picking up speed at the thought of Wolfe. Captain Wolfe Stovia. *Vikomt* Wolfe Stovia now that his father, Syracen, was dead. A few years my senior, Wolfe had proven himself steadfast, loyal, hardworking, and a strong soldier. He was one of the youngest Captains in the history of the Guard. And I didn't trust him one iota.

He wasn't long in arriving.

Wolfe strode into the room like his namesake. Sleek and watchful, wily and dangerous. As handsome as any man in Phaedra, the servant girls went into twittering spasms whenever he was near. It made me feel rather queasy, to be honest.

His light blue eyes washed over the room, resting on me a moment, his expression inscrutable. I was so thankful he looked like his mother's side of the family. I didn't think I could have coped with a young version of Syracen stalking the palace halls. Wolfe bowed deeply and smiled at Haydyn, almost flirtatiously. "Princezna."

I rolled my eyes as Haydyn smiled prettily back at him. She may as well have batted her eye lashes invitingly the way her eyes raked him over. Strikingly tall, broad, a thick head of silky chestnut hair, olive skin and beautiful almond shaped eyes. His was a strong face, masculine, powerful. I disliked it greatly.

"Captain," Haydyn sighed at him. "I need you to send some of the Guard on an errand for me."

I watched as Wolfe listened carefully to the news, his expression tightening as he learned of our situation. "I will send nine of my best men out, your Highness. Three to each province."

"Thank you, Captain." Jarvis got to his feet wearily, helping Ava out of hers. "We appreciate it."

As they were about to depart I cleared my throat, drawing their gaze as I stood. "May I suggest we keep this between us? And stress the importance of keeping this information confidential to your men… *Captain*," I bit out the word.

Haydyn's eyes widened. "Of course, Rogan is right. We don't want to cause panic until we have all the facts."

Wolfe nodded, but he never took his eyes from me as he smiled sardonically. "Of course, Princezna."

I glared at him as he took his leave, followed by Jarvis and Ava.

Solemnly, Haydyn and I walked back to her suite, Matai close on our heels. I was afraid to mention what had just been discussed.

"I keep waiting for you to stop being unpleasant to Captain Wolfe." Haydyn threw me a reproving look.

I snorted. "You'll be waiting a *loooong* time then."

"Rogan, really," she clucked. "He's not his father, you know."

I shrugged. I knew Haydyn thought it was unfair of me to treat Wolfe badly but I couldn't help it. He was a Stovia. No matter how much he ingratiated himself to Haydyn or into the Rada's trust, he would always be my enemy. His father had taken my family and I had destroyed his in return. I was suspicious of his loyalty to Haydyn, when any normal man would have wanted vengeance for his father's death.

Haydyn did not share the suspicion. She sighed dreamily. "I don't understand how you can be so mean to him. He's so handsome and strong."

I laughed softly at Matai's choked grunt behind us and Haydyn threw him a teasing look over her shoulder. He would take his revenge for that. We stopped at her suite and I checked the hallways both ways. It was clear. I nodded at them and Haydyn grabbed Matai's hand, disappearing into her suite with him. I stood guard. Protecting Haydyn as always. Protecting her secrets. Protecting her love for Lord Matai. I felt a twinge of unfamiliar longing at the sound of her and Matai's intimate laughter beyond the door. Haydyn was akin to my younger sister, and yet she knew more of that mysterious intimacy between man and woman than I did. All I ever wanted was to be a source of wisdom and support for Haydyn. How could I be when she was far worldlier than I was? I was nineteen and un-kissed, never mind…

I ducked my head, feeling silly and adolescent. I did not seek love. I'd never wanted it… but romance… perhaps. I shook my head. I had no time for romance. I was far too busy facilitating Haydyn with hers.

Chapter Three

"Mm," I moaned, the sweet chocolate and fresh cream cake making my eyes flutter shut in rapture. "Cook, you've surpassed yourself," I mumbled through my bites.

Cook grinned broadly, rolling out pastry as servants bustled around us in the massive kitchen. Valena giggled from her seat across from me, cream sticking to the corner of her mouth. "I swear, Rogan, the sweetest expression you ever have on your face is when you're eating Cook's desserts."

I raised an eyebrow teasingly at her cheekiness and reached across to swipe the last of the cakes from her plate.

"Hey!" She leapt forward to grab it back from me but I held it out of her reach. If we had been standing face to face rather than sitting across a long table, she would have taken it easily. Valena may only be fourteen but she was extremely tall. At least five foot ten, a good three inches taller than I was. "Oh don't, Rogan." Valena's eyes widened as I pretended to pop the cake into my mouth. "Cook's only made a few today."

Cook shook her head at my teasing. "I swear it could be eight years ago with the way you act, Miss Rogan."

"Well I wouldn't have to act that way if you made more than just a few cakes." I shoved the cake back to Valena, my eyes greedily watching as she scoffed it down in seconds. "Oh, you didn't even take time to enjoy that. Sacrilege. I should have eaten it."

"But it was mine." Valena grinned through a mouthful. "You're too honorable to have taken what was mine."

I laughed at the manipulative twinkle in her eye. "Where has she learned such false charm and deviousness?" I asked Cook, shaking my head.

Cook snorted. "You!"

Valena burst out laughing and I was truly thankful she had finished eating the cake, otherwise I'd have been speckled with chewed pieces of it.

"Valena!"

We all spun around at the sound of Raj's frantic voice, the kitchen coming to a standstill as he fell into the room. Falling into a room was something Raj never did and we all stared at him wide-eyed as he shrugged himself back into order. But my heart was thumping as Raj smoothed back his white blonde hair and straightened his waistcoat. "Valena," he said more quietly now. "I need you."

Valena didn't ask any questions. She jumped up from the table and made her way towards him. Raj shooed her in front of him and then turned his pale eyes on me. "You too, Rogan."

I shared a brief, worried look with Cook and hurried after the healers.

"What's going on?" I asked.

"I've been called to the Princezna's suite."

I forgot all ladylike manners and lifted my dress, running as fast as I could through the palace halls to Haydyn's apartments. Servants gaped at me as I blurred by them and I wanted desperately to shout back at Raj to hurry up. But if he did that, if he ran with me, then everyone would know something was wrong with Haydyn. What was wrong? And hadn't I known all along that there was something the matter? I cursed myself for not pressing her further, but ever since Jarvis and Ava had imparted the news of the hostility in Phaedra a few weeks ago, I was afraid to burden Haydyn further.

I found Matai inside her suite. No other servant. Only him, hovering worriedly over Haydyn who was lying sprawled on the floor. "What happened?" I rushed towards her, throwing myself down beside her. Her skin was deathly pale, her hand limp in mine.

Matai met my gaze with dark, fierce expression in his eyes. "I don't know," he whispered to me. "We were only talking... and then she... she just collapsed on the floor. I was afraid to move her. I've called for Raj... I didn't want anyone else to know..." he trailed off as Raj and Valena came into the room, Valena shutting the door behind her.

Raj shoved me out of the way.

"What's wrong with her?" I demanded.

"Give me a minute, Rogan, for havens sake," Raj replied through gritted teeth.

My heart stopped as Haydyn groaned, her eyes fluttering open. As they focused, they widened in panic. "What happened?" she asked hoarsely.

"You collapsed," I bit out, my worry translating to anger.

Her eyes found Raj. "Why?"

Raj shook his head. "Lord Matai, help me move the Princezna to the bed."

I stood back, and Valena gripped my hand reassuringly. I squeezed back.

"Lord Matai, Rogan, please leave Valena and I alone with the Princezna."

I objected immediately, "No. I'm staying right here."

"Rogan." Matai grabbed my arm. "For once do as you're told." I wasn't even given a chance to struggle. Not that I could. Matai was as big as Wolfe. He thrust me outside the suite and shut the door behind us, his large body blocking my way in.

"I need to be in there with her."

"No. You want to be, there's a difference."

"Matai."

"Stop it, Rogan," he hissed, a flash in his eyes revealing his concern. "For once… just stop it."

I slumped at his tone, my heart pounding so hard I felt sick with it. "What's wrong with her, Matai? She won't tell me."

"I know." He grimaced, crossing his arms over his chest and leaning back against the door. "She's been over tired lately. I've tried to talk to her about it but…"

"She keeps saying nothing is the matter," I finished.

"Yes."

Our gazes met and held. We both knew something was *definitely* the matter.

It seemed forever before Raj beckoned us back into the suite, and yet it had probably only been fifteen minutes. Matai struggled to keep me back at a distance to give Haydyn room. Determined to be at her bed side, and smaller and spryer than he, I ducked under his arm and raced to her.

"What's the matter?" I grasped Haydyn's hand. She was sitting up in bed now, color back in her cheeks. She surprised me with her bright smile.

Matai stood hovering at the end of the bed. He threw Raj a belligerent look. "Well, man, what the hell is going on?"

I rolled my eyes. Matai really needed to do a better job of hiding his feelings for Haydyn.

Raj smiled indulgently, glancing from Haydyn to Valena. "Both Valena and I have checked the Princezna over. We could only feel the darkness of exhaustion. We took it away. As you can see, the Princezna is feeling much better." He strode towards her now. "As for this not sleeping, I'm going to get one of the servants to bring one of my tonics up from my stores. It should help greatly, Princezna."

"Thank you, Raj." Haydyn nodded, her eyes twinkling gratefully. "I appreciate your help."

I pulled away from her now, mad at her for frightening me. "Next time maybe you'll do as I ask and see Raj before you collapse on the floor," I snapped.

The others looked a little shocked at my attitude. Not Haydyn. She looked remorseful, sensing the truth behind my annoyance. I hated that she knew me so well. "I'm sorry, Rogan. I promise not to frighten you again."

"Pfft." I turned from her.

"Rogan?"

"If you're all better I have things to do."

I felt Matai and the healers glare at me but I shrugged it off.

Haydyn narrowed her eyes on me. "Yes, you do have things to do." She threw back the covers and got out of the bed with a surprising breeze of energy. "Tell Jarek to ready my horse and yours. We're going to the marketplace."

I clenched my jaw and nodded tightly before striding across the room to the door. The marketplace? She knew I hated the marketplace. She was deliberately trying to bedevil me.

"Oh, and Rogan."

I stiffened, not liking that sing-song tone of hers. It meant she was up to something. I turned slowly. "Yes, Your Highness."

Haydyn smirked at me. "After you speak with Jarek, please find Captain Stovia. We'll need an escort."

I made a face at her and departed, her sweet laughter trickling behind me. Despite the distasteful thought of being in Wolfe's presence, I smiled softly at the sound of her laughter and shook my head at her mischief.

***

"There you are," I called softly to Jarek, finding him working in the Silver Stable. We had stables almost as large as the palace because half of the Royal Guard was cavalry. There were a number of stable boys, and Jarek, a lad my age with a quick wit and warm smile, had been a stable boy up until recently. The old Stable Master had passed away suddenly and I had suggested Jarek for the job. Yes, he was young, but we had been friends ever since my arrival at the palace and I had never met anyone with such an affinity for horses. There had been some upset at first when Haydyn made him Stable Master, people assuming he was too young, and not responsible enough. But he had the stables in tip-top shape in no time at all, proving himself worthy.

Jarek looked up from checking a chestnut bay's hooves. He grinned at me and stood up. "Where else would I be?"

"I don't know." I shrugged playfully, sauntering leisurely toward him. "The Jewel Stable. The White Stable. Or the kitchen. Cook made cakes today."

He sucked in a breath, his eyes wide with teasing upset. "And I missed them?"

I snorted. "Jarek, you would have missed them even if you'd been there. Valena and I had devastated the plate within five seconds."

"Valena," he clucked, "She's getting to be too much like you."

"Everyone keeps saying that." I frowned. "And what's wrong with being like me?"

Jarek stilled and cocked his head, his eyes bright as they washed over my face. "Nothing. Absolutely nothing."

Despite myself, I warmed at his attention. We had been friends for a long time but our conversations had taken a decidedly flirtatious turn of late. And he *was* extremely good-looking. However, that was the problem. I knew too many maids, and even a few noblewomen, who had shared Jarek's bed. Despite that reckless voice inside my head eager to uncover the mysteries of bedroom intimacy, I didn't want to be just another girl he'd tumbled.

I cleared my throat. "Haydyn wishes to go to the marketplace right away. Could you ready Midnight and Sundown?" Our horses.

Jarek threw me a look for dismissing his flirting, but nodded. "Is the Guard going with you?"

I grimaced. "Yes."

He laughed. "You don't sound too excited about it. Here's a thought." He stepped close to me, so close I had to crane my neck to look up at him. My heart thudded in my chest. "Why don't I be your guard for the day?" He bent down, his hot breath blowing across my ear as he whispered. I shivered. "I'd take good care of you."

"And Haydyn?" I murmured, my whole body vibrating with awareness of him.

Jarek laughed softly. "She has Lord Matai." He drew back only a little, our noses almost touching. "You can have me."

"Well isn't this cozy?"

I closed my eyes at the voice of interruption. Arrggh, how I hated him! Jarek sighed and stood back from me and I turned to face Wolfe. He leaned against the stable wall glaring at us. "Apparently I'm escorting you to the marketplace. When was that message going to be delivered? A week, two…?"

I glared at him. "Clearly it already has been."

Wolfe snapped up off the wall and strode towards me. Dear haven, he was tall. He towered over me and Jarek. "You," he bit out at Jarek, "The horses. Now. Hers," he flicked a distasteful look at me, "The Princezna's, Lord Matai's, my own, and three of my Guard."

Jarek crossed his arms over his chest defiantly, not in the least intimidated. "Which three?"

"Worth, Vincent, and Chaeron's," Wolfe replied through clenched teeth.

Jarek nodded tightly and then threw me a grin, his eyes devouring me purposefully. "I'll speak with you later, Rogan."

"Jarek." I grinned back at him and watched him leave, biting my lip in thought as he swaggered out of the stable and into the next. Feeling Wolfe's eyes on me I turned and met his sharp look with one of my own. "What?"

"What?" He guffawed, eyeing me incredulously. "The Princezna has been unwell and everyone is agreeing to her outing to market, and you're in here flirting with the stable boy."

"Stable Master," I corrected, poking him in the chest with the word. "And don't take that self-righteous tone with me as if I don't care about Haydyn."

Wolfe snorted. "Do you care? You were supposed to come and inform me so I can protect you at market, and you're in here with your legs practically wrapped around Jarek."

How dare he? I sucked in a breath at the accusation. "You're lucky I don't slap you for that insinuation. Jarek is my friend. I was here asking him to prepare the horses and I was just about to come and find your sorry self to inform you Haydyn required your company into market. *Not* that I should have to explain myself to you."

Wolfe eyed where Jarek had departed before turning his disbelieving, disdainful eyes on me. "I'm sure that's exactly what you were planning to do."

I didn't care if he believed me or not. I sighed, as if I were bored by him. "That comment deserves only one response." And that was to march out of there without another word.

***

The city of Silvera grew quiet, parting as we moved through the crowds on the cobbled streets, the noise level hushing and then rising as the people gathered back together behind our entourage, like a wave crashing to shore behind us.

I rode beside Haydyn on Midnight while she rode Sundown. Matai rode on Haydyn's other side and three of the Royal Guard rode at our backs. Wolfe was atop his magnificent stallion in front of us, his eagle eyes watching the crowds as we made our way past taverns, apothecaries, inns, bakers and butchers and candlestick makers. The marketplace was in the massive Silvera Square, where people from the neighboring provinces came to sell their wares. Haydyn always had a particular interest in the artists and craftsmen of Raphizya and the beautiful glass works of Vasterya.

"I've decided to hold a ball." Haydyn smiled at me after waving once more to Silverians who bowed and curtsied as we trotted past.

I raised an eyebrow at the unexpected idea. "A ball?"

"Hmm." Haydyn grinned excitedly, seeming all her young seventeen years. "A ball. I'll invite all the Rada and all the noblemen and women of every province. A way of showing our solidarity in an unsettling time."

"A ball?" I still wasn't convinced.

"I think it's a fine idea, Princezna." Matai smiled at her.

I sighed. "No one asked you, Lord Matai."

"Rogan, be nice," Haydyn tutted. "Anyway, Lord Matai is correct. It *is* a fine idea."

My heart jumped a little at the determination in her voice and I felt hope blooming in my chest. Perhaps Haydyn was finally taking charge. And I might not like fancy balls but… it *was* a good idea. If only because it was *her* idea.

Her face fell when I didn't respond. "Don't you think it's a good idea, Rogan?" She looked so worried.

I cursed inwardly. Why did everyone's opinion matter so much to her? She was as smart and capable as any of us fools whose advice she solicited. I sighed inwardly, wishing she'd remember she was fair and just and royal— she should not concern herself with my opinion, or anyone else's for that matter.

Instead I gave her a soft smile. "Lord Matai's right. It's a fine idea."

Moment of anxiety over, Haydyn grinned cheerfully as we entered the marketplace. Again all went quiet at the sight of us. Gradually, however, as we trotted over to the stables the noise level rose again.

"I want you to seek out the finest fabric for me, for my new ball gown, as well as the finest for yourself," Haydyn commanded gently as Matai helped her dismount. I was so shocked by the request I dismounted without help, forgetting I wasn't supposed to do that in public. But Haydyn very rarely used my magic and never for something as frivolous as fabric shopping.

Already my body was crackling inside, drawing me towards a fabric stall deep in the crowds of the square. "Fabric?" I queried softly.

"Hmm." Haydyn nodded, smiling prettily at me. "We want to look our best for such an important event."

"Not the key to world peace? Not the answer to shutting down a rookery or controlling rogue gypsies? *Fabric*?"

Haydyn sighed wearily. "Must I repeat it, Rogan, when we both know you're being facetious?"

I shrugged. "Well, I just had no idea that the form of our fashion was so incredibly important to settling Phaedrian disputes."

"More facetiousness. Lovely."

I rolled my eyes. "Fine. Away I go to seek and order the fabric." I glanced between Matai and her. "What are you going to do?"

Haydyn gazed a little too adoringly at Matai. "Lord Matai's going to escort me around the market while I choose some gifts to present to our guests at the ball."

I threw Matai a look of mock horror. "Lord Matai, may I say now how much I have enjoyed knowing you, for I fear it will be the last time I look upon you. Death by boredom." I winced.

He grinned at me. "I'm sure I'll survive."

"Well you don't have to sound so put upon," Haydyn sniffed.

I laughed, thinking about her well known generosity. "And just where are all these gifts going? We didn't bring a cart?"

"I'll borrow one. Or buy one. I am the Princezna."

I almost rolled my eyes. She asserts her authority when shopping. Wonderful.

"Well, don't let me keep you. Off I go. Shan't be long." I moved as fast as I could away from them and into the crowds before Haydyn demanded I take an escort.

I breathed deeply of the thick smells of the market. It was a strange mixture of pungent sheep's wool, beats, chocolate, oil, sweet meats, bread, perfume, paint… oh it was a fragrance of all the variety of the market. Usually, I hated the crowds, preferring my escape to be down at the cliffs some miles from the palace. I loved the peace and quiet of watching the surf of the Silver Sea crash against the cliff walls. For some reason it reminded me I was alive. But never alone. No. There was always a guard with me some way in the distance. Today, as I swept past people—some who recognized me, some who didn't—calling out to me to buy their wares, desperate for what they assumed was a noblewoman to purchase something expensive from them, I loved the market.

Because I was alone. All alone.

Free.

I was quick on my feet, dodging persistent sellers, and hopefully any of the Guard who may have followed me. In no time at all I found the stall with the fabric that called to my magic. I saw it instantly. Velvet, the color of lapis lazuli, made from the finest silk in the textile factories in Ryl. Haydyn would look wonderful in it. I reached out to stroke the beautiful fabric when a hand clamped around my wrist.

"No, no, miss." I looked up into the ruddy face of the market seller. "Not the right color for you, miss. Come see some of my silks." He tried to pull me towards the more expensive material. I tugged at his grip but he was determined.

I grew irritated by his persistence. "Sir—"

"With a face and figure like yours, you shouldn't hide behind the heavy textures. Fine silks, miss, fine silks for you."

I tugged again. Oh yes, *this* was why I hated the marketplace.

A large hand came down on top of the sellers, ripping it from my own and holding it tight. Both the seller and I looked up into the intimidating and angry face of Wolfe Stovia.

"You dare to lay your hands on the Princezna's Handmaiden?" Wolfe growled at the man.

The seller blanched as he looked at me, recognition finally dawning. "Oh, My Lady, I meant no disrespect."

Wolfe grunted and shoved the man away. "Lady or servant, I see you trying to forcefully coerce a woman again and you and I will have words."

I'd never seen anyone look so ill, so green. "Apologies, My Lord. I was over excited. It won't happen again. Apologies, My Lady." His head bobbed up and down at me.

Oh for havens sake. "I'm not a lady," I huffed, angry at Wolfe for drawing attention to the situation and blowing it out of proportion. The overbearing lout. I glared at him. "You, sir, are a bully."

Wolfe merely frowned at me. "And you, girl, are the Handmaiden of Phaedra and as such a lady. You are not to allow strange men to touch you."

I curled my lip disdainfully. "I'll allow a mountain man of Alvernia to touch me before I take advice from you, *Stovia*." Dismissing him, agitated by his presence, his ruination of my pretense at freedom, I turned back to the seller. "I want three bolts of the lapis lazuli velvet and one bolt of the emerald silk chiffon." I relaxed a little at having completed my task for Haydyn, but then my body hummed with energy again and I turned without thinking toward a stall some quarter of the way back into the middle of the market. The fabric that would suit me most was in there somewhere. Damn Haydyn. Damn being an Azyl.

I spun back on the seller. "Have the fabric delivered to the palace and ask for Seamstress Rowan. You'll be paid well for your troubles."

He nodded, doing this obscene half bow/curtsey thing that made me throw a growl in Wolfe's direction. Turning sharply from them both to make my way to the fabric stall my magic called me to, I drew in a breath at the pleasant sandalwood scent of Wolfe as he fell into step beside me.

I stopped abruptly. "What are you doing?" I snapped.

Wolfe shrugged, refusing to look at me, refusing to leave. "Just one of the more unpleasant jobs of being Captain of the Guard. Protecting *you*."

Pulling a face, I began walking again. "We are droll, aren't we?"

"Some people think I'm charming." He grinned flirtatiously and executed a graceful half bow to a passing tavern girl, who eyed him seductively over her bare shoulder.

"Some people don't know any better."

"Ooh is that judgment I hear in the voice of the lady who was flirting with a mere stable boy this morning."

I gritted my teeth. "Stable *Master*."

Wolfe raised one annoying eyebrow. "As if that makes it any more palatable? You know he's bedded every girl in the palace? You're not special."

I could feel my blood boiling under my skin, as it did whenever I was forced to be in the same presence as this man. I tried to take deep, calming breaths. I did. I really, really did. It didn't work. "Who I choose to converse with is of no consequence to you, Captain Stovia. And may I remind you to whom you are speaking?" My answer was thick with condescension but he deserved it.

"So there is a snob buried under all that 'I'm not a lady, I'm not a lady, I'm just like everyone else,' piffle?" He mocked.

"I do not speak like that. And I *am* just like everyone else. *Except* when it comes to you. You will talk to me like I'm royalty, *Captain*. As in… don't speak to me at all."

The usual cool and collected Wolfe stiffened at my insults, his face taut with anger. Our dislike was definitely, *definitely* mutual. "If you want to get snooty, Rogan,—"

I flinched at his use of my given name. He'd never called me Rogan before. Not to my face anyway. It had always been My Lady, despite my lack of nobility.

"—may I remind *you* that I'm the one with Lord before *my* name. Don't speak to me like I'm dirt beneath your shoe."

Arrogant beast, I shook my head. Just like his demon father. I laughed humorlessly, a cold, brittle laugh that caused him to wince. "You don't need to remind me who you are, *Vikomt Stovia*." With that I veered from him, pushing my way through the crowds to escape him. I looked back to make sure he did not follow. He didn't, however, I watched him nod at someone and then glance at me. Within seconds, Lieutenant Chaeron had pushed his way through the crowds to walk by my side, his hand on the hilt of his sword. I wanted to be annoyed at the immediate sense of suffocation his presence caused me, but then I recalled Jarvis' words of warning and relaxed. There was a reason behind Haydyn's idea for a ball. Quite suddenly I was glad for our trained Guard. We had never needed them before.

But then there had never been crime in the different provinces before.

Chapter Four

"What about Matai, Haydyn?" I whispered, knowing he stood outside her bedroom suite. She glanced worriedly at the door, before pinning me to the wall with a hurt look.

"Please, keep your voice down, Rogan."

I tried. I shuddered, trying to take deep breaths. But I was so mad at her. I wanted her to wake up! My head swam with all Ava and Jarvis had told us.

That morning, Haydyn had been called to the Chambers to speak with Jarvis and Ava. Last night Wolfe's men had returned, and they hadn't returned bearing good news.

"So… it's all true?" Haydyn had asked as she sat clutching my hand tight in hers. I had ignored the pricking, wincing pain of her long nails digging into my skin and had tried to squeeze her hand in reassurance.

Jarvis had nodded, looking years older since the last we had seen him only a few weeks before. "All three complaints prove true. Javinia is in unrest and it seems rumor of the unrest is spreading through Sabithia. Alvernia is worsening. Even the Valley grows more uncivilized. Apparently Arrana is the only civilized city in the province. And as for the rookery in Vasterya… well it exists."

"Oh no." Haydyn had grown limp beside me, her young eyes round and fearful. "What do we do?"

Ava and Jarvis had shared a look.

I had immediately become suspicious. "What?"

"Well." Jarvis had cleared his throat. "Of course we should send reinforcements into Javinia, and someone should speak with Markiz Solom Rada in Pharya—he needs to send his guard out to police the rookery. I don't know why he hasn't already."

"I do," Ava had murmured and I knew what she meant. Markiz Solom was my least favorite of the Rada. Spoiled, entitled, weak.

"What about Alvernia?" I'd narrowed my eyes on them.

Again they'd shared that nervous little look.

"Well." Ava had smiled at Haydyn brightly. "We have a wonderful suggestion."

My intuition had told me it wasn't that wonderful. "Suggest it then."

"Rogan," Haydyn had admonished but I hadn't even acknowledged it. I'd had an awful premonition.

Seeming unconcerned with my attitude, Jarvis had leaned forward across the table, his eyes all grandfatherly and wise as he'd focused his attention on Haydyn. "You are of an age now, Princezna, and it's time to discuss the possibility of you marrying and carrying on the Dyzvati line."

I'd sucked in a breath, feeling Haydyn stiffen under my touch. "She's not a broodmare," I'd bitten out.

Jarvis had flinched at my tone. "I didn't suggest she was, Rogan. Please disband with the attitude."

"Rogan, please." Haydyn had patted my hand. "His Grace is right. I am of age."

As I'd watched Ava and Jarvis share pleased looks, I'd known deep in the pit of my stomach what they wanted of her. "You want a match with Alvernia."

They'd seemed shocked at my deduction and Jarvis had shifted nervously for a moment. Vaguely, I'd noted Matai stiffen at the door.

Jarvis had found Haydyn's eyes again, his expression soothing and manipulative all at one. It had made me want to pull her away from him. "We think you might want to consider Markiz Andrei of Alvernia—son of Vojvoda Andrei Rada. It would greatly improve relations between the two provinces and may be a brilliant stepping stone towards civilizing the north."

My mouth had fallen open as I'd watched Haydyn's reaction. She'd grown pale and still, deliberately not looking at Matai. She'd glanced at me only to wince at my expression. And then she'd straightened in her chair, her chin rising defiantly. "I think it's a very good idea. And one we must consider. Vojvoda Andrei and his son are invited to the ball next month are they not?"

"Yes," Ava had replied happily, relief sparking in her eyes, "They are Princezna. They're staying at the palace with the rest of the Rada and their families. It will be a wonderful opportunity to get to know one another and further any plans for a betrothal."

"Splendid." Jarvis had clapped his hands together and Haydyn had smiled, relieved to have pleased them.

The walk back to her suite had been ice cold, Matai refusing to look at either one of us, and Haydyn trembling the whole way. Matai had opened the door for us and as soon as we'd entered he had shut it carefully in our wake, not saying a word.

"I just can't believe you're even considering marrying some stranger."

Her cheeks grew pink with deep blush, and I knew she was growing equally angry with me. "It may be for the best of Phaedra. I'm finally doing something worthy of a leader and you're angry at me?"

"You're not doing something worthy of a leader. You're doing what someone else wants you to do. As always!"

She flinched, hurt widening her eyes. I immediately felt awful but words of apology stuck in my throat.

"There was never a future for Matai and me," she whispered sorrowfully, pleading with me to agree with her. "He's not of a high enough rank."

"You can have any future you want, Haydyn. They need you!" I implored, pointing out the window. "Not the other way around. You can do what *you* like, love who *you* love, *be* who *you* want to be. And there is nothing that they can do about it, because *they* need *you*."

Haydyn trembled, clasping onto the post of her bed. "No." She shook her head, growing more wane by the second. "Something's wrong with Phaedra and I have to fix it. Jarvis knows how. The betrothal is a good idea," she gasped, seeming out of breath.

I was too angry to pay attention. I wanted to stamp my foot like a child, my head bursting with the pain of hitting the brick wall she insisted on putting up. "Haydyn, it's a good idea. But not the best idea. Not the only idea. Surely we can come up with something else. You don't—"

"Rogan—"

"—know if Andrei of Alvernia is a despicable lout like the rest of the mountain people are supposed to—"

"Rogan—"

"—be. He could be—"

"Rogan!" Haydyn gasped out and fell towards me. My heart flared in panic and I rushed to catch her. As my arms encircled her before she hit the ground, her eyes rolled back in her head and she grew limp, lifeless in my arms.

"Haydyn." I shook her, a nauseating fear growing in my chest. "Haydyn." I shook her harder but her eyes wouldn't open. She was so pale. So deathly pale. I choked on a sob. "Haydyn! Wake up!" I shook her harder, a sob breaking out from the pit of my stomach. "MATAI!" I screamed now. "MATAI!"

Chapter Five

The room was silent. Like death had crept into the palace and snuffed out all the candles, all the cheer, all life. I looked around at my companions and swallowed past the constriction in my throat.

"I've called you all here for a reason," I whispered and cleared my throat to be heard.

After Haydyn had collapsed in my arms, Matai had burst into the room in the company of Wolfe. Apparently he'd heard me and Haydyn arguing and had stopped to enquire about it. Unable to rouse Haydyn, I'd silently made my way through the Palace, terrified of spreading my panic. Quietly, I had ushered Valena and Raj to the suite. When Raj told us gravely he and Valena needed more time to discover Haydyn's unwaking illness, deep suspicion and fear had begun to coalesce in my chest so I sent a messenger out for Vojvoda Jarvis and Grofka Ava. I'd met them in the grand entranceway and had brought them to my suite, where Wolfe and Matai waited.

They paled at the news of Haydyn's collapse. Outraged to learn it wasn't the first time. I bore the brunt of the glares.

Finally, Valena called us through to Haydyn's suite. Inside we were greeted by a very grave Raj. And then he confirmed our worst fears. Haydyn had fallen ill to the Somna. The rarest of illnesses in Phaedra, the Somna, more colloquially known as the Sleeping

Disease, was a mystery to us. No one knew where, why or what caused it. There had been fewer and fewer records of the Somna over the last centuries, but every now and again it took hold of someone without warning. It caused a growing lethargy that soon caused the victim to fall into a coma-like state. If the victim was lucky enough to have a Dravilec close by, the healer could hold off death by healing the sleeping person from starvation and dehydration. If not, death was inevitable... unless one could find the rare leaves of the Somna Plant, the only cure to the Sleeping Disease.

A plant that was said to be extinct.

I gazed around the Chambers of the Rada at Jarvis, Ava, Matai, Wolfe, Valena and Raj. Only we knew Haydyn was dying. That's why Phaedra was falling apart. Unbeknownst to her, her magic was waning with her illness.

I thought of my harsh words to Haydyn, the words that had been my last. I flinched and then gritted my teeth. They wouldn't be my last. Haydyn was *not* dying. Not while I had breath in my body.

"Someone, command me to seek the Somna plant," I urged, almost violently.

Wolfe's eyes widened as everyone shifted, as if waking out of a coma themselves. "Of course," he whispered, and they all seemed to admonish themselves for not having thought of it before. "Rogan—"

"Not you," I interrupted. I wouldn't be ordered to seek anything from another Stovia again. I ignored Wolfe's faux wounded expression and turned to Jarvis. "Vojvoda."

He nodded militantly. "Rogan, I want you to seek the Somna Plant."

Waves crashed over me and I shuddered at the current of energy that dragged on and on. I'd never been hit with my magic like this before, my nerves buzzing and twanging, my muscles twitching. But as I saw the Somna Plant buried in the northern most point of Phaedra, I knew why. I had never had to seek anything so far from me before. "It exists," I exhaled in relief, my heart in my throat, tears pricking my eyes. I felt them all exhale with me.

"Where?" Matai croaked.

I smirked unhappily at the thought of my journey ahead. "The Pool of Phaedra."

Ava gasped. "In the Mountains of Alvernia?"

I shrugged. "Is there any other?"

"You're going to retrieve it, aren't you?" Jarvis gave me a worried look.

I curled my lip at the question. How dare he question my honor? "Of course, I am," I huffed, my brain whirring with what needed to be done. "We'll send word ahead to Vojvoda Andrei Rada that I and some of the Royal Guard are coming to visit his province. Let him and everyone else think Haydyn's sending me to feel out a possible betrothal between her and the Markiz. Everyone knows Haydyn defers to my opinion, so no one will question it. In reality, I will spend only a day or so at Arrana and head into the mountains to retrieve the plant." I looked around at them all sternly, not taking a moment for fear of interruption. "Back here Haydyn has decided she would like some peace from palace life. She's going to stay in her cottage in Land's End. Only Matai, Raj and…" I took a moment to think who would be most trustworthy. "…a chaperone for appearances sake so we'll send Seamstress Rowan with you. She can be trusted." I stared them all down. "No one must know the truth but us and Rowan."

They all gazed at me like they'd never seen me before. Jarvis gave me what could pass for a warm look as he nodded. "It's an excellent plan, Rogan."

"How long will it take you to retrieve the plant?" Valena asked quietly, her fingers worrying the handkerchief in her hand. She hadn't stopped crying since she'd helped Raj uncover Haydyn's illness.

Unwillingly I looked to Wolfe. He was the only one who knew the provinces well. He cocked his head to the side thinking about it. "Without interruption? With the Royal Guard—"

"Not all of them." I shook my head.

"My Lady, crime rate is rising. There is no way I'm taking the Handmaiden of Phaedra across our land without an army."

"Stop calling me the Handmaiden of Phaedra."

He shrugged. "Just being respectful."

"I'd believe that if you didn't add this mocking tone to the title every time you say it," I sighed, realizing our arguing was hampering the progression of the plan. "Fine. Twenty men."

"A hundred."

A hundred men? How conspicuous. I gave him a look that told him I thought it was ridiculous.

Wolfe grunted. "Fine, fifty."

I opened my mouth to argue and Jarvis held up a hand. "You will take fifty men with you, Rogan. That's an order from the Rada."

I grimaced but deferred to his wishes with a brittle nod. "Alright. So how long will it take us?"

Wolfe shook his head. "Difficult to say. Depending on weather and any other unforeseen circumstances I would guess anything between three to six weeks. What will I tell my men?" He queried Jarvis.

"I assume you can trust Lieutenant Chaeron with the truth. Otherwise, just what Rogan outlaid. This is merely a diplomatic trip on behalf of the Princezna. If trouble brews and you must tell your men then you must, but otherwise keep it between you, Rogan and Chaeron. May I suggest you leave Second Lieutenant Worth back at the Palace, just in case you and Rogan don't make it back in time before trouble arrives here?" Jarvis shuddered at the thought of crime in Sabithia, as did we all as we shared anxious looks.

"Of course." Wolfe stood, projecting strength and capability. They all looked to him as if he would take care of everything. I hated him for that. "I'll see to my men."

"I'll see to Haydyn's quiet removal from the Palace," Ava said, standing unsteadily to her feet. "Lord Matai, will you find Seamstress Rowan, explain everything. She will need to pack a few things. Raj, Valena, Lord Jarvis, we need to get the Princezna out of the Palace." She turned to me and, taking me by surprise, she drew me into a soft hug. I stiffened at the touch. No one but Haydyn and Valena ever hugged me. "Good luck, Rogan. I know you can do this. We shall see you in a few weeks' time."

I nodded, pulling back, trying not to choke on my tears. "I better gather my things together." I strode to Valena and drew her into a tight embrace. She bent down to soak her tears on my shoulder. "You take care of her. And yourself."

"Be careful, Rogan." Valena pulled back, brushing at her tears. "Please."

I promised I would and marched from the room, only now feeling what Haydyn must feel every day: the weight of an entire world on my shoulders.

And now, like her, I would have given anything to ask someone else to help me carry my burden.

Chapter Six

Haydyn lay before me on her bed, peaceful and pale, her eyelids not even twitching to assure me she was dreaming somewhere inside herself. My throat felt so tight, so sore, and I gripped the bed post lest I reach forward to shake her as I wanted to— to shake her awake and scold her for terrifying the living daylights out of me. Her chest rose gently, slowly, and I let go of the breath I was holding.

"You're going to be alright," I whispered, bending down to brush a kiss across her forehead. I knew every feature, every freckle of her as well as I knew myself. I choked back a frightened sob and pulled away from her. "I promise."

***

I strode out into the courtyard where the Guard were busying themselves with their horses and the cart that would travel with us with supplies. I tugged on my leather riding gloves, my cloak billowing at my back as wind rushed in from the east. My heart thudded rapidly in my chest, my whole face tight with tension. I willed my expression to relax into a soft smile when I realized Jarek was watching me carefully as I approached him and Midnight.

"Thank you, Jarek," I acknowledged, taking Midnight's reins and stroking my mare's glossy blue-black coat. Midnight nickered and bounced her head towards me in hello.

"So." Jarek eyed me skeptically. "A diplomatic trip on behalf of the Princezna?"

Not meeting his eyes, I nodded as I continued to stroke Midnight. "Yes. Haydyn's interested in improving relations with the Alvernians."

"It's such a hastily put-together outing." Jarek shook his head. "My boys nearly broke their backs getting the horses ready under Wolfe's command. Usually a trip such as this would take a week of preparation at least."

I shuddered, hating to lie to an old friend. Instead I opted to trust him with a little of the truth. I looked into his eyes and he froze instantly at the solemnity of my gaze. "Alvernia is worsening," I told him quietly, glancing around to make sure no one else was listening. "I'm going with Captain Stovia to discern the situation for myself and see what can be done. Speak of this to no one, Jarek, but Haydyn may consider a betrothal to Vojvoda Andrei's son."

Jarek's eyes widened. "Are things really that bad?"

I nodded.

He sighed wearily, shaking his head at the news. "I swear, I'll tell no one, Rogan. It would cause unnecessary panic."

Smiling at his understanding, I took his hand. "Thank you, Jarek. Haydyn will be staying at her cottage in Land's End while I'm gone.

The news has troubled her and I think it would do her good to get away from palace life."

Jarek squeezed my hand. "And what of you, Rogan? You're to bear the burden of travelling and worrying and making the decisions? It hardly seems fair."

I felt warmed by his concern and gave him a soft look. "I make no decisions. I merely offer an opinion. Which we all know I do often, and well, on many subjects," I teased.

"I will miss you while you're gone." He raised my hand and kissed it softly, his eyes twinkling as they captured mine. Such a charmer, I shivered. I knew deep down that as soon as I was gone Jarek would be flirting with the next prettiest maid that came along. But there was comfort and ease in being with Jarek, in being in Silvera, and to leave him was to leave the city and all the security I had known since I was blown adrift from my family so many years ago. I felt a sudden panic at having to leave and abruptly pulled my hand from his.

"I won't be long, Jarek," I replied briskly as he helped me into the saddle. "Take care of everyone."

He nodded, patting the rump of my horse, and stood back as Wolfe cantered into the courtyard from the stables.

Wolfe eyed me gravely. "Ready?"

"As I'll ever be."

I was surprised and annoyed as Wolfe sent Lieutenant Chaeron before us so that Wolfe could ride beside me, the Guard at our backs.

Before I could offer suggestion of an alternative travelling formation that involved him being *gone* from my side, Wolfe cleared his throat. "Vovjoda Jarvis has instructed me that we will have to stop in Peza for the night to visit with Grof Krill Rada, and in Caera to visit with Vojvodkyna Winter Rada."

Visiting nobility on social calls on a journey to save Haydyn's life? Were they insane? Remembering rumors of an affair between Wolfe and Vojvodkyna Winter a few seasons ago I wondered if Jarvis had actually been the one to come up with those instructions at all. I threw Wolfe a disbelieving look. "That's ridiculous."

Wolfe shook his head. "No, it's not. We can't expect to travel through the land with fifty of the Royal Guard and not have word reach the Rada that the Handmaiden of Phaedra is on a diplomatic trip to Alvernia. The Rada would be insulted if we didn't stop in to visit with them. Just be thankful we're only travelling through Raphizya and Daeronia."

"Thankful," I scoffed. "Thankful? It's your fault for making me bring fifty bloody men with me. We could have gotten through the provinces undetected otherwise."

"Oh really?" He asked, his eyebrow arched mockingly. "So if you took off through Phaedra with a couple of men you would retrieve the plant faster, is that right?"

I sniffed. "Exactly."

"And how would we explain your disappearance at the palace?"

I smirked. "I'm at the cottage with Haydyn."

Wolfe grunted at my quick response. "Fine. What about the fact that even if you were disguised as a lumberjack people would know you were raised a lady. You're a target, Rogan. Everything about you is a target, and I doubt even a few men would be able to help you out of the trouble you would get in if I weren't here supervising you."

I was stunned by his utter arrogance. My expression must have said as much because he chuckled at having irked me so much I was speechless.

"Perhaps I better swap places with Lieutenant Chaeron?"

I wanted to kick him off his horse. "I think that would be wise," I muttered through gritted teeth.

Very quickly I had the soothing presence of the older Lieutenant Chaeron, who was happy to oblige me with pleasant, easy conversation. We passed slowly through the city as folks dodged out of the way of the massive entourage. I was surprised when Wolfe began leading us toward the Flower District, the wealthy neighborhood where Matai and Wolfe lived—where all nobility and wealthy business owners had beautiful townhouses. The route lengthened our journey out of the City. I was even more surprised when we drew to a halt outside one the townhouses.

"What's going on?" I queried Lieutenant Chaeron.

He nodded to Wolfe as the Captain dismounted from his horse. "Captain Stovia wanted to personally inform his mother of his departure. She worries." He smiled at me as if I would be moved by the familial image he created. Instead I had gone cold inside at the thought of Wolfe and his mother. Of the man missing from their lives. I shuddered and looked away from the house, fighting to keep my composure as images of Syracen flashed through my mind, always followed by my parents' horrified faces as they died, of my little brother lifeless at my feet.

"Miss Rogan, are you alright?" Lieutenant Chaeron asked softly.

I nodded, throwing him a brittle smile. I liked Chaeron. A few years ago I had asked him to stop calling me My Lady like everyone else. He swapped it for Miss Rogan, and it felt a little easier to swallow.

I was about to speak, to reassure him, when the door to Wolfe's home reopened and he appeared with a short woman at his side. He turned and kissed her hand and she smiled anxiously at him. Then she turned and waved at the Guard.

"Safe trip, good men!" She called softly.

"Thank you, My Lady!" Some of the men called back. She smiled prettily, still very attractive for her age, not even a hint of a gray hair in her chestnut tresses. Her eyes travelled over our entourage and then finally found me. Vikomtesa Stovia froze, her lips falling open. She appeared aghast by my presence. She turned to Wolfe and whispered something and he too stiffened, shaking his head and muttering to her. She nodded, seeming to gulp, and then looked back at me. I could have sworn the woman looked scared. Seeming to shake herself, her blue eyes switched from me to Chaeron.

"Lieutenant Chaeron, take care of my Wolfe won't you?"

Lieutenant Chaeron grinned as Wolfe rolled his eyes at his mother before patting her hand and bouncing down the stone steps to mount his horse with an ease and agility that made me envious. "Of course, My Lady!" Chaeron called back.

I looked away sharply, shaken by the Vikomtesa Stovia. Even more so by her reaction to me… as if I was the one to be feared, not them.

***

As soon as we were out of the city, Wolfe pushed us on at a fast pace. When we could we skirted around villages, when we couldn't we slowed so as not to cause suspicion. I hated those moments, having to wave to the villagers like I was royalty, when in truth I was a farm girl just like many of the Sabithians. Once we were out of the village and onto the main trade roads, Wolfe picked the pace back up and we followed suit. My body began to ache three hours in, my bottom numb in the saddle. I tried not to show my discomfort. We wouldn't be stopping today as we had gotten a late start. We would be riding on until night fall.

Lieutenant Chaeron seemed to sense my ever-growing discomfort and began to talk to me about his family. We shared stories of farm life, and agreed that the people of Vasterya seemed very similiar to those of Sabithia . But not once did I actually ever mention my family, and Chaeron didn't pry. Everyone knew my sad tale.

Everyone knew I didn't *discuss* about my sad tale. Instead, the Lieutenant made me laugh as he spoke of his younger sister and her comical attempts to catch the man of her dreams in their village in the north west of Sabithia near the stone quarries.

"Donal is from coal mining country in the north east of Sabithia," the Lieutenant grinned. "Quiet, reserved people. He moved to Laerth to live with cousins, start a new life in farming. He wasn't prepared, I don't think, for the overwhelming attentions of my sister."

I laughed as he described her outrageous tactics to get Donal.

"She succeeded though?" I asked, not nearly as uncomfortable as I had been.

Lieutenant Chaeron snorted. "Kirsta had him wed in less than two months. They've been married three years now and have two children. More to come I suspect."

His was a warm sounding family, what I'd always imagined my own would have been like, had we been given the chance to grow with one another. I swallowed my numbed grief and encouraged him to tell me more about his own wife and children.

As night fell we crossed first the River Silvera, and a while later, the River Sabith, and as we passed through small woods we saw lights twinkling in the distance between the trees. Coming out of the woods, I swatted at another insect that had decided my skin was a tasty treat. Not even twenty four hours in and already I was feeling the irritation of travelling.

"Sabith Town." Wolfe stopped his horse, turning to us as he pointed at the large town in the distance. "We'll rest here for the night."

I swear I almost swooned in relief. And I was *not* a swooner. I grinned at the Lieutenant, and with renewed energy The Guard loped into a canter, the men and the cart still trailing behind us in the woods. I was assured they would catch up.

Seeming to know the town, Wolfe took us straight to a large inn on the outskirts of it. I was thankful that we wouldn't be trotting our way through the quiet streets at this time, waking everyone from their beds.

The inn keeper, a tall, stout woman with arms like rolling pins, came swaggering out to us, and I raised my brow at her manners. Then I smiled. Her robust confidence reminded me of Cook.

"Well, what a fine sight!" She called heartily as Wolfe dismounted. They shook hands and it became clear to me that she and Wolfe were already acquainted.

"You bring me much business, Captain Wolfe." She nodded to us all, her eyes landing on me. She dipped me a graceful curtsey at complete odds with her ambling gait. "My Lady!" She called up to me. I was beginning to realize that this woman never spoke. She barked. "Well." She turned to Wolfe. "You'll be needing a room for that fine lass. As for you and your men, well, I have five rooms free that I'm sure a good few can share. The rest will need to bunk down in the stables I'm afraid."

"That's fine," Wolfe assured her. He spun around to address Lieutenant Chaeron who dismounted. "Lieutenant, I'll ask you to take a room in the inn. See how big the rooms are, see how many of our men can share. I'll bunk in the stables with the rest."

Taken aback by Wolfe's order, having thought he would've been too spoiled to 'rough' it with the rest of the men, I forgot myself and began to dismount. I was almost to the ground when I felt a hand on my lower back and was eased to the ground. I knew his scent before I even turned. "I can manage," I bit out.

"I know," Wolfe replied coldly. "But appearances, My Lady, appearances."

I made a face and he rolled his eyes at me.

"Child," he muttered and then took my arm like a gentleman. I tried to tug it away but he held me fast. "Can you behave for one night, Lady Rogan?" he hissed. "I have to show you to your room."

"You're such a fusspot," I exhaled and allowed him to walk me into the huge inn. I gaped in wonder at the openness of it. To our left was an arched doorway that led into a large eating area and bar. A fire crackled at one end and I shuddered at the thought of its delicious heat. To our right was a narrow hallway I guessed led to rooms and before us a massive open stairway that led to the rooms upstairs.

"Room 11, Captain." The inn keeper approached us, grinning broadly. She thrust the key towards us and Wolfe took it before I could.

"Thank you, Mags, you're a wonder."

She blushed at his smile and I groaned inwardly. Dear haven, if a woman like Mags fell for Wolfe's charm, no woman alive was safe.

"I'm sure I can find the room all by myself. I'm a big girl, you know."

He grunted at that and led me upstairs.

The room was surprisingly nice. And large. A four poster with clean cotton sheets and woven quilts sat at one end, and lo and behold a lovely fire already lit flickered brilliantly at the other. Very nice. Not that I gave positive commentary in front of Wolfe.

"I'll have Mags bring you up a meal." Wolfe strode around the room, peering here and there. What in haven was he looking for? "Everything seems in order." He marched stiffly back to the doorway.

"What? No rookery thieves behind the changing screen?" I asked sarcastically.

Unimpressed, Wolfe stared right through me. "Just lock the door behind me."

I shrugged in answer just to annoy him and as the door was closing in his wake he said, "And stop flirting with my men, My Lady. Some of them are married."

My cheeks flamed in outrage, and without him to bear it, the door took the brunt of my thrown travelling bag.

Chapter Seven

Although Wolfe had promised to take it a little easier on us after having hurried us through the first day, he still kept up what I considered a grueling pace. He only allowed us a fifteen minute break, and although I understood (more than anyone) the importance of getting the plant in good time, I didn't think we'd get there any faster if we all died from exhaustion. Moreover, the men were a little befuddled by how quickly we were moving considering this was supposed to be a casual diplomatic trip.

I managed to antagonize Wolfe into giving us a half hour break.

By the third day of our journey we were close to reaching the northern border of Sabithia. The night before we had been given shelter by one of the wealthiest farmers I had ever met. Chaeron told me no one knew how they bred their sheep or worked the wool, but the Farmer Soel and his family made plenty of money around Phaedra, providing the rich with the finest wool. As Farmer Soel had welcomed me into his home, I had found his face familiar. Clearly, I had seen him at the marketplace in Silvera. I had been led inside with Lieutenant Chaeron. The rest of the men were either camping outside or in the stables. Wolfe had insisted I be chaperoned, but at the glare I drew him he had immediately suggested Lieutenant Chaeron accompany me while he kept an eye on the men.

After a wonderful sleep it had been jarring to get back on the horse, but as the hours wore on I realized my aching muscles were growing used to the saddle. Thank haven for small mercies. The light was fading as we cantered into what Chaeron called Lumberland. Most of northern Sabithia was covered in forestation, and the province purchased most of its wood for housing, furniture etcetera from these companies. Wolfe carefully followed signs that had been posted to allow travelers to pass through safely, careful not to put us in the path of falling trees and such. By the time we drew clear of the forest and into a clearing where a small village stood— a lumber factory on the outskirts marring its quaint beauty—the day had grown dark as it gave into night.

People were still milling around and noise levels rose at our sudden appearance. Wolfe held a hand up to us and the Lieutenant stopped. I pulled on Midnight's reins to halt her. We watched quietly as Wolfe approached a tall man who stood with his sleeves rolled up, his face grimy with sweat. At whatever Wolfe said the man nodded quickly and disappeared off into the door of the factory. Only minutes later, he returned, followed by an equally tall, strapping man perhaps in his late fifties. This man grinned broadly at the sight of us. He spoke to Wolfe for a moment before the captain led him to us.

"My Lady. Lieutenant," Wolfe addressed us quietly. We were all a little tired today. It *had* been especially hot. "This is Jac Dena. And this is the village of WoodMill. Jac owns the largest lumber company in northern Sabithia."

Jac grinned proudly and nodded his head at me, his eyes washing over me wide and astonished. "Nice to make your acquaintance, My Lady."

I nodded my head, unsure what to say. And to be truthful too tired to think.

"Jac has graciously invited Lady Rogan and Lieutenant Chaeron to stay with him and his family. He's going to prevail upon the rest of the village to give The Guard shelter for the night."

"Thank you, Mr. Dena," I acknowledged softly, desperate for some food and sleep. "That's extremely kind of you."

"Oh not at all, not at all, My Lady." He shook his head, still grinning. "We are honored to offer hospitality to the Royal Guard and the Handmaiden of Phaedra."

I glared at Wolfe. Damn him and repeating that stupid nickname. He smirked unrepentantly back at me.

***

Not too much later, I found myself seated beside the Lieutenant at a homely table, in a homely kitchen, with wonderful homely aromas that made my stomach clench in anticipation. Jac's home wasn't overly large but it was comfortably furnished, and from the state of things it was clear his family had everything they needed. His wife was a pretty, petite woman who stammered in my presence and flittered around us like a little butterfly around too many flowers. Jac sat at the head of the table, and, after arguing quite profusely, I sat across from his two sons instead of at the other end of the table where Mrs. Dena normally sat. I wasn't coming into someone else's home and acting like some kind of overbearing Kralovna. Mrs. Dena finally took a seat and we all began serving ourselves. I became uncomfortably aware of Dena's two sons' staring. My cheeks flushed under their scrutiny. The eldest, Jac Jnr, couldn't be much older than me, and the youngest, Leon, not much older than Haydyn. I had never before been the target of such open attention and I squirmed in my seat. From the corner of my eye I saw Chaeron grip his knife a little too tightly.

Thankfully, Jac drew my attention from them, asking questions about Silvera. I tried my best to answer them graciously and articulately. After all they had opened their home to strangers and I was more than thankful to be off my horse for a while. I'm sure Midnight was equally thankful.

"By gee…" Leon suddenly exhaled, sitting back in his chair, his dark eyes fixated on me. I stopped with my fork halfway to my mouth, my eyes wide with surprise. The boy looked as if he was picturing me naked. I flushed harder. "You are the prettiest thing I've ever seen. And that's including Shera. Shera's the prettiest girl in WoodMill, but she isn't as pretty as you."

"Leon, don't—"

But Jac Snr's reprimand was cut off by Jac Jnr, who slapped his brother across the head. "Don't be speaking to royalty like that, Leon. And don't be speaking about Shera at all. I told you to stay away from my girl."

"She's not your girl!" Leon yelled, going purple with anger very quickly. I unconsciously slid towards the Lieutenant as the boys argument grew wilder, none of the two listening as their parents demanded them to stop. I flinched as the discussion became aggressive in light of some personal revelations.

"What do you mean you kissed her?!" Jac Jnr bellowed. He dove onto his brother, the two crashing to the ground. I jerked back from the table at the sight of fists meeting flesh, images of Kir on the muddy ground, a giant soldier towering over him in the dark, flashing through my mind. I stumbled away from the fight, feeling hot shivers cascade across my skin. Seeing my reaction, the Lieutenant strode across the room and shoved Jac Snr (who was very little use considering his size) out of the way. He grabbed the two boys as if they weighed nothing and tore them apart with little effort.

"Enough!" He shouted at the two and then glared at Jac Dena. "I suggest you discipline them."

Jac nodded, his face red with embarrassment. "I am so sorry, Lieutenant. I've never been so ashamed in my life." He grabbed his sons, growling at them as they disappeared from the room. I looked at Mrs. Dena who looked so confused and alarmed by her sons' behavior that I immediately grew worried.

My eyes clashed with Lieutenant Chaeron. A silent message passed between us. This was it. The Dyzvati magic was beginning to fail in Sabithia. People who were inclined towards temper would no longer be affected and soothed by Haydyn's evocation. They would react as they would do naturally, without thought, only with the heat of anger no longer tamed by my friend and her magic. It never even crossed my mind that it might be natural for brothers, close in age, to fight so. To Phaedrians, under the Dyzvati spell for so long, *natural* was to curb any instincts that may disrupt the peace, despite any inward feelings of anger, passion or violence.

That night Chaeron insisted on sleeping on a pallet in the room the Dena's gave me. I didn't question it.

Chapter Eight

Wolfe was visibly upset when Chaeron told him what had happened the next morning as we readied to leave. He glanced around to make sure none of the men were listening nearby and then looked at me, his gaze penetrating. "Are you alright?" He asked tightly.

I nodded, perturbed by his apparent concern.

Wolfe looked at me a moment too long, his eyes telling me he was worried by the news. Instinctively I wanted to reassure him somehow.

And then I remembered who he was and turned my back on him to mount Midnight.

***

It rained in Raphizya. Not light showery rain to ease our hot skins but hard, pelting rain that fell down on us in large drops, furious at having been dominated by the sun for so long. My cloak was soaked to my dress like a second skin making movement on the horse difficult. Not to mention I had to keep pulling my cloak closed, my muslin dress leaving little to the imagination plastered to my body. We stopped at an inn that night and I stood naked by the fire for so long the backs of my legs were blotched red. I didn't care. I was blissfully warm.

The next day the sun was back out but not so hot, and we gathered ourselves together again for a milder, more comfortable journey. I winced at a chorus of sneezing from the men behind me and prayed that none of them were very ill.

When Wolfe stopped us for lunch it was in a wide open field. In the distance we saw cows and sheep in neighboring farm lands. The grass was as green as green could be, as green as a master painter's imagination, and a single, beautiful willow tree attracted the men as they dismounted. Some gathered around the tree, talking and laughing as they sipped thirstily from their water canteens and munched on bread we had bought from the people of WoodMill. I fed Midnight an apple and then left her to graze by the men, needing a moment of peace from them. I didn't wander far, just enough so that their voices were bells on the wind. Wolfe sat laughing with Chaeron and a few others, munching on some oatcakes. I shrugged off an uncomfortable feeling that had begun to grow within me. Part of me felt as if I'd misjudged Wolfe somehow— unfairly blamed him for his father's deeds. So far he had proved himself strong and fair. His men loved him, obeyed him, and trusted him despite his young age. Surely that told me a little something of his character. I winced and thought of my parents, mentally slapping myself for my soft musings. If I felt this strongly, this hateful towards Syracen for what he did, surely Wolfe felt the same way about me and my exposure of Syracen? Frowning, I pulled my gaze away from him and grew interested in two of the men training off to the side. They parried and thrust at one another with their swords— easy, fluid, strong. My heart skipped a little as a sudden interesting idea took hold. I lifted up my skirts and strode towards them.

"Officer Stark, isn't it?" I enquired softly as I came upon them. "And Officer Reith?" They seemed surprised that I knew them by name but I had an excellent memory.

"My Lady." They both offered little bows.

"Please." I held my hands up. "It's Rogan. Or," I noted their appalled looks, "Miss Rogan, if you must. But I'm not Lady anything."

"Miss Rogan," Officer Stark cleared his throat, "how can we assist you?"

I smiled at them. Now… I couldn't flirt. I was terrible at it. But I had learned from Haydyn that a soft smile went a long way. And she was right. Stark and Reith puffed up their chests under my feminine attention. "I was watching you train. You're both very good."

They flushed and began murmuring 'thank you'. I calculated their heights with the happy realization they were the perfect men to ask of this. Not too tall, nor too broad.

"I wonder if you might teach me how to use a sword?"

Reith's jaw dropped before he remembered himself and straightened, clearing his expression. "A sword, Miss Rogan?"

I offered him an even bigger smile for calling me Miss Rogan. "Yes. Nothing too difficult of course, but I do think with us travelling into Alvernia that it may be of use to me to know how to defend myself a little."

The men shared a look. I breathed an inward sigh of relief. They weren't too shocked by the idea. In fact Officer Stark nodded determinedly. "You might be right there, Miss Rogan. Shall we show you first how to grip the sword?"

I grinned excitedly, unable to believe they had acquiesced so easily. I was so used to being treated like Haydyn— like I was a piece of precious glass that would shatter at the slightest touch. Reith, being the shortest of the two, circled me a little uncertainly and then came up behind me, his arms going around me to show me how to hold the sword. So engrossed in their teachings, laughing with them as I thrust the sword like a limp noodle, I didn't hear his approach until…

"What the bloody hell is going on?"

Reith jumped away from me as if I was poisonous, his face flushing as he looked at the person behind me. Wolfe.

I turned around. "We wer—"

"I wasn't asking you," Wolfe snapped, glaring at the men. "Officer Stark?"

Officer Stark coughed, shifting uncomfortably. "Miss Rogan asked us to show her some basic sword training, Captain. We didn't see any harm in it."

"Any harm? Any *harm*?" Wolfe seethed. "She could have walked into the damn thing, for havens sake."

Blood flooded my cheeks like boiling water and I bit my tongue from screaming at him like a banshee. "Captain Stovia," I fumed. "I am not a doll. I am perfectly capable of avoiding the sharp end of a sword."

"And," he ignored me entirely, knowing how much it would enrage me further, "*Lady* Rogan is to be addressed as such."

"I asked them to call me *Miss* Rogan," I retorted.

He growled, "Well I'm un-asking them." His own cheeks were flushed now as his blue eyes sparked like hot chips of aquamarine at his men. "From now on, if *she* asks for anything, you ask me first before you acquiesce to her request."

"Yes, Sir." They both mumbled, heads bowing a little.

Wolfe turned on his heel and began marching away, his spine stiff with irritation.

"I have a name!" I called out to him lamely. *She* indeed.

As soon as he was out of earshot, Officer Reith whistled, "I don't know what it is about you, Lady Rogan, but you're the only one who ever makes Captain lose his composure."

I frowned at him and Officer Stark nudged him, his eyes telling him to shut up.

"Oh right." Reith swallowed, looking embarrassed and a little guilty. So they had remembered I had inadvertently had Wolfe's father killed then, had they?

"Yes," I replied wryly. "People react oddly when they're talking to their arch-nemesis."

I walked away feeling deflated, only to stiffen when I heard Reith mutter to Stark, "I'm not sure that's what gets Captain so hot."

I grimaced and kept walking, my eyes finding Wolfe as he ordered the men back onto their horses. Of course he saw me as his enemy. Why else was he always baiting me? I wasn't an idiot— Wolfe hated me as much as I hated him. And I'd be waiting when he took his chance for vengeance.

If only I knew how to use a sword.

Spoilsport.

***

I wasn't speaking to Wolfe for humiliating me in front of his men and he wasn't speaking to me for enlisting his men's help behind his back. He rode ahead the entire way to Peza and I glared at his back without distraction. Lieutenant Chaeron kept making amused little sounds from the back of his throat but I ignored him, somehow thinking if I stared long and hard enough Wolfe might suddenly be knocked off his horse and onto his ass.

Having sent one of the men ahead to let Grof Krill Rada know we were arriving, Grof Krill's guards met us at the gates and escorted through Peza to the Grof's home. I stared in wonder at Peza, completely oblivious to the people and their waving and exuberant calls of welcome. I was amazed by the similarities to Silvera. It was as if Silvera had been copied by a master artisan and plunked down in Peza. The architecture was the same, the street plan was the same, and even some of the market square was the same, if only a little smaller. The difference, however, was the awesome splashes of vibrant color everywhere. Tapestries hung on the outsides of buildings, and there were murals painted on brick work. I winced at the thought of having to clean and replace those tapestries, and at having to refresh the murals every few years. But this was the city of art and it made sense that the people wished to display it wherever they could

The Lieutenant caught my astonished expression and grinned at me. "Remarkable, isn't it?"

"Extremely." I smiled, truly charmed by the colorful city.

The Grof's guard quickly led us out of the hubbub of the city to a gated district, where large mansions surrounded a beautiful park. When they pulled to a stop outside the largest mansion, I gaped openly. The building with its pillared columns and gothic arches was a jumble of architectural ideas and yet somehow it worked— intimidating and palatial.

"Captain Stovia," the Captain of the Grof's guard announced loudly, "Vikomtesa Laurel Sans," he pointed to the smaller mansion next to this one, "has graciously offered her house and stables for some of your guard. The rest of your men will find rooms and shelter with his Lordship. Some will have to sleep in the stables, but I assure you they are large and comfortable, Captain."

Wolfe nodded. "Thank you, Captain." He turned to Chaeron. "Take some of the men to the Vikomtesa's and introduce yourselves. Get some rest. We leave early tomorrow at sunrise."

"So soon, Captain?"

We all turned towards the voice that belonged to a tall, elegant man, who strode towards us from the house, a huge wolfhound following at his heels. A footman opened the massive gates for Grof Krill Rada. His eyes immediately found me. "Rogan," he called up to me familiarly and I noted both Wolfe and the Lieutenant share a disapproving look. "It's been a while."

The last I had seen Grof Krill was three years ago. I had taken him for a quiet man, watchful and intelligent. We had barely spoken, at least not enough for him to speak to me as if we were old friends. Remembering why I was there, however, I offered a polite smile. "My Lord." I bobbed my head. "It is good to see you. I trust you are well."

He smiled, his eyes travelling down the length of me. "I am now."

I narrowed my eyes at his open flirtatiousness. I didn't remember this side of him.

"Well, someone help the Lady Rogan down from her horse," Grof Krill snapped and Wolfe dismounted quickly, his jaw taut with anger at having to be told to act like a gentleman. For some reason that annoyed me and I reached for him without complaint as he drew me down from my horse. His eyes widened marginally at my acceptance of his aid. He held me a moment too long, my heart picking up speed as our suspicious gazes clashed with one another. Seeming to remember himself, Wolfe shook a little and stepped back.

"Rogan." Grof Krill breezed past Wolfe to loop my arm through his. His eyes were half-closed, seductive, as he said, "I have such grand plans for us this evening. How does dinner and the Opera sound?"

Exhausting, I thought. "Wonderful," I mumbled.

"I'll accompany you," Wolfe's tone drew us to a halt inside the driveway.

Grof Krill arched an eyebrow at him. "Oh you will, will you?"

Wolfe strode towards us, his face stony and dangerous. He matched Grof Krill in height and outweighed him in strength. "Lady Rogan goes nowhere without a Royal escort, My Lord."

The Grof sniffed, quite obviously put out. "We'll be accompanied by *my* guard."

"I said *Royal* escort, My Lord," Wolfe reiterated arrogantly and then dismissed the Grof by turning to the Lieutenant. "Take the men to the Vikomtesa's now, Lieutenant Chaeron. Have the men ready to leave by sunrise tomorrow."

***

Dinner was a strange affair.

I was continually befuddled and astonished by Grof Krill's outrageous flirting. He had never treated me with such overt flattery before, nor Haydyn even. And surely the women at court would have mentioned Grof Krill if he was such a lady killer. No. I definitely remembered a somber man, who was refined and reserved. I hadn't known him very well but I had thought him one of the more intelligent members of the Rada. What on haven had happened to him?

I patted Strider's (the wolfhound) head as it lolled in my lap, his eyes staring up at me adoringly. I really shouldn't have slipped him that little bit of chicken. We shared a frustrated look with one another as Grof Krill told me how beautiful the ladies of the opera were this season— *although nowhere near as beautiful as you, Lady Rogan*, he added. I nearly snorted at that. Just what did this character want from me?

Somehow I managed to get through dinner despite the Grof's appalling bad flirting and Wolfe's monosyllabic responses to questions posed by Krill. I felt so tense I was sure one pull of the laces on my dress and I would snap like a piano wire.

Things deteriorated badly from there. I had no dress to wear to the opera so Grof Krill provided me with one. I flushed as his maids helped me into the red dress. *Red.* I had never worn red. And it was a deep, scarlet red in plush velvet. Not to mention I had never worn my neckline low like that before. Oh it was very fashionable, and all of Haydyn's dresses were cut just so, but I had never really been comfortable with my figure, which was a little more voluptuous than what was fashionable. I blanched as they pulled my hair up off my neck, fastening pins here and there with an expertise that boggled the mind.

I bit my lip as I saw the finished result in the mirror. I looked like a modern lady of Peza. But I wasn't modern. If you were clever like Haydyn, modern was elegance and refinement without being flashy and bold.

Modern on me was a little too dark and declaring.

"I can't wear this." I turned on the two girls who had made me up so prettily. "Isn't there another dress I could wear in a style not so bold?"

The maids gasped at me, "No, My Lady, you must wear this. You look wonderful."

I flinched at my reflection. I looked like someone else, and there were too many facets of my persona out there in the verse that already had nothing to do with me. I didn't want to add another one to it. I slumped suddenly, exhausted. I just had to get through this evening and then I'd be done.

"Fine," I sighed and brushed past them without another word.

As I descended the grand staircase in Grof Krill's home I watched on quietly as Wolfe entered the entrance hall. The Grof had obviously lent him evening wear as well, the crisp darkness of the tailored suit causing his hair to burn gold under the chandelier. I stopped to gaze on him as he stared up at a huge painting of the Silver Sea crashing against the cliffs, the palace up in the distance. His eyes washed over it intensely as I studied his handsome profile. What was he thinking? He looked so stark, so alone.

I suddenly felt as if I knew him.

A strange flutter in my lower belly made me stumble and as I righted myself I realized I'd drawn Wolfe's attention. I warmed uncomfortably at his unwavering stare and met him in the middle of the hall. His jaw clenched tightly as he took in my attire.

"What?" I snapped, already feeling stupid and in no mood for his quips.

Wolfe cleared his throat. "You look beautiful."

I wanted to slap him. How dare he make fun of me when I felt so vulnerable? "Can you just cease with the sarcasm for one night, Captain?"

His mouth fell open at my rebuke but his riposte was interrupted by Grof Krill.

"Rogan!" We turned abruptly as he greeted us. For a moment he looked astonished at my appearance and then he smiled—a real, genuine smile—as he took my hand and placed a gentlemanly kiss upon it. "Why, you look beautiful, Lady Rogan."

I relaxed, believing *he* actually meant it. I gave him an almost grateful smile. "Thank you, My Lord."

I heard a choked noise beside me but carefully ignored the good Captain as the Grof escorted me out.

***

The opera was wonderful. The singers' talents were breathtaking, the sets incandescent. My senses were overwhelmed by the vibrancy and decadence of the opera hall, the wealthy audience and vivacious stars that took to the stage, and the scent of jasmine in the air. I had been to the opera in Silvera with Haydyn but there was something different about being at the opera in the homeland of opera. Even the stares of the nobility who recognized me from society events back in Silvera did not sway me from the stage.

It would have been an un-spoilt evening if Grof Krill hadn't begun his insincere pursuit of me again. His hands kept reaching to brush my arms, my skirts, and one time even my breast as he passed me. I threw a quick look at Wolfe, but thankfully he hadn't noticed.

At the moments when I was sinking into the oblivion of the effervescent opera crowd, Grof Krill would touch me and jar me back into the reality of his uneasy company, making me careful not to lean too close to him. By the end of the opera I was at once moved and exhausted.

With Wolfe at our back, Grof Krill took my hand as he led me out of his opera box and through the crowds outside it. He began descending the stairs before me, rather than taking me down side by side, and I knew his plot instantly as he 'accidentally' tripped on a stair, pulling me down so I was captured in his arms.

I grew flush with anger at his games and apologies as he kept a hold of me, pretending to balance my footing, even though I already had. I struggled a little in his arms, desperate not to cause a scene. I felt a hot grip on my arm and looked up at Wolfe who spoke daggers with his eyes as he glared at Grof Krill. I immediately let Wolfe pull me away and looped my arm through his as the three of us descended the stairs. No one else had noticed our little tussle, thankfully.

My mind whirled with confusion. I knew now why Grof Krill didn't flirt or seduce. He was awful at it! Which begged the question… why was he trying so hard to seduce me?

I was grateful as Wolfe helped me into the carriage and sat beside me before Grof Krill could.

And then I froze as I realized I'd been thankful to Wolfe.

Thankful for his presence.

Fear and shame shuddered through me and I sidled a little away from him as the carriage departed from the opera hall.

***

I practically ripped the dress off, having shooed away the maids who were waiting for me in the guest suite. I dug through my travelling bag in an unidentified rage and drew on my nightgown, almost tearing it. I was so angry. Angry and confused and I didn't know why. I took a breath, pouring cold water from the ewer into the basin and splashing my face. I stumbled and flopped down onto the stool by the dressing table, studying my face intently. Gradually my eyes blurred and I grew numb as my face became more and more unfamiliar. Tears trembled on my eyelashes and I didn't know why.

"You're just tired, Rogan," I whispered to myself.

Snick. Snuck.

I stilled at the sound of a key turning in the lock in my door, my heart pounding in my chest. I shot to my feet, eyes wide as my hands delved quickly through my travelling bag until I drew out the dagger Matai had given me before I left. Heart racing, sweat breaking out across my shivering skin, I tip toed barefoot across the room like a skittering rabbit and took up behind the door. Slowly, sinisterly, it opened inwards. A black, booted foot appeared first and then a large elegant hand on the door shut it behind him. I stood behind the familiar figure. Disgruntled at my height, or more so his, I lunged up and looped an arm around his neck, drawing him down so I could press the dagger in my other hand to his throat. He let out a startled yelp and halted, immobilized at the feel of cold metal.

"Grof Krill," I growled, shocked and terrified that he had come into my room. I couldn't let him know I was scared, willing my body not to tremble.

"Now, Lady Rogan." He held his hands up away from his body, the key to my room glittering in one of them. "I mean you no harm."

I pressed the dagger closer so that it pinched, and he hissed in pain. "No harm, indeed. What do you want with me?"

"Your magic."

I was so taken aback by his answer I inadvertently loosened my hold and he ducked out of it, spinning to face me. I thrust the dagger at him and he took a wary step back. "What do you mean?"

"I need your help," he replied, his eyes sad, desperate, yet still wary on the dagger.

I made a face. "Would that be why I was subjected to your abysmal attempts at seduction this evening, My Lord?"

He flushed, groaning as he ran a hand through his hair in frustration. "I'm not a very good flirt, My Lady. Please accept the apology of a foolish man."

"Why the flirting?"

He shrugged. "I thought if you liked me, you might be more inclined to help me."

"With what?"

"I want you to find the woman that I love."

I shuddered as the wave of my magic crashed through me. I felt her. Beautiful and gentle Ariana, who worked in Javinia… as a governess. I threw Grof Krill a speculative look, glad he had no idea that my magic had already obeyed his command.

"The woman you love?" I queried softly, suddenly curious despite my exhaustion. Then I felt a spark of indignation. "You intended to seduce me to help you so I could reunite you with the woman you love?"

Grof Krill winced. "Not my brightest or nicest plan."

I huffed. "I should say not."

His shoulders slumped, his throat working as if trying to hold back the emotion. "I wouldn't have, My Lady, but… Ariana. My lovely Ariana. She was a ward of my friend's, the Baron Roe. The daughter of a friend who had died when Ariana was twelve. I hadn't seen the Baron for years, we had been school chums. He moved back to Raphizya from Daeronia three years ago. Ariana and his daughter, Drusilla, were of an age, both seventeen. I fell in love with Ariana almost instantly." He sighed. "She wasn't like those twittering idiots at court. She's intelligent. Quiet. Gentle, but passionate. I miss her every day."

"What happened?" I whispered, finding myself lost in his heartbreak despite his terrible behavior.

He smiled humorlessly. "We were like two peas in a pod. We loved one another very much. But my aunt found out about my love for Ariana and was furious I would consider marrying someone of low birth. She blackmailed Ariana. She had somehow gotten wind of Drusilla's affair with one of the stable boys and threatened to expose her." He snorted. "So cliché, I know, but a word from my aunt and Drusilla would have been ruined. And Ariana loves Drusilla, so she took up the situation my aunt offered her and disappeared. My aunt wouldn't tell me where she'd sent her. My aunt died a year ago, leaving me no clue. I've hired people to find her but nothing. My aunt was a conniving bitch but a clever one."

"So you want me to seek her?"

He nodded, coming towards me in his excitement. I held the dagger back up. "I won't hurt you, Lady Rogan."

"No, you won't," I bit out. I was split in two by him. Part of me ached for him, and the other distrusted him as I did most men. What if he'd hurt Ariana somehow and she had *wanted* to disappear, wanted to stay disappeared. A plan formed in my mind. "You better leave, Grof Krill, before I scream for Captain Stovia and you are charged with trying to force the Princezna's Azyl to work for you."

"No." Krill shook his head. "I would never force you. I just want your help."

"I can't help you, My Lord. My duty is not to you. I work only for her Highness. Now please leave."

I watched the light dim in his eyes, his face growing instantly haggard. "Of course, My Lady. I shall leave you in peace. I apologize for my untoward behavior. I overstepped."

He left quietly, the door closing behind him. Futile though it was, I turned the lock.

I sighed wearily. I would never sleep now. Instead I hurried to the dressing table and rummaged through the drawers until I found stationery. I dipped my pen in ink and quickly began my letter...

Dear Ariana,

You do not know me. I am Rogan of Vasterya, Princezna Haydyn's Handmaiden and one of the Azyl. I have been fortunate enough to enjoy the hospitality of Grof Krill Rada of Raphizya whom I am told you are acquainted with. I write to you on behalf of a desperate man who tells me he loves you. I have not informed him where you are, although the Grof did command me to seek you, so if he lies and yours was not a relationship of mutual love then fear not, he will not find you. Did you know the Grof had no inkling of his

aunt's blackmail until after your disappearance? Did you know his
aunt is dead thus freeing your dear friend from any consequences of
her blackmail? Grof Krill desperately seeks you, Ariana. He has
been looking for three years. I doubt he will ever give up. He loves
you.

If you love him... please return to him.

Yours Sincerely

Rogan

I sighed and folded the letter into an envelope, addressing it to
Ariana. I snorted at my own foolishness. The girl would probably
think the letter a hoax. I shrugged and pulled on a dressing gown.
Still, it was the only thing I could think to do for him without putting
all my trust in his sincerity. I hurried from the room, my candle
flickering shadows across the walls as I made my way through the
mansion and out into the cold stable yard. I shivered and rushed to
the stables, coming across a man on guard whose hand immediately
leapt to the hilt of his sword before jolting in shock, in recognition.

"My Lady," the officer whispered, rushing toward me. "What are
you doing out here? Are you well?"

I nodded, my teeth chattering together. "Here." I thrust the
envelope at him. "You must find a messenger immediately and have
this delivered in Javinia." I handed over the coins for payment to the
messenger.

Like a good soldier, he nodded unquestioningly. "Of course, My
Lady. But please, I insist you return inside."

I smiled. "I have every intention of doing so." And without another word, I hurried back toward the mansion, that deep, buried, romantic part of me hoping my letter reached Ariana.

Chapter Nine

I didn't think I had ever been so tired. Not quite trusting the Grof, I had been unable to fall asleep and had sat frigidly up in bed until sunlight started to spill through the cracks in the curtains of the guest suite. By the time the maids arrived to help me dress I was already washed, had adorned a clean simple riding dress, and pulled my hair back in a conservative plait. I knew they were shocked by my 'unladylike' behavior— a lady who took care of herself? Haven forbid. I imagined I'd be a prime bit of gossip amongst the servants of Grof Krill's home when I left. I was so numb with exhaustion I couldn't really give a damn.

The Grof was not at breakfast and the butler informed me Wolfe had already eaten and was preparing his men in the stables. I scoffed down some toast and black coffee hoping it might wake me up. All it did was make me jittery. Knowing Grof Krill would not be seeing me off after last night's embarrassing encounter with me, I made my way outside to find the Guard waiting for me. I felt annoyed that no one had come for me sooner. I hated being the one to keep everyone waiting, as though I was *that* woman. Tiredness made me grumpier and I huffed in annoyance as Lieutenant Chaeron helped me mount Midnight with a cheery, "Good morning."

"Lady Rogan." Wolfe urged his horse towards me from the front of our cavalcade. He nodded a dismissal at the Lieutenant who left my side to mount his own horse, Snowstorm, whom he sidled away from us, giving us some privacy. I frowned against the morning sun, wishing suddenly I was more inclined to wearing bonnets, but they annoyed me. I liked to be aware of my surroundings, and bonnets cut off too much of my peripheral vision.

"Captain Stovia," I mumbled, hoping I wasn't in for a lecture of some sort. This could end in a screaming match. A weary one, but I'd give it my best effort.

His blue eyes were pale as the sun shone off them, pale and concerned as they checked me over, as if searching for injury. "Are you alright, Lady Rogan? After last evening, I mean?" He twisted his mouth in consternation as we both remembered Krill's appalling behavior.

I nodded sardonically, suppressing a yawn. "Yes, Captain, I am fine. Grof Krill explained his unseemly behavior last night and apologized."

Wolfe stiffened at the news, his eyes narrowing. "Oh he did, did he? And what exactly did he tell you?"

I shrugged. "He was trying to ingratiate himself to me. He wanted to use my magic to find someone."

"That piece of…" Wolfe sucked in his breath, turning around in the saddle to glare bloody murder at Krill's mansion. For a moment he looked ready to dismount and head inside. I rolled my eyes, yawning whilst he was turned away. The man really took his duties too seriously.

"Never mind," I assured him and he snapped back to face me, anger still etched his features. "I assure you I knew from the start that he was up to something, Captain. I'm not the sort of woman men make fools of themselves over."

I grew uncomfortable as Wolfe stared at me, seeming to digest what I had said. And then he snorted and gathered his reins. "And yet so many of them do."

Too tired to question that cryptic comment as he rode off to take the lead, I merely acknowledged Lieutenant Chaeron with a tremulous smile and we took off riding side by side, the Guard at our backs.

I barely remember leaving Peza, my mental state had practically shut down and my body was slowly following it. Everything was a blur as I fought to keep my eyes open, my body tense so it didn't fall asleep. But as the city disappeared behind us and the land grew quieter, passing many farms off the beaten track, my body grew happy for the peace, and thus began to give in to its need for respite. I began to feel a little nauseated with the exhaustion and fought to keep my head up. We couldn't waste any more time after stopping off at Peza. Every time my eyes slid shut for brief moments, Haydyn's smiling, beautiful, serene face danced across the blackness of my lids, and sparks of aching pain shot out of my heart and across my chest. I snapped my eyes open and gripped the reins harder, determined to go as fast as Wolfe was leading.

My body was in total disagreement. Perhaps three, maybe four hours into our journey all I was aware of was the heat of the sun burning through my dress, the distant sounds of the clip clopping of horses hooves, and murmured chatter that resembled insects buzzing around my head. The sounds didn't make sense.

And then I was lying outside in the grass by the cliffs in Sabithia. It was a hot summer day and my mind lazily began to drift into slumber.

"Miss Rogan," I heard a voice call in the distance. My eyes popped open at the happy sound and I stood up leisurely. I gazed behind me to see Haydyn approach, and was shocked to see her all alone. She was barefoot like me, her toes dipping deliciously into the cool grass at our feet.

"Your Highness." I teased back. "I missed you," I said as she took my hand.

"I missed you too."

We grinned at one another and then turned to stare out at the calm sea from the cliff edge.

"That water looks wonderful," I whispered.

Haydyn squeezed my hand excitedly. "You know today it looks calm enough to swim in."

I shook my head. "We're too high up."

She chuckled. "Be adventurous, Rogan."

Frowning I took a step closer to the edge, the drop at least fifty feet, probably more. "It'll kill us."

"Not today." Haydyn shook her head. "Trust me."

Heart pounding at the thought, I gripped her hand tighter. "Together? On three?"

She laughed, exhilarated. "One. Two. Three!"

"Miss Rogan!"

And then I was falling.

Blissfully falling.

***

I didn't want to peel my eyelids open. Everything ached in that sore, yucky—even my muscles were tired—kind of exhaustion. I felt strange and disorientated. Where was I? I slowly opened my eyes and found myself staring up at an unfamiliar ceiling. It was dark. Night time. Only a few candles around the room lit it enough for my heart to start pounding at its strangeness. Where the hell was I?

"Ah, Miss Rogan, you're awake."

Calming instantly at Lieutenant Chaeron's voice, I turned my head on the soft pillow and found him sitting in a chair by my bedside. His brow creased with worry as he leaned over me, offering me a glass of water. He helped me sip it and then settled back in the chair.

"What happened?" I asked hoarsely. "Where are we?"

He made a clucking sound with his tongue, a little disapproval marring his usually friendly expression. "You should have told us how exhausted you were. You could have been killed."

Now I was very confused. All I could remember was talking to Wolfe earlier outside Grof Krill's mansion. "What happened?"

"You fell asleep on your horse." He sighed like a wearied parent. "If I had jumped off my horse one second later you would have landed on the ground, and possibly have been trampled."

I swore softly at the thought, chastising myself for my stupid pride and hell bent determination to get to Alvernia in record time. "You caught me?"

He nodded and patted the hand I reached out to him. "We've stopped at a nearby farm. We've all been resting. We're going to stay here through the night. Captain is not at all pleased with me or you."

I groaned. "I've slowed us down."

Chaeron patted my hand again. "That's not why he's angry. He wishes you had told him you'd had no sleep. He takes your safety very seriously. We all do."

I nodded vaguely, feeling my lids start to flutter again as I mumbled, "He needs to find himself a hobby."

Distantly I heard the Lieutenant chuckle, and then he whispered, "Sleep well, Miss Rogan."

Chapter Ten

Not a big fan of guilt, I smothered the feeling with anger and directed it at Wolfe. The next morning he barely acknowledged me. He was cold, distant with me, and it irritated me more than it should have because generally I liked his indifference. But his annoyance with me only compounded how stupidly I had behaved, making me feel like the simpering debutante I was so adamant I wasn't. Lieutenant Chaeron threw me a few bolstering looks and as usual tried to keep up a pleasant conversation with me as we rode through Raphizya. Wolfe was taking things deliberately slower and it smacked of condescension. I huffed in the saddle, wanting to speed up, and poor Midnight faltered a little at my mixed signals. I leaned over to stroke her face, apologizing quietly in her ear for taking my impatience out on her. I forced myself to relax in my seat and ignored Chaeron's knowing grin.

With my renewed energy it didn't feel like such a long ride that day. Before I knew it we were crossing the stone bridge across the River Kral, called so because it was the longest in Phaedra, passing through not only Raphizya but Vasterya as well. We were closing in on Ryl, the second largest city in Raphizya, famous for being the only city in Phaedra that wasn't a capital, and also for its factories. Almost as large as Peza, it was home to factories that mass-produced textiles, paintings, pottery and lots of other knick-knacks, designed by the artisans of Peza. The factories sustained much of Raphizya, supplying employment and a large exportation income.

Knowing the plan was to stay with Matai's cousins, Mr. Zanst and his wife and their two small children, I wasn't surprised when Wolfe led us through the outskirts of the city towards the Factory District. Ironically, the Factory District wasn't in fact where the factories were. The Factory District was home to the mansions and large townhouses of the *owners* of the factories. Mr. Zanst owned a large textile factory and was said to be wealthier than his Vikomt cousin, Matai. I had met Mr. Zanst and his wife at court before, two of the few people outside the titled nobility who were invited to stay at the palace during the spring and autumn Seasons of Sabithia. They were a nice couple, friendly and open, and a refreshing diversion from the titled nobility and all their manners and 'do's' and 'don'ts'.

When we arrived Mrs. Zanst was there to greet us, her husband not yet returned from his office at the factory. Attractive and young, I hid a smile as some of the Guard tried not to stare at Mrs. Zanst. They had been deprived of female companionship for longer than some of them were used to and she was a lovely sight. Sighing, I dismounted with Chaeron's aid and was immediately enveloped in a friendly hug by Mrs. Zanst.

"It's such a pleasure to see you again, Lady Rogan." She smiled widely at me as she stood back to take in my appearance. "I must say you're looking very well for a young lady who's been travelling.

And without a carriage no less." She frowned, looking over the Guard.

I shrugged inelegantly, happy to be around someone who didn't care if I shrugged inelegantly. "I thought a carriage would be more of a hindrance than a help."

Mrs. Zanst didn't seem to agree but she said no more, clasping my hand in hers as we walked inside, leaving the Guard to their organization. It would seem there wasn't enough room in the stables or the mansion for all of them so some would have to venture into the city for accommodation. I rolled my eyes as many eagerly volunteered, knowing that the excitement was due more to finding a bed partner than an actual bed.

"Oh," I gasped as we stepped into the entrance hall. "Your home is lovely, Mrs. Zanst." And I meant it. Her expression brightened, a little flush of pride cresting her cheeks.

"Thank you, Lady Rogan. I do try."

In all of the homes of the wealthy I had ventured into the floors of the entrance hall, hallways in general, were always white and black marble, or, as it was at the palace, pure white marble with crystalline sparkling under foot. But Mr. and Mrs. Zanst had forgone the cold, marble aesthetic of the wealthy, and instead had beautiful, wide slatted, light wooden polished floors that reflected the light from the stunning but simplistic chandelier that spiraled down from the ceiling in one trim arm. I stared at it a moment, surprised by its originality. It was like a piece of artwork. Careful not to encumber the light, airy quality they had created, there were no drab oil paintings to be found or heavy tapestries, only pale buttercream walls, one of which was adorned with artwork—a mural, depicting a brilliantly blurry forest with gorgeous wood nymphs and other charmingly rustic creatures. A few silver mirrors were dotted here and there, wall sconces in the same vein as the chandelier, and flowers of the softest pastels.

"It's like a fairytale," I whispered. "Haydyn would love this."

Mrs. Zanst blushed even harder. "Do you really think so?"

I nodded sincerely, giving her arm a friendly squeeze. "You, Mrs. Zanst, have a gift for interior design."

"Oh, I'm pleased you think so. Many of the women here," her voice dropped to a murmur, "Think my taste unfashionable."

"To the contrary, your taste is a fashion setter. Wait until we get you back at the palace to decorate Haydyn's private parlor, Mrs. Zanst, then all the ladies will be after you to design their homes for them."

Wide-eyed, she pulled me into her equally quaint and beautiful parlor. "Do you really think so?"

***

Having inadvertently received a friend for life in the charming Mrs Zanst I felt bad when I tricked her. Desperate for some time alone, to be away from the Guard and the Factory District that was buzzing with the news of our arrival, I knew I had to make my escape before the neighbors started calling on Mrs. Zanst to meet me. Having faked a headache and fatigue from the journey, I was shown to a spectacular guest suite with wonderful views of Ryl. There I hastily wrote a note to Mrs. Zanst telling her where I'd gone so she wouldn't worry, and then threw on a dark cloak, creeping out of the room. I had to hide twice— once in another bedroom and then in the music room on the second floor. I halted at the sound of children squealing and realized the nursery must not be far off. Afraid of being found by an impish child I scurried down the next flight of stairs and then cursed under my breath when I came face to face with the butler.

"May I help you, My Lady?" She bowed gracefully, the tallest female butler I had ever encountered.

I gulped, thinking fast. "I'm going for a walk. Mrs. Zanst suggested I follow the Factory District out to the right to get to the city…"

She frowned, shaking her head. "That can't be right, My Lady. Mrs. Zanst must have meant for you to take a right and then a left once you reach the entrance to Factory District."

I smiled inwardly. "And that just takes me directly into the city?"

"You can't miss it, My Lady."

"Thank you."

And as easily as that I was out the door. I held my breath, almost skipping as I shot out the driveway and through the gates. As I hurried along I peered towards the back of the house and saw some of the Guard still organizing themselves at the stables. Afraid to be spotted, I took off at a run, no longer caring which of the neighbors saw me.

As the wind rushed into my face, tearing my eyes, my skirts fluttering a hindrance around my legs, I grinned and pushed harder. It felt wonderful, so freeing.

Skidding to a stop at the end of the Factory District, I peered over my shoulder to make sure I wasn't being followed. I couldn't see anyone. I smoothed my skirts down and straightened my cloak and began walking sedately towards the city which called to me with its noise and smell. There were still a few hours until night fall. Plenty of time to have a look around.

Quite suddenly I found myself in the hubbub of the city, where there were lots of people rushing around as if they had somewhere important to be. In fact, as I gazed around at the rather drab appearance of the city, with its industrial towering factories in the distance and the squab little shops, I realized how different it was to Peza, considering the wares that were created here.

Or so I thought.

Like stepping into an oil painting I was gobsmacked when I walked through an arched alleyway. I found myself lambasted by color as I entered the market square. Everywhere were people and stalls in a multitude of hues, where quiet sellers stood patiently offering help and information. Never before had I seen such serious, hushed sellers. But as I walked around the stalls, my eyes widening every now and then, I realized why. Their products were beautiful, no matter if they were mass-produced— products that sold themselves. I stopped suddenly, drawn to a stall with beaded jewelry. The jewelry I owned was of the finest precious metals and stones, nothing like this. But I fingered a bracelet made with pleated leather. Three beautifully painted beads in emerald, aquamarine and rose decorated the end near the clasp. A little bird of silver metal hung between the beads.

I saw my mother taking a bracelet from my hands as a child, pressing a soft kiss to my head and telling me it wasn't to be played with, but when I was older it would be mine. It had been a leather rope bracelet, no beads, but a little bird had hung from its center.

"How much?" I asked a little dazed, holding the bracelet up.

The seller smiled gently. "Five coppers, miss."

Five coppers? That was all. I picked it up, as well as another similar to it, only it had different colored beads. Haydyn would like it, I was sure. "I'll take two."

She smiled pleasantly at me again and took the money. She then wrapped the bracelets separately in tissue paper before popping them into a little paper bag for me. I thanked her and walked away, bemused by my impulsive buy. I wasn't really much of a shopper.

I wandered for a while amongst the glitter and awe of the splendid market and then eyed a confectionary store in indecision. Finally, at the little growl my stomach gave, I shrugged and went inside to buy a cream cake. I took the cake back outside to stand back from the crowds at the corner of the shop where it met a narrow lane between buildings. I could eat my cake in peace here.

Although the cake was good, I couldn't help feeling a little unsatisfied as I ate it people-watching. It was nowhere near as good as Cooks, I grimaced. I wondered if Valena was eating all my cakes as well as hers. Smiling wryly at the thought, I wiped at a smudge of cream on my lip and readied myself to make my way back to the Zansts. I was lucky to have gotten away for this long. And I just knew I was in for a severe lecture from Wolfe. Perfect.

Just as I made to take a step forward, I heard a scuffle from behind me. My heart spluttered with dread.

But it was too late.

A grimy hand clamped down on my mouth, dirty and sweaty, and my feet left the ground as I was dragged back into the darkness of the alley. I tried to scream against the hand but all that came out was a muffled whine. I beat at the head behind me, trying to wriggle free from the strong arm around my waist.

"Stop it, or I'll break your neck," A gruff voice spoke in my ear and I shivered as decayed breath hit my nostrils. I stilled, feeling the strength in his hold.

"Do it," someone else said.

How many were there? I turned to see just as a musky hood came down over my face, drowning me in darkness. Panicked, I began to thrash and beat out at my attackers. More hands clamped down on me, muffled grunts and curses as they tried to lift me off the ground. I was terrified, furious to be so helpless and vulnerable with one of my most valuable senses disabled.

The familiar sound of a sword hissing from its scabbard halted us all, and my heart fluttered as one of my captors grunted, "Deal with him."

One of the Guard! I'd never been so thankful to be followed. Trying to listen to the fight that had broken out, I stupidly let myself be thrown up onto what I assumed was a hard shoulder. Grunts and a shout of pain found my ears. I hoped the officer's sword had just found one of my captor's bellies. The clatter of steel hitting stone made me tense. Then all I could hear was flesh smashing into flesh, grunts, groans, hisses of pain.

"Stop or we kill the girl."

I heard heavy breathing and then silence.

Fearful, I began to squirm now, beating down on whatever body part I could find.

"Stop it, or we will kill your bodyguard!" the voice below me growled as an insolent hand swatted me hard on the bottom. Tears of humiliation sprung in my eyes but I stopped fighting, realizing they had both I and the officer in an untenable position. If one of the Guard had let himself be disarmed, then there must be too many of them to fight.

"What will we do with 'im?" A rough female voice asked from somewhere to my left.

"Bring 'im. 'e'll only send people after us otherwise."

We were really, truly going to be taken? I began to fight again in earnest, taking pleasure in the yelp of pain I produced when I bit what I assumed was an ear through the hood over my head.

"Bloody 'ell! Prick her!"

A sharp, short pain flared in my arm and I cried out. Heat rushed up my arm at a dizzying speed and flooded my brain in a gush of warmth and bright colors. The colors burst like fireworks in the night sky until they faded, leaving only a numbing darkness.

Chapter Eleven

A shaft of light shot up under my eyelids causing a sharp pain to ricochet through my head, eliciting a small moan through my dry lips.

"Rogan?" A familiar voice asked.

I jolted at the voice and then groaned, peeling my eyes open. I turned my head and winced at the cold stone beneath it. A tiny window was the source of the annoying light in another wise dank, cold cellar. I scrambled quickly to a sitting position, grit and dirt pinching my hands. Panic set in as I found Wolfe sitting near me, looking tired and pale as his eyes searched my face.

"Are you alright?" He asked softly.

I shook my head, trying to get my bearings as I looked around the large room with the low ceiling that had nothing in it but us and a changing screen in the corner. A door made of thick metal bars stood at one end. I felt like I was in a dream. I couldn't remember how I had gotten here. Flashes of images, of unfamiliar faces, swept through me. I remembered being jostled. And someone trying to feed me. And dreams. I felt like I had been dreaming forever.

"Where are we?" I croaked. My throat felt like it hadn't been used in a while.

Wolfe sighed and pushed a cup of water to me. I gulped it thirstily. "Do you remember being taken in the market at Ryl?"

Instant fear shot through my body and I trembled, dropping the cup. "Where are we?" I whispered again, searching frantically about me now. I could still feel that clammy, dirty hand over my mouth, those hands on my body as they tried to restrain me. "You were the one that followed me?"

He nodded gravely. "We've been kidnapped by the Iavii."

My jaw dropped. That was the last thing I had been expecting. Although, to be honest, I didn't know what I'd been expecting. The last time I'd been kidnapped it was for my power and I had just assumed this was the same situation. Maybe not. "Those gypsies from Alvernia that have been causing havoc in Javinia?"

"The very ones." He grimaced. "They drugged us. We're in Javinia, but we've only been out for a few days I think, which means we must be near the border."

My heart thudded in my chest and I felt sick. "A few days. At the mercy of those people?"

Wolfe's jaw clenched and he turned away from me in frustration. "Well you would have to defy orders and take off on your own somewhere."

Heat, angry heat, shot through me, waking me up. "Oh it didn't take long for the lecture to start, did it, Stovia?"

"I'm not the one that got us into this mess," he hissed, gesturing around at the cell. "They have a Dravilec, Rogan. And they're well-armed and can fight. God knows what else they've got."

"A Dravilec?" I was momentarily thrown by the fact that gypsies would have a mage amongst them, considering there were so few left.

"Yes. The healer took the effects of the drugs away so we would wake up. I was then promptly told who they were and what they wanted with us."

Feeling belittled and guilty I mumbled fearfully, "What *do* they want with us?"

He laughed humorlessly. "They find themselves fortunate enough to have in their hands the Handmaiden of Phaedra and the Captain of the Royal Guard. We're bargaining chips, My Lady. They're going to hold our safety ransom in exchange for land from Markiza Raven."

I scoffed at the ridiculousness of it. "Are they idiots?" I made a face. "Even if they managed some temporary agreement with Novia, once we're free we'll just send in the entire Guard to arrest them for what they've done."

Wolfe shook his head. "Not if they keep us hostage for a while. They know how much the Princezna cares about you."

An awful understanding dawned. "You mean... they mean to keep us here... indefinitely?"

"That would be my guess." He nodded. "They'll promise to look after us, keep us alive. But they won't hand us over until they're certain of their position. If ever."

Acid curdled in my stomach and I dragged myself along the floor so I could lean my head against the wall. The tight, fearful knot that had begun to grow in my chest since we learned of the growing crime in Phaedra enlarged painfully. "This is because of Haydyn... isn't it? Because her power is waning?"

Wolfe sighed and followed my lead, leaning back against the wall, his light eyes hard as flint. I looked away, unnerved by him when he had that focused, ruthless look in his eye. "Yes. It is," he replied finally.

"We have to get out of here." I shook my head and jumped up to rush at the cellar door. My legs felt wobbly after having not used them for a while but determinedly I held my balance.

"Rogan..."

I pulled at the door but it was worthless. Ignoring the prick of tears behind my eyes, I peered through the bars. There was nothing there to see. Just a narrow, dark staircase leading upwards into the house. I whirled around, my eyes narrowing on the window. I ran at it but couldn't reach it. I twisted around to glare at Wolfe. "Can you get up for a minute to see if these bars will shift?"

He pinned me to the wall with a disgusted look. "I'm the Captain of the Royal Guard, Rogan, not an idiot. I tried the window and the door as soon as they left us in this damn cellar."

I deflated instantly, but refused to show my fear. "Well, we have to do something."

"The only chance we get is if they let us out of here."

Reluctantly hearing the wisdom in his statement, I nodded and made my way back over to my spot at the wall. I slumped down to the ground and stared straight ahead. It was then I became aware of how much I needed a bath. I wrinkled my nose. Being kidnapped was not fun.

Wolfe grunted and muttered a curse under his breath.

"If you've got something to say, say it," I snapped.

"Oh it's nothing," his words were laced in heavy sarcasm, "Just relaxing, you know, thanking my fortunate stars for being the one who was put in charge of protecting you."

"Hey!" I whipped around to scowl at him. "No one asked you to protect me! To follow me!"

He rolled his eyes. "I'm the Princezna's Captain, Lady Rogan, and you are the most important person in her life. Not to mention the last of the Azyl and the only bloody person who knows where the Somna Plant is! It's my job to protect you. And you make it *very* difficult."

"I went for a walk!"

"And got us kidnapped by creepy… Iavii… people!"

"Oh dear haven," I groaned, and leaned back against the cold brick wall, closing my eyes. "Will you be done with it, already?"

He spluttered, "Be done with it? Be done with it? Do you have any idea what this could do to me? What if I can't get us out of here, Rogan? What if something happens to you?"

"Be calm. It's not like they'll blame you and you'll lose your position." I sighed heavily. "I can't believe I've been kidnapped with Captain Wolfe Stovia. Talk about cruel punishment."

"You are such a brat."

I smiled, glad I was annoying him. "And you are such a pompous, untrustworthy snake."

I felt his indrawn breath without looking at him, and determinedly squished the guilt that seized my body.

Before he could reply, the key turning in the door made us both sit up, alert and wary. A huge, burly man with long dark hair pulled back into a messy queue strolled into the cellar. His intimidating figure seemed to take up the entire space as he watched us like a predator studying its prey.

"We've brought ye food." He had a slight accent, his words rolling and unrefined. He nodded at someone and a young man came into the room carrying a tray. "One move and I run ye through," the big man warned, his hand going to the hilt of a sword strapped to a belt around his hip.

I looked at Wolfe for guidance but he just kept his eyes trained on the larger of the men. The young man came forward, keeping his distance from us, and laid the tray down on the ground. He looked up at me as he picked one bowl off of it and slid it towards me. As he did the same for Wolfe's bowl, his eyes never left me, and I squirmed under his strange regard. He watched me with a clinical interest that was extremely disturbing. I waited for Wolfe to do something. But he just sat there.

"I need to use the… I have need of… I need to relieve myself," I finished, blushing at my impulsive outburst.

"Relieve yerself?" The big man grinned. "Ye mean ye need to use the piss pot?"

I flushed even harder at his crassness but nodded, hoping he would let me out of the cellar so I could find my bearings.

"There's one in the corner." He grinned even harder. "Behind the changing screen."

I was horrified. "You are jesting?"

He shook his head. "If ye're that desperate, ye'll use it."

Disgusted, I could do nothing but wait with bated breath for them to leave and then I turned on Wolfe. "Why didn't you do something?"

He shrugged and grabbed the bowl and bread that had been left for him. "He had the upper hand. Moreover, I'm hungry."

I think my jaw may have hit the ground at how blasé he was. Infuriated with not only him but myself, wishing I had somehow had a life that prepared me more for the kind of hogwash that kept happening to me, I snatched my bowl up and bit out, "Wonderful. Just wonderful. Let me know when you decide to start working on that whole protecting me bit you keep spouting."

He threw me a look but didn't retort… which annoyed me more than I would have liked.

When we had finished eating he finally said, with a mischievous smile in his voice, "You know if you need to… *relieve* yourself… I could hum, or sing so you're not embarrassed, you know by the noi-"

I blushed so hard my face could have warmed the guard around a camp site. "I understand your meaning." I stopped him.

"I'm just saying I—"

"You could sing, yes, yes, very funny."

He nearly choked himself to death laughing when three hours later I made him do just that, as I darted behind the changing screen to use the chamber pot.

Worse still, he actually had a very nice singing voice.

Chapter Twelve

"I really am getting tired of people manhandling me," I murmured, covering my fear with bravado and ignoring the bite of the dagger at my neck. I tried not to think how ironic it was that only a few days ago I had someone else in the position I was now in.

"Rogan," Wolfe murmured back in warning.

I shrugged and the gypsy at my back pressed the blade harder against my skin. I winced as it cut.

Wolfe growled in outrage, making a move toward me. The two, huge gypsies holding him in their grasp reeled him back in.

"I told ye, the girl gets it if ye make a move to attack." The man holding me was the one from yesterday, with the messy queue and hand-me-down gentleman's clothing. The hand he wrapped around my waist tightened and he pulled me back against him so I was flush with his body. "And ye," he whispered softly, threateningly in my ear, "keep it quiet. Or I'll find a far more pleasurable way to occupy yer mouth."

Aghast and repulsed, humiliated at being treated this way in front of Wolfe, who eyed the gypsy as if the man had just signed his own death warrant, I immediately decided it would be best if I shut up. The four men in the cellar with us were huge. What on havens did these people eat?

"Now," the gypsy continued, "We're going for a little walk outside. And ye're both going to behave." I noticed how measured his words were, as if he had to concentrate on his enunciation.

I tried to catch Wolfe's eye to see if he had a plan, but the gypsy pushed me ahead and I stumbled, my throat nearly catching the blade edge again.

A menacing growl rumbled from behind me. "If you want me to behave, you better stop putting her life in danger," Wolfe warned in a tone that would have intimidated a lesser man.

The gypsy grunted but he was more careful with me as he took us upstairs. The overwhelming light made my eyes tear. I really only caught a glimpse of a cozy parlor as we were taken out the front door of the modestly-sized farmhouse we were being kept in. As he dragged me down the porch stairs, my eyes widened at the fields in front of me. Dozens of tents scattered the farm. There were dogs and cats running around, horses grazing leisurely, and even some sheep and cattle in the distant fields. In the center was a huge stone campfire, unlit but still surrounded by the comings and goings of the gypsies.

"Come on," the gypsy grunted and pushed me ahead. We made our way past a few tents, people stopping to stare at us curiously. Finally, he drew us to a halt at a small tent made from blue, purple and red patchwork and dropped the dagger from my throat.

"Vrik," a soft, seductive voice called to him and we all turned as a dark-haired beauty sauntered over to us, her hips swishing her drab skirts back and forth. The worn blouse and gray skirt did nothing to detract from her exoticness. My spine stiffened in insult as she perused me with a sneer before instantly dismissing me. Worse, she turned to Wolfe and her eyes widened appreciatively. She even licked her lips. "Are these them?" she asked Vrik without taking her eyes off Wolfe.

The gypsy behind me answered so I assumed he was Vrik, "Yes. Selena wants to see them."

She nodded without question and then turned back to undressing Wolfe with her eyes. My heart picked up pace as I watched Wolfe stare back at her, expressionless. "Can I have this one, Vrik, when ye're done with him?"

He snorted. "Scarla, we haven't even sent the message off to Javinia that we have them. A little patience, please."

She flashed her black, cat-shaped eyes at him. "But I want him!"

"I'm sure the lad will be more than happy to see to ye when we reach an agreement with Markiza Raven. But until then he's a prisoner, alright."

Scarla pouted and reached out to trail a hand down Wolfe's chest. Wolfe flinched. "I'm not happy about this, Vrik. Perhaps I should speak with papa?"

"Papa will tell ye the same thing. Now leave, Scarla."

It was obvious these two ill-mannered being were siblings. Scarla huffed a little more and then went up onto her tiptoes to whisper in Wolfe's ear. I don't know what she said but I don't think I had ever seen Wolfe blush before. My heart thumped and my own cheeks flushed. I looked away quickly, gritting my teeth.

When Scarla left, Vrik grabbed my arm tight and thrust me into the tent, the other men and Wolfe at our backs. Immediately my eyes adjusted to the dimness of the tiny tent. I stopped, startled by the sight of the older woman in front of me. It was very nearly bare inside. There was grass beneath my feet, and except for the bizarre placement of a gorgeous old library desk and chair that would have looked more at home in a study at the Palace, there was no other furniture. The old woman sat patiently behind the desk.

"Here ye are, Selena. Our prisoners." Vrik pushed me towards her and I caught myself on the desk. "Let us know if ye see anything that'll tell us about any future land agreements that we may come to with that damn Rada."

Selena looked at him blankly, as if he were below her interest. "Take the girl back outside. I wish to speak with the boy first."

As I was dragged back outside I threw Wolfe a questioning look. But he was staring avidly at Selena. Who an earth was this woman? What was going on?

Finding myself at the mercy of other gypsies' curiosities, I turned so my back was facing camp. Vrik just stared at me, his arms crossed over his chest.

"What's going on?" I asked, more than a little impatient now.

"Be quiet."

"Who is Selena?"

"I said be quiet."

"You are really rather rude."

The beast actually bared his teeth and growled at me. "And ye are getting on my last nerve, Princezna."

Trying to pretend that his animal behavior didn't bother me, I sniffed. "I'm not a princezna."

He made a face. "Ye look it and act it."

I did not, I huffed. I think all and all I had been taking my abduction extremely well. Especially considering the terrible memories it brought back of being carted off by Wolfe's father. I hardened in remembrance and snarled back at him. "You haven't seen anything yet."

Vrik raised an eyebrow, looking me over. And then he had the audacity to grin. "Ye might be fun after all, Princezna."

Before I could offer a disgusted retort, Wolfe was pushed out of the tent with the two gypsies at his back.

"What happened?" I asked quickly, moving towards him. Vrik instantly gripped my arm and wrenched me back.

Wolfe growled at him and then turned back to me, his lip still curled disdainfully. "Nothing. The old woman's useless."

One gypsy walloped Wolfe across the back of the head.

"Stop it!" I yelled at the offending gypsy, and was rewarded with a bewildered look from Wolfe as I was shoved past him and back into the tent.

"Anything?" Vrik asked Selena without any niceties as I was forced to stand before her.

Selena shook her head. "He was blocking me somehow."

"Blocking ye?" Vrik asked, stunned. My head swiveled between them, completely at a loss as to what they were discussing.

"Hmm," she answered. "Keep a careful eye on him."

My patience snapped. "What is going on?" I demanded, my eyes burning into the old woman.

She arched an eyebrow at me and then smirked at Vrik. "We've got a live one here."

Vrik chuckled, a dark, sinister kind of chuckle that sent shivers slithering down my spine. "Seems so."

Selena smiled at me and I got the strangest feeling she liked what she saw. "Give me your hands."

I tucked my hands behind my back. "Why?"

She winked. "I'm not going to hurt you. Just give me your hands... or I'll make Vrik hold you while we do this."

I snapped my hands out so fast she cackled. "Don't think she likes you too much, Vrik, so I wouldn't be getting any ideas."

Vrik grunted behind me.

Selena snatched my hands in her extremely cold ones, and I felt every wrinkle and crevice of that sandpapery touch shoot through me.

She was a mage.

Seeing the question in my eye, Selena nodded. "I'm one of the Glava, little Azyl."

Dear haven, they had one of the Glava and a Dravilec among them. I immediately wondered if they had been collected as Syracen had done with me, Valena and Kir. "Your specialty?" I asked softly.

"I'm a reader."

"You read people's minds?"

"No. Just their future."

I gulped and shook my head, trying to withdraw my hands. "I don't want to know my future."

She cocked her head curiously, her eyes washing over me as she gripped them tighter. "What happened to you, girl, to make you so afraid of the future?"

"Well for a start I was kidnapped by the Iavii."

Vrik smothered a chuckle behind me as Selena glared.

"*We* won't hurt you, girl. No. You fear something else."

"You said you can't read minds."

She laughed softly, condescendingly, like I was a small child before a teacher. "I don't need to read minds to know that a young, intelligent, pretty girl with her whole life ahead of her should be excited at the prospect of the future. You clearly aren't. So why are you frightened instead?"

"I'm not frightened by it. I'd rather live it when it comes, than know about it now. A piece of information can change a person. I'd hate to change the way I'm supposed to live my future."

Her whole face lit up as she grinned. "What a wise thing to say."

I exhaled heavily, acting the spoiled brat in the hopes it would get me out of there. "Can I go now?"

"No." She tugged harder on my hands and I lurched forward. A sick feeling swirled in my stomach as Selena closed her eyes. She was still for so long, my heartbeat getting louder and louder, I was sure they must hear it in this tiny, sparse tent. Finally, Selena grinned. Her eyes popped open. "Nothing to fear," she assured me. "You'll marry one of the Glava and be very happy about it."

I scoffed and pulled my hands free. "Doubtful, madam, as I have no intentions of marrying anyone. Ever," I emphasized. I began to feel better. Perhaps she wasn't really one of the Glava after all.

Selena shrugged. "I'm never wrong."

Wolfe was right. This was nonsense. I rolled my eyes and pulled away from her. "Can I go now?"

Seeming to laugh at me, which irked and unsettled me, Selena nodded and Vrik strode forward frowning. He grabbed my arm and I winced. I was going to be covered in bruises from where he kept gripping me.

"That's it?" he hissed at Selena. "Nothing about an agreement? About land?"

She shook her head, holding her hands up. "You know I only get what's most important to them."

"And you determined marriage?" I snorted and turned to Vrik. "You might want to purchase yourself a new reader. This one is definitely broken."

Growling at me again Vrik forced me forward and out of the tent. Wolfe was nowhere to be seen. My heart sputtered and panic seized my chest. "Where's Wolfe?" I asked and received no answer. Vrik tried to pull me back towards the house but I wouldn't let him, digging my feet into the ground. "Where's Wolfe?"

"He's fine," Vrik grunted and used both hands to pick me up and put me down in front of him. He pressed his hands into my back and pushed me forward. I struggled all the way.

"Damn it, tell me where he is?"

"He's fine," he reiterated. "Now get yer arse in this house before I do good on my earlier promise to shut ye up in a way that I'll definitely enjoy, but ye won't."

A flood of rage took over that I should be so vulnerable to this man, and I elbowed him deliberately as he pushed me forward. "Just tell me where he is?"

"Having a better time than me probably."

I stilled, my heart now thumping so hard it made me ill. Was Wolfe off with the gypsy girl whilst I was being mauled? Irritated beyond rationality I kicked back and caught Vrik in the thigh. He yelled and yanked my head back by my hair as he forced me, kicking and shoving me, into the house and down the cellar stairs.

"Where's Wolfe?" I screamed for the millionth time and was again ignored as I was thrown into the cellar.

I landed with a painful grunt, my ribs hollering in my pain as they impacted with the stone floor.

I heard a curse and then Wolfe's face hovered over mine. "Rogan, are you alright?"

He was here? In the cellar? I groaned and relaxed, thumping my head against the hard ground. "Ouch." I was such an idiot. They'd brought him back to the cellar to wait on me. Honestly, I was terrible at this 'being kidnapped' situation.

"Rogan?" I felt his fingers on my face and the blood whooshed in my ears. My eyes flashed open and my heart lodged somewhere in my throat at his close proximity. I could see the hints of gold striations in his blue eyes, his dark lashes enviably long. Suddenly I felt a strange queasy feeling in the pit of my stomach and squirmed at the concern in his face. Distrusting it, I pulled back with a flinch and watched the concern melt to his usual blank arrogance. "I take it you're fine." He sighed and moved away from me.

"Yes, I'm fine." I struggled to a sitting position, willing my heart to slow. I pushed my skirts back down into some semblance of modesty. Not that it mattered. I was torn, smelly and unwashed. Feeling Wolfe's unwavering gaze I stopped fussing and glared at him. "What?"

"Nothing." He shrugged. "I've just never heard you say my name before."

"What?"

"You were yelling 'where's Wolfe?' over and over again."

I flushed, not wanting him to misunderstand. "I thought they were separating us and we have a better chance of escape if we're kept together. And you've heard me say your name before."

Wolfe shook his head, smiling wryly. "No. It's always Captain or Stovia or Captain Stovia. Then there's *Vikomt*— you usually spit that one at me."

Uncomfortable for reasons unknown and not wishing to have anything that could qualify as an actual conversation with him, I decided to ignore his questioning. "Well, *Vikomt*, how do you suggest we get out of this?" I gestured around the cellar. "Now that we know they have a Glava and a Dravilec in their hands."

Something flickered in Wolfe's eyes at my question, something akin to disappointment, and then he looked away. He cleared his throat. "I'm wondering how many more of the mage they have here. I'm hoping they've not been..." he threw me a mystifying look before he continued quietly, "collecting them."

My throat worked at the memories but I refused to drop my gaze. I knew my eyes hardened, however. I saw it in the way Wolfe's eyes blazed back at me. I didn't know fully understand what his expression meant, but I guessed it could only be anger—memories of his own destroyed family.

"So what do we do?" I murmured, wearily wondering when this truce between us was going to end and Wolfe was going to take his vengeance.

"The only thing we can. I heard the other two guards talking about the festivities this evening. Apparently, you and I are attending. When we're there I'll create a distraction. You have to keep your wits about you, Lady Rogan. Watch me all the time. When I make my move, you make it with me and we run."

I blinked owlishly, hoping I'd heard wrong. "That's your big plan? A distraction?"

He smiled cheekily at me. "Yes. It's good, right?"

"You're going to get us killed."

"Well, since you got us kidnapped in the first place, I think it's only fair."

Chapter Thirteen

I kept my expression blank as I was studied by this man, this older version of Vrik, who stood by the campfire, shadows and light flickering across his dark skin, pin pricks of light reflecting in the blackness of his gaze. I tried not to shiver.

Around us the hubbub of noise was now a hushed tide, rising and falling with little bursts of laughter and conversation as the gypsies enjoyed ale and food around the fire. Wolfe stood beside me in the darkness. We were guarded by Vrik and three other men, but not tied up, not held tight. It was as if for now they wanted us to feel less like prisoners and more like guests. At the sound of a whimper my eyes followed it to a girl sitting on a log, squashed in the middle of two rough looking women. Her head was held back by her thick locks, tears streaming down her face as one of the woman held the dagger she'd been using to cut her apple up to the girl's eye. My face tightened in anger at their bullying and the man before me frowned, turning around to follow my gaze. He seemed amused by my reaction and turned back with a lazy shrug. "She's one of the Caels. Her brother was particularly annoying in handing over some land so we took her as punishment."

My blood ran cold, crystallizing to ice until I felt frozen solid in my anger. "And what of her brother, her family?"

He shrugged again. "Dead."

Waves of nausea crashed over me. The man seemed to flicker before me, his features merging with the man who had destroyed my life. They even had those same black eyes. "You son-of-a-bitch," I spat and was immediately wrenched back into Vrik's tight hold. I felt Wolfe stiffen beside me but I couldn't look at him. Not with the memories. Not now.

Not caring if my outburst would provoke a lash of anger, I waited sullenly for a reaction. To my surprise the man burst into laughter, his eyes moving past me to his son. "Ye were right, Vrik. She's feisty. She'll do well here."

Determined not to show fear, I lowered my eyes to regain composure, and then lifted them when I was able to project boredom. "What do you mean?"

The man waved the question away as if he was batting away an annoying pest. "First, introductions. My name is Tiger. I am leader of the Iavii."

"What do you want from us?" Wolfe asked impatiently.

Tiger seared him with a look and then smirked at him. "I only want ransom from *ye*. Ye," he shook his head chuckling humorlessly, "The famed Captain of the Royal Guard. I was expecting... *more*."

"Really?" Wolfe shrugged. "Funny, you're just what I expected— a fucking leech, sucking land that's not yours and growing fat on it. Like a bully," he nodded at the girl who was being tormented, his eyes blazing in indignation, "in the schoolyard, taking what doesn't belong to him and having the audacity to call himself Kral."

My heart thudded at Wolfe's impassioned speech, my eyes savoring this image of him. An unexpected feeling of warmth for him seized me by surprise. He looked at me when he was finished and I dropped my gaze, glad for the shadows of the night that would hide my blushing cheeks. I frowned, confused.

"Yes," Tiger growled. "That's what a pampered prince who's lived in luxury and peace his entire life would think. We've travelled for too long in Alvernia, across Daeronia. We like Javinia, it's warm. It's home. Gypsies no more, we want land. But ye wouldn't understand that. Ye haven't had to suffer the harsh lands of the mountains and deal with uncivilized folks like us. Uncivilized breeds uncivilized."

"No." Wolfe shook his head. "You chose to act this way, *be* this way. Dyzvati magic stifles emotions and actions that can lead to unrest and chaos. Not having that magic doesn't turn people into automatic animals. It just makes sure those that would act that way can't. Don't blame this on magic or lack thereof."

"Shut him up," Tiger spat at the man beside Wolfe, but I lunged between them before he could hit him.

"No!" I cried, putting my hands up to stop the blow. The man looked to Tiger. Tiger scowled but shook his head and the gypsy lowered his hand. I relaxed and glanced up at Wolfe only to find him glaring at me. Ignoring him, I addressed Tiger, "What do you want?"

Tiger sighed. "Tomorrow morning I send a message to Novia for Markiza Raven. In it, she will be told I hold ye both ransom, yer lives for land. Then we'll have to wait whilst she informs the Rada and the Princezna. When we get the land we'll keep our promise not to kill ye. *He*," he stabbed a finger at Wolfe, "will be kept as a prisoner until such time as I see fit to release him."

"And Lady Rogan?" Wolfe bit out through gritted teeth.

Tiger smiled, his eyes running the length of me in a way that caused my stomach to flip. I almost gripped Wolfe's arm I was so discomfited by that look. "Lady Rogan is something ye're not, Captain." He strode towards me, seeming mesmerized. I flinched as he reached up and gripped my chin lightly. "She is one of the Azyl… and I find that I am in need of an Azyl."

"You're a collector." I glowered at him disdainfully.

He didn't seem to care. "Yes. But ye're different. I've heard good things about ye. When Selena is impressed, I'm impressed." Abruptly he let me go and turned to gesture behind him. "Bird!" he called. Almost instantly the tall, skinny boy who had served us our food earlier, the one who had stared at me so detachedly, appeared before us. Tiger put his arm around the boy affectionately and grinned at me. "This is my adopted son, Bird. Say hello, son."

Bird smirked at me. "Hello son."

I almost rolled my eyes at his rehearsed insolence.

"Bird," Tiger continued, "is one of the Glava."

My jaw dropped. "Another mage?"

"Ye said it yerself, I'm a collector. I found Bird when he was five years old."

I almost launched myself at him and was surprised to find Wolfe's hand on my wrist, squeezing it in restraint. "You mean you took him!"

"Semantics." Tiger waved my accusation off. "Bird, show them what ye can do."

His eyes laughing at me, Bird turned and looked at the Cael gypsy girl. She gave out a frightened yelp as we watched as her hair floated up into the air, strand by strand. She began to whimper and the two women beside her laughed and scooted away from her as first one arm popped up into the air and then the other. Finally her entire body rose from the log as if propped up by unseen arms. Panic suffused her and she began thrashing and screaming as she rose steadily higher, terrified tears streaking her cheeks. "Stop!" She shrieked. "Make it stop!"

None of the gypsies around me seemed too distressed by the sight, although I noticed a few on the other side of the campfire glare at Bird in disgust. I, too, was disgusted. I felt sick at the sight and was just about to reprimand them when Wolfe snarled, "You've had your fun. Let her go."

Bird arched an eyebrow at Wolfe's demand and then looked to his father. Tiger was smiling at Wolfe. "The boy thinks he's a hero."

"Please," I added, pleading with my eyes. Tiger frowned and then nodded at his son who dropped the girl. She fell with a hard thump onto the log and let go a howl of pain. "You bastard!" I yelled, forgetting myself.

"Now, now," Tiger admonished and then shot Vrik a wide-eyed look. "Ye're right, son, perhaps she would do better for ye. I'm not sure Bird can handle her spirit."

"Then give her to me." Vrik reached a hand out and wrenched me to him. I was completely taken aback by the claim as so far he'd been relatively unemotional, even when he was threatening me with disgusting acts.

"No!" Wolfe lunged for me, but was dragged back by the two gypsies. They held him fast and tight as he violently resisted their hold.

Bird shrugged. "She's not much to look at, papa. I don't care if ye give her to Vrik."

Vrik ran a hand down my cheek so softly I trembled, fighting the urge to be sick as these men decided casually which one would rape me. "I didn't see the appeal at first either, but the more she snaps and snarls at ye, the prettier she seems to get." He chuckled and then ran a hand down my waist, my hip and around to squeeze my bottom painfully. "Plus she's luscious enough to bear healthy children." I winced at his manhandling, afraid to look at Wolfe who was struggling and cursing at them all.

"I've changed my mind." Bird turned to his father like a petulant little boy who had just discovered the toy he had given away did something interesting he hadn't known about. "I want her."

"Very well," Tiger agreed. "We'll do the handfasting on the morrow."

Marriage! I began to struggle in Vrik's arms who growled, "Papa, she clearly doesn't want him, give her to me."

"I don't want any of you!" I screamed, fighting against him, but he wouldn't yield. "You can't do this to me!"

Tiger strode forward and pulled his hand back. I braced myself. His palm cracked across my face with a slap hard enough to roll my eyes back in my head. Harsh heat shot up the left side of my face and my eyes watered at the sharp needles of pain. "You'll be given to Bird. The Glava marries the Azyl."

So that was Selena's game, I slumped, telling me I would marry one of the Glava. Old, manipulative witch.

Suddenly a shriek echoed around the campfire and I opened my eyes to see the fire in the center of camp roar high, high into the night as if it had been jerked awake from a deep sleep. The gypsies stumbled away from it, fleeing the site as the flames licked out at them like arms trying to snatch them back into the death of its embrace. Wide-eyed I looked to Wolfe and found his eyes narrowed in concentration. Bird screamed and Vrik let go of me as a wall of fire encircled his father and adopted brother. Slack-jawed, ignoring the blazing heat stroking my skin I stared at Wolfe, feeling the crackling of his magic. *His magic? His magic!*

Wolfe was one of the Glava?

He reached out, not even looking at me, and yanked me to him, his arms encircling my waist as I was pulled back into him, his chest to my back. Another fire shot up around Vrik and his men, another around tents. Wolfe, still holding me, strode forward and grabbed the girl from the Caels who sat immobilized in shock on her log. He ripped her out of her seat and holding our hands he began running, a wall of fire blocking the men so we could escape. Wolfe headed towards the house where two horses grazed. The girl seemed to come out of her daze at the sight.

She ran towards the mare and jumped up into the saddle like an acrobat. She grabbed the reins expertly, turning the horse to the west. Her terrified eyes caught Wolfe's and they swam with gratitude. "Thank you!" She yelled and then kicked her heels against the mare's flanks and bolted out of there.

"Where is she going?" I yelled against the noise of the chaos behind us, still shocked numb and cold despite the heat of the fire at my back.

"Back to her clan," Wolfe grunted. "Come on, Rogan, move." He vaulted up on the stallion and then reached a hand down for me. I just stared at, still not believing what he had done, how powerful he was.

"Rogan!" He yelled and pulled at my arm. Shaking myself of my stupor I reached for him and let him haul me up onto the horse. His arms came around me, squeezing me tight as he took hold of the reins and pushed the horse into a gallop, heading north east.

Chapter Fourteen

We rode in complete silence, pushing the horse to his limits to get as far away from the Iavii as we could. Wolfe had been right, we were very close to the border and soon, just as the stallion's coat was beginning to sweat, we came to a stop on a hill and gazed down a valley into the distance where the glass factories of Vasterya shaded the border. It had grown much bigger since I was a child. There were lots of dark, crooked buildings surrounding the factories, like a small city.

This was the rookery.

"We need to be extra careful here," Wolfe said quietly behind me, his voice pinched tight with tension. He dropped the reins, and I turned awkwardly to see what he was doing. He was shrugging out of his emerald military jacket. He threw it on the ground behind us.

"Won't you be cold?" I asked, shivering a little myself.

He shrugged. "Doesn't matter. From now on I don't want anyone to know who we are until we're returned to The Guard."

Seeing wisdom in that, I nodded and let him move the stallion forward. I still hadn't asked about the magic. For the first time I felt real and true anger toward Wolfe, not angry at him because of his father, but hurt and angry at his *own* deception. No one knew that, like Syracen, Wolfe was one of the Glava. An immensely powerful one if I was to go by the destruction he had caused to get us out of the gypsies' grasp. I stiffened as I realized why I was angry.

"You alright?" Wolfe asked softly behind me and I nodded, trying to ignore the heat of him at my back and the way my body wanted to relax into his.

I was angry because somewhere along the way I had stupidly begun to trust this man. Stupid, stupid, stupid! How could I? Were the nightmares, the memories, that huge gaping hole in my heart, not enough to remind me not to trust a Stovia?

I stewed in silence, feeding off Wolfe's tension as well. He was probably waiting on tenterhooks for me to ask why he had hidden the fact that he was a mage. Dear haven, what awful vengeance he must have been planning! And yet, that was so in contradiction to the man I had come to know...

Stop it! I yelled at myself. I didn't know him, I didn't know him at all, and it was that silly kind of... *girlish* thinking that was going to get me killed.

***

One minute we had been in the country and the next we were inside the walls of the town, of the rookery. The change in atmosphere was intense, slithering over me and clinging to my skin in sickly chills. There was a malevolence here, echoing in the way people hurried past us, not even glancing at us, their heads down as they determinedly rushed to get home or inside out of the dark, dank streets. The streets weren't kept clean. Urine and waste mixed with the smoke and smells from the glassworks. Houses and shops were shabbily constructed, soulless and frightened-looking buildings jammed together in crooked rows. There was little light here, street lamps sparsely spaced between streets.

I could feel Wolfe's astonishment at the state of the place, his shock as great as my own. This was unbelievable.

"How could Markiz Solom Rada let this happen?" I whispered solemnly and turned to find Wolfe warily eyeing a boy who was watching us too avidly.

"I don't know," he bit back. "We should have been told. We would have stopped this."

"What will we do?"

"I have a few coins I kept hidden, the Iavii didn't get them. We'll find somewhere with lodging so we can eat, rest, and send a message to The Guard in Ryl."

"Will they still be there?"

"Yes. They'll send some men out to search but they won't move perchance we return to them. I'll tell Lieutenant Chaeron to bring the men and meet us in Caera at Vojvodkyna Winter Rada's home as planned."

I gave a brittle nod, thinking his plan sound, and wondering whether he'd go through with it or decide to take his vengeance whilst The Guard was gone. He could kill me, and Haydyn would die, and then he could blame it on the Iavii. I winced at the thought.

Even to me it sounded a little melodramatic. I sighed, deciding to trust him. For now. "We need to get a move on. We've already lost too much time."

"I know."

Wolfe eventually had to stop and ask someone where the nearest inn was. We were pointed in the direction of a drinking tavern we were told had rooms above to rent. There was a stable behind the tavern and we secured the horse, handing over coin to the stable boy who kept guard over the clientele's horses.

Shivering now, the night growing late, we headed into the tavern. Eyes immediately swung to us, conversation growing hushed. I was surprised when Wolfe's hand slid into mine, and I jolted at the fissures of pleasure that shot up my arm at the feel of his rough, warm fingers entwining with mine.

He gave a slight shake of his head, his blue eyes startling in the light of the barroom, warning me not to make a scene, to just go along with him. I responded with a subtle nod and he relaxed a little, leading me past the chairs and tables, ignoring the other patrons completely. Noise level rose again as we approached the bar, and the huge burly barkeeper came over to us, a wide grin appearing in amongst his massive, ginger beard.

"Well, good evening. What can I get you?" He was all friendly smiles. I relaxed a little at this warm welcome, such a jarring contrast to the streets outside.

Wolfe nodded congenially back at him. "Good evening. We would like a room if you have one available."

The barkeeper's eyes lit up, I gathered at the thought of earning the extra money from renting a room. He looked me over before turning back to Wolfe with a wink. "Aye, I'd be wanting a room too if I were you."

Despite having overheard such talk amongst The Guard and servants back at the palace, I flushed red at the insinuation.

Wolfe squeezed my hand and shrugged at the barkeep. "My wife and I are tired, we've been travelling a while," he lied and I knew it was for my sake and my sense of propriety, a sense of propriety that seemed a little misplaced considering everything we'd gone through. "I'd like a room and some food sent up. Also, we had a little mishap on the road. You wouldn't have some clean clothes we could buy from you?"

The barkeep's grin grew wider. "Not a problem, lad." He reached under the bar and brought up a key. "Room two is available." He pointed to stairs hidden in the shadows of the back of the room. "Just up there. I'll have my wife bring you a dinner plate and some clothes."

"And some hot water," I interjected, desperate for some kind of bathing.

"Of course. That'll be three and twenty."

I tried not to gape at the outrageous costs, knowing we were deliberately being ripped off because of how desperate we looked.

My eyes rose to Wolfe's face but the only sign he gave of being annoyed was the slight tension in his jaw.

"Two and twenty," he haggled and I raised my eyebrows as the barkeep laughed.

"I don't think so, lad. Three silver pieces."

"Two and fifty."

The bar keep shook his head still laughing. "Tou are a funny one, lad. Alright, two and ninety."

Amazed, I watched as Wolfe shook his head again. "Two and seventy."

"You're robbing me." The barkeep shook a finger at us, still seeming amused. "But fine."

Wolfe handed over the money and took the key. He almost dragged me out of the barroom and up the stairs.

"Are you trying to pull my arm out of the socket?" I snapped wearily as we stumbled up the stairs and onto the landing. Still Wolfe refused to slow down until he had the door open. He hauled me inside, slamming the door shut with the heel of his boot.

"I was trying to get you out of the bar before I had to fight those bloody men over you."

My eyes widened at his comment as he strode towards the fire in the room and set about lighting it. The room was small with only a queen-sized bed. I took note of the bed with a strange thump of my heart. "What are you talking about?"

Wolfe snorted. "These people have been left to live in squalor for too long. We should have known about this. Instead we sit on our plush cushions in Silvera, thinking the world outside happy and adoring and at peace. This isn't peace," he sneered, pointing outside the window as he turned to glare at me. "Where have we been, Rogan? We've let our people come to this and we dare to look down our noses at them. Those men haven't seen anything as fine as you in a long time and I was making bloody sure we were out of there as fast as possible before they took it upon themselves to have you."

I shuddered at the thought. "I didn't notice." Exhausted, I flopped down onto the bed. "I look a mess."

Wolfe sighed and looked away, provoking the fire to life. "Wearing rags you would still carry yourself like a lady. You have the skin of a lady."

Ignoring the silly flutter in the pit of my belly that he had noticed anything about me, I tried to enforce our old dynamic and retorted stupidly, "I'm not a lady, Captain. I'm a farm girl."

Wolfe stood up and strode towards me, his eyebrow arched. "You've been raised a lady, Rogan. That makes you one."

I rolled my eyes at him, but before I could retort with a pert comment a knock sounded on the door. The barkeep's wife arrived with two barmaids. They brought us food, clothing, and hot water, and quickly left, the girls throwing wide-eyed looks at Wolfe, hiding giggles behind their hands. Clearly, they too had never seen anyone like Wolfe before. After all, *he* really was a Lord, and carried himself like a gentleman. He didn't seem to notice their attentions and as soon as the door closed he locked it. Without really looking at me, he picked up the dress they had brought me and threw it towards me. "Get cleaned up and dressed. There's a screen behind you."

I tried to quell the flutters in my belly at the thought of stripping naked in the same room as Wolfe. Determinedly, I walked around to the back of the changing screen.

"There must be some stationary in here," Wolfe muttered and I heard him pulling at drawers and rummaging. At his sound of triumph I suddenly felt a relief that we could get a message to The Guard. It had been a number of days since we'd been taken in Ryl and strangely I missed the comforting presence of Lieutenant Chaeron and the rest of the men.

A crash sounded from downstairs and I jumped, my dress falling to the floor. "What on haven…?"

Wolfe grunted as yells followed more crashing. "Tavern brawl."

A tavern brawl? Dear haven, we were far away from home, weren't we? "Oh," I managed and tried to relax at the sound of Wolfe's pen leisurely scratching against paper. If he didn't seem too concerned then I wasn't going to be.

My undergarments were in desperate need of a wash and I peeled them off with a sigh of relief. I'd just have to leave them here and make do with the rough, blue dress the barkeep's wife had brought me. It would scratch my skin but I'd rather that than have to put dirty undergarments back on. I draped them over the top of the screen, vaguely aware that the scratching of pen against paper in the background had stopped. Taking the cloth and hot water I gave myself a quick scrub down, trying to be fast so the water wouldn't be too cold when Wolfe got around to using it. After a moment or so I thought I heard Wolfe make a strangled sound and then the scratching of pen against paper started up again.

"Nearly done," I told him, thinking perhaps he was getting impatient with me. I drew on the blue dress, a demure, work-worn thing, but it was clean and surprisingly not too rough against my skin. I'd be colder without my undergarments but I thought perhaps I could get Wolfe to procure a cloak for me.

When I stepped out Wolfe was staring at the screen as if in a daydream.

"You better hurry," I said taking my undergarments off the screen and rolling them into a ball. "The water's getting cold."

He nodded, his lips pinched tightly together. When he brushed past me he barely spared me a glance. I arched an eyebrow at his behavior but said nothing. I'd now given up any attempt to understand Wolfe Stovia.

Speaking of which…

I tucked into the food, my trembling stomach glad for the energy boost, and waited as Wolfe, once clean and changed into an old pair of trousers, shirt and waistcoat, ate his meal. Then I couldn't stand it anymore. We were both sitting by the fire, enjoying the peace of the moment, and I couldn't stop myself from ruining it.

"So you're a Glava?" I asked quietly, even though there really was no question of it.

Wolfe stiffened immediately and turned slightly to glare at me. When he made no reply I grew irritated.

"Why didn't you tell anyone?"

"I don't want to talk about," he dismissed me, getting up and taking coverings from the bed to make a pallet on the floor.

"Seriously?" I jumped to my feet. "You just destroyed an entire gypsy camp and *you* don't want to talk about it?"

"No, I don't."

How could he possibly expect me to just let something like this go? "How can you expect me to trust you when you've lied about this?"

Wolfe snorted and finally glanced over at me. "You don't trust me anyway, Lady Rogan."

I ignored that, especially because it might be true, and snapped, "I demand to know, Captain Stovia."

"I could give a fuck what you demand to know. I'm tired and I'm going to get some sleep. You should too."

His coarse language should have shocked me but I knew he'd deliberately used it to rattle me, to stop me from pressing for information. Surely he knew me better than that? "The Princezna will be so eager to hear that a mage was living in Silvera all this time and he didn't see fit to tell us."

This time I stumbled back under the force of Wolfe's severe look. "You better keep this to yourself, Rogan."

My eyes flashed at his tone, my hands going to my hips in a stance of defiance. "Are you threatening me?" Furious, the words were out before I could stop them, "Dear haven, you are just like your father!"

I'd never seen Wolfe move so fast. One moment he was on the other side of the room, the next he was inches from me, his large hands gripping my upper arms, shaking me hard for what I had said. His eyes were white and his face mottled red with a rage I'd thought *I'd* only ever felt. "I'm *nothing* like my father!" He roared. "*Nothing!*"

I flinched, taken aback that this side of him existed. I felt myself pale under the fury directed at me. Seeing my startled and wary expression Wolfe cursed and let me go, his hands visibly trembling as he stumbled away from me.

Not knowing what to do, my heart pounding in my chest, my cheeks burning, I just stood there as he bedded down on the floor. The silence was so thick, so uneasy, I'm sure someone intruding in on us wouldn't have been able to breathe under the weight of it.

"You better get some sleep," Wolfe broke the silence, in a quiet, defeated voice that made me feel guilty for some strange, inexplicable reason. Surprised that my legs could move after what had occurred, I ran over to the bed and slid under the sheet that he'd left me. At the sound of movement on the floor I turned and watched as Wolfe searched for something. His hands finally found his trousers and he delved into the pocket and pulled something out.

"Here." He threw something white and papery up onto the bed. "Thought you might want those back."

Frowning, curious, I reached over and picked up the item.

It was the paper bag with the bracelets I'd bought for me and Haydyn.

"How did you…?" I asked softly, unsure of the feeling constricting my throat.

"You dropped them in the alley. I picked them up before they drugged me. They seemed important when you were buying them."

A sharp pain shot across my chest and I held in a noise of distress. Wolfe had been with me the entire time at the market. Why had he taken the time to rescue the cheap little bracelets that only meant something to me? How had he known that they were important?

I shuddered and rolled over, fighting back tears, wishing that the man on the floor could stay black and white… the way he had always been to me. He was the last man in Phaedra I should ever trust, should ever feel anything toward.

But those shades of gray just kept creeping in.

Chapter Fifteen

It was an understatement to say I was sore, cranky and sleep deprived the next morning. My brain would not stop peddling as I lay in that bed listening to Wolfe shuffle about uncomfortably on the floor. There were moments I felt I couldn't breathe I was so confused, lost, and afraid of what I might be feeling towards him.

Suffice to say that come daylight we weren't really talking to one another, only grunting responses at each other. Wolfe had breakfast brought up to us, still convinced I had the potential to cause trouble in public, and we shoveled down some horrible porridge as quickly as possible. We then solicited the help of the jolly barkeep to retrieve a messenger for us. We had to wait in a dark corner of the nearly empty tavern (*imagine all the trouble I could cause in an empty room*, I snorted at Wolfe) looking anywhere but at each other. Finally a surprisingly tidy, well-put-together young man came in and spoke to the barkeep, who pointed at us. Turned out the young man was the best horseman in the rookery and made good money as a messenger. The barkeep swore we could trust him. So Wolfe handed over the sealed letter and money, and ordered the messenger to the Zanst's home in the Factory District in Ryl. We received a few raised eyebrows at that, the barkeep and the messenger probably wondering who in haven we were acquainted with in the Factory District.

"Can we leave now?" I asked quietly, not quite able to keep the petulance out of my voice. The messenger was already gone and on his way and Wolfe had just been staring across the barroom as if in a daydream.

He flinched at the sound of my voice and I ignored a little pang in my chest that I refused to believe was hurt. "Yes," he replied in a low, scratchy voice and I took some satisfaction in the fact that he hadn't slept either. "Let's go." He grabbed me by the elbow and pulled me to my feet.

"You don't need to manhandle me," I hissed as he took me out of the room, waving goodbye to the barkeep.

"Just stay by my side while we're here, alright," he snapped back.

I sniffed. "I would have thought you'd be happy to see something happen to me."

"I'd be happy if you suddenly lost the will to speak."

I made a face at him but he ignored me, still holding me a bit too painfully by the arm as he strode across the back yard to the stables. There was nothing and no one in sight.

Including our horse.

"What the…" Wolfe growled, letting go of my hand as he peered into the stables. My heart thudded in my chest as I spun around, scanning the back of the building.

Our horse was gone.

I drew in a shuddering breath. How on earth were we going to make it back to Ryl?

A muffled thud sounded from over my shoulder.

"Wolfe—" I spun around only to find him crumpled on the ground, unconscious, a trickle of blood running out from his hair onto his forehead. Standing over him were three of the dirtiest, vile-looking thugs I had ever seen, each holding disturbing, make-shift weapons. The tallest leered at me, his yellowing teeth flashing menacingly as he bounced a mallet off the heel of his palm. The second tallest was an older man, not quite as grubby, his hand-me-down, unwashed clothing that of a gentleman's. His large hand sat on the hilt of an old but deadly-looking sword. The third appeared to be the youngest and as he jabbed the air teasingly with a dagger, I thought perhaps he might be a little deranged. He had a wild look in his eyes that sent a shudder down my spine. I wanted to drop down next to Wolfe to check if he was alright, amazed that these ignorant-looking thugs had crept up on us so quietly. Wolfe would never live it down if his men found out how easily he had been felled… again. The fact that I was the common denominator in his failed protection had not escaped me.

A sound from the thugs drew my eyes back to them and I stiffened my spine at their leering regard. "What do you want?" I asked, proud that I kept tremors of fear out of my voice.

The tallest, who I deduced was the leader, quirked an eyebrow. "My, my, we are a haughty little thing, aren't we?"

Wolfe chose that moment to groan and my heart thudded in relief.

"Aw shit," the older man spat, "we need to get them back to Boss, Jesper, before this 'un wakes up."

"You two pick him up." Jesper gestured to Wolfe and then his eyes devoured me. "I'll take care of her."

Oh dear haven, what the hell had Wolfe and I gotten ourselves into now? I wanted to collapse and shriek and weep with exhaustion and fury. Didn't these people know my friend was dying? That if I didn't save her then we were all doomed. I was doomed! I couldn't possibly live in a world without Haydyn. How dare they do this?

My patience snapped.

As he reached for me I kicked up between his legs as hard as I could. He let out a bellow of pain and dropped to his knees in shock. Before any of the others could make a move I slammed my booted foot into the hand that held the mallet and Jesper cried out, the weapon tumbling from his hand as he clutched his injury to his chest.

"Get her!" He yelled as I dove for the weapon. I came up brandishing it wildly as the two thugs crept towards me, the light of violence in their eyes.

"I'll cut you up, you little bitch, if you don't play nice," the young one hissed at me, swiping the air with the dagger.

"She's not to be injured!" Jesper shouted, getting to his feet now.

"I won't harm her Jen-Jen," the young thug sing-songed. "No, she'll like what I do to her, won't you pretty pretty?"

Revulsion hit my gag reflex as I realized exactly what he intended for me. But he didn't know who he was trifling with. There was no way anyone was getting near me. I had a job to do. I had to get to Alvernia and no other son-of-a-bitch was slowing me down!

Conjuring all the strength I had in the world I pulled my arm back and launched the mallet with all my worth at the young thug's head. It made perfect aim, clocking him across his skull with a sickening thud. His eyes fluttered and he fell back with a dull sound, comically sprawled across the concrete in unconsciousness. I breathed a sigh of relief.

The older of the thugs stared at his downed colleague in surprise and Jesper cursed. "For goodness sakes, lass." He shook his head in disbelief and then glared at me. "Now you've downed Little Sin. We'll have to come back for him. You won't get me or Dandy here, alright. We ain't gonna hurt you, am under orders from Boss not to. So, Dandy here is going to take you and I'm going to take the boy here, alright? Now if you don't make a fuss I won't slit the boy's throat."

He said it so calmly, as if he were talking about the weather rather than killing Wolfe.

"What do you want?" I whispered, wishing Wolfe would wake up.

"That's up to Boss to tell you, lass."

I had no choice but to walk with Dandy as Jesper carried Wolfe over his shoulder, an impressive feat considering how large Wolfe was. He grunted and groaned about Wolfe's weight the whole time we walked. My outrage grew as we strode through the dull, dank streets of the rookery, my pleading eyes trying to catch those of the people passing by. They flinched under my regard, their eyes washing over my companions in fear, and they turned from me as quickly as possible, pretending they hadn't seen a thing. I knew then that I was in the hands of one of the rookery gangs. Someone back at the tavern must have sold us out to them. Wolfe had been right all along. We spoke too well, held ourselves like a lady and a gentleman. I could only imagine we were being kidnapped for possible ransom again.

Jesper and Dandy slowed as we approached a large crumbling building, the glass panes of its windows broken and cracked, the wide double doors covered in splashed paint. Jesper banged on the door three times and it swung open immediately. A young man with two large knives in his hand stood back and nodded at Jesper.

"Got 'em then, Jesper?"

Jesper laughed and swatted Wolfe's bottom. "Looks like it don't it."

The boy eyed me as Dandy pushed me inside and as I gazed around the wide open space with the large ovens and broken glass, with the grains of sand littering the floor (among garbage, old food and even rats – I shuddered) I realized we were in a disused glass works. At the back of the room was a wall, the upper half blocked in with glass that was cracked and shattered in some places. A doorway led into darker places beyond. There were pieces of old furniture here and there, a dismal attempt to make the place look cozy. I froze as my eyes took in the flickering candlelight and the gang of men and women who lounged around the room, their beady eyes watching me. They were like a plague of rats. I shuddered again.

"Take 'em through the back to Boss' room 'e said." The boy jerked his head towards the back of the room.

"He in?"

"Nah. 'e won't be long 'e said."

Jesper grunted and shifted Wolfe up on his shoulder. I kept close to him as possible as we walked through the room, Jesper calling greetings to gang members who smirked and leered at me. I felt a tug on my skirts and turned to see a young, haggard-looking woman clutching at me. She sat sprawled over an old chair and I stumbled back under her regard as she licked her lips at me. "Jesper, asks Boss if I can have this one." She grinned up at the man before turning that wicked smile on me. I blushed in understanding which made her laugh throatily. Jesper clamped his hand down on my arm.

"She's for Boss, Nalia. Don't get any ideas."

Nalia's lips twisted into a pout. "But I wants her. She's pretty, like silks. You knows how I likes silks, Jesper."

I shivered and hurried away as Jesper grunted and pushed me forward. We were silent as we made our way through steel gray hallways, until Jesper came to a stop and thrust his foot against a door, shoving it open. My eyes widened even further when we entered what could pass for a normal room in this hovel. A brass framed bed sat in the corner covered with colorful quilts and cushions. A fireplace that was obviously used had a tin bathtub in front of it, and a cozy armchair off to the side. Little knick-knacks were placed here and there on the mantel. Other pieces of well-made furniture scattered the room, men's clothing haphazardly draped here and there. And it was clean. Surprisingly so.

"Boss' room," Jesper grunted and then dropped Wolfe on the stone floor as if he were nothing more than a sack of potatoes. I cried out and rushed for Wolfe just as his eyes began to open. "Shit!" Jesper sighed and reached across the bed for something. In the next moments I watched helplessly as he tied Wolfe— who was coming around far too slowly for my liking —up against the heavy brass bed.

"You next." Jesper strode towards me and I tried to kick out at him again. He dodged and clucked his tongue at me. "Not that again, you little bitch."

He lunged at me, trying to wrench my arms behind my back but I shrieked and punched and pummeled at him, vaguely aware of Wolfe now shouting and struggling from his prison on the floor. Then Jesper's huge hand came towards my face and cracked it back with an almighty blow. I felt like I'd run into a brick wall. My legs gave way and I was barely aware of Jesper tying my hands behind my back and throwing me onto the bed. Water streamed out of my right eye and I hesitantly lifted my cheek, wincing at the throbbing pain.

"Stay here, and behave!" Jesper cried. "Boss will be in soon."

I struggled into a sitting position as the man slammed out of the door, a key turning in the lock.

Feeling his gaze on me, I looked down at Wolfe. His eyes blazed back at me.

"Are you alright?" He asked hoarsely, his gaze on my cheek, his jaw clenched so tight I thought it might shatter.

I huffed and shimmied toward him, trying to get a look at the cut on his head. "Am I alright? Wolfe, they knocked you unconscious." I sucked in a breath of sympathy at his wound. "We need to get that cleaned up. Are you feeling well?"

He winced now, stretching his legs out before him and pulling at the ropes. It was futile. He slumped wearily. "I feel a little dizzy."

"You were out a while."

"Noted. Where are we?" He glanced around the room.

I sighed. "We're in an abandoned glass works. We've been taken by what I assume is a rookery gang."

Wolfe cursed and then whipped around, vengeance burning in his blue gaze. "Did any of them touch you?"

I grinned, thinking about Little Sin. "I knocked out the one who tried."

Wolfe quirked an eyebrow. "Knocked out?"

I quickly told him how I had incapacitated Jesper and then launched the mallet at Little Sin. Wolfe shook his head in amazement. "Perhaps I *should* let the men train you," he murmured.

I smiled back at him smugly. "I told you so."

He rolled his eyes. "Can you never take anything graciously?"

I snorted. "Not from you."

Wolfe shook his head, hearing the teasing in my voice. He tugged at the ropes again. "We need to get out of here, Rogan."

Ignoring the shiver that rushed down my spine every time he said my name, I stumbled inelegantly onto the floor, trying to maneuver myself in front of him.

"What are you doing?" I could hear the amusement in his voice.

"I thought you could use your teeth to get the ropes off my wrists," I explained over my shoulder, thrusting my arms backwards at him.

"Rogan, please tell me your kidding? Have you seen how thick this rope is?"

"Well, how else are we—"

I hushed at the sound of a key turning in the lock, and barely registered as Wolfe brought a leg up, pulling me back in towards him so I was sitting between his legs with a sense of being shielded. I felt his indrawn breath on the back of my neck, the tension from his body crackling against the tension in mine.

We waited, hearts racing, and the door swung open. At first I couldn't make out anything except a tall, strong figure of a man. And then he strode inside, slowly, leisurely… and I let go a yelp of surprise.

 I recognized those green eyes and jet black hair, that defiant smirk. They were all now in a taller, older man with a harder face that was no less handsome than it had been as a young boy.

"Kir!" I gasped.

The smirk on his face fell as he came to a halt, his eyes drinking me and Wolfe in. "Rogan? Wolfe?"

"Kir!" I laughed a little hysterically, relief flooding through me.

"Holy mother of—" he dropped to his knees and grasped my shoulders, his strange eyes wide on mine. "I can't believe it's you."

"Well it is," Wolfe grunted from behind me. "Fancy untying us?"

Stunned, he sank back onto his heels, taking a moment. It was then realization struck.

"You're Boss?" I asked softly, trying to keep the condemnation out of my question.

Kir must have heard the accusation anyway, for he flinched and looked away. "Yeah," he admitted. "I'm Boss."

Wolfe struggled to be seen from behind me, so I moved out of the way, letting him peer around my shoulder, trying not to inhale that wonderful woody spice that was all Wolfe. "So, any intention of letting us go then?"

Kir and Wolfe shared a long look. "I can't believe it's you. How are you?"

I was surprised by how congenial the two were, considering Wolfe's father was Syracen and the fact that Kir had had to live with the bastard for a year. There seemed to be so much more in Kir's question than I understood.

Wolfe nodded slowly. "I'm alright, Kir. Except for being kidnapped that is."

Seeming to shake himself, Kir nodded, a flush of embarrassment cresting his cheeks. He gestured at me. "Turn, Rogan. Let me get those off of you."

I shimmied out from Wolfe's embrace and managed to twist, holding my hands out behind me.

"I'm going to use a blade, so keep still."

As soon as I was loose, Kir moved around me and freed Wolfe. He eyed the top of Wolfe's head and frowned. "I told them not to do any damage. Mind you," his gaze flickered over Wolfe as he slapped him on the back, "considering how big you've gotten, they probably had no choice."

Wolfe grunted and stumbled to his feet, rubbing his wrists. "Not that it isn't good to see you, Kir but why the hell did you have us kidnapped?"

Feeling lost in this reunion, I too slowly rose to my feet, watching the two men as they faced off with another. There was no tension or animosity between them. In fact they both appeared happy to see each other in one piece. I was growing steadily more confused by the second.

Kir shrugged, looking between us both. "I didn't know it was you. I got word that a fancy gent and lady were here and I knew the Markiz would be interested."

I gaped, feeling even more disorientated and lost. "The Markiz?"

Kir nodded grimly. "Things have been changing in Vasterya for a while now, Rogan."

Wolfe growled, "Changing how?"

Gesturing to the bed, Kir slumped down into the armchair. As I took a seat beside Wolfe on the bed I noted how much older Kir appeared than Wolfe, despite them being of the same age. It was almost as if Kir had seen too much. Whatever he had gone through had made a physical impression on him.

"Who do you think set the rookery up, Wolfe?" Kir exhaled slowly, seeming pained to be having to explain this.

I was still completely lost but Wolfe drew in a breath, "Markiz Solom."

"What?" I squeaked, any color in my cheeks surely having completely leached out now. What on haven were they talking about? Why would the Markiz create the rookery?

"The Markiz cottoned on to the fact that the Princezna's powers were beginning to weaken in Vasterya. Suddenly all these plans and feelings he had buried inside himself were bursting forth, being allowed free reign. With no word from Silvera that there was anything wrong with the Princezna, tipping him off that there was some kind of cover up going on, the Markiz began making plans."

"What kind of plans?" Wolfe asked softly, and I knew that menacing quiet did not bode well.

Kir shrugged again. "I was working for him. He found a Glava useful and he paid me well. When things began to change he put his plan to take the sovereignty over into action."

My stomach plummeted and I felt like I had been kicked in the ribs. "Take the sovereignty over? Is he insane?"

"Yes." Kir nodded. "Quite possibly. He's started training an army. He paid me to start the rookery up, hoping that a gangland at the border would put off visitors who may take tales back to Silvera. So far it's worked."

Wolfe was frowning. "I sent men in only a few weeks ago. There was no mention of an army."

"No, there wouldn't have been. The army is trained out in the west near the sand dunes. And the people of Pharya are almost religious in their belief in the Markiz and would never betray him. Without the Dyzvati power these people are easily brainwashed, especially with food and money." He snorted and gestured around him. "Even I've been brought low by it."

I narrowed my eyes on him, suddenly understanding his role in this. "You would have let him do this? Bring an army into Silvera? Betray Haydyn?"

My old friend remained expressionless as he replied in a flat voice, "I suspected Haydyn was unwell and that it was being dealt with. I expected this madness to be over soon and for me to return to working for the Markiz who would remain a Markiz, not a Kral."

Remembering the boy who had fought so savagely against Syracen when he hurt me, who had taken a lashing unlike anything I had ever seen, I wanted to believe him, but there was a hollow darkness in Kir's eyes that hadn't been there those many years ago.

Wolfe cleared his throat, breaking the strained look Kir and I shared. "So what were you planning on doing with us?"

"Making sure you weren't spies. I thought the Markiz would pay good money for you. And he certainly would pay good money to get his hands on the Captain of the Royal Guard and the Handmaiden of Phaedra." Kir shook his head, grinning wryly, not seeming to believe we were here. "But he won't find out about you. I would never let any harm come to either of you."

I exhaled sharply, my relief palpable. "Thank you, Kir."

He threw me a boyish smile, one so genuine we could have been children again planning new ways to harass Syracen, consequences be damned. He studied me and I felt his gaze sharpen. "I knew you were pretty, Rogan, sweetheart, but I had no idea you'd turn out so well."

I felt Wolfe stiffen beside me at the compliment and tried not to blush at Kir's roguishness. He had been like that as a young teenager as well. In fact he'd once kissed me on the cheek when Syracen was visiting at the palace. Kir had gotten away from him and had come to find me. I think I'd been hiding out in the gardens, terrified to be in the same building as Stovia. Sensing my unease, Kir had teased me into playing a game of tag with him. A few games in and we heard Syracen bellowing for Kir from the bottom of the gardens. Kir's eyes had hardened but when he saw me watching he'd turned his bright smile on me and swooped down, planting a kiss on my rosy cheek, telling me he'd be back for me.

"You're just the same," I laughed, shaking my head at him.

His eyes told me he disagreed before he turned to Wolfe. "What about you, Wolfe? How is life treating you these days? Got a wife yet?"

Wolfe grunted.

Kir didn't seem to be bothered by Wolfe's monosyllabic response and instead stood to his feet. "You look like you both could do with a bath and some food."

Immediately panic set in, Haydyn's face swimming before me. "Actually, Kir, we really need to be going."

"Where are you heading?"

For some reason I wasn't sure we should share that information with Kir and wasn't surprised when Wolfe replied, "Ryl."

We weren't going to Ryl. We were going to Caera, but if anyone had intercepted the messenger then he would verify that we had wanted him to contact people in Ryl. Plus, The Guard was in Ryl. No rookery gang could outfight The Guard.

So, Wolfe didn't quite trust Kir either. I felt a pang of guilt that I shoved to the side. Nothing could get in the way of saving Haydyn. Not even an old friend.

Kir nodded. "Well, you'll need horses. I can get you horses. But I have a lot of explaining to do to the gang and well... you both look like you could do with some freshening up and some rest. Let me have the bath filled, and Wolfe you need to take care of that wound."

We didn't argue with Kir. Mostly because I think we were desperate for a bath. It was the spoiled upbringing in us both. Kir had a couple of the men fill the bathtub with hot water and I left the room with Kir while Wolfe bathed. He took me to another room down the hallway, away from the gang members. It too was kept quite clean, a couple of armchairs here and there, painted theatre posters covering the chipped walls. I sat down, confused by the strange mix of alien and familiarity in being with Kir. I smiled in thanks as he handed me a glass of water. I drank it greedily, much thirstier than I had realized.

My eyes widened at the touch of Kir's fingers on my face, but he was just tipping my cheek to the side for a better look. His green gaze darkened to the color of the forest at night.

"Who did that?" He bit out.

Not really caring if I got Jesper in trouble, I told him. Kir cursed profusely before softening his expression as he took in my fright. His fingers were gentle on my skin as he stroked my cheek.

"I'll kill him for that."

I shivered, pulling away when his gaze dipped to my mouth. "Please don't."

He quirked an eyebrow, drawing back. "You don't want me to punish him for beating you?"

I smirked. "I think I punished him enough."

Kir laughed. "I forgot how bloodthirsty you can be. What did you do to him?"

I told him and Kir laughed harder until I joined in.

Wiping tears from his eyes, he sighed, appearing relaxed for the first time. "Oh I have missed you, little Rogan."

Smiling sadly, I shrugged. "It's been a long time, Kir."

"It has," he agreed. "But we went through a lifetime together in only a year."

As we both remembered, a chilly silence fell over the room. I flinched, still hearing his screams as the Captain of Guard lashed him over and over again with the horsewhip.

"Do you dream about it?" he asked me so quietly I almost didn't hear him.

I looked away, my teeth clenched tightly together. I gave him an imperceptible nod.

His rough hand clasped mine and I turned slowly to look at him. "No one understands, Rogan. How could they? No one understands but you."

I nodded, feeling as if the last eight years were melting away and I was huddled in Kir's arms as we cried together by a campfire, The Guard ignoring us as we sobbed in a grief only we could understand. In Silvera we saw one another once or twice a month but I remembered how empty I felt when I heard he had run away, like some of kind of bond had been snapped. "You left me," I whispered.

His features hardened as if he was in pain and he grasped my hand tighter. "I had to get away, Rogan, please understand."

"I do," I replied softly. "I do."

"You could stay. Here. With me."

Shock froze me and I stared back at him wide-eyed.

His mouth quirked up at the corner. "It's not such a strange request, Rogan. We were close once. We loved one another as children."

I felt pin pricks of tears at those words because they were true. We had clung to one another with a fierceness born of our grief and protected one another whenever we could. "I can't stay, Kir. Haydyn needs my help. I can't stay."

"She *is* ill then?"

Biting my lip, I gripped his hand tighter, pleading with my eyes. "Please don't tell anyone."

His eyes widened and he cupped my cheek. "I would never do anything to hurt you."

I believed him.

But…

"What about Wolfe?" I drew back a little, feeling as if I was drowning in a riptide of memories and sorrow… and affection.

Kir frowned. "What about Wolfe?"

"You seem surprisingly friendly with him considering you had to live with his family for a year."

I watched him closely as his eyes narrowed, his mouth thinned. "I have no problem with Wolfe. He was a good lad when we were young. As much a victim as we were."

W-w-what? I struggled to breathe evenly.

My heart began thudding in my chest. How could Kir… what did Kir know that I didn't? How could Kir forgive when I couldn't? "What do you mean?" I was desperate to know, I needed to know.

He leaned in close to me, his expression quizzical. "Why do you care?"

"I-I… I…" I had no answer for him. And even if I did I would have been distracted by the heat that sparked to life in his eyes, his mouth descending towards mine. Kir was going to kiss me! My heart flailed as if it were being strangled. Was I going to let him?

"Boss."

Kir pulled back, his eyes closed tightly, muttering curses under his breath. He whipped around and I followed his gaze to the door, completely shaken by what I'd nearly let happen.

Jesper was grinning at us knowingly. "The Hawks want to talk to you, Boss."

"The Hawks?" I queried, confusion wrinkling my brow.

Kir smiled and pulled me to my feet. "My gang is called the Hawks."

I threw him a sardonic look. "Why? Because you always catch your prey?"

He grinned wickedly. "Always, beautiful Rogan. Always."

I rolled my eyes at him and he laughed, and by the way Jesper's mouth fell open in surprise I was guessing it was something Kir didn't do often.

"I'm sure Wolfe will be finished with the tub. Why don't you go along and check and I'll be back soon with some food."

I nodded and we headed down the hallway together. When he and Jesper disappeared around a doorway, I was so in a stew about what had almost happened I forgot to knock and just barged into the room.

"Oh," I gasped as Wolfe stood before me shirtless, droplets of bath water falling from the strands of hair at the nape of his neck to his shoulders, running in tantalizing rivulets across his muscled abdomen. He was beautiful. My gaze followed the trickle like a magpie with a diamond… and then I gasped again at the raised scar on his lower stomach. "Oh m—" I cut off at the agitated noise he made at the back of his throat. He wrenched a shirt on over his head, covering what I had just seen.

Wolfe had been branded.

A dark, horseshoe burn scar branded his lower stomach. Who would do such a thing?

"Wolfe—"

The door burst open slamming into my back and I stumbled forward.

"Oh, Rogan, I'm sorry." Kir righted me as he came in, patting my shoulder in apology. "It's just we have a problem." He slammed the door shut.

"What kind of problem?" Wolfe refused to look at me.

"I'm about to have a bloody mutiny on my hands if I don't hand you over to Solom."

I paled, instinctively wanting to edge closer to Wolfe. Reminding myself I was an independent woman, I stiffened my spine. "So what do we do?"

Kir's gaze pinned Wolfe to the wall. "I'm sorry, brother, but I had to."

Panic made my heart gain tempo. "Had to what? What's going on?"

"Does she know? About your…?"

Wolfe nodded stiffly.

Kir relaxed then. "I know you tried to keep it hidden, but it was the only thing I could barter with."

"I understand."

Understand what? My head swiveled back and forth between them so much I was sure it was about to spin off. "Understand what?" I snapped in burning frustration.

Finally, Kir turned to me. "I told them about Wolfe being a mage."

I gasped. "You knew?" Suddenly I felt hopelessly betrayed. What was it that these two men shared? Why was Kir so amiable to Wolfe? Why couldn't he have told me he and Wolfe were friendly with one another? Why was I the only one that didn't really know Wolfe?

Kir nodded. "Yeah, I know. I managed to convince the Hawk's that we could sell Wolfe to Solom."

"No!" I yelled, outraged at the idea. "Over my dead body! No!"

The two of them raised their eyebrows at me and then grinned.

What on haven were they grinning about?

I growled in frustration as the truth dawned on me; for a moment I had forgotten my decision to trust Kir, but I wasn't amused at him taking an opportunity to get rise out of me. "You're not really going to sell him, are you?"

Kir huffed in indignation. "Of course not. I'm going to let them think I am. They're sending a messenger to Pharya to have someone come and collect Wolfe. That someone should be here in a few days. For now I want you to rest up for the night and have some food. And then tomorrow when I come to get you, we're going to pretend Wolfe blasted me with his powers and you escaped. In actuality I'll be letting you out the back door."

"There's a back door?"

He grinned. "Of course. I'll have a couple of horses waiting."

Relief washed over me and I impulsively threw my arms around him, drawing him in for a hug. Kir laughed softly and tugged me tight against him. "Thank you," I whispered.

"Worth it just for the hug."

Later, after I too had had a chance to bathe and both Wolfe and I were fed, Kir apologized before leaving and locking us in the bedroom. Wolfe had claimed the armchair so I lay down on the bed, thinking about Kir, about Wolfe, and about the horseshoe brand marring Wolfe's body.

"I was surprised at your vehement refusal to let Kir sell me to the Markiz," Wolfe suddenly said. "I thought you wanted me dead."

"I thought you wanted me dead," I replied honestly, turning to look at him. His handsome face was a mask of complete shock that soon melted into anger.

"What do you mean you thought I wanted you dead?" He snapped.

I was so tired. So sick and tired of my world turning upside down on me again and again. I wanted wildflowers and summers by the stream. I wanted tobacco in the air and lemonade on the tongue. Fighting tears, I turned my back to him, curling up to sleep.

Why would Kir protect Wolfe? Why was there friendship and trust between them?

Why did Wolfe protect me and look out for me?

"Never mind," I finally answered. "I'm just starting to realize I don't know you at all."

"Yes you do," was his hoarse response. "You just hate that I'm not what you need me to be."

Trying desperately to ignore that enigmatic comment, I slammed my eyes shut.

Chapter Sixteen

Kir's old bed was not comfortable. But I think my not sleeping had more to do with my awareness of Wolfe. I kept seeing that brand on his stomach, the pain in his eyes when he caught me looking at it, and the soul deep look he and Kir shared as Kir asked him if he was alright. There was something I was missing. How could a man so committed to the protection of the crown and the principles of honor and loyalty be a charlatan underneath, waiting for his moment to exact revenge?

Oh right. Because his father had been one.

But Kir wasn't hateful to Wolfe like I was. In fact, if my instincts were right (and who knew these days) I suspected Kir was protective of Wolfe. Why? Again, what was I missing?

Had Haydyn been right all along? Was I wrong to condemn Wolfe for the actions of his father?

My guilt was compounded by Wolfe's tossing and turning. My whole body trembled with tension as I listened to his soft groans as he sought some kind of comfort in sleep. The need to offer comfort took me by surprise and I had to curl my fingers into fists to stop myself reaching out to him. When at last his breathing evened out, my body did too, relaxing into the lumpy mattress beneath me. With his fall into slumber, I finally found my own.

Too quickly I was awoken, someone shaking my shoulder. Having been dreaming of Haydyn as I had been most nights, I automatically assumed in my semi-conscious state that she had come into my bedroom again and had some delicious secret to tell me. Last time she'd awoken me this early it was to tell me she'd fallen in love with Matai and had given her virginity to him the night before.

"What now?" I mumbled, swatting at her with my eyes closed. "You with child?"

"What? Rogan, wake up," an irritated voice snapped at me. Wolfe.

I shot up on the bed and cracked my head off of his. "Ow." I winced, my eyes watering as I pulled back. Wolfe's face hovered inches before mine, his pale blue eyes narrowed in pain. He rubbed at his forehead, already swollen in the upper corner from the cut he took to it yesterday.

"It's like waking the dead," he grouched and pulled back.

I rubbed my cheek sleepily and then cried out at the tender pain that shot up my face. "Ow, that hurts," I whimpered and watched warily as Wolfe's face turned black as a thundercloud.

"If I see him again, I'm going to kill him."

No need to ask who he was talking about. "Does it look really bad?" I was afraid of the answer.

Wolfe walked over to me slowly and hunkered down to his haunches so we were at eye level. The air whooshed out of my body as he reached up tentatively to touch my bruised cheek, his features etched with concern and some other emotion I couldn't quite decipher. I had the sudden urge to buss into his touch like Haydyn's cat, Z, when one of Cook's cakes was in the vicinity. A hot shivery rush of tingles exploded across the top of my skin as our eyes connected. My stomach lurched. I couldn't breathe. I needed him away from me.

Clearing my throat, I knocked his hand away and stood up, brushing past him, almost knocking him on his ass. There was a mirror above the fireplace, dirty and broken, but it had enough of a reflection to show the red and purple swelling on my right cheek. Beautiful.

I sighed and caught Wolfe's eyes in the reflection. "Is it almost time?"

He nodded, frowning, and then he broke our gaze. A strange tension sprung up between us. If I were honest with myself it had been there since we'd been taken by the Iavii. For someone who had spent the last eight years arguing with and bitching at Wolfe I had never once felt this horrible, ill-at-ease way around him. I didn't like it. Not one bit. I was so afraid of what it meant, so afraid of disappointing my family's memory.

"I—"

I don't know what I was going to say but it didn't matter because the key turned in the lock in the door and suddenly Kir was there, smiling at me and befuddling me even more.

"You ready?" He asked, shutting the door and striding in, every inch the confident rookery gang leader.

I didn't look at Wolfe. "Yes."

"Great—" Kir cursed under his breath as he reached me, his hand cupping my chin. "That looks sore this morning."

Feeling Wolfe's burning gaze, I gently tugged out of his hold. "I've had worse."

Kir grew serious. "I remember."

Not really strong enough to take a trip down nightmare lane with him, I put my hands on my hips, trying to exude the strength I wasn't feeling. "Alright, so now what?"

"Now you make your escape. Remember," his gaze switched between me and Wolfe, "To get out, you take a left, a right, and the back door is at the top of the hall. I left it unlocked." Now he just stared at Wolfe. "When you attack me you have to make it look real."

Wolfe's face tightened.

Kir sighed heavily, his lip curling up almost condescendingly. "I mean it, Wolfe."

I wasn't surprised when Wolfe made no response. Clearly, he didn't want Kir to get hurt.

Coming to the same conclusion I had drawn, Kir pulled back his shoulders, his own expression determined. There was a dark, mischievousness in his eyes I didn't trust. "Fine." He shook his head, throwing Wolfe a warning look. "Then I guess I'll just have to make you want to."

When his long arm came out and caught me around the waist I squawked in undignified surprise and instinctively pushed against his hard chest as he crushed me to him, his other hand winding into my hair to bring my lips against his in a hard, punishing kiss. The hand on my waist slid down my back and squeezed my bottom. I yelled into his mouth, trying to get away. Quite abruptly that muffled exclamation was given free reign as his body was wrenched from mine, soaring across the room and straight through the door. That's right. Straight *through* the door. Not the doorway. The door. I gaped in befuddlement at Kir collapsed around the wooden splinters of the door in the hall, groaning as he drew himself up into a sitting position.

"Come on." I blinked down at the large, familiar hand wrapped around my wrist and then up at its owner. Wolfe. A very angry Wolfe.

I was dragged out through the fragments of the doorway and into the hall, only to be pushed behind Wolfe at the sound of yelling to the right of us. Jesper came hurrying down the hallway with Nalia at his back. Wolfe stared them down in concentration. I felt the heat of his energy as the two thugs were thrown back down the corridor from whence they came, their bodies crashing sickeningly against the wall before crumpling in an unconscious heap.

Another groan caught my attention and I gasped as Kir wiped at a large gash on his arm. "Are you alright?" I made to rush towards him but Wolfe grabbed my arm again to wrench me in the opposite direction. "Stop!" I yelled at him, whipping back around to check on Kir.

"I'm fine, Rogan," he assured me, wincing as he pushed a large chunk of door off of him. "Go. Just go."

We shared a long look as Wolfe continued to haul me up the narrow corridor, and just as we turned left I mouthed 'thank you', unexpected tears threatening to brim over. He gave me a knowing nod just as I disappeared.

"So you not only manipulate elements but you have telekinesis too?" I hissed at Wolfe as we hurried along this next hall.

"Shut up, Rogan."

I raised my eyebrow at his tone. I could either argue with him or get out of here. Mind made up, I yanked my arm free from him and picked up my skirts. As I ran, Wolfe ran with me, and we burst out through the back door…

…Only to be confronted with two of Kir's thugs smoking tobacco and staring in confusion at the two horses tethered to a drain pipe on the next building.

Their roll ups dropped to the sodden wet ground as their mouths fell open at the shock of seeing us. Wolfe didn't say anything. He merely flicked his hand and the two of them went soaring past us. At the sounds of flesh hitting brick (I thought I might have heard some bones cracking too) I decided now was not the time to question Wolfe about his abilities. Instead we moved together, hurrying to untie the two horses Kir had managed to procure for us. With me at Wolfe's back we hurried off into the streets of the rookery, the horse's hooves echoing against the buildings in frightening volume. Amazingly, the horses worked against the slickness of the cobbles with more proficiency than I could have expected, and we were heading out of the rookery, past the glass works, and into the green of the Vasterya I remembered, at harried speed.

As we galloped down the muddy trade road, passing farm country, Wolfe slowed a little until my horse was abreast with his.

"Rogan." He sighed, licking rain from his upper lip, seeming afraid to meet my eye. "We need to get somewhere safe. I know you don't want me to ever use your magic, but…"

Understanding that he wanted permission to use my magic to find a safe place to stop, I decided it was the perfect opportunity to get some answers. "If I let you, will you tell me everything?"

He scowled at me, his eyes so blue against the stark dullness of the day. "What do you mean?"

"You!" I gestured to him, anger flaring out from my chest to batter against him in the rain. "Tell me why you hid whatever magic you have? I want to know about you and Kir. I want to know about the horseshoe."

"That's none of your business, Rogan!" Wolfe shouted back to be heard over the weather and the horses.

He was right. It was none of my business. But not knowing was driving me crazy and I needed to stay focused on Haydyn. This distraction had to be dealt with. "I'm making it my business."

"If we don't find a safe place to stay that's on you!"

"No." I shook my head. "That's on you. What's so important you can't trade this?"

"It's private, Rogan. You know *private*, as in none of your business, as in you don't need to know!"

"Yes, I do!"

"Why?"

For a moment I couldn't meet his eyes, and my stomach lurched again as my brother's laughter taunted me. I clenched my teeth, hoping somehow it would hold me together. Finally I met Wolfe's curious, frustrated gaze. "I don't know why."

I don't know what Wolfe saw in my eyes, but he searched long enough to find it and finally nodded. "Fine."

"You'll trade?" I asked in surprise.

"I'll trade."

"Then ask away."

"Rogan, I need you to find us someplace safe to stay and get us there by a safe route."

My magic washed over me in a warm wave and I was almost sorry when it was over and my skin turned cold again in the downpour. I felt the pull of the little farm over the border into Daeronia. I grinned wearily, glad at the thought of the danger free journey I felt ahead of us. "Follow me."

Chapter Seventeen

Being a mage came in handy. It took us a few days but we crossed the border into Daeronia with little problem (except hunger and exhaustion) and soon our olfactory senses were bombarded by the sweet yeasty smell of the large brewery to the west of us as we headed towards Caera. It would take another half day or so to ride onto Caera, so I took us off the main trade road and into the fields towards a tiny farm owned by an elderly widow my magic told me would help us.

She was surprisingly wily, peppering us with questions. Since my magic told us it was safe, Wolfe thought it was alright to tell her he was one of The Guard and we had gotten into some trouble at the rookery in Vasterya.

"Oh, I heard about all that trouble at the border." She nodded, leading us past her little sitting room and into a larger farm kitchen. The smell of home-cooked stew caused my stomach to rumble. I clutched it in embarrassment. The widow threw me a sympathetic smile and gestured to the table for us to take seats. "Sounds like the two of you were lucky to get away."

"Yes, ma'am, we were," Wolfe agreed. "We really appreciate you helping us."

"No thanks needed." She bustled about, ladling huge amounts of stew into a bowl. I felt the saliva building up under my tongue. "I ain't got much room in the house I'm afraid but I've got a barn outside with a nice warm hayloft. I got some blankets you can take up there that should keep you cozy for the night."

Even though normally I wouldn't fancy a night in a barn it was just so nice to be treated with some hospitality again I didn't care. "That sounds perfect." I smiled gratefully as she put a bowl of stew and a cup of ale before me. I shared a happy look with Wolfe and we broke bread, scooping the stew up as if we hadn't had a decent meal in ages. And to be honest we hadn't. The old widow was almost as good a cook as Cook.

"This is delicious," I managed between mouthfuls and she smiled cheerily, watching us scoff it down, seeming happy to have someone to feed again.

After our bellies were full we sat with her for a while, engaging her in conversation that we somehow kept focused around her life. Finally, seeing her eyelids droop, I suggested we get some sleep. Handing over some blankets and an oil lamp, the widow sleepily wished us a good night and turned to ascend the stairs to her own bed.

The barn wasn't huge and when we climbed up into the hayloft we glanced at one another. It was certainly cozy. I flushed at the thought of being in such close quarters with Wolfe. Without a word to one another, we spread the blankets out and then carefully sat down. I could feel the heat from his skin inches from mine, the scent of him tickling my senses. I shivered a little, my stomach doing that strange flipping thing again.

Finally I couldn't take the silence. "So, you're quite a powerful Glava?"

Wolfe tensed beside me and I bit my lip, wondering if he was going to go back on his word and not tell me all I wanted to know.

"Well?"

He exhaled so heavily I almost felt badly for pressing him about it.

Not badly enough to stop. "Wolfe?" I placed a tentative hand on his arm and he jolted in surprise, looking down at it there. Those eyes of his lifted up slowly until they were stuck on mine and I flushed, breaking the connection as I removed my hand from his arm.

"I hid it," he answered quietly, snapping my attention back to his face. "I hid it."

"But why?"

He shrugged, staring off into the dark rafters ahead of us, his jaw taut with suppressed emotion. "Because... because I was afraid the magic meant I was like my father."

That vulnerable sentence reached out to me to take me by the shoulders and shake me awake. My heartbeat picked up its pace and I began to get this sick feeling in my stomach.

How could I have been so wrong?

"Kir… Kir said you were as much a victim as me and him. What did he mean?"

Wolfe's eyes slanted towards me, a well of dark pain and anger fencing in his gaze. I knew he didn't want to tell me, that I was using his sense of honor in keeping his promise against him. If I were any kind of good person I would have reached out and told him it was alright, he didn't need to tell me anything. However, my own selfish need to discover the real Wolfe won out. I stared back at him, waiting.

"My father…" his voice cracked but he refused to look away. "He didn't treat me and my mother very well. As you know… he was a cruel man."

Ice crawled across my skin. "What did he do to you?"

"Mostly manipulative mind games to make us feel inferior, subordinate. But when Haydyn's father was dying —when he died —as you know things got worse. For us as well."

Thick silence fell, robbing me of my voice. In truth, I wasn't sure I wanted to know what Syracen had done to Wolfe. It was one thing for a man to abuse strangers, but to hurt your own flesh and blood…?

"He uh… he horsewhipped my mother a few times."

Bile rose in my throat as I remembered the agony Kir had gone through. To do that to your own wife… "And that scar… the horseshoe?" I didn't really want to know, did I?

A bitter, twisted little chuckle escaped Wolfe and he shook his head. "I made the mistake of attacking my father when he took the whip to my mother. Kir helped me because my mother was kind to him. My father beat Kir... but me... he took a hot horseshoe to and branded me. He told me I was his son not hers. Like horseflesh I belonged solely to him and as such he expected me to obey him as my master."

I couldn't comprehend what he was confiding. My chest flared with sharp, needling pain. Hot tears prickled in my eyes, and I couldn't speak. My throat had closed up with hurt and anger for him.

With guilt.

All these years I had been horrible to him, painting him with the same brush of his father, so sure he would want to hurt me for what I did to Syracen.

"I got my revenge though. I helped Kir escape."

So that explained their camaraderie.

Kir knew Wolfe better than I had. Why did that hurt so much? I clutched my stomach tightly. Wolfe must loathe me for the way I had treated him. The pain sharpened in my chest and I almost couldn't breathe. Suddenly I was truly afraid Wolfe hated me.

"I'm so sorry," I whispered, a stupid tear leaking out and rolling down my cheek. I brushed it away impatiently and was surprised when Wolfe caught my hand.

He stared, seeming amazed, watching as I lost my fight with another tear and it escaped. His thumb caught it, rubbing it softly into my cheek. I was so aware of him... so close to me, my whole body tense to the point of trembling, and my heart raced madly. "Are you crying for me, Rogan?"

I nodded and then shook my head stupidly. "I'm sorry."

"Why are you sorry?"

"Because he hurt you. Because I've treated you terribly because of him." I shuddered trying to calm myself. "I thought you detested me, that you were planning to take some kind of vengeance for my part in getting Syracen killed."

When his touch left me, I was confused. I wanted him to touch me again but I was also thankful he didn't. I could breathe easier when he wasn't so close.

Right now his brow was deeply furrowed with thought. "That's why you're snotty with me?"

Snotty? How dare he—

I shook it off, amazed by how easy it was to become irritated with him. I threw him a look for his choice of word but sniffed in acknowledgement. The corner of his mouth quirked up and I could tell he wanted to laugh at me. He smothered it with his hand, rubbing it across his mouth in concentration. And then he nodded. "I think I understand. But you should know I felt nothing but relief when he was killed. My mother and I were free. Our lives completely changed that day. For the better."

I wanted to reach out and offer some kind of comfort, some kind of apology that would make up for the last eight years of disdainful attacks against him. Haydyn would be pleased to know she had been right all along about him, I thought wryly.

When Wolfe tensed beside me I grew uneasy. I understood when he asked, "What exactly did my father do to your family, Rogan?"

The rage burst open across my chest like a tidal wave after a land-shake and I drew in deep shuddering breaths to calm my memories. Finally I asked softly, "Are you sure you want to hear about that?"

"Only if you're up to telling it."

So I told him about a perfect summer's day ending in tears and bloodshed and a never ending impotent agony. His golden skin grew paler and paler as the story went on. I even told him about Valena. When I grew quiet I hadn't even realized I'd been crying until Wolfe, eyes bright with sorrow, handed me a handkerchief. I wiped at my tears as another smog-filled silence descended over us.

For a while all I could hear was our soft breathing and blood rushing in my ears.

"No wonder you hate me," Wolfe choked and his shoulders slumped over. For the first time in a long time he looked like a little boy again and I didn't want to be the one that had done that to him. Especially since I was coming to realize…

"I don't hate you," I replied softly, sure my heart was going to burst it raced so fast. It only sped up even more as our eyes collided, his searching mine in desperation. The color returned to his cheeks and he licked his lips nervously.

"You don't?"

I shivered at the hoarseness in his voice and shook my head, my cheeks burning. "No. I realize now that this person you've been, Captain of the Guard, that's really who you are. I'm sorry I didn't treat you the way you deserved."

He smirked. "I wasn't exactly charming to you either."

I laughed softly. "You were just reacting in kind."

He snorted. "Yes, I suppose I was. It was galling you know. You're so sweet to everyone else."

I wrinkled my nose. "Sweet, I'm not sweet."

"You can be."

My cheeks burned hotter. I shook him off, embarrassed. Heaving a sigh I pushed him teasingly. "You're a good man, Wolfe," I admitted.

Those gorgeous aquamarine eyes of his widened at the praise and he smiled slowly, such a naturally wicked smile it flipped my stomach over again. "Really?"

I nodded.

But then abruptly, his smile dropped, his eyes dimming with sadness.

"What?"

Wolfe shook his head. "I'm still the man whose father killed yours."

Not for the first time, I didn't know how to respond. My soul was a mess inside, completely confused and bewitched. Because now I knew that this sick guilty feeling inside was my growing feelings for

Wolfe, and the subsequent shame I felt for betraying my family. Caring for the son of the man who had killed them… how was that *not* a betrayal of their memory?

Turning his body in towards me, Wolfe shifted a little closer and I trembled at the look in his eye. Unconsciously, despite what I had only been minutes ago screaming at myself, I tilted a little closer to him too, drawn to his heat like an addict to opium.

He cleared his throat. "I wanted to kill him, you know."

I frowned. "Who?"

"Kir." Wolfe snorted, shaking his head ruefully. "I wanted to kill him... when he kissed you."

My breath caught as our eyes locked. Suddenly I knew what that indecipherable look was he sometimes gave me. Wolfe… *wanted* me? Wolfe? Wolfe who gave every woman at the palace a fit of the vapors when he spoke to them? Wolfe who had a reputation for being incredibly discriminating with women? For goodness sake, according to palace gossip, he had had a love affair with Vojvodkyna Winter Rada, the woman whose court we were heading to—an incredibly beautiful, sophisticated, young widow. And he wanted me? *Me?*

"I—"

Whatever banal thing I would have said was cut off as Wolfe reached out to slide his hand behind my neck. I gulped, feeling so hot I thought I was going to combust. The way he looked at me… I shivered… no one had ever looked at me like that before. Like I was the most—

"You're so beautiful," Wolfe told me hoarsely, and maybe it was naive but as he looked at me I believed he really thought so.

And then I wasn't really thinking much because his mouth was on my mouth.

He brushed his lips across mine in soft, feathery butterfly kisses, beautiful and frustrating all at the same time.

"Wolfe," I muttered in complaint and his lips smiled against mine. "Cruel," I whispered.

He took it as a challenge. I was gripped closer, his arms wrapped around me, binding me to him so I was flush against him, my arms trapped. And his mouth…

His kiss was hard and persistent now and I pushed into it, intoxicated by the feel and scent of him all around me. A little strangled sound erupted from the back of my throat at the feel of his tongue against my lips and he took the opportunity to sweep into my mouth, drugging me with the unfamiliar dark pull of the kind of kiss Haydyn had told me about but I'd never experienced. I stilled, unsure of what to do, letting him kiss me and enjoying it, but afraid to participate in case I did it wrong. Wolfe suddenly stopped, breaking the kiss. He pulled back to frown at me.

I blushed, feeling like an idiot. Wolfe was used to experienced women, not nineteen year old girls who were as sensual as the straw we sat on.

"You've never been kissed properly before?" He asked softly, stroking my flushed cheek. I was still wrapped tightly against him and despite my embarrassment I didn't want to pull away from him. I was addicted. *Wonderful.*

"No." I shook my head, feeling like a schoolgirl.

"But I thought you and Jarek—"

"Me and Jarek, what?!" I snapped back, my eyes flashing angrily. What in haven was he insinuating exactly? Or had Jarek said something? Had Jarek spread lies about me? No, he wouldn't... would he?

Wolfe arched his eyebrow arrogantly. "What was I supposed to think? You're always flirting with him."

Arrgh! I hit my hands against his chest trying to pull away from him but he only held me tighter, grinning now, which made me madder. "You are the most—"

"I'm glad I was wrong." He cut me off, his eyes narrowing with lustful intent. "Now kiss me back."

I shuddered, my earlier annoyance disappearing in a puff of smoke. With my usual aversion to being vulnerable I jutted my chin out defiantly. "I don't know how, so maybe we should stop."

Wolfe smirked. "Not a chance. Just follow my lead, mimic what I do." His breathing grew labored as he leaned in towards me. I shook terribly as his lips reached for mine again and I felt his arms flex around me. This time his kiss began a little gentler as I tentatively opened my mouth. When his tongue touched mine I followed it with my own. Wolfe groaned against me and I felt it reverberate through me in delicious waves. I gasped at the feeling taking over me. This must be what Haydyn was always talking about. The kiss grew more frantic and I freed my arms so I could wrap them around him, my breasts flat to his chest, every inch of my body as close as I could get to the heat of his. We collapsed back against the blankets, Wolfe's body covering mine, his thigh pushing my legs apart. I shuddered at the feel of him against me, my brain no longer able to work against the sparks and explosions that were shooting off around my body as his drugging kisses went on and on, his strong hands sliding up and down my waist seeming desperate to touch me but afraid to move higher or lower. When I arched into him Wolfe shook against me. I felt him reluctantly pull away, both of us gasping for air as he rolled off of me. I didn't know what to do with my body— my nerves were twanging, my hands shaking. I noticed Wolfe's were too as he exhaled heavily, running a hand through his hair I had mussed up.

"We have to stop. You drive me crazy, Rogan," he whispered gruffly. "You always have."

My heart was struggling to calm down and I laughed at the strange, wonderful but awful turn of events. "Well, you took the perfect revenge."

He turned his head to look at me and he grinned smugly, taking in my flushed face.

I swatted at him. "Very nice."

"What?" he laughed, rolling up onto his elbow and reaching out to brush my hair off my face. "After spending the last few years panting after you it's nice to know you want me back."

My eyebrows rose in surprise. "The last few years?"

Laughing softly, Wolfe reached for me, pulling me into his embrace, tucking my head under his chin. I automatically snuggled against his heat. "Let's stop with the questions for now, Rogan. We need to sleep."

I was skeptical that after our kissing session I would be able to fall asleep. But surprisingly, with Wolfe keeping me safe, I drifted off quickly into a dreamless slumber.

Chapter Eighteen

I couldn't see her in the crowds. Where was she? This was her night. Smiling benignly at a Raphizyan Baron and his insipidly vapid wife, I made my way out of the noisy ballroom and into the foyer. I had already asked Vikomt Matai, her new personal guard, if he had seen her. He had turned his back for one minute and she was gone. I knew the man felt terrible, losing the Princezna in a crowded ballroom two weeks into his new post. I tried to reassure him. Haydyn could be a minx and he'd have to get to know her better to understand her better. Once he had, looking after her wouldn't be a problem. Two footmen stood guard at the entrance.

"Have you seen the Princezna?" I asked anxiously, before reminding myself to stop twisting my hands together nervously in case they thought something was amiss.

One of the footmen stepped forward a little. "Her majesty left the ballroom a few minutes ago, My Lady. She was headed in the direction of the orangery."

I nodded my thanks and lifted my gown, my steps picking up pace as I followed the luxuriously gilded hallways of the palace to the large orangery in the east wing. It had views of the Silver Sea in the distance and was one of Haydyn's favorite places. Not that you could really see the views past the exotic plants and citruses Stena, the gardener, had populated the glasshouse with. Briefly, I closed my eyes, wondering what an earth I'd find when I got to the orangery. This was supposed to be Haydyn's proper debut as Princezna of Phaedra. She was sixteen now, no longer a child. But something had been plaguing her all day.

I stepped inside the humid air of the orangery, the scents somewhat overwhelming. I'd never understood the attraction of the place. Haydyn said it made her feel like she was somewhere else. I relaxed a little at finding her sitting on a bench at the back of the orangery. She glanced up, unsurprised to see me there.

"Haydyn," I whispered, moving towards her, the rustling of my skirts sounding overly loud in the quiet of the glass room. With a deep exhalation I sat beside her, our elbows bumping. "Why aren't you at the ball, enjoying your debut?"

She huffed, "It's not as if they haven't seen me at a ball before."

I stopped myself from snorting out loud. "True," I muttered, desperately trying to keep the laughter out of my voice. Sometimes it was so hard to teach her to be responsible when I agreed with her summations. "But this is a special evening and you really should return to your guests."

Haydyn shrugged.

I frowned. "I know you aren't blind to the superficiality of some of your court but you've never treated them with disdain. You've always been so friendly and polite to everyone. Tonight, I'd be surprised if you had stretched your lips once into a smile. I even thought I misheard you telling Lady Viskt that if the people of

Alvernia were half as well-fed as her cat, Phaedra would have no tribulations. Now I think I didn't mishear it at all."

She laughed lightly. "No, you didn't. But, Rogan, she's awful. All she talks about is that bloody cat of hers. As if the Princezna wants to discuss an overfed spoiled brat of a cat that scratched me last time she brought it to court, over her donating money to the charity I wanted to start for the mountain people of Alvernia."

A wave of fondness made me smile softly at her. "Dear, not everyone is as open-minded about the Alvernian mountain people as you."

She snorted. "Including you."

I shrugged, unabashed. "The southerners are under the same evocation as the rest of us. If they wanted to live more civilized they could."

"But—"

"You know I'd be more positively inclined towards this rapidly failing philanthropic idea of yours if I thought for one second it had been your idea."

Blushing, Haydyn shrugged. "Darren is very passionate about these issues."

Now I did snort. "Darren is an arrogant troubadour with an overinflated sense of importance. He's never even been to Alvernia! The furthest he's been is Ryl. Not exactly the best troubadour if you ask me... travelling minstrel my left butt cheek."

Haydyn burst into raucous laughter, shaking her head. Once she'd controlled her giggles, she stared up me with love shining bright in her eyes. "Perhaps you're right. He did write me the most awful poetry the other morning. Something about hair the color of the moon and a sweet lady granting him a boon. I think he may have been trying to get me to kiss him."

I narrowed my eyes. "You didn't, did you?"

Pinching her lips together she gave a sharp jerk of her head. "No. I did think about it but he's not really what I expected. None of this is." She swept the room with a dainty hand.

"What do you mean?"

"I don't think I can do this," she confessed hollowly. "Decisions and choices, and pandering to the court. It's all so much responsibility. The coronation ceremony is only two years away, and then I'll be crowned Queen. Somehow that makes it sound all that much more frightening."

"Why don't we go away?" She clutched my arm frantically, her emerald eyes pleading with me. "We'll jump on a boat and sail the coast to Alvernia. See for ourselves what the people are really like."

"Hay—"

"Or we could take off on Midnight and Sundown, head for your old family home in Vasterya. We could run through the fields and play by that stream you always talk about. It sounds like paradise."

I smiled sadly at her and drew her into a hug. "Haydyn, you know we can't."

"Why not? You're the only one I care about and the only one who cares about me. We'll have a grand adventure."

"You know you care about the people here, Haydyn. You're just overwhelmed, and that is to be expected." I turned so I was facing her, my eyes serious, older than my years. "Phaedra needs your magic, Haydyn. And it needs your goodness. I know it's a lot to ask of a young woman, but we've all had to sacrifice something for our land."

Immediately her eyes welled up with tears. "Oh, Rogan, you must think me terribly selfish and childish."

"No. I think you're young. I think you're scared. But I know how smart and kind and good you are. And like you said, you have me. I'll help you through. I'll always be there for you. You're all that matters, and nothing will get in the way of that. Nothing..."

...a stripe of heat across my face tingled, slowly bringing me out of sleep. I peeled my eyes open, blinking against the stream of sunlight coming in from a crack in the rafters.

Where was I?

It took me a minute but then it all came flooding back and I stiffened. I rolled my head to the side. The place where Wolfe had slept was empty. He was gone. My heart raced. No, he was probably just in the house, I reassured myself. I groaned and sat up. Despite feeling less exhausted, I still ached all over. *All over.* Why, oh, why had I kissed Wolfe last night? I groaned, burying my face in my hands. It was such a silly, stupid thing to do!

You were exhausted.

Yes. I was exhausted. I wasn't thinking clearly... *clearly.*

I was in the middle of rescuing my best friend, my sister—the one person in the entire land of Phaedra who meant anything to me. I couldn't be distracted by kisses from the most inappropriate man imaginable. His father killed my family. He was a Vikomt and I was a farm girl. He would marry and I... definitely *would not*!

But what to do now? When I went into the house, how should I act? My stomach churned. I dreaded an actual conversation with him about it. Oh surely Wolfe would know it was a mistake. A bleary-eyed, adrenaline-rushed error in judgment. I should act like nothing happened. I bet that was exactly what he would want. I nodded, happy with the decision, and scrambled down out of the hayloft, nearly falling on my bottom I trembled with nerves so badly. The sun was bright and hot outside the hayloft and I winced at the thought of riding to Caera in this heat. Heaving a huge sigh, I braced my shoulders as if readying for battle and headed into the widow's house. Wolfe was nowhere to be seen, but the widow was bustling around in the kitchen, and the smell of breakfast was heady and thick in the air. My stomach grumbled a plea.

"There you are." The old widow smiled at me. "I hope you slept well."

I nodded, confused. Where was Wolfe?

"Your man is out back getting washed up at the trough."

I glowered. "He's not my man. He's my…" I realized I didn't know how to finish that sentence.

Chuckling softly, the widow lay out the breakfast for us. "I'm just going out to feed my pig. Be back in a minute."

"Thank you." I gestured to the food gratefully and sat down, answering her cheery smile with a half-hearted one of my own. I never knew confusion could be so physically disorientating. Shrugging it off, I began to dig into the delicious food, salivating as it melted on my tongue. Perhaps we should take the old widow back with us, employ her in the palace kitchens. My lips twitched at the thought. Cook wouldn't be amused by that turn of events. Ah Cook. I missed her. And Valena. And Haydyn… but that went without saying.

At the sound of a creak behind me, my ears perked up, and then his familiar scent hit me. I felt Wolfe behind me. The press of his lips against my neck startled me and I flinched back from him, staring at him incredulously. Immediately, Wolfe took a step back, a wary aspect in his gaze. Whatever he saw in my expression made him snort in disgust and he took the seat beside me to tuck into the breakfast.

"Last night was a dream then?" he asked with a definite edge to his voice.

I took a moment, shaking off the delicious tingling sensation on my neck where he had kissed me. I desperately tried to ignore the way my stomach flipped at the sight of his aquamarine eyes and wicked mouth. Finally, when I thought my voice wouldn't come out all breathy and give me away, I replied, "Not a dream. Just a mistake."

Somehow Wolfe managed to glare at me out of the corner of his eye, and it wasn't hard to fall back into the way of things, bristling at the condescending look he slid on and off his face as easy as a mask. "A mistake?" he seethed, shaking his head. "I should have known you'd wake up as skittish as mouse. I shouldn't have left."

"It's got nothing to do with that. And I am not skittish! I never skitter."

He rolled his eyes. "You're being skittish. But I'm willing to forgive your less than pleasant reaction and give you some time to think about things."

Whatever else I had been feeling, whatever doubts, whatever confusion, rushed out of the window at his patronizing attitude. That familiar heating of my blood took over my mouth. "You arrogant, condescending, arrogant—"

"You said that already." He flicked his fork at me, amusement playing on his lips.

He thought I was kidding. He thought we were having a disagreement. I took in a deep breath, willing my nerves to calm. "I'm completely serious, Captain," I told him softly, hating how he flinched as I reverted to calling him Captain. "I'm sorry to have misled you in any way... but what happened last night won't happen again."

Wolfe gazed at me a moment, perhaps trying to calculate how earnest I was. Finally he shook his head, angry confusion in his beautiful eyes. "Rogan, don't. I know this is... difficult... but we can figu—"

"Don't." I stood up quickly, my plate rattling back on the table. "I'm going to wash up." Before he could argue any more with me, I hurried out of the kitchen, brushing past the bewildered old widow. The trough was right out back, hidden in the shade of the house so the water was still chilled. It felt delicious, shocking, and refreshing as I splashed it up into my face, rubbing water droplets into my neck and behind my ears. It wasn't perfect, but it would do. For a while I just stood by the trough, gazing around at the open land around the old widow's home. The land here wasn't as lush and green as Vasterya. There was a browny-bronze tinge to everything that suggested the land existed in a state of near autumn all year round, contrary to the heat of the sun. There was more rainfall in Daeronia during the summer months than anywhere else bar Alvernia. It was colder too, the further north you crept. I decided I liked the air in Daeronia, however. Not only were we still close enough to brewery land to smell the sweetness in the air, but it was joined by a crisp freshness that you just didn't get in the other provinces during the summer months. It was always so humid everywhere else.

Deciding I had prolonged my visit to the trough as long as I could, I headed back into kitchen, heart pounding, dreading what was awaiting me. Wolfe stood watching for me, his expression carefully blank.

"There you are," he said gruffly. "I have the horses waiting."

The old widow came bustling back into the kitchen, a pack clutched in her hands. "Here." She thrust it at me. "Here are some provisions just in case, but you should reach Caera before nightfall."

I thanked the widow as did Wolfe, before Wolfe gestured to the doorway. His eyes had hardened. "Ladies first."

My instinct (call it years of disliking him) was to be peeved with him, but *I* had been the one to wrong *him*, so I pinched my mouth closed and headed past him.

"Be patient," I heard the old woman say and Wolfe grunted. I glanced back with a little furrow between my brows as the two shared a look – her amused, his exasperated. Curious, I threw him a questioning look and then quickly whipped back around at his ferocious glare.

It was going to be a long ride to Caera.

***

We rode the horses hard to Caera. With the two of us angry at me, I felt emotionally and physically exhausted when we reached the city. I almost wept with relief as we crossed the beautifully-sculpted bridge over the River Cael and into the gates of Caera. I had never been to Caera before but I'd heard about the bridge. It was wide enough for horses and carts to pass one another and was made of thick, sturdy stone, polished to brilliance. On either side were walls made of the same stone that reached Wolfe's shoulders in height. Massive stone statues stood guard at either entrance – two ethereal female mage at the entrance and two powerful male mage at the exit. Some say it was Vojvodkyna Winter's sense of humor: Caera was a woman's world and the rest of Phaedra was mans. Statues of winged creatures beckoned from the walls of the bridge and I stared wide-eyed. How much money had Winter put into this bridge? It was beautiful... but wasn't it a waste? I was sure Jarvis would think so.

As soon as we were inside the city walls I felt Wolfe's urgency to get to The Guard. We hurried through the thronging masses as they hurried to and fro. The marketplace in Daeronia would be busy— they didn't have anything to export except beer and coal so much of the business was in import. I had to admit as I followed Wolfe out of the main streets to quieter cobbled ones, I was impressed by the Vojvodkyna's white stone city. It really was spectacularly beautiful. Much like her Grace. I winced, suddenly remembering we were heading to the home of Wolfe's ex-lover. I gulped.

That wouldn't be awkward at all.

Unlike the other wealthy districts of Phaedra, the Radiant District was a walled district with a gatekeeper. When Wolfe explained who we were, one of the soldiers disappeared behind the carved wooden doors keeping us out. Wolfe glared his disapproval at the three other guards who tried desperately not to shift their feet uncomfortably. I almost sympathized with them. I knew how stinging that glare could be.

"Captain!"

We both turned at the sound of Lieutenant Chaeron's voice as he came through the gates, directing the guard to open them so we could trot through.

"It's good to see you, Lieutenant." Wolfe nodded down at him. Chaeron nodded back. Men were such funny things.

I smiled brightly at Chaeron. "Lieutenant. So good to see you."

"You too, Miss Rogan." He looked up at me with concern as he walked by my horse. "I do hope you are well, Miss Rogan."

Realizing he was genuinely distressed that I had been taken while under his protection, I sought to reassure him, "Of course, Lieutenant. Captain Wolfe and I looked out for one another."

We both ignored the grunt from the said Captain's direction.

"The Vojvodkyna has a suite waiting for you. She realizes how exhausted you must be and has given you leave to retreat to your room."

Given me leave? I wanted to snort at that. I was going to my bloody room, leave or not. I didn't say that though. That would make me sound jealous. And I wasn't. Not a bit. "How kind of her."

Some of The Guard was waiting outside of Vojvodkyna Winter's spectacular stone white mansion that was a surprisingly small replica of the Silverian Palace. Hmm. I raised an eyebrow but kept quiet. I wouldn't have been able to comment, even if I had wanted to. The soldiers circled me and Wolfe, peppering us with questions, anxiety, remorse, until Wolfe actually took pity on me and ordered his men aside so I could go inside.

"Lady Rogan," Wolfe called to me as I walked away. I stiffened at hearing him so formal but I told myself it was only because we were among the men again. I turned slightly, face expressionless.

"Yes, Captain?"

"I would prefer if we stayed here for a few days instead of one. To regain our strength."

I returned his nod with a brittle one of my own. I could understand the wisdom in the suggestion, despite my desperate need to get to Alvernia... except I wondered if it was just wisdom on Wolfe's part or if he wanted some extra time with the beautiful Vojvodkyna? Shaking off the strange pang of pain I felt, I followed Lieutenant Chaeron who introduced me to the butler, a beautiful older woman. Her auburn hair was tied back in a fierce knot, and streaks of silver darted through it at the sides. I was surprised that Winter had such an attractive butler, thinking perhaps her vain enough to want to be the prettiest woman in her home. But when the butler called for two maid servants to help me to my room, I came to a better understanding. The two maids were stunning young creatures, their auburn hair and wide blue eyes a striking counterpart to their dark work clothes. Then again, even their work clothes were the finest I had seen. It was then something obvious occurred to me: Vojvodkyna Winter Rada was obsessed with beauty. So far the servants resembled her in coloring. It was strange, to say the least, and I wasn't just being snotty because of her history with Wolfe. I honestly found it a little narcissistic. Not a little. A lot. As I followed the stunning little creatures to a lovely bedroom suite where a bath already awaited me, as well as tray of food, I snorted at the maids' beauty. The Royal Guard must be in haven here.

***

It was a wonderful sleep. Comfortable. Warm. Luxurious even. I did dream of Haydyn again, but I had given in to the idea that until I saved her, she was going to be a regular visitor in my subconscious. The next morning I awoke to a maid setting a tray over my lap. She informed me I had missed breakfast, but that once I was refreshed I was invited to join the Vojvodkyna in her parlor for tea. Not particularly looking forward to that I made an agreeable noise from the back of my throat before tearing into my toast in frustration. The maid stared at me a little wide-eyed, probably unaccustomed to a lady taking her anger out on harmless toasted bread, before giving me a tremulous smile. She bustled around the room, laying out a dress for me from the luggage the Royal Guard had kept safe. I nearly sighed happily. It would be nice to wear clean clothes.

***

I followed another pretty maid to a room with white double doors edged in gold. A handsome footman with burnished brown hair and pale blue eyes pulled the door open for me and I swept inside, my gaze going back to the footman who was strangely familiar.

"I see Arnaud has captured your attention," a husky voice curled around me, drawing my gaze in its direction.

Immediately my spirits depressed. I forgot the impact of Winter's beauty. Contrary to her name, Winter was more autumn in coloring. Striking auburn hair, wide cobalt eyes and fine features. Her pale skin was the only thing about her that could be considered winterish. No wonder Wolfe had wanted this woman. Which really made me wonder what an earth he found appealing in me? She was all sunny autumn morning and I was all... thunderclouds and rain with my dark hair and dark eyes. Wolfe—

Wolfe! I turned around again to stare at the footman but he was gone, the door closed behind him. The footman had Wolfe's coloring! My gut twisted and my jaw clenched.

"He's rather delicious, isn't he?" Winter laughed, a throaty laugh meant for seducing boys and men.

I frowned at her, my thoughts taken over by Wolfe. It took me a moment before I realized she had meant Arnaud and I replied with a half-smile, "Very."

Winter drew to her feet quickly, her white dress as stunning as a ball gown, the neckline cut low, the waist cinched so everyone could see how tiny it was. I smoothed the plain gown I wore, wondering why on earth I was letting the obvious differences between us bother me. I had never cared before.

"Come, sit down, you look exhausted." Winter clasped my hand gently and led me to the armchair. I took a seat slowly, surprised by the genuine concern on her face as she eyed the bruise that was now fading on my cheek. "You've been through such an ordeal. The Vikomt Stovia told me all about your abduction by rookery gang members." She shook her head in disgust. "I had heard of this so-called rookery in Vasteryian Borders but to actually face the reality of it. You're very brave, Lady Rogan. You are to be commended for handling it so well."

I smiled in spite of myself. "Thank you, Your Grace." Wolfe hadn't told Winter about the gypsies. He'd only told her a half truth, a truth she was already aware of. Good. We were sticking to the plan. Not panicking anyone with the growing unrest in Phaedra.

"Tea?" Winter asked.

I nodded, feeling tongue-tied. I really didn't know what to say to this vivacious creature. Haydyn was always so good at talking to the Rada. I winced. Then again, Haydyn was as beautiful as Winter—perhaps more so.

"Arabelle." Winter waved a dainty hand to the maid in the corner and the girl came forward at a graceful float. She had her servants as well trained as debutantes.

Once tea was sorted, Arabelle was dismissed and Winter relaxed more into the settee. "I do hope you slept well last night, Lady Rogan. I gathered you might need the rest."

"I did." I actually smiled at the thought of the luxurious bed upstairs. "Thank you, Your Grace, for your hospitality. It feels like sun after a very long bout of rain."

Pleased with my poetic thanks, Winter hurried on to pepper me with more questions about my wellbeing until I began to feel guilty for judging her so harshly. She didn't seem like a shallow socialite at all. In fact, if I remember correctly, Haydyn had told me she liked the Vojvodkyna. She said Winter was smart and opinionated and cared not who knew it— the kind of woman I might have called friend...

Just as we were discussing Haydyn's plans to hold a ball next season in the hopes of addressing some Phaedrian issues, a knock sounded at the door and Wolfe came striding in. He looked like his old self again. At the sight of him my heart did a little *thump thump* I bitterly ignored.

"Vikomt!" Winter rose to her feet, her eyes alight with happiness at the sight of Wolfe. His returning smile was wide and brilliant and he bowed over her hand slowly, pressing an intimate kiss to the corner of her wrist. I felt a painful twist in my chest. Seeing them together, as they turned to me, I processed just how handsome they looked. How right. Winter was a little older than Wolfe, but with his maturity and sense of responsibility the age difference seemed inconsequential.

"My Lady." Wolfe nodded at me, his expression blank, and eyes indifferent. I felt like scowling at him in outrage. Instead, I nodded back as if I were unaffected by the difference in temperature of his greetings to me and the Vojvodkyna.

"Oh, My Lord, it is lovely to have you to tea," Winter said to him in that husky undertone, leading him to the settee to sit closely by her.

I did not think it was deliberate, but now Wolfe was in the room nothing else existed for Winter, and she huddled into him, availing him of her recent deal with a factory owner in Raphizya that she swore would bring more income and work for the people of Caera. Wolfe listened aptly, his eyes never leaving her, drinking in the vivid, intelligent woman's proximity. I felt completely cut out, and the longer they sat talking, the more irrationally angry and hurt I grew. I felt as if a small creature was gnawing on my ribs.

I was jealous.

Hatefully, painfully jealous, and there was nothing I could do about it. If only there was some way I could not be attracted to him. I mulled over this for a moment. There was Haydyn. Once Raj administered the cure and she was well and back to full strength perhaps she could evoke feelings of disdain for me again. I chewed on the idea for a bit before dismissing it. No. Haydyn needed all her strength for the peace evocation. Well that was that then. I just had to avoid Wolfe at all costs.

"Well." I stood slowly, smiling brightly, falsely down at them. "Thank you for tea, Your Grace, but I promised Lieutenant Chaeron I would meet with him."

"Oh, of course." Winter smiled happily at me.

"Good day, Your Grace. Captain." I managed to meet his eyes before hurrying past them.

"Lady Rogan, wait," Wolfe called out in clipped, demanding tones.

Not wanting to respond but knowing it would prove to him how annoyed I was by his attitude with me, I spun slowly and raised a condescending eyebrow at him like I used to. "Yes?"

"Where are you going?" He demanded.

"I just told you," I snapped.

Winter raised an eyebrow at my attitude and Wolfe narrowed his eyes at me. And then as I looked at them pressed together on the settee I decided I *was* angry. Just two nights before, Wolfe had been kissing me. Me! Now he was romancing his old lover under my nose! Arrggh! I had been correct to walk away. Correct! I had been nothing but an amusement. And Wolfe had been nothing but another Jarek.

"I don't remember any such plans," Wolfe snapped back.

"I want Lieutenant Chaeron to train me. With a sword. Considering what happened. You yourself said it wasn't a bad idea."

He frowned. "It's not. But I'll train you."

The thought of him putting his arms around me made me quail in fear. Not because I was frightened of him. But because I was frightened of myself.

"No, thank you." Without another word I spun around and left them to stew in the wake of my rude departure.

Chapter Nineteen

Training with Chaeron the day before had really taken my mind off the Wolfe situation. I was still not amused that Chaeron hadn't taken my word for it that Wolfe was allowing me to be trained to use a sword and had gone off to ask permission from the man himself. But when he returned a little sheepishly I decided that learning to fight back was more important than being peevish. Chaeron had proved to be a patient and adept trainer and I really felt as if I had learned something from him. I now knew how to hold the hilt of a sword properly, which apparently was more important than I gave credence to. He was teaching me how to use an opponent's weight and height against them, considering most men were going to be taller and stronger than me. I was still being backed into a corner, but I was getting there.

"Lieutenant." I waved to him as I crossed the courtyard. He and a few other soldiers were already busy at practice. "May I join you today?"

"You've come back for more punishment, Miss Rogan?" Chaeron grinned teasingly.

I raised my eyebrows in mock hauteur. "I'm nothing if not resilient, Lieutenant."

We smiled at one another before he set about procuring me a sword. We went over a few basics again and he had a few of the men, of different heights and weight, come at me, calling out instructions on how best to deal with their attack. "See how Smythe keeps attacking low— despite my best efforts to break him of the habit— he's trying to sneak past your defense. But now you know the pattern of his thrust and parry you can use it against him, sweep up, strike at him as his sword comes at you..."

We had only been training for a half hour when Wolfe appeared in the courtyard. The men hurried to appear vigilant, even though there was nothing about to be vigilant for.

"Lieutenant." Wolfe nodded at Chaeron. "Why don't you and the men take a break?"

I frowned as Chaeron nodded and gestured for the men to follow him out of the courtyard, dispersing them in seconds. "You just got rid of my sparring partners."

Wolfe remained expressionless. "Follow me."

I narrowed my eyes at his command. What on haven did he want? Still furious at him, I considered telling him to stick his sword where the sun didn't shine.

But curiosity won out.

I followed quickly as he led me out of the courtyard and down the stone servant's steps that led into the walled gardens. I hurried along trying to keep up with him, my heart thudding in my chest as I gripped the hilt of the sword in my sweating hand. What could possibly be wrong to have put Wolfe in this strange state of tense

calm? When he disappeared into the high hedges that hid us from the
view of the house, I'd had enough.

"Wolfe!" I called quietly, sharply, drawing to a halt. When he
spun around startled, I bit my lip. Damn it, I'd used his name again.
Shrugging off my embarrassment I glared at him. "Well. What is the
matter? I'm not following you any longer until you tell me what is
going on."

Wolfe shrugged lazily and headed back toward me, his
movements languid and sleek. Sometimes he reminded me of an
overlarge cat. And like Haydyn's cat, Z, I didn't trust his body
language - it signaled an approaching attack. "I merely wanted
privacy to continue your training."

I felt an angry flush color my face. "I was in the middle of
training. I don't need your help."

"I'm the best swordsman in the Royal Guard," he said without
arrogance, and I knew it was true. "Don't you want to learn from the
best?"

"I was learning from second best, which is quite alright with me."
I thrust my chin in the air haughtily, running my eyes down the
length of his body with a look of distaste. "Why don't you return to
your mistress, Captain? I've heard she enjoys a bit of swordplay." I
don't know what possessed me to say something so indecent!

Wolfe laughed, a true happy laugh that sent a shiver rippling
through me. I took a step back but he followed until I was pressed up
against a hedge, the branches pricking into my skin through my

dress. He loomed over me, inches from me, intimidating me. "Are we going to spar or not?"

Determined I could withstand his nearness, I gave him a stubborn nod and pushed him back. He immediately encircled me, his arms coming around me and covering my hand on the sword.

"I've already been shown how to hold it," I said hoarsely, my skin tight and sensitive at his close proximity. I could feel his breath in my ear, his hard thighs through my skirts.

"You've not been taught how to hold mine," he replied in a low voice, his lips brushing my ear. My cheeks must have bloomed bright red as understanding dawned. The lascivious son of...

"Why you—" My indignation trailed off into silence at the surprisingly sweet kiss he pressed against my neck. He held me tight as if trying to offer comfort more than passion. I almost melted into him. But then I have an excellent memory...

...I swear, I've never met a man who knows how to use his mouth quite so well...

Winter!

I stiffened. I remembered overhearing her one night at the palace two summer seasons ago. She and her friends had been discussing her liaison with Wolfe with pride and relish...

...I would pay all the gold in Phaedra to be showered in that man's kisses...

Feeling stupider than stupid, I shoved away from Wolfe, hard, so he staggered a little. Turning to face him, I found his eyes bright and narrowed with frustration.

"I'm not one of your women," I hissed, hating the sting of tears in my eyes. "Go back to Winter."

His face hardened immediately and he bristled. For a moment I had forgotten how much larger he was than me, his height casting me into shadow. "I don't want Winter," Wolfe growled. "It's been over between us for a long time."

I wanted to believe him. Wolfe wasn't the kind of man who lied. And I knew, deep down, as I sneered at him — because it was easier this way— I was deliberately choosing to believe otherwise. I shook my head at him, the message in my eyes clear. I felt his glare burn through my back as I hurried out of the gardens and away from him.

***

Dinner was excruciating. I wore my best dress, which wasn't saying much considering all I had packed were travelling gowns, and sat next to Chaeron hoping his soothing presence would get me through it. Winter sat at the head of the table with Wolfe at her side. As per usual she was dressed as perfectly as a doll, flawless, refined. A lady.

Wolfe and I refused to look at each other and I knew Chaeron was confused by the tension at the table. A tension that grew worse when it became apparent that Winter had cooled towards me.

The few times she deigned to speak to me it was with a tight little smile and hard eyes. My protective Lieutenant bridled beside me at her rudeness, but as Winter was Vojvodkyna and Chaeron a mere Mister, I placed a quieting hand on his arm to reassure him and received a blistering look from Wolfe for my trouble.

I had never been so thankful to get away from a room in my life. I shook off the Lieutenant's apologies on behalf of her Grace and hurried to my room to lock myself inside.

But I couldn't sleep. I kept thinking of our journey ahead in the morning. Soon we would be in Alvernia and I would have to brave the mountains for Haydyn's cure. But brave them I would and then hurry home to bring her back. I needed her more than ever. I refused to think of what was happening back in Silvera. If I did I'd start to panic and lose the little focus I had.

Finally, after having tossed and turned the sheets into a tight tangle around my legs, I shoved my way out of the bed and into a dressing gown. Winter had a library on the ground floor. I would pick out a book and read for a while in the hope that it would send me off to sleep.

I was surprised to discover the sconces still alight out in the hallway, and as I walked it became apparent that the Vojvodkyna kept her house alight even during slumber hours. I clucked, shaking my head. The lady really was wasteful. I hurried through the lit hallways and tiptoed down the stairs, my bare feet cold against the marble floor. I hopped quietly from rug to rug to save my poor feet –

they'd taken quite a battering already on this journey. As I drew closer to Winter's parlor the sound of low voices drew me to a halt. *Was that Wolfe?*

Heart thudding in my chest, blooding rushing in my ears, I sidled along the wall until I drew up to the door. Peering tentatively around the doorframe I sucked in a breath at the sight before me. I hated that I wanted to cry. I hated that he made me feel that way.

Wolfe was sprawled in an armchair, his long arm draped over the edge, a brandy snifter dangling from his fingers. Winter stood over him, between his legs. She gazed down at him longingly.

I felt like screaming.

"Darling, you're being impossible," Winter purred as she leaned down, bracing a hand on each arm of the chair. "I've missed you. Two nights in the same house and not even a peck." She finished by pressing her lips to his cheek.

To my horror, Wolfe groaned, that familiar groan that I thought was all mine. Stupid fool. Stupid, inexperienced child.

But then he shocked me by pressing a hand to Winter's shoulder to push her away. With a sigh, Wolfe rose to his feet, towering over the Vojvodkyna. I watched as he brushed his fingers gently down her cheek. Winter stared back at him wary and bewildered.

"I told you no," Wolfe said in a low voice. "I'm sorry, Winter."

Holding in my breath, and squashing the little voice inside me that said 'ha, I knew he was telling the truth', I waited for Winter's response. She didn't seem like the kind of woman who would take kindly to being rebuffed.

Indeed she turned from him, her spine ram rod straight. "You can't possibly love her," she whispered. "She's nothing special. She's not even beautiful."

My jaw dropped. I may have questioned curiously who on Phaedra they were discussing but I knew how much Winter admired beauty… and I was anything but beautiful.

"I think she is," Wolfe whispered back and I felt my heart pound so hard it was as if the organ itself was swelling. My legs trembled, and my toes curled into the marble floor.

Winter shook her head and turned back to gaze at him, her eyes flashing as her lip snarled in disappointment. "I'm such a fool." She rolled her eyes heavenward. "Even back then your eyes used to follow her everywhere. I told myself you were only doing your job, watching over her."

"I'm sorry," Wolfe repeated, looking helpless. I'd never seen him thus. I didn't like it.

"Stop saying you're sorry. So what? You're going to give up what we could have again for a girl who doesn't even like you?"

That awful pang resonated again and again like a vibration in my chest as Wolfe flinched. I felt like crying out to him. It wasn't that I didn't like him. It wasn't that at all. I just couldn't *be* with him.

"Rogan is confused." He rubbed his forehead in that familiar way of his and my heart beat faster. "But I'm willing to wait."

Winter shook her head, as if she thought him a fool. Mayhap she saw something in me that he didn't. "You *actually* love her?"

My breath caught.

Wolfe sighed and walked over to the table. Slowly he placed his brandy snifter on it and then straightened, reaching for Winter in a comforting gesture. "I do. I love her."

At his pronouncement I thought I might be sick. I felt the blood rush out of my face and abandon my body. No. *No.*

Clutching my stomach in fear, I quietly backed away from the door and snuck down the hallway, my legs not seeming to be a part of my body as they took me upstairs and back to my room. For a while I just stared at nothing, balancing on the edge of my bed, my heart fluttering wildly.

Wolfe loved me.

Wolfe.

Loved.

Me.

How had this happened?

I thought of the way I had hurt when he told me what Syracen had done to him, what the sight of the horseshoe brand did to my heart. Of the way I had come to enjoy arguing with him so long as it meant being in his company. Of the way my stomach flipped when he turned his wicked smile on me, and the way my body came alive when he kissed me. Of the ache, deep and gnawing in my chest when I thought he and Winter had resumed their affair.

Oh, haven no. I closed my eyes, frustrated tears clogging my burning throat. I couldn't love him back. I just couldn't.

There were too many obstacles between us. Too much history. Too much hurt. The blood of the man who had destroyed my family ran in his veins. I wouldn't. I wouldn't betray my family by marrying Wolfe. A Glava. I thought of Selene and her prediction. Well, I'd prove her wrong.

From now on I was putting a world of distance between me and Wolfe. Soon he'd stop loving me. He'd be fine. He was a catch. He could have any woman he wanted.

And me?

Well I only wanted one thing and Wolfe kept getting between me and it.

Focus. Utter focus on retrieving the Somna Plant.

Saving Haydyn. Just the thought of her name: I knew it would help me keep Wolfe at a distance and give me the strength to go it alone.

Chapter Twenty

He knew what I was doing. The frustration and anguish on Wolfe's face when I gave him formal, clipped responses to his queries almost undone me. But I chanted *Haydyn* over and over in my head to keep me strong. And after the third hour, Wolfe finally glowered at me like he really hated me and sped off in front. Feeling Lieutenant Chaeron's curious gaze I stared straight ahead, my eyes blank, features expressionless. The quicker Wolfe disliked me the better this would be.

Despite the horror of the significance behind our journey across Phaedra, despite the terrible close calls I'd already had with the world's less civilized creatures, and despite the turmoil my entire body was undergoing being near Wolfe, I actually looked forward to venturing into the coal mining district of Daeronia. I'd heard the people were close knit and friendly. So as we trotted into the first village on the main trade road, I was more than a little surprised by the chill in the eyes of the villagers as we passed through. It was dusk, and people strode quickly to their homes, covered in soot and grime. Others, clean and rugged, headed in the opposite direction towards the mine. But all of them stared up at us with hard eyes and bristling bodies. I gaped at them in confusion, my eyes drinking in their squalid little homes and their gray little world. No one stopped to greet us, and Wolfe, who rode a few meters in front, made no attempt to stop to speak with them. The lines of his own body were stiff and I noted his hand sat on the hilt of his sword. Swallowing nervously now, I kept my eyes front, my mind whirring with bewilderment. We were in the southern-most village in Daeronia. It was more than possible that the evocation was gone from here. Shuddering, and sharing a glance with the Lieutenant, we shifted the horses forward at a faster trot. Wolfe crossed a little wooden bridge on the other side of the town and stopped in the clearing beyond it. He turned and the Lieutenant and I did the same. None of us said a word. We just waited for the entire Guard to make it through the village. When the last two men trotted over the bridge and joined us, I finally let go of my breath.

"That was chilly," I said quietly to Chaeron.

He answered with a brittle nod and looked over at Wolfe questioningly.

Wolfe sighed. "It's nearly dark. We should camp here. I think we'll be fine as long as we don't ask them for a place to sleep." He flicked a glance at me before staring straight ahead again. "I'm afraid it'll have to be a campfire bed for you, My Lady. I hope that doesn't distress you too much."

I wanted to nip back at him. He had said it loudly to needle me in front of his men. I looked at him, sensing the anticipation about him. He *wanted* me to nip back. He wanted something, anything from me. Trembling a little, I turned away from him. "I think I can manage well enough, Captain."

Feeling his questioning gaze on my face, I slid off my horse, letting my hair fall and cover my burning cheeks.

"Tyler, Szorst!" Wolfe called out to two of the men. He slid from his horse and approached them, holding out a bag of coins. "Go back into the village and procure us some coal. It should keep us warm at camp and perhaps soften the locals to us." He nodded in the direction of the bridge to some of the villagers who had come out of the village to peer at us making camp. Their entire bodies radiated with hostility. As the two men started off on foot I worried my lip between my teeth, watching them. Remembering the looks on the coal miners faces I decided that sending the men in alone was a bad idea. But I couldn't very well say that to Wolfe and I couldn't rush off alone— that had not worked out well in the past.

"Lieutenant." I approached Chaeron quietly as he settled the horses with some water.

"Yes, Miss Rogan?"

Telling Chaeron I thought his men were in danger wouldn't work. The Royal Guard was somewhat arrogant about their prowess and didn't take lightly to having it called into question. I'd have to go about this a different way. "We've been riding all day and I really would like to stretch my legs. Would you walk with me into the village?"

He frowned at me, suspicion in his eyes. "Miss Rogan, you saw how unfriendly the people were."

"Then perhaps a few of the other men would like to stretch their legs with us," I used my take no prisoners tone that Haydyn hated.

She could never defy me when I used that tone. I usually brandished it on her when she was daydreaming during her tutorials or refusing to get out of bed.

I blanched at that last thought. Shaking off the familiar growing panic that thrummed continuously beneath my skin, I raised my eyebrow at Chaeron as he just stood there. As my look intensified he finally drew himself up. "Of course, Miss Rogan."

As we passed two men, Chaeron called to them to come with us, and then informed Wolfe that he was escorting me into the village. Discerning the coming argument by the look on Wolfe's face, I drew out my heaviest artillery and stilled him with a look so cold it made him pale.

I gulped down my guilt and hurried on, my skin prickling and muscles twitching at the feel of his eyes on my departing figure.

As soon as we crossed the bridge I felt the charge in the air, a sense of violence and anticipation. Chaeron and his men must have felt it too because suddenly we were hurrying back into the town and through the narrow streets to get to the main village courtyard we'd come through. Sure enough, Tyler and Szorst stood with their hands on the hilt of their swords, surrounded by a group of angry coal miners, spitting and shouting at them. Just one spark, I thought. That's all it would take.

"Halt!" Lieutenant Chaeron bellowed and I flinched in surprise. He sounded terrifying and intimidating, and looked it too, as he strode forward with the two guards at his back. The villagers stumbled a little but did not move away from Tyler and Szorst who looked relieved to see us. "An attack on the Royal Guard is a high offence and will result in imprisonment!"

Some of the villagers seemed to deflate, their faces drawn and wary. Others grumbled but slumped away. Others grew even more aggressive. One man, a tall stout man with a round face hardened with hatred, stood forward from the group to face Chaeron.

"Who gives a damn about The Guard?! We're left to stew in this forsaken place, working our fingers to the bone in 18 hour shifts in the mines under order from management! Three months ago we worked good hours, decent hours, until management started adding an hour here and there until eventually we exist on no sleep, bad food and broken bodies. Our children grow sick! Our wives grow weary! Where is the Royal Guard in that, I ask you?"

Chaeron was as shocked as I at the explosion, and the rebel rousing yells of agreement. What on Phaedra was going on here? What this man said, it couldn't be true? But as I looked around at the desperate faces, I found the truth in their eyes.

Impulsively, I strode forward past Chaeron, who tried to reach for me and missed. "There must be some mistake," I implored to the man. "We didn't know."

He looked at me with such revulsion I flinched. And then he made a groggy noise in the back of his throat and spat in my face. Chaeron's blade was against his neck before I even could comprehend what had happened. Humiliated and ashamed, I wiped at the phlegm dripping down my cheek and glowered at the man who now stood stiff against Chaeron's sword.

"Your name?" Chaeron growled in his face.

"Den. Den Hewitt."

"Den Hewitt, you just committed a crime. Do you know who this lady is before you?"

The rebel-rouser paled somewhat as he really looked at me, his eyes showing a little of his panic as he wondered who he had just offended. "No," he replied hoarsely.

"You just assaulted the Lady Rogan of Silvera. The Princezna's Handmaiden."

The gasps of the people around us made me want to curl inside myself. Den blanched, fear turning his mouth white. Still shocked at his treatment of me, a woman, a lady, I let him stew on it a while. They thought his punishment would be grave indeed. However, although stunned by his offence, I was more concerned by his accusations.

"I didn't know." He wilted a little.

"No. I imagine you did not." Chaeron shifted the sword from his throat. "Den Hewitt, I charge you with assault against the Lady Rogan of Silvera. You will be placed in my custody and taken back to Silvera for trial."

"Lieutenant." I shook my head, not wanting this man punished severely for an act of stupidity born out of frustration.

"But Lady Rogan?" Chaeron frowned.

"All I want is an apology." I crossed my arms over my chest.

Hewitt looked between the two of us, his expression filling with hope as he waited for Chaeron's decision. The Lieutenant finally nodded although his eyes blazed against the decision, and Hewitt breathed a sigh of relief before turning to me. "I am so sorry, My Lady. I am so sorry."

I nodded. "If you had merely told us your grievance we would have dealt with it, Mr. Hewitt. I assure you that none of us were aware of these conditions you speak of. Let us return to our camp quietly and I will speak with the Captain of the Guard. He will investigate the matter." It was perhaps obnoxious and forward of me to assume Wolfe would take care of this situation, but I couldn't leave these people as they were. They were so volatile. Just one spark…

After thanking me and apologizing some more, relieved at escaping a close call, the men and I withdrew from Hewitt and turned back for camp. I could feel Chaeron's disapproval simmering beside me, but I shrugged it off. I was the one who had been spat on. I should be the one to mete out the punishment.

Before I could approach Wolfe, Chaeron was charging ahead. He cornered the Captain and began speaking to him frantically. At any other time I would have been annoyed, but I *was* trying to keep my distance from Wolfe.

By the time Chaeron was done, Wolfe's face was hard as stone. With an efficiency and lethal determination that demonstrated just why he was Captain, Wolfe rounded up a group of ten men and they mounted their horses. As they cantered towards me, I stood to the side and kept my eyes on the grass. I saw Wolfe's horses' hooves come into view and then stop.

"Next time, ask me before you offer my services," his harsh voice caught me by the back of the neck and tipped my head upwards.

I scowled at him. "Are you saying you would leave them this way?"

He frowned back at me. "You know I wouldn't. But I don't appreciate taking orders from you, Lady Rogan."

My apologetic smile was brittle. "Apologies. It won't happen again."

Again, seeming startled and disappointed by my compliance, Wolfe nodded and began to pull away. Just as I was relaxing, sure Wolfe would take care of the issues the villagers had put forth, he threw over his shoulder, "I'm fining Den Hewitt for assaulting you."

"But I don't want that!" I cried, rushing to catch up with him. I could see the other men trying to look uninterested in our exchange. "You can't do that!"

Wolfe drew to an abrupt halt and glared down at me. "I can do anything I want. I am the Captain of the Guard." He seethed, his face mottled red with anger. "He assaulted you, Rogan, and that I will not stand for." Abruptly he turned and jerked his reins, galloping over the bridge and into the village, unmindful of his surprised Guard who took off after him. Surprised by the abrupt departure? No.

They were surprised that Wolfe had betrayed his familiarity with me in front of them and used my given name.

***

It was with a mixture of relief and pain I realized Wolfe had had enough and was no longer speaking to me. He returned to camp some few hours later and told Chaeron what had happened. I tried to eavesdrop, but the collective snoring of The Guard drowned out their voices.

The next morning Wolfe refused to look at me let alone speak to me, and as we moved off away from the village, I had to ask Chaeron for the details of Wolfe's venture into the village.

Apparently Den Hewitt had not exaggerated. After investigation, Wolfe discovered the Manager of the mine, a wealthy Baron no less, was working the villagers to the bone to keep up with the competition from the local mining communities surrounding them. Discovering sick children and ill workers, worn out and hopeless, Wolfe was furious. The village had had two deaths in the last month. Exhaustion and dehydration. He fined the Manager (and Den Hewitt) and threatened him with criminal charges if he did not return to the normal working procedures. To ensure his obeisance, Wolfe left two of his men to guard the workers and sent a messenger to Vojvodkyna Winter Rada explaining the situation, and asking her to send some of her men to relieve the Royal Guardsmen and to order a replacement Manager for the mine.

I rested easier knowing Wolfe had taken care of it. I had known he would. I sighed wearily and stared straight ahead, worrying about what we would find in the next village we passed through. I had so much to tell Haydyn once she was awake and well. Our problem wasn't just the evocation. Our problem was that outside the cities governed by the Rada, the people were ignored and left to go about their business ungoverned. That had to change. I straightened my spine with determination. When this journey was over and my task complete, Phaedra was in for some changes. For the better.

Chapter Twenty One

To my utter relief the next few days in Daeronia passed uneventfully. We stopped in two other mining communities and neither of them was suffering under the conditions of the first. From their disposition to the state of their homes, to their fervent hospitality, they were fire to the southern coal mining village's ice. And I? I was confused. Perhaps I had merely wanted to put the Manager of the coal mining village attitude down to Haydyn's evocation, but the northern coal miners had great attitudes, and surely if the evocation waning was the problem then they would be the ones to feel the affects more so than the south.

My forehead spent a lot of time in a perpetual state of wrinkles.

The situation with Wolfe hadn't changed. If anything it had worsened. Anything he had to say to me he had Lieutenant Chaeron pass on to me, and the night we dined in the home of the Manager of a large coal mining town called East Winds, Wolfe flirted with their twenty-year old daughter as he ignored my existence. *I* ignored the fist of agony in my chest. His attitude was of my own making and I had no right to feel anything toward him.

We had been following the River Cael and were closing in on the border between Daeronia and Alvernia. My stomach had now formed into a constant knot of anxiety, the need to get to the Pool of Phaedra an obsession, sharp and unrelenting. I was impatient when Wolfe stopped us by the river for our midday break, and was about to voice my disgruntlement when I remembered I hadn't spoken to him for three days. Plus, it was unseasonably hot, not even a wisp of that crisp Daeronian breeze that I had come to love. Telling Chaeron I needed a moment alone, I wandered along the river bank that flowed on the left side of the trade road, as the men gathered near the woodland on the right. They stopped, sliding down to lean against tree trunks and eat the hard biscuits that had come to form their unsatisfying daily diet. I was still in sight, but I used the horse to cover me as I took off my shoes and stockings to dangle my feet over the bank into the river. I sighed at the wonderful feel of the cold water on my skin and thanked the haven I hadn't had to walk too much. My stupid soft 'lady's' feet would be ruined. Reluctantly, I pulled my feet out of the water and reassembled my clothing before Wolfe sent someone to collect me. However, as I walked back to the men, my eyes darting over them, there was no sign of Wolfe or Chaeron. Puzzled, I searched them out. Where were they? Just as I was about to draw near the first group of men I caught a flash of color out the corner of my eye a little way in among the trees. Wolfe's green military jacket. He'd had to borrow it from one of The Guard, who now wore a plain jacket provided by the Vojvodkyna. Curious as to why Wolfe and Chaeron were huddling in the woods, I eyed the men to see if any were watching me. I was somewhat disappointed to see that none of them were.

That was brilliant guarding for you.

Rolling my eyes, I snuck away from the men and edged closer to Wolfe and Chaeron. Leaving my horse, I stopped a few trees back from them, hidden in the shade.

"I just don't know if it's a good idea," Lieutenant Chaeron exhaled.

"I have to," Wolfe insisted, his voice flat.

"I could do it."

"No, it has to be me." Wolfe shook his head. "If Rogan's going up into the mountains then I'm going to be the one protecting her."

Chaeron sighed again. "Things are difficult between you as it is."

"I know. But I won't let my feelings get in the way of my duty. Which is to protect her."

"What will I tell the men?"

"Tell them I've taken Rogan on a tour of Alvernia, to let her see for herself what the area and the people are really like, so she can report back to the Princezna."

"They'll think it's insane. They'll wonder why you've gone alone. Perhaps even speculate…"

"If any one of my men utters a derogatory word against Lady Rogan I want you to deal with them."

Chaeron sucked in his breath as if insulted. "You know I would, Captain."

"Good. Tell them the Alvernians are paranoid, suspicious. A Royal entourage traipsing around their land would be seen as an act of aggression. Tell them that Lady Rogan and I are going incognito."

"Alright." There was a moment of silence between them before Chaeron peered at Wolfe with genuine concern. "Wolfe," he said softly, surprising me *and* Wolfe by using his given name, "You've never been into the mountains. A few of the men here have. They'd be better suited to escort Miss Rogan."

Wolfe shook his head determinedly, his jaw set. "I won't let her go into that without me…" he shoved a hand through his hair in obvious frustration, appearing vulnerable and lost. "It would drive me crazy."

Chaeron placed a hand on Wolfe's shoulder. "Alright."

I backed away as stealthily as I could, the blood rushing in my ears from what I had overheard and the blood flooding my cheeks for having been eavesdropping. I walked numbly back to the men with my horse beside me, and saw nothing and heard nothing as we mounted back up and set off. Wolfe was furious with me but he still cared. Cared enough to foolishly follow me into the heart of the Alvernian Mountains where the chances of us both coming to harm was great. No. I shook my head, ignoring Chaeron's concerned looks. I wouldn't go into the mountains with Wolfe. I had to keep my distance. I had to stay focused on finding the plant and I couldn't do that if I was worrying about Wolfe.

I had to get away from him somehow.

When we reached Arrana I had to leave and set off into the mountains alone. It didn't matter if I had an escort or not. Only I knew the way to the Pool of Phaedra and my magic would get me there without getting me lost. I just had to be careful and remember the route up so I could get back down the mountain without faltering.

***

That night, we made it to Arrana. Smaller than the other cities, Arrana was also more heavily fortified, with a massive fifteen foot wall snaking around its border. Like one of the keeps used thousands of years ago when the mage first came to Phaedra, the city had a moat and drawbridge, and armored guards. We had to wait for permission to enter, and as we crossed the sturdy bridge into the city walls, I frowned in disapproval. There were no wars in Phaedra. No need for city walls and moats and drawbridges. I understood the Vojvoda was nervous of the mountain people of Alvernia— I was nervous of them and I had to walk right into their midst —but his fortification sent the wrong message. It isolated Arrana. It made it a lone entity, and broke it from Haydyn's Phaedra.

What must the people of Alvernia think? Or any people who crossed the border into Alvernia? It was unwelcoming and superior. Worse… it was aggressive.

This too would have to change.

***

This would never do, I thought glumly, watching Markiz Andrei
follow the servant girl's bosom with his eyes while his father,
Vojvoda Andrei, tried to convince me that his son would be a
brilliant match for Haydyn. I found it difficult swallowing my fish as
I dined with them. I studied the junior Andrei as he smiled at me and
I bemoaned the vapidity behind his eyes. The poor boy wasn't
lascivious or cruel. He was just… silly and… well not very
intelligent. He was so wrong for my Haydyn. Haydyn needed
someone as clever and as passionate as she was, someone who stood
up for her and to her.

Someone like Matai.

All of a sudden I felt unbearably sad.

I let Wolfe and the Vojvoda do all the talking. I smiled enough so
as not to seem unpleasant and bored, but I was sure the Vojvoda was
puzzled as to why Haydyn would send an advisor on her behalf who
had barely opened her mouth once to speak. But I felt buried by the
troubles of Phaedra. Buried and useless. I needed Haydyn to wake
up. I had needed her to wake up before she fell ill. I only hoped that
she would once I provided the cure and told her all I'd learned. To
begin with, marrying Andrei would be a terrible mistake.

So lost in my problems, I barely noticed that Wolfe had managed
to finagle it so he was the one to walk me to my room. As we drew
closer and his arm brushed mine, I began to come out of my stupor

as my skin came instantly alive at being so close to him. I glanced at him quickly and looked away. We hadn't talked or been this near to one another in some time. Not since Caera.

"In the morning you and I will leave for the mountains." Wolfe stopped abruptly and I drew to a halt, turning to him. We looked one another in the eyes for the first time in days. "We're going to pretend we're taking a tour of Alvernia and its people, but in reality we're going to get that plant."

I knew if I didn't try to dissuade him after all we'd been through he'd be suspicious. I had to give a little argument, even though I already had my plan at the ready. "Do you really think that's wise… considering?"

"Considering?"

"Considering you hate me." I held my breath, waiting for him to dispute it. I knew he cared. I just needed him to admit it. Haven, I wished my heart would make up its mind!

I felt a sharp pain somewhere near the said organ when he shrugged. "It's my duty."

I bit back a hurt retort. "Fine. I want it noted that I dispute the idea. For future reference."

"Noted."

I nodded and turned to go into my room, disbelieving that that would be the last thing I said to him before heading into the wilderness where I might never return. I stilled as his hand wrapped around my upper arm. I glanced up nervously as he sidled closer, his eyes challenging me to stop him. I didn't. I let him kiss me. I thought it would be a hard kiss meant to dominate, but instead he surprised me with a soft, seductive brushing of lips and tongue, meant to melt. Even as he kissed me, giving me what I wanted, I ached with longing.

When he pulled back Wolfe's cheeks were flushed and he gazed at me again with that soft curl of his lip, bright gold in his blue eyes. "I want it noted that I don't hate you. For future reference."

Not able to stop it, I felt a small smile tilt up the corners of my mouth. "Noted. Although I must protest that you keep forcing unwanted kisses on me."

"It's the only way to get one. Unwanted indeed." He raised a knowing eyebrow at me.

Arrogant knave.

I shook my head, feeling sad and happy all at the same time. "Why do you persist, Wolfe?"

His grin was slow and wicked as he stood back from me, allowing my body and mind to breathe again. "Strategy."

"Strategy?"

He cocked his eyebrow. "At first I thought imposed isolation would make you miss me—"

"Why you arro—"

"—but then I realized that it's being near me you can't resist. And there are only so many kisses you'll take before you give in to me completely, Rogan."

Ignoring the flush of excited heat that shivered through me at his hoarse tone and serious eyes, I gripped the handle of the bedroom door behind me and guffawed. "We'll see, Captain. We'll see."

I slammed the door in his face, growling at the sound of his cocky chuckle as he walked away.

For a moment all I could do was stare at myself in the mirror, touching a mouth that now tingled with the taste of Wolfe. I closed my eyes, hating that thrum in my body that never used to be there before he first kissed me.

I wasn't even sorry for kissing him. I was thankful that our last moment together—before Wolfe truly did come to dislike me—was sweet, in that dysfunctional way of ours.

Shrugging him off as best I could (he still lingered in the air around me), I scrambled about, ringing the bell for a servant, and getting my coins at the ready. Grateful when a young girl in rough servants clothing appeared, I explained to her what I needed from her and showed her the coins. She stared at them in wonder. There was more money there than she probably earned in two years of hard work.

"Well?" I asked, my heart stuck in my throat.

For an answer she scooped the coins up and pocketed them, grinning from cheek to cheek. "I'll help ye, My Lady," she replied in the soft burr of the Alvernians.

Breathing a sigh of relief, I went over again what I needed, and then waited for her return. She wasn't long in reappearing with a few bundles in her hand. In one was a pack with food supplies and a canteen of water. In the other was boy's clothing stolen from one of the stable boys. Hurriedly, the girl helped me into the trousers that hugged my figure in a way that would make me blush if Wolfe ever saw me in them, and I pulled on the overlarge shirt, waistcoat and warm overcoat to see me through the bitter cold nights in the mountains. The boots she brought me belonged to her, they were worn and soft, but still foreign to me, and I hoped my feet would cope in them. Lastly, I pinned my long thick locks in a bun and hid the hair under the woolen cap she had brought me. Hopefully in the dim light, if I kept my head low, I could pass for a boy. If I removed the overcoat no one would ever believe it. I just had to make sure I never removed it. Lastly, I stuffed the dagger Matai had given me into the pack.

Thanking the servant profusely, we hurried through the darkened house and out to the front gates where she had a horse all ready and waiting for me. Once mounted, I gave the house one last look. Wolfe was going to be furious. But I was counting on him not to be foolish enough to follow me into the mountains without The Guard. He knew my magic wouldn't get me lost. But he didn't know the way. The Guard would keep him right... and slow him down.

I sighed. I had to put all my trust in Lieutenant Chaeron. He wouldn't let Wolfe leave without him.

Chapter Twenty Two

Fear wasn't something new to me. I'd first encountered the feeling, with its dripping jaw of sharp teeth and painful unbreakable hold of gnarled fingers and claws, when Syracen killed my parents and I ran through the fields with my brother. For months, maybe a few years, that fear never really went away. And then it had shown up in little spurts these last few weeks, perhaps not as toothy as the first time, and maybe not as adept at keeping me in its hold, but it had been there, smiling at me and laughing.

Now it was back.

I was blind, galloping out of the city walls and down into the valley beyond Arrana. It took a while for my eyes to adjust to the night, and with my heart already racing at the thought of getting caught I wasn't sure my poor horse would escape me being sick on it. But I held strong, my hands biting into the reins as I widened my eyes, desperate for them to acclimate to the darkness. By the time I had put Arrana at a fifteen minute gallop behind me I could see more than just shapes and shadows ahead of me. I drew the horse to a stop, sorry that I didn't know his name so I could soothe him. I could feel his tense muscles beneath me as he attuned to my own tension.

The land before us dropped into a steep valley that stretched for miles, the mountains peeking up over it in the distance.

I suddenly realized I was all alone. I snorted at the irony of it. All I'd ever wanted was a moment of peace, to be truly alone, and now that I was I was terrified. This land before me was alien and unknown. I didn't know the people, I didn't know the towns. My magic was the only thing keeping me together, that and the coat that was protecting me from the cold night air. I had never known it to be this cold at night during the summer months. Stroking the horse's face, I leaned over and murmured soothing words in his ear. His ear flicked against my mouth, tickling me, and he scuffed his hoof back, giving a little snort. He was ready then. I smiled. At least I'd have him with me for the journey through Silverian Valley—named so because it was the one area in Alvernia, other than Arrana, that was closest in temperament to the Capital City. But in Alvernia that wasn't really saying much. I reckoned it was called so more out of hope than reality. I trembled a little, thinking of the reports from the Vojvoda that the Valley people had grown more uncommonly uncivilized. I'd have to move through it inconspicuously, in a hurry.

With a jerk of the reins we took off, the horse steady on his feet as we followed the steep trade road down into the valley. Once on level ground we increased our speed, hoping to put as much distance between myself and Wolfe as possible. The last thing I needed was him catching up to me.

In the dark I didn't see much. I wouldn't have even if I'd wanted to I was so determinedly concentrating on getting to those mountains. The trade roads were rougher in Alvernia, less travelled, and we stumbled a few times along the way until I had to pull the horse into a less frantic pace. I'd wear him out if I didn't stop soon anyway. Exhausted and tense, every little noise that I heard over our galloping making cold sweat slide down my back, I was thankful when the sun broke the horizon. It burst out over the mountains until the brownish-green rolling plains of the valley became visible. We grew closer to the mountains towering over the valley in the distance, mountains like monsters beckoning travelers into nightmare. Thick, brutish, looming trees the Alvernians called the Arans covered what appeared to be every inch of the mountains— the lushness of those deep, black-green trees a sharp contrast to the sickly pallor of the plains I was passing through. The mountain people of Alvernia lived among those trees, their homes shrouded by their darkness, and their lives sheltered in ignorance and uncivilized isolation.

My stomach lurched and I pulled the horse to an abrupt halt. Thankfully I made it off the poor horse and to the side of the road before I vomited up last night's fish.

***

After a quick break I was back on the horse, racing him faster than ever as the mountains drew closer. I didn't see much from the trade roads, only a farm or two visible from the road, but I wasn't interested. My magic was beginning to hum and vibrate through me the closer I drew to the Somna Plant. The Silverian Valley wasn't huge. Most of Alvernia was covered by those mountains. It could be crossed in under a day, and as mid-morning crept past, the horse and I finally drew into the shade cast by the mountains. Up close they were utterly mammoth. I watched a bird circle up ahead and then fly in among the trees. Disappearing forever.

I rolled my eyes at myself. "Stop being maudlin," I sighed.

Soon we drew around a bend in the road and the Aran trees stood before me, an entrance up into the woods, dark and waiting. I slowed the horse and trotted forward. The horse snorted again, feeling my thighs squeeze against him in my fear. My stomach was so full of butterflies they were brimming over and touching my heart, their stupid wings tickling against the organ and urging it to react in kind. When we drew closer I could make out a wooden sign nailed to one of the trees, the words:

ALVERNIN MOWNTINS

TRED WIF CAYR

carved crudely into the wood. I closed my eyes trying to draw in breath and calm. Shakily I slid off the horse, leading him over to a humble lane cut into the fields around us. Pitched into the ground was another sign in the same carving.

HEVERS FARM

I soothed my night companion who had gotten me this far and thanked him, before hitting his rump, sending him into a jolt up the lane where hopefully the Hever's would find him and take care of him. I couldn't take him up into the steep mountains. It would slow me down and be unfair to him.

For a moment I stood at the opening of the woods, looking up the hill into the gloomy inside of the forest. I could hear the crick and twitch of the woods themselves, branches snapping, woodpeckers pecking. Insects buzzed around me, small animals skittered over crushed leaves and twigs, and in the far, far distance I even thought I heard the howl of a dog. I shivered. I imagined the overwhelming aroma of the forest might calm me with its musky floral, honey, laurel, and freshly cut-grass smells all breathing beneath the heady scent of rich, dark soil. It *was* wonderful. But I was still quaking.

With another deep breath I straightened my shoulders and took my first step into the mountains.

"Only for you, Haydyn," I whispered, and continued on in resignation.

The climb was almost immediate. One, two, three steps and the ground began to tilt upwards. There were no more signs posted to the trees giving me directions to towns or settlements or whatever it was these people had in here, but I was following my magic, managing to keep to the rough track that already wound its way up through the mountains. The longer I climbed, the more I began to wonder where the people were. My ears were practically pinned back, my body and heart jumping at every little noise. I must have

stopped and spun around a hundred times, my eyes probing through
the trees for signs of life. So on edge, the nerves in my body had
taken on a life of their own. I wasn't going to sleep tonight.

I climbed for hours, my feet beginning to blister inside the maid's
boots. I fought off the pain by refusing to think about it, thinking
only of the growing darkness within the woods, how cold it was
becoming. By dusk I was beginning to panic that there were no signs
of life. My magic told me the Pool of Phaedra was still days off yet
and I had hoped to find some safe place to shelter for the night. Safe,
I snorted. Was that even a word in the Mountains of Alvernia?

I stopped suddenly, my ears kicking back at a familiar noise.
Water! The trickling noise in the distance set my heart racing again.
Surely where there was water, there were people! I followed the
noise, tripping over a thick root and taking my first tumble in the
woods. I landed on soggy leaves and damp soil, little dirty circles
staining my trousers at the knees. I grunted and got back up,
determined not to feel foolish considering no one had seen me. The
noise drew me to a stream and I followed that stream, making sure it
didn't pull me too far from the direction of my magic.

Surprise rippled through me as the woods broke beyond me, the
stream leading out of the trees and into the open mountain. This part
of the mountain had been cleared. Stretching before me, encircled on
all sides by the Arans, was a town. Shacks, I gathered were houses,
dotted here and there, some by the stream, some further off until they
looked like little black squares from where I stood. Lights

shimmered in the dark. An extremely well-lit larger shack, some way in the distance, caught my eye.

"Can I be helpin' ye, son?"

I jerked and then froze, my mouth falling open, my eyes wide, my palms and underarms instantly giving into cold sweat. Slowly, afraid of what I'd find, I turned to confront the gruff voice with its strange burr. A huge man, exactly what I had in my mind when I thought 'mountain man', stood before me, burly, tall and suspicious of me. He was wrapped up warm in worn clothes, a furry hat covering his head. I gulped at the sight of the huge axe laid casually against his shoulder.

I felt threatened by more than just his height. I was a woman alone and I had been caught by a strange man. But then I realized… he'd called me 'son'. Glancing down at my boy's clothing, feeling the boy's cap on my head, I exhaled in relief. He thought I was a boy. I deepened my voice and tried to emulate a rough accent.

"Just lookin' for a place to rest before I pass through."

He straightened a little, eyeing me closely. "Oh yeah? And where you be headin', boy?"

I'd never heard such an accent before. It was clipped and tight with trilling 'r's, dropped 'g's' and a grammar I couldn't get my head around. I shook myself from my momentary distraction and thought about my answer. It was well known to everyone in Phaedra that the Pool of Phaedra was considered mystical and fascinating. There had been many an adventurer who'd dared the mountains to find it. "The Pool of Phaedra."

The man smirked at me. "An' what would a sprite like ye want with the Pool?"

I shrugged. "I'm on a spiritual journey and that is all I wish to say on the matter."

He laughed and I bit my lip. I'd sounded far too well-bred. But he didn't say anything, just chuckled, "Well don't be gettin' all ornery, yer business is *yer* business." He laughed again, shaking his head. There was something jolly about him and something reassuring in his eyes. I began to relax.

"My name is Brint," he told me, his booming voice carrying beyond us. "Brint Lokam. I'm about the closest thing Hill o' Hope has to a Mayor."

"Hill o' Hope?" I asked in confusion.

Brint grinned and gestured to the open land before us. "Hill o' Hope." He winked at me. "We here at Hill o' Hope have what some folks call an ironic sense o' humor," he drawled out the 'i' in ironic comically.

I couldn't help but return his smile. "My name is Ro—" I stopped, remembering I was supposed to be a boy. "Rolfe. My name is Rolfe."

"Nice to meet ye, Rolfe. Well, ye don't look like ye can cause much trouble. Why don't ye join us at Hope Tavern?" Brint pointed to the larger shack all lit up in the distance. "They'll give ye some gristle and grub, maybe a splash o' ale." He winked again. "It's no much but it's somethin'. Plus, folks are in a good mood lately what with the Iavii people who used to crawl all over these parts havin'

taken off for greener pastures. Once yer done fillin' up, ye can come

back with me." He jerked a thumb over his shoulder and I noticed

the shack up the hill behind us. A single light flickered in the

window. "The wife will be more than happy to put a pallet by the

fire for ye so ye can get some rest before movin' on in yer spiritual

journey."

I smiled reluctantly at his teasing. I knew I probably wouldn't get

a better offer so I nodded in thanks and began following him down

the hill towards Hope Tavern. My first encounter with an Alvernian

mountain person was not unfolding as I'd always imagined. That

preconceived idea in my head was only further slashed to ribbons

when we entered the tavern and Brint introduced me to the roughest-

looking people I'd ever seen. Even rougher than the gypsies and the

rookery thugs. I couldn't decipher age among them— they were all

so weather-beaten and worn, laughter wrinkles tickling the corners

of everyone's eyes. Despite the obvious fact that their life was hard,

that they didn't have much of anything, they were so friendly and

jolly and happy with one another. I couldn't believe what I was

seeing and hearing. No, they weren't well-mannered as a rule, but in

spite of that, no one was ill-mannered to me. And, if I were to go by

the stories they regaled me with, in amidst this uncivilized, isolated

community of theirs was a true civilization of apparent camaraderie

and teamwork.

More shocking for me still, I watched the barkeep—who had

thrust a plate of strange food and the darkest ale I'd ever seen at me (but for free, so I couldn't complain)—kiss a man who slid over the bar and wrapped his arms around him. Wide-eyed, I glanced around to see if anyone was looking but no one cared. Brint caught my look and laughed, explaining the two men were old lovers. Back home in Silvera, I knew of rumors of men who preferred other men, but society pretended it didn't exist, happy to ignore it as long as the men in question kept it hidden. I'd always believed in every kind of freedom and it amazed me that up here, in the heart of savage country, people were freer and more loving than anywhere else. The worry in my chest began to ease. The situation in Alvernia wasn't nearly so bad as we'd been led to believe. Mayhap Haydyn need never marry Andrei, whose father perpetuated the ignorance I had grown up with.

It was true.

Once again I had been ignorant and prejudiced.

I decided then and there, as I enjoyed the rambunctious, raucous company of the people of Hill o' Hope, that I would never again draw an opinion until I knew everything about the subject upon which I spoke. I thought of Haydyn's long forgotten failed philanthropy regarding these people. If we'd listened to her, we would have done a lot of good. Once again I was ashamed.

After I'd eaten, I had relaxed back beside Brint, listening as his neighbor Abe regaled me with the story of Brint, who organized a search party for a little girl who'd been kidnapped by the Iavii.

"We were lucky that the group who'd taken wee Amelia were few, because no matter what, Brint would be ah takin' us into the woods to fight the buggers and bring her back."

I stared wide-eyed at Brint who looked marginally embarrassed by the story. "And did you?"

"Oh indeed," Abe went on. "We snuck up on the buggers and dealt them out a booting they wouldn't forget. We got wee Amelia and brung her home to her folks. The Iavii departed the mountain no' too long after that."

"You were very brave." I nodded, lifting my cup to them.

"Are ye brave?" A girl suddenly appeared at my side, swishing her dirty skirts and smiling at me, her teeth yellowed from having not taken care of them. I squinted, feeling warm and fuzzy from the ale. She would have been pretty had she been allowed the life of a lady.

"No," I replied promptly.

"Ye've come into the mountains by yer lonesome. There's a certain amount of bravery to be said for that." She brushed her fingers down my face before abruptly dropping into my lap.

Bewildered by her sudden proximity it took me a minute to realize she was reaching to kiss me. I squealed under my breath and jerked back, thankful as her weight was lifted off of me.

Brint gave her a look and patted her bottom. "Be on with ye, lass. This one is shy."

The girl huffed in disappointment, striding off before throwing me one more longing look. My cheeks must have bloomed bright red because Brint was laughing at me again.

"Tera is a bit free with her favors." He shook his head. "Gotten worse since the Iavii have gone. Everyone be a bit more relaxed these days."

"I can't believe the gypsies were that awful to their own." I bit my lip. Up here, Haydyn's evocation did not reach and it was up here that life was hard enough.

Brint glowered now, looking as fierce as I first imagined him to be. "We weren't their own. You never knew which Hill they'd come barrellin' into next, takin' that which wasn't theirs to take."

"Then I'm glad they've left you alone."

"Me too, son. I pity the buggers who they be botherin' now though."

I grunted. I would be one of those buggers.

I shook off my memories and smiled, looking around me. "The mountains aren't anything like I was told they'd be. Everyone is so friendly and nice."

Once again Brint's lips thinned and he leaned in close to me. "In Hill o' Hope we are. We be good people. But don't ye be gettin' all mistaken, son, there are folks in these here mountains who've gone crazy with the isolation. Ye watch yerself in this journey o' yers. Stick to the trails. There's a place one Hill from here called Shadow Hill. Ye be bypassin' around the outskirts o' Shadow, ye here. No nothing there for strangers but a world o' suspicion and sorrow. And the closer to the pool ye reach, be warier. There be dogs in packs up that way, hungry and feral as any an animal starvin' and uncontrolled."

I gulped. The fear came back again. I should have known it couldn't be as easy as I'd begun to hope. Hah, I snorted inwardly. Hill o' Hope. It was really called so because it gave hope that the mountains were as kind and easy going as the people here. But according to Brint, I'd be foolish to think that. And I was going to take his advice.

"Thank you," I replied softly. He nodded at me grimly, as if seeing past my deception and into the truth of me. He seemed concerned for me.

"Come." He stood to his feet. "Let us get ye home and to some sleep."

It was even colder out now. I thought about the nights ahead. I wouldn't have a home to sleep in, or a roof to shelter me to give at least the pretense of safety. I thought of Brint's warning. The thought of sleeping under the stars was nothing compared to the thought of facing the horror he had not spoken of but had been there in his eyes nonetheless.

Chapter Twenty Three

Brint's wife Anna was just as friendly and caring as her husband. She laid out blankets by the fire for me and stoked the fire to life to keep me warm. She insisted that in the morning I stay for breakfast, but I explained I had to leave extremely early. I was afraid of Wolfe and The Guard catching up to me. Anna ignored my protests, insisting she and Brint were early risers. But I knew I couldn't stay. However, I told them I would, and made sure I thanked them enough so they'd know, when they found me gone in the morning, that I had been tremendously grateful to them.

I slept a little, but I was so nervous for the day ahead that I was up before the sun broke the horizon, and was slipping through Hill o' Hope before their roosters woke everyone up. I held on to my magic like a child holding a parent's hand tightly in the marketplace, terrified of being lost to the wildness of the mountains.

The morning air was chilly, but as the sun rose and began filtering through the trees I grew warm in the humid environment of the forest. I had to take off my jacket, sure that with no one around the fact that the trousers were beyond indecent on me wouldn't matter. Stopping at midday for a quick snack and some water, I mulled over Brint's words of warning. He'd told me the next town (Hill) up from theirs was full of good people, the Hill o' Hope's close neighbors. But I decided I wasn't taking any chances like I had last night. I'd been lucky with Brint and his people. Remembering how badly things had gone in the past, I wasn't going to press that luck. Instead, I took the outskirts of the town, keeping to the trees and treading slowly and quietly so as not to draw any attention. Through the trees a town, smaller than Hill o' Hope, flashed in and out of view. Children helped their parent's milk cows, sort out wool that was being clipped from the few sheep they had, collecting eggs from hens. They worked together in tandem, a machine of teamwork, just like Hill o' Hope.

By late afternoon I was exhausted. My shirt was soaked with sweat underneath the waistcoat I wore and my feet were screaming in pain from the ever growing blisters populating my soles, toes and heels. If I kept walking I didn't feel it so much. But then I'd make the mistake of stopping for water, and when I moved off to walk again the screaming pain would start over tenfold.

I pushed on through the night until my eyes began to droop. At the sight of a tree with a large root curling around the soil like an arm, I took off my pack and slumped down behind it, hidden from view from anyone beyond it. Every muscle in my body screamed at me. The pain in my feet made me whimper. I shook my head in disgust. When had I become this soft, genteel creature who couldn't withstand a little exertion? I felt miserable and incompetent. When I lived on the farm I could run for miles without stopping; I could climb trees like a trapeze artist; walk and climb and walk some more and never want to stop. Life outdoors had been second nature to me. Now I was pampered and useless, and everything my parents had abhorred. I thought of Wolfe and had to hold back frustrated tears. I just kept betraying them over and over again.

Even more angry at myself for being pitiful and maudlin, I exhaled and looked around me at the little bed I'd made for the night. A large spider with spindly brown legs crawled slowly up from the soil onto my leg. I felt the tickle of it through the fabric of my trousers. Gently, I leaned over and scooped up the spider, putting it down on the ground behind me so it could scuttle off and not get squashed beneath me as I slept. Watching it, I was reminded of my little brother. He had hated spiders. Terrified of them he had said he didn't trust their fast little legs. It was the only thing he ever squealed at and I knew to come running to rescue not only him but the poor spider from his fear. Despite the spider, he would have loved this, I thought, gazing up through the thick branches of the Arans above me, hardly able to see even a drop of sky. He would have thought this was quite the adventure.

I dug through my pack and pulled my dagger out, clutching it in comfort as I waited for exhaustion to give into the inevitable. Somehow I did drop off to sleep, fatigue tugging me under despite my nervousness about being alone in the mountains.

My neck tingled, the feeling turning to something sharp enough to pull me out of semi-consciousness. I groaned and slapped my hand to the spot and pulled away a huge centipede, its legs clambering frantically as it dangled between my fingers. I squealed under my breath and threw it away, shuddering as I touched my neck to make sure there was nothing else there. I winced. The damn thing had bitten me!

I jumped to my feet, flinching at the forgotten blisters, and shook myself out. Not sure I was safe from the insects, who obviously liked the Aran root as much as me, I curled into a ball in the open soil, glancing around to make sure there was nothing else near me.

Oh haven I hated this!

Thankfully, I must have drifted back to sleep, for I woke up lying flat out on my back, the ceiling of the forest above me now giving way to the blue of the sky.

The blue of the sky! What time was it? I cried out and lunged sleepily for my things. It was definitely past sunrise. Probably mid-morning. I'd missed a good few hours of light for walking. Grumbling at myself, I chewed on a biscuit and sipped from my canteen as I hurried upwards, remembering to hold back the whimpers from the pain in my feet and body. Those first few steps were agonizing, the breath whooshing out of me. I sucked in air and took a few more tentative steps, building momentum and chanting Haydyn's name like a mantra to get me through. At the thought of Shadow Hill I began chanting inwardly as I was sure I must be growing closer to the Hill. I didn't want to be heard.

By afternoon, the sun was stronger than ever and wearing me down. But my feet. My feet were unbearable. At the constant sound of the stream to my right, I gave in. It didn't deviate from the direction of my magic, only from the worn track that kept me from the thick of the woods and all the plants and twigs that would trip me. The thought of cold water against my sore feet was too terrible a temptation to ignore. I headed off, taking my steps carefully, until I found the wide stream rushing past at a refreshing pace that made my dry mouth ache. I could almost feel its soothing waters on me. I smiled wearily and sat down, pulling off my boots hesitantly.

"Aaahh mmm…" I whimpered as the boots knocked against sores. I pouted like a little girl as I peeled my stockings off, a garbled shout of pain escaping before I could stop it as the stocking, stuck with sweat, ripped open a blister. I glared at the boots. Perhaps taking them off hadn't been such a good idea. They might not go back on without a fight. Slumping at my losing battle with my feet I slid them into the stream, wincing at the stings here and there. And then the cold water did what I had hoped it would, numbing my swollen appendages until I didn't feel a thing. When they'd had enough, I kneeled over on my knees and ripped off the jacket and waistcoat so I could scoop water up to clean my neck and behind my ears as best I could. Feeling sweat along my hairline, I tugged the cap off and uncoiled my hair, sighing in satisfaction as my scalp drew breath.

The crack of a branch made me flinch and stiffen.

I was terrified to look behind me.

I heard the heavy breathing and my heart spluttered in absolute horror. A smell drifted upwind. Stale. Dirty. Human.

"What be here then?" He growled in my ear.

Chapter Twenty Four

There was no chance for me dart out of his grasp and escape him. Huge arms encircled my waist, dragging me back from the stream as if I weighed nothing more than a sack of flour. I shrieked and reached behind me, clawing at skin and pulling at hair. The stranger merely grunted until I was shunted up on to his shoulders, high, high, off the ground. He was huge. I wriggled and screamed and fought and pummeled, and was merely slapped at for my troubles, as if I was as insignificant as a flea. My heart raced so fast it hurt, bile threatened to rise in my throat, and I was shaking so hard my teeth chattered together. Frustrated tears welled in my eyes. I was so stupid. Brint had warned me about the Shadow people. Had I listened? No. I'd wandered off the path because my feet hurt! Not only that, I'd unbound my hair.

I beat at the man's back once more with fury. "Put me down!" I cried out, exhaustion making my voice weak.

How was I to escape these people? My feet hurt, I had no energy. I was useless. Once again kidnapped and taken. I could only hope the people showed me mercy.

The stranger's hand slid around to my buttocks and he squeezed me painfully, making me shiver in revulsion. "Good," he commented gruffly. "Very good."

What the haven did that mean?

The more we trekked, the more I felt my magic wailing at me to turn back. He was deviating from my path! Just as I was about to yell at him again, he slowed, walking up a few stone steps before I heard the creak of a door. I swung, looking around us. We were still in the woods! As we entered the dimness of a tiny shack, an awful realization dawned on me. He wasn't one of the Shadow Hill people. And we were all alone.

As he set me on my battered feet, I ignored the pain and tried to dart away from him. His huge sweaty hands wrapped around my waist and he pulled me back forcefully against him. I shuddered at the feel of his wet lips against my neck, fighting the urge to be sick. I yelled in outrage and raked my fingernails along the skin of his hands. The stranger growled and burled me around. I caught a glimpse of a rough face, drooping eyes and a toothless mouth surrounded by a beard, before his meaty hand walloped me across the face. Ringing burst into song in my ear as I crumpled to the ground, dazed, my left cheek blazing with heat and throbbing with pain. Disorientated, darkness fell over my eyes.

A few minutes later as I came to I felt a tugging at my feet and looked over to see the huge Mountain Man tying my ankles together with rope. Disbelief cleared my head and I pushed out my legs, trying to get away from him. With horror, I realized he'd already tied my wrists so tight with rope that the slightest movement chafed them painfully against the scratchy material. Distantly aware of his hands sliding along my leg, I searched the room, looking for anything, a weapon, some way out. I lay on a soggy pallet in the far corner. And there was nothing. Nothing else in the room but a large hunting knife, a pail and a door. There was one window. Tiny. Not nearly big enough to climb out. No. No.

My eyes widened as I felt his hand crawl up the inside of my thigh. I snarled at him and shook his hand off of me. Mountain Man did nothing but smile and crawl alongside me, the stench of his body odor making me gag.

"Now, now," he admonished and I shrunk back at the bright lust in his eyes. My stomach roiled and my lips trembled. Tears splashed down my cheeks. I knew why I was here. I choked on a sob and he grinned wider. "No tears, wife." He shook his head, and his hand was back on me, touching me where no one had touched me before. I roared like an animal in his face and he flinched back in surprise. Then he gave a huff of laughter. "Good wife."

"I'm not your wife!" I screamed through tears and snot. "Let me go, I'm not your wife!"

I was rewarded for my rebuttal with another heavy slap, across my right cheek this time. My teeth pierced through my lip at the impact and blood trickled slowly down my chin. I glared under my lashes at the Mountain Man, and watched incredulously as his eyes followed the blood. My heart stopped at the brightness in his gaze. The lust had deepened. I swallowed back a rush of vomit.

Mountain Man reached out and touched the blood wonderingly. "Yer ma wife," he growled, pushing his face in mine. I closed my eyes, holding in my breath so I didn't have to inhale the stink off him. "I find ye. Ye be ma wife."

Brint had warned me, I shook. Brint had told me there were people out here gone crazy with the isolation.

"I'm goin' huntin'. But I be back. I be gone a while. But I be back, wife. I be back and feed ye wife. And then ye be seeing to my husbandly needs." He stroked himself and I turned away sharply, biting back screams and denials. Little whimpers escaped between my pinched lips.

I shuddered at the feel of his fingers soft on my face. Then they gripped hard, jerking my head around to face him. I didn't have to open my eyes to know his face was inches from mine. His lips came down wet and hard on my mouth, his beard scratching my face as I struggled against him, my lips tightly closed. A large hand encircled my neck and squeezed. I gasped, giving him the opening he needed. His tongue forced its way into my mouth. I gagged on the foul taste of him, his rancid stench clogging my senses. No matter how much I jerked my head this way and that, he followed, his lips drinking me in like a fish gulping for air. The skin around my mouth was raw from his beard and wet from his fetid saliva. I was running out of air, close to hyperventilating when I felt his hand squeeze my breast.

Fury ignited within me— fury at myself and at my stupidity. Fury at this man, this Mountain Man who thought he could just take me like I was a deer in the woods. It coursed through me in an unthinking rush. Instinctively, I brought my tied hands up, suffusing as much strength and force into the upswing as I could, and nailed him between his legs.

He broke away from me with a strangled shout and fell back, clutching where only minutes before he'd been stroking. I immediately vomited on the crude wooden floors beside the pallet. The room now reeked with the vilest of human stench as I emptied what was left in my stomach.

I struggled to draw breath, the room spinning around me. I had to get out of here. I had to.

I thought of my kidnapping by the Iavii people. Of Kir's rookery gang. None of it had been so bad as this. Nothing this horrific had happened to me in a long time. I didn't think anything could match watching my parents and brother die. But if I stayed here... if this man used me and broke me...

I sobbed, tears blinding me as I drew my tied hands down onto the floor and used my upper body to drag myself along the wood. The door was just there. I could get to it.

A bellow echoed around the shack and I was jerked back like a rag doll, thrown against the back wall of the hut, a sickening vibration shooting through my body as my head made impact. I slumped back on the pallet and watched through blurry eyes as the Mountain Man approached me, his face blazing with hatred, lechery and anger. I became alert at the sight of the large hunting knife in his hand.

"Bad wife," he growled, brandishing the knife at me. "Teach ye a lesson I will."

I beat at him uselessly with my tied hands as he grabbed me by my shirt front to hold me. And then he tore the shirt open, revealing the curve of my breasts.

"No!" I cried out and swung my hands back up, catching his jaw. The Mountain Man barely blinked.

"Yer goin' to behave." He pointed the knife right in my face and I glared back at him, ignoring the hot tears rolling down my cheek. I took deep breaths as he smiled at me. I let a shaky calm envelop me. If this was to be my end, then I wouldn't give him the satisfaction of enjoying my fear. I jutted my chin out defiantly.

The Mountain Man tut-tutted and gently placed the tip of the blade at the bottom of my throat. I shivered at the menacing cold touch as he gently drew it down my skin, scratching me, until he came to the rising curve of my left breast. The blade pressed deeper and I muffled a cry of shocked pain. He scored a shallow cut along the top of my breast, watching my expression the whole time. I felt blood trickle from my wound and clenched my jaw to keep from looking at what he'd done to me.

Mountain Man pulled the blade back, grinning the entire time, his eyes alight with excitement. The knife disappeared into a pouch on his hip and he stood up. He was huge. Massive. His entire shadow cast me into darkness in the shade of the shack.

He tugged at his trousers and licked his lips. "I like red on ye, wife. It's good. When I get back, I be bedding ye ma wife. Bedding ye with a little more red."

At that he abruptly turned and left, picking up some crude hunting gear I hadn't seen before. It lay near the door. The door opened and I searched it greedily for a lock. It slammed shut behind him and I heard his footsteps disappear. Struggling to draw breath I heaved a sigh of relief, not only to be alone, but because… there was no lock on the door!

At his sudden departure, the realization of what had just happened to me and was going to happen to me if I didn't get out of there, came rushing in like a storm against the cliffs in Silvera. Terrified sobs broke out of me in rib-cracking force, and I shook and shivered, damning my stupid pride and fear that had made me venture into the mountains without Wolfe.

"Stop it," I bit out angrily, impatiently brushing the tears from my face with the tips of my fingers. I couldn't just sit here wallowing. I had to get out of here. The longer I stayed the more likely he would return. If that happened we were all doomed. Haydyn was doomed. I had to get to that plant. I had to get back to Haydyn. And when she was awake, I'd tell her all that had happened. All that I had discovered. That there was good and bad people all over our world, and that background, upbringing, proximity to the Dyzvati evocation made no matter. I'd lived my life with blinkers on, convinced that my harsh jolt out of innocent childhood somehow made me wiser than the rest. But I wasn't. I was still a child who'd only been thrust into womanhood on this journey—this journey to save Phaedra from losing the evocation. This journey that had taught me —I sucked in a painful breath — we didn't need the evocation. What we needed was a stronger government. We needed to take care of our people no matter the province they belonged. The evocation wouldn't change the issues that made people act out as soon as its strength waned. But perhaps a better governing of them could bring us closer to fixing the issues, and bring us closer to ridding the world of men like the one who had come upon me and taken me as if I were a body without a soul...

All this I'd tell Haydyn... if I ever got out of this.

With renewed determination I thumped my bound hands down onto the floor, ignoring the bites and splinters from the wood. I began to drag myself along the ground. I didn't have great upper body strength but I might have managed more easily if it weren't for the stinging pain of my feet and the throbbing cut on my breast needling my brain, trying to slow me down.

I made it to the door, but I was already soaking with sweat. It took me another five minutes to wobble up onto my feet so I could pry the door open. As soon as it opened and the fresh air of the forest rushed against me, stealing me from the stink of the shack, I was submerged in dizziness. I leaned against the doorframe to collect myself.

Finally, I opened my eyes. My magic reached out to me, beckoning me back onto the path. If I could manage to hobble far enough away, perhaps I could find some way to untie the ropes.

Carefully, concentrating, I balanced my body just right and hopped down onto the first step out of the shack. I wobbled a little, making my heart pitch in fear, but I was still standing. I took another breath and hopped again. This time I lost my balance and went crashing with a painful oomph onto the forest floor. A little winged bug stared up at me before flying off. I growled in fearful frustration and tried to pull myself into a standing position. Five falls later and I was back up.

That's the pattern of how the day went. I couldn't even remember how far I had fallen and hopped and dragged myself to. I kept freezing at every sound in the forest, trying to hear over the blood rushing in my ears. By nightfall, I was covered in sweat and mud and forest. But with no coat and a ripped shirt, I was thankful for the heat of the exertion. The shack felt long gone now, but still I remained terrified. I had no idea how far I'd come.

Night had fallen a few hours past when I heard a loud snap of a tree branch. I stilled, my heart fluttering like a snared animal. I glanced around sharply, trying to see movement in the dark. A large plant rustled and I whirled around. I could feel eyes on me. Boring into me. Trapping me.

A rush of warm fluid slid down my leg inside my trousers.

The rustle sounded again, another crack of tree.

Beady eyes appeared in the dark, low to the ground. I let go of my breath, my whole body sagging as some kind of possum darted out of the bush and away from me. Realization dawned and I looked down in the dark at my trousers. Already I could smell the stench of urine.

Silently, I began to cry.

***

I made another mistake.

Sometime during the late night, perhaps early morning, my mind blank with agony and exhaustion, I had fallen again. I had only intended to take a minute to collect myself. But when my eyes finally peeled back open it was because a stream of sunlight was begging them to.

I blinked, confused. Where was I?

"Finally, ye be wakin'."

The nightmare that had unbelievably been real came rushing back at the sound of the Mountain Man's voice. I closed my eyes as I was roughly turned around, the taste of dark soil on my lips.

"Open yer eyes!" he bellowed in my face, the putrid breath bringing back memories of the day before.

Not wanting to, but somehow needing to, I did as he demanded, opening my eyes to see his ugly face inches above mine, his large hands gripping my upper arms.

His eyes blazed with rage. "Ye goin' to be gettin' it bad, wife, for runnin' off."

I was dragged up into his arms. It took me a minute to wake up, but as soon as I did I started struggling. I was in so much pain already his pinches and slaps didn't stop me from giving him hell as he strode in long lurches back to his shack.

The magic screamed at me again, as he pulled me from its path.

When the shack appeared, I stopped struggling, and slumped in his arms. We had walked perhaps thirty minutes using his long strides.

It had taken me hours to get thirty minutes away from this beast.

I gave a roar of rage and clobbered my bound hands against his head in impotent wrath. He snarled back at me, giving me a wounded look as if he was the victim, and not I. The fact that this man was clearly deranged made it worse. There would be no reasoning with someone like him.

I was thrown down on the pallet as he slammed the shack door shut. The stench of dead meat filled the shack and I gagged at the carcass of an animal in the other corner of the small room. But the carcass was the least of my worries.

My heart froze as the Mountain Man began undressing. I struggled away from him, my back pressed against the wall of the shack, my eyes frantically searching for a weapon as the Mountain Man loomed over me naked.

Fuck the chafing! I pulled my wrists back and forth frantically, desperate to be free. I could hear him laughing as he lowered himself to the ground, but still I kept rubbing my wrists back and forth, growling and crying at the agony as I ripped my wrists raw, the wetness of blood joining the savage sawing. Saliva and tears dripped off my chin as I refused to look at the man before me, refusing to give in.

I slammed back against the wall, wide-eyed as he crawled over me, straddling me. I looked into his face with so much hatred I hoped it incinerated him. His stench overwhelmed me as it had the last time, and my stomach lurched in response. His stale sweat and bad breath would have been enough to make me sick, but the odor of blood and old meat swam out of him as well. He smelled like death.

I closed my eyes and pushed away from him as his hands pawed at me, the muscles in my body twanging and twitching like the taut strings of a lute.

"Ye better start playin', wife, or I'm goin' to get mad."

Despite his threat, I couldn't stop flinching from his touch. I couldn't have even if my mind had told me it was the safest thing to do. Instead I incurred his anger over and over again, pushing and struggling and jerking to get him off of me. One of his huge hands slid down over my face, and he pushed me, slamming my head off the wall. The minutes after that were distant and unclear. My head lolled on my shoulders, and I could only see and hear images. I swore I heard Wolfe's voice, saw Haydyn's face.

But they weren't here.

As the present came back to me, my situation had worsened. I was flat on my back on the pallet, the Mountain Man still straddling me. My shirt had been ripped completely open by the knife in his hands. I was covered in little shallow cuts.

I gave a garbled cry and swung at his head with my hands, a weak hit, but enough to give me a moment to summon my energy. I bucked under him, trying to throw him off. I swung at him again, causing him to jerk away, giving me the momentum I needed to shake him off. I screamed like a banshee the entire time, using it to draw my adrenaline into usefulness.

The Mountain Man roared back at me and clambered over me, the knifeless fist swooping down and connecting with my face. I felt blood gush out of my nose, my eyes watering, and I fought down more vomit. He used my disorientation to unbutton my trousers.

"No, no," I mumbled, tasting the bitter copper of my blood. I shook my head. No. I began to hyperventilate as his body drew flush with mine, his face hovering above me with lascivious eyes and a lusty grin. I threw up again.

It didn't discourage him.

I heard the clatter of the knife as he threw it away and one hand pressed my head, left cheek down, into the pallet. I imagined it was to keep the vomit off him. He tried to tug my trousers off. I felt my eyes roll back in my head.

The Mountain Man flinched, a startled cry falling from his mouth. I looked up out of the corner of my eye and saw him staring straight ahead at the wall, his eyes wide. He snarled and rolled off of me and my own eyes widened at the sight of an arrow sticking out of his back. I threw my tied hands out and dragged my body away from him, gasping at the vision of a man, cast in the shadow of the doorway, a huge machete clutched in his hands. Beside him stood a girl. Young. Perhaps Haydyn's age. She held a crossbow pointed at the Mountain Man. I watched in a stupor of horror and hope as the Mountain Man lunged to his feet to attack the intruders. The girl let another arrow fly with expertise and calm. Mountain Man staggered back as the girl immediately armed the crossbow with another arrow. The man beside her laid a gentle hand on her shoulder, holding her off.

I wanted to complain. To tell her to shoot. Mountain man was still standing. But as I watched Mountain Man, I noticed his face go slack. Pale. And then his eyes rolled back in his head. He collapsed with an almighty thud.

"This her?" the man at the doorway asked softly, nodding at me.

"Stupid question, papa. Course it's her," the girl answered lazily, as if she were encountering an everyday situation.

I slid away from them. I couldn't trust anyone here.

The man nodded grimly and moved tentatively towards me, making me shimmy back further. I hit the wall again and glowered at him. He stopped, and as my eyes adjusted to the light, I saw his face. He appeared upset. Concerned. "I'm not goin' to hurt ye, little one. I'm goin' to untie those ropes for ye, so ye can be gettin' yerself together."

My heart beat unsteadily as I glanced between the two strangers. I so needed to believe them. "Who are you? What did you do to him? Don't come near me!" I screeched as he edged closer.

He sighed heavily and the girl huffed, "Well that be a grateful response. We isn't goin' to hurt ye!" She shook her head. "Papa, she's as soft as goat's cheese. No wonder she be landin' in this mess and causin' a rumpus!"

I blinked in confusion, still dazed from my beating. Who was this girl? This man?

"L, be nice," the man admonished softly. "Help the poor girl, will ye. She's been through what ye like to call an *ordeeul*."

An ordeal? I wanted to scream. *An ordeal?* Being kidnapped by the Iaviia, running from rookery thugs, that was an ordeal! This... I shook my head. I looked back over at the Mountain Man and then back at the two people who had attacked him. Had they really saved me? Why?

The girl— L, her father had called her —sighed. "Look here, Rogan, we isn't goin' to hurt ye. We're rescuing ye from Crazy here. My arrow was tipped in a poison he won't be comin' back from. Bugger won't be hurtin' no one again." She curled her lip in disgust at the Mountain Man.

I was barely listening. I had stiffened in surprise. "How do you know my name?"

The man sighed now. "My girl is one o' the blessed. A mage. She's got the Sight."

"A Glava?" I raised my eyebrows incredulously at her.

"That be me," L huffed. "I felt yer terror. So papa and I set out to rescue ye. Now… ye goin' to repay our kindness by no' takin' a fit o' the vapors as we untie ye?"

There was something genuine about the girl's gruffness and her father's gentleness. Relief crashed over me and I began to shake uncontrollably. Tears glittered in my eyes but I fought them back, noticing L watched me carefully. "Of course," I managed, relaxing somewhat.

The man reached for me slowly and gently cut the ropes around my wrist.

He hissed at the mess. They were red and bleeding, skin shredded off entirely in places. I imagined, overall, I wasn't a pretty sight, covered in blood, bruises and vomit. Not to mention my trousers still stank of fear. "Ma will have to be puttin' some o' her special medicine on to be sortin' that mess out."

I didn't argue. I couldn't continue on in my journey without getting cleaned up and hopefully fed. When he had cut the rope from my ankles, which were in much the same condition as my wrists, I numbly refastened my trousers and tried to pull the shirt together. L stilled my hands, briskly pulling off her jacket and tugging me into it. She buttoned it for me. Up close now I could see her eyes. A multitude of emotion lived in them. She wasn't as unaffected by the state she'd found me in as she'd like me to believe. I stumbled forward on my blistered feet and L exhaled again, throwing her father a look. "Ma will need to be sortin' her feet out too if this one is to be gettin' to the Pool."

It took me a moment, as L and her father reached to help me out of the shack, their arms around me as I hobbled along with them, to realize L's comment meant she knew who I was and why I was here.

"Where are you taking me?" I asked wearily, as we wandered into the woods. I numbed myself to the pain, only focusing on my relief.

L's father answered, "Back to our home so ye can get cleaned up. I'm Jonas, by the way."

"Hello, Jonas. Thank you for rescuing me."

L coughed.

"You too, L."

After a moment of silence the numbness and overwhelming relief gave way to a need for answers, for more reassurance. "Where is your home? What else do you know, L? Is it—"

"Questions later, Lady Rogan," L sniffed. "Let's just be gettin' the blazes out o' here."

I obliged her, not once looking back.

Chapter Twenty Five

L and Jonas took me back onto the trail path and my magic hummed contentedly as we headed in the right direction. I hobbled between them a while, little whimpers and grunts escaping out of me at the pain.

"We be headin' near the outskirts of Shadow Hill," L whispered abruptly. "Ye need to be keepin' that pain quiet."

I didn't reply. I just heeded her warning.

Sometime later, when I heard voices way off in the distance, I guessed we were at Shadow Hill. Jonas and L had grown tense beside me and were walking almost tentatively. I could tell they were worried I'd somehow give them a way, but after what I'd just gone through I had no intention of putting myself in a position to be abused again.

There was a horrible moment when we heard the woods crashing to our right— the whips and rustles of trees and plants, the hard thud of a heavy foot in the soil. My rescuers looked at each other wide-eyed and then quickly pushed me behind a thick tree trunk, warning me with their eyes to stay there. They scurried off to find a tree each to hide behind. I didn't dare look behind me, or peer around the tree. My heart *thud thud thumped* in my chest as I heard a man whistling and humming under his breath. I then heard a hissing noise and saw

L roll her eyes from her place behind the tree across from me. I think perhaps the man was relieving himself.

After a while the humming and noise of him crashing through the woods faded into the distance and a grinning L came out from behind her tree, Jonas behind her. I glowered at her. I'd never met a girl as cocky as this one. Without a word, they put their arms back around me, helping me, and we set off again.

Half an hour later, quiet tears rolled down my face. I was in agony. The back of my head throbbed, my cheeks felt stiff and bruised, as did my mouth. The cut on my lip stung. The rise of my breast throbbed, my wrists felt raw, the pain from the broken skin was sharp and nipping. My ankles were the same. I tried not to let my legs get too close together so they didn't rub off one another. And my feet: they felt shredded and swollen.

I expected L to make a comment on my tears but she just looked at me and picked her pace up a little. I tried to keep up, and as dark fell over us, L and Jonas led me off the trail path into the thick of the woods. Wariness clung to me but I tried to shrug it off. L and Jonas were helping me. I really believed that. But my body, still in shock from what had happened, still regarded everyone with fear and suspicion.

We walked perhaps another hour, this time deviating enough from my magic for it tug at me, like a child pulling a friend's hair in frustration. I didn't care this time. I needed to rest. Just for a minute. Only a minute.

Finally a well-built shack appeared in a tiny clearing in the woods. There was a vegetable garden outside, and a goat tied to the wooden framing of the porch. It was the homeliest looking place I'd seen since venturing into the mountains, like something from a fairytale. As we hobbled up the rough-hewn path the door to the house burst open, candlelight from inside streaming out to greet us. I almost wept in relief. A woman's silhouette framed the doorway, a child's face appearing from behind her skirts.

"Thank haven," the woman whispered into the night. "I was gettin' worried."

"Ma, we need some o' yer medicine," L called out to her as we drew towards the porch. Jonas and L helped me hobble up the steps until I was facing the woman. Her expression changed instantly as she took me in, her smile disappearing into angry concern.

"Dear haven, what did he do to that child? Get her in here." She gestured us inside briskly. It was easy to see who L had inherited her gruffness from.

In I went with them, looking down at the little boy who stared at me in horror. I gazed around in wonder. We were in the sitting room/kitchen of their home. Two rocking chairs sat on either side of a large, glowing fire. I was huddled over to the table that took up most of the room. There were empty plates and cups on it. In the kitchen the smell of stew wafted out to me and my stomach clenched. There were two doors, one at the back and the other on the wall opposite the fire. I gathered that it led to their bedrooms. Their home was warm and welcoming and cozy. My body gave way at the relief and I crumpled between Jonas and L, both of them crying out to catch me.

"For havens sakes," L complained. They picked me up, dragging me over to a seat at the table. I slumped back in it, thankful to be off my feet.

"L, there's water boiling over the fire. Bring it." L's mother scooted into a chair opposite me and smiled softly. "Ye be Rogan, that right?"

"Yes, ma'am," I replied politely.

Her grin widened. "Ma'am. Ye be hearin' that L. Perhaps ye can be learnin' some manners."

L grunted.

"I be Sarah Moss. Ye met L— Elizabeth, but she be preferrin' L —and my husband Jonas. And that one there." She nodded warmly at the little boy. "Is Jonas Jnr. We just be callin' him Jnr."

"I'm pleased to meet all of you," I wheezed out. "You have no idea." Tears I couldn't control spilled over my lids.

"Aw lass," Sarah tutted. She turned to L, who had placed the hot water before her. I watched through blurry eyes as Sarah rolled up a cloth and dipped it into the water. "L, why don't ye and yer papa make us up some bowls o' stew, eh?"

L and Jonas did so without complaint.

I, on the other hand, waited warily as Sarah leaned over with the wet cloth and dabbed at the blood on my face. I winced as she touched my bruises. My nose must have been swollen as well. I was so glad I couldn't see myself.

For a while all Sarah did was wash away the blood on all my cuts. She drew a deep breath and put the cloth aside. When she turned back to me, it was with only her hands. At the touch of her soft fingertips on my face, my eyes widened at the tingling rush of energy that shot through my nose. My eyes teared up as the swelling disappeared, as my cheeks returned to normal, and the cut on my lip disappeared. Not a word did I say as she turned those healing hands to all my wounds, even my feet.

Sarah looked exhausted by the time she settled back in her chair. L and Jonas had ladled out the stew and were already busy eating.

"You're a Dravilec," I whispered in amazement.

She nodded. I shook my head, glancing between Sarah and L. A Dravilec and a Glava in the same family. L caught my look and seemed to understand. She smirked at me.

"How is that possible?" I asked.

Jonas replied, "I have Glava in my family history. Sarah, Dravilec."

That really wasn't what I meant. What I had meant was that for a world whose mage were apparently dying out I'd encountered many of them. Haydyn's evocation wasn't the only thing in Phaedra changing. More mage were being born. I chewed my lip. I wondered what this meant.

Of course, the Moss family didn't know I'd encountered many more like them, so my puzzlement was bemusing for them. I shrugged it off. This wasn't the time.

At Sarah's insistence I ate the stew given to me. I ate it slowly, my stomach still fragile. But as I ate the stew and warm bread, and sipped the apple juice Sarah had made, my body began to shut down in a sudden lassitude, now that it felt safe.

"No, no, Lady Rogan." Sarah shook me and I was surprised that it didn't hurt. Of course. She had healed me. I smiled dopily at her. I could have kissed her for that. "We need to get you washed up first."

Again I was too tired to argue. Sarah shooed the rest of the Moss' from the room and set about undressing me. I let her wash me, as my own mother had done years before, too exhausted to be embarrassed. She was gentle with me, even rinsing my hair out and plaiting it into a coil on my head. At last she pulled one of her own clean, soft, cotton nightgowns over my head, and taking me by the hand she led me into the room at the back of the house. It was small, with two single beds and a chest of drawers opposite them. Floral curtains were pulled across the window. In the bed closest to the door lay Jnr, already fast asleep. In the other bed was L. She sat up in cotton longjohns (it didn't surprise me she didn't wear a nightgown to bed) with the bedcovers pulled back.

"She alright?" L whispered.

"She will be," Sarah replied softly and took me over to her daughter. "She just needs sleep." She turned to me now. "Ye can share L's bed. She don't mind."

At that moment I didn't care if she did or not. I crawled over the bed and slipped in under the covers. L craned around to look at me. "Make yerself at home," she grunted and then slid in too, pulling the covers around us. She reached over and pulled the other side of the quilt up so that I was completely covered. "Night ma," she turned back to her mother.

"Night, L. Proud o' ye, lass."

"Thanks ma."

I must have fallen asleep as soon as my head hit L's pillow because I didn't remember a thing after that.

Chapter Twenty Six

The next morning I awoke snuggled up next to L. She had given a huff of laughter because I'd trapped her in my embrace and she couldn't get out without waking me up. I had blushed beetroot, but she'd merely shaken me off when I tried to apologize.

Apparently everyone else was already up for breakfast. It was mid-morning, L told me. They'd let us rest longer. I was grateful. I already felt so much better than I'd ever thought I'd feel again. L gave me clothes to wear. We were of a similar height. I pulled on the soft trousers and shirt, warily eyeing the stockings and boots she gave me.

The boots were a little big but I pulled them on. I knew my feet were going to be a wreck soon. As we dressed for the day, L mentioned I'd woken her up with my nightmares. I couldn't remember that and I apologized profusely. She shook me off again.

"I only mentioned it because…" She seemed embarrassed and I raised an eyebrow at that. "Well because ye might be wantin' to talk about what happened to ye. Ye can talk to me." She shrugged and turned away from me.

I smiled sadly at her back. "Thank you, L. I don't…" I bristled at the way my body still clenched in fear at the thought of the Mountain Man. "I can't just yet, but thank you."

L shrugged again and headed into the main room.

Breakfast was delicious. Eggs, toast, goat's cheese. More of Sarah's delicious apple juice. The Moss' were kind and considerate of not only me but each other and I enjoyed their teasing banter at the breakfast table. Their home was happy and warm. It was so nice to see that again after what I'd encountered up here in the Alvernian Mountains. It soothed my jangled nerves.

L told me she knew about Haydyn and the Sleeping Disease. None of them looked particularly worried by that and I realized it was because it didn't really affect them way up here where the evocation didn't reach. But as L went on, I gathered they realized the importance of the evocation for the rest of our world. They knew there was no stopping me. And I could see in L's eyes that she knew for me it was personal, and that I felt about Haydyn the way she felt about Jnr.

"So the Pool of Phaedra." L shook her head. By now I knew she was seventeen, Haydyn's age, but she spoke to me like I was twenty years her junior. "Quite a quest. Ye've certainly made a muddle o' it so far, isn't ye?"

"L, be polite," Jonas scolded.

L gave him her favorite gesture. A shrug. "Just sayin'."

I gave her my favorite expression. A glare. "I'm doing my best. I won't stop until I get that plant, even if I have to face a million Mountain Men to get it."

I watched L's eyes glimmer with a hint of respect at my determination.

"Well, I be gettin' an idea," Sarah piped up. "Our L is as tough as they come, knows these here mountains better than anyone. If ye follow yer magic to the Pool, L will be keepin' ye safe and right."

"Although I don't appreciate bein' offered up as a guide without my say so I do see the wisdom in the suggestion," L agreed. "I'll do it."

I rather liked the idea of having a savvy, crossbow-toting mountain girl with me but I didn't want to endanger anyone else. "I appreciate the offer, but you don't have to help me. You've already done so much."

L glowered at me. "I don't offer help unless I be wantin' to. I'm comin'. Isn't no yes thank ye, no thank ye about it. I leave yer lily white arse to saunter through these here mountains and Phaedra will be doomed—ye be eaten alive by the Aran and Phaedra fallin' to nothin' without that Princezna o' yers."

Minutes before I'd thought having her along might be a wonderful idea. Now I grimaced. With L's obnoxious, superior attitude I met as I well have brought Wolfe along.

Then I remembered the Mountain Man.

I eyed L's crossbow leaning against the wall at the fire.

I pasted a strained smile on my face. "Thank you. I appreciate it."

***

We left soon after, both of us outfitted in warm jackets, each with a pack of supplies. L carried her crossbow and I carried one of Jonas' hunting knives. I'd lost my pack and dagger at the stream when the Mountain Man had taken me.

We took off at a brisk pace and I marveled at how rejuvenated my body felt, as if I had never undergone what I had. The boots didn't begin to rub as quickly as the maid's from Arrana had, but when I did eventually feel pain niggle, I ignored it.

Our march upwards was quiet until we broke for a late lunch. I was sweating in my jacket already. As we sat to nibble on the biscuits and bread Sarah had given us it soon became apparent that L was bored with the quiet.

"Ye don't talk much for a fancy person with fancy learnin'."

I shrugged.

I thought that would be the end of it, but as we began walking again L encouraged me to tell her about my 'fancy' society life. Anything I said or explained to her was answered with phrases such as, "Well that just sounds stupid." and "What would ye be wantin' to do that for?"

Surprisingly, I began to enjoy L's chatter. Her speech may have been of the mountain people but its rough slaughter of our language belied a keen mind and sharp wit. I couldn't help but agree on some of her assessments when I told her about some of the scandalous things society members got up to.

L was pragmatic and straightforward, much as I'd always thought I was. She knew the mountains well, traipsing through them without a care, physically stronger than I. I puffed a little to keep up with her. She began to wonder how I'd survived this far without her, especially when I squatted to relieve myself and she saved me just in time from squatting on poisonous leaves. After that L began pointing out the different species of plant in the forest, what each of them was called and what their properties were capable of. I was amazed by how knowledgeable she was on the subject and she told me her grandfather had taught her before he died a few years ago.

Hours later, when we stopped for the night, my magic vibrating through me stronger than ever, L didn't build us a fire. When I asked why, shivering in my jacket, she told me it would attract the mountain dogs. My heart had thudded in my chest as I remembered warnings from Brint about the dogs. I was glad L said we should huddle together for heat.

We fell asleep with our arms tight around one another.

***

"Who's Wolfe?" L asked as I tripped over a tree root I hadn't seen. I picked myself up, dusting the soil off my hands. It was early morning, we'd already eaten, and we'd been walking for half an hour.

I glanced sharply at L.

She smirked at me, her young fresh face bright with amusement. "Ye said his name in yer sleep, last night. And the night before."

Whatever she saw on my face, it had her laughing. "Ah I be seein'. I just got a wee picture o' ye kissin' a fine-looking specimen o' a man. Wee bit soft perhaps, but mighty fine."

I felt the heat of indignation. "Wolfe is anything but soft," I snapped.

L grinned mischievously. "He yer man, then? Yer betrothed?"

Like a thirteen year old I blushed, shaking my head. "It's complicated."

I was rewarded with a scowl. "I can be keepin' up."

With a weary sigh, I went on to tell L about my family, about what Syracen had done to them. That Wolfe was Syracen's son. How all these years I'd thought Wolfe had been after revenge. How I had recently discovered what Syracen had done to Wolfe. That Wolfe had feelings for me. That I had feelings for Wolfe but I knew that acting on them was a betrayal of my family. I talked myself hoarse, surprised by how much I'd come to trust this girl in so little time. L listened patiently, her eyes betraying her interest and her sympathy.

Still, when I was finished, she scratched her cheek and said gruffly, "Well, I isn't no expert on these here things but from what ye be tellin' me, sounds to me as if ye be gettin' things a wee bit backward."

"Backward?" I puffed out of breath, glowering at her back. L turned around and caught the look. She chuckled at my expression and reached down to pull herself up the suddenly steep incline of the mountain.

"Well yer parents tried to protect ye, told ye to run. They died for ye basically."

"Yes," I replied through clenched teeth, hissing the 's'.

"Well that be sayin' to me that they was good folks. They just wanted ye to be free and happy."

I frowned, wondering at the direction of her point, and if she was ever going to make it. "Yes?"

"Well if this Wolfe man—haha, wolfman." She chortled and then noticed my belligerent expression. "Never mind. If this Wolfe makes ye feel free, makes ye happy, don't that all that be matterin' to yer parents?"

"But his father killed my parents. Being with his son would be a betrayal of their memory."

"That don't be makin' no kind o' sense. Ye brought yer parents murderer to justice, Rogan, and ye saved Wolfe and his mother from a life o' misery at that evil-doer's hands. And this Wolfe person, he sounds like he be an upright kind o' fella. And don't he be some kind o' nobility?"

I swept the sweat off my forehead, my fingers trembling. "A Vikomt."

L grunted. "Lass, ye be gettin' yerself a rich man. That's every parents dream," she joked.

When I didn't respond, she threw me a wicked smile that transformed her from ordinary to pretty. "Ye joined giblets with yer Wolfe, then?"

I frowned, searching my brain for a translation.

L laughed at my confusion. "Has he bedded ye, Rogan?"

I rolled my eyes at her forthright question, my cheeks flushing red despite myself. "No," I bit out.

L sobered quite abruptly. "Ye a maiden then?"

"Yes. Aren't you?"

"O' course."

I nodded, having expected as much.

"Think on this then, Rogan…" she stopped to freeze me in her guileless gaze. "What if I had no' got to ye? Is that how ye would have wanted it? Raped and abused by a stranger in these here mountains, instead of it bein' right and true with the man ye love?"

I felt cold. Stumped. Panicky little flutters shaking off the ice she'd created inside me with her directness.

"If there be one thing these here mountains learn us, Rogan, it be life is often harsh… and always temporary. Don't run from love because ye lost so much o' it as a child. Instead… love while ye can."

Gulping back the emotion clogging my throat, I somehow managed to respond, "Is that what you intend to do, L?"

She threw me another quick grin before turning back up the mountain. "As soon as I be finding love like ma and papa's."

As I followed her, I felt myself drowning in L's practicality. I had been since the moment I met her, and now that pragmatism of hers was starting to make sense. And with Wolfe, I didn't want it to make sense.

"My plan wasn't to marry – *ever*."

She snorted at that. "My plan for this week was to show Jnr how to be layin' a trap without takin' his hands off. Instead I'm stuck up in these here mountains with the dumbest smart person I ever be meetin'."

"You know, L, I'm feeling overwhelmed by your kindness and charm."

"I try to leash the potency of the charm but it's too exhaustin'." She grinned crookedly back at me.

I shook my head and burst into reluctant laughter.

***

By the third day we had made it up through the Alvernian Mountains with little mishap. We'd heard a few howls in the distance that had given us pause to worry but so far we hadn't come across the mountain dogs.

My magic told me we were close. Very close.

It was mid-afternoon, and the mountain had already begun to plateau under our feet. L suddenly drew to a stop as a new scent drifted by us in the wind. It smelled like lilacs and damp moss.

"I guess we be here." L smiled at me. At my confused look she pointed in front of her and I walked around her, my feet throbbing but I didn't care. Light sparkled through the trees in front of me and I grinned in relief.

"We're here."

Together we took off at a run and burst out of the trees into the bright light. Before us the grass at our feet slid down towards a glistening lake, enclosed on all sides by higher ground. A small waterfall cascaded down from one of the mountains, descending into the lake, causing puffs and foam to rise in the water. Fresh lilacs and orchids bloomed around the edge of the lake, interspersed with dewy plants and buttercups. I stared in amazement. It was the most enchanting place I'd ever seen.

"Wow." L nudged my shoulder. "Impressive."

I nodded, smiling in awe. "The Pool of Phaedra." I was finally here. My lips trembled and I felt tears prickle behind my eyes.

"Yer no' be gettin' all watery are ye?" L teased.

I gave her a little push and she laughed. I don't know what I would have done without her. Impulsively, and so unlike me, I threw my arms around her and pulled her into a hug. At first she tensed with surprise… and then tentatively she put her arms around me and hugged me back. When I eventually stepped back from her she gave me a look, pretending she was bemused by my affection. I grinned at her and then walked around her, following the tug of my magic.

It took me to behind a large rock by the edge of the lake. Behind it grew a blue plant, the color of the lake itself, vivid and alien, the sweet smell of molasses drifting up out of it.

"The Somna Plant?" L asked from behind my shoulder.

I nodded, reaching for it.

"No' much left."

No, there wasn't. "I'm taking it all," I whispered, reaching for my pack. "We have alchemists back in Silvera who might be able to plant this to grow more crops. Mayhap they can withdraw its properties and discover other uses for it."

"Alchemists. Properties. Who cares, Rogan, just be gettin' the damn thing and put it in yer pack." She glanced around warily now.

I frowned as I carefully pulled the plants out by the roots and wrapped them in cloth. "What's wrong?" I asked, putting the plant into my pack just as carefully.

L exhaled shakily. "Well, I don't be wantin' to alarm ye but I be sensin' we might be hittin' a spot o' trouble on the way back down."

My heart thumped in my chest, visions of the Mountain Man making me dizzy. "Trouble? What trouble?"

She shook her head, her eyes narrowed in frustration. "I don't be knowin' yet. Sometimes my gift, as ma calls it, has a warped sense o' humor."

With one last longing look at the Pool of Phaedra, L and I hurried back into the woods. I trusted that L had been paying attention to the route we'd taken, and as I followed her, having taken note just in case, I saw that she had. I shouldn't have expected anything else.

We were both tense and anxious as we moved swiftly through the Arans. All I wanted now that I had the plant was to get back to Silvera and Haydyn as quickly as possible.

When the wood creaked and cracked around us we would come to a stop, warily cocking our heads, our eyes wide as we studied the landscape around us. There would be nothing. We'd look at each other, me frightened, L ready, and we'd head off again, our departure faster downhill that it had been going up.

Dusk passed into dark and still we strode through the woods, desperate to get back to L's home. For now, L searched the woods, looking for the perfect place to bed down for the night. When more time passed, my feet aching, my stomach growling, and still L hadn't stopped, it was almost on the tip of my tongue to beg L to just choose somewhere already, when the hair on the back of my neck rose.

A low growl sounded from my left and I drew to an abrupt halt. L heard it too and spun around to look at me. Her eyes flicked to the direction of the sound. "Mountain dog," she told me quietly. Slowly, silently, she took her crossbow and brought it up, aiming somewhere out to my left. "I thought we might be comin' upon one o' these dung bred lowlifes."

Frightened but needing to see for myself, I turned my head slowly. My eyes widened at the sight of the large dog merely meters from me. Its body was skinny but muscular, it's coat rough, with little bald patches here and there. Its sharp muzzle was pulled back over its sharp teeth, saliva dripping from his rotting gums. Its eyes feral.

"We've got to be takin' this mutt down and then be goin'. Its pack can't be too far behind it."

Just as the dog moved to attack, L shot the arrow. It plunged with perfect aim into the dog's flesh. It whined and collapsed mid jump. I exhaled in relief and turned to thank L only to yell out to her as another dog lunged out of the woods and onto her. It took L down, its jaws clamping on her shoulder as she struggled under it, trying to reach for her crossbow which had fallen out of her hands, as well as keep the dogs teeth off of her.

I acted without thought.

With the hunting knife in hand, I leapt on the dog, plunging the blade deep and up into its belly. It jaws lashed out at me, missing me by an inch, before it whined and slumped unconscious on top of L. I grabbed the top of her arms and pulled her out from under it. The dog's blood stained her trousers.

Her own stained her jacket, where the dog had ripped it open and tore into the muscles of her shoulder. It was deep. She swayed a little and I reached to catch her. In her usual gruffness L batted me away.

"We need to go."

When she took off at a run, I followed, anxiety gripping my chest. L was running on adrenaline right now. When that dissipated, I needed to get her home to Sarah as soon as possible.

Finally L drew to a stop, the pallor of her skin worryingly pale. So white. I pulled out the cloth the Somna Plant was wrapped in and put the plant back into the pack. With a briskness L couldn't argue with, I removed her jacket and shirt, tying a tourniquet up over the awkward wound. It would stem the flow of blood but that was it. Hastily, I put her shirt back on as she lolled in my arms. Next her jacket. I forced a couple of sugary biscuits on her and some water. And then I wrapped my arms around her, watching over her, trying to keep her awake.

Chapter Twenty Seven

I'd never been so thankful in my life to see a house.

Of course our trip going down the mountain was faster than going up, but with L growing weaker by the hour we weren't as quick as I would have liked in getting her back home. For once I could pride myself on doing something right on this trip. I was glad I'd paid attention to the route we'd taken, for L was worryingly disorientated the rest of our way back to her home. In those hours with her, looking after her, keeping her conscious, I felt more like myself again. This person, this young woman in control, was me again. And with my old determination I pushed both L and I to our limits, not stopping for food or rest, until I had her back to Sarah. I wasn't letting anything happen to the girl who had saved my life twice without ever asking for anything in return.

As if she sensed us the door to the shack flew open, and Sarah rushed to meet us as I dragged L up the Moss' garden path.

"What happened?" Sarah's eyes blazed with worry.

"Mountain dog," I bit out, relief making me weak. Thankfully Sarah took hold of L and carried her the rest of the way into the house.

When I stepped over the threshold I took in Jnr staring wide-eyed at his mother as she laid L on top of the table.

"Jnr, heat up some water," Sarah threw over her shoulder as she ripped L's clothes away from her wound. She hissed at the sight of it and I turned away, seeing how putrid it had grown with infection. Sarah stroked her daughter's face tenderly. L barely registered the touch. "L, my love, ye got yerself a fever. I'm goin' to be sortin' that out, alright, honey."

I just stood there, gazing on uselessly. This was all my fault. I should never have taken L with me. Sarah caught the guilt and concern on my face and smiled reassuringly.

"Now don't ye be lookin' like that, Rogan. Things happen up in these here mountains. L's goin' to be alright."

Jnr struggled with the pot of hot water so I hurried to take it from him before he splashed the water and burned himself. Sarah took it from me quietly and set about cleaning L's wound. She stirred a little at her mother's touch. And then, as she had done with me, Sarah put her fingertips on the wound and shot her energy into L. I watched in amazement as the wound began to close, the color returning to L's face with surprising swiftness. L's eyelashes fluttered and she groaned, looking up into Sarah's happy but now fatigued face.

"Ma." Her head rolled and she saw me standing over Sarah's shoulder, wringing my hands. To my surprise she smiled. "Knew ye wasn't completely useless." She turned to Sarah now. "Here, Ma, Rogan saved my life."

"Well don't that be somethin'." We all turned at the sound of Jonas' voice. He stood in the doorway to the house, his eyes bright on his daughter and then on me, a dead rabbit slung over his shoulder. He winked at me and then stepped further into the house. A shadow moved behind him and my heart faltered. There was a man with him, taller, broader. As he stepped inside beside Jonas, his familiar eyes bored into me, inscrutable and probing.

"Wolfe!" Jnr shouted happily and flew past me to hop at Wolfe's feet. "This be my sister, L, Wolfe." He pointed at L lying on the table. I glanced at L as she pulled herself into a sitting position. Her eyes flicked between Wolfe and me, giving me a knowing look.

I exhaled and looked back at Wolfe.

I shook my head.

I couldn't believe the fool had come after me. Where was the damn Guard?!

When our gazes locked, despite the inscrutability of those pale eyes of his, a delicious relief, like coming home after months of miserable absence, swept over me.

***

It was strange sitting around the Moss' kitchen table with Wolfe. I knew I'd only known the family a few short days, but I had a bond with L that made me feel closer to all of them, and it was strange to share them with Wolfe. We hadn't spoken yet about my running off on him, and he wasn't unpleasant to me. However, I knew that was more for the Moss' sake than anyone else. We'd been eating for five minutes, and having already exhausted L and I's rescue of one another from the mountain dogs, Jonas and Wolfe sat discussing hunting techniques while Jnr desperately tried to get in on the conversation, completely enamored by Wolfe. As he did with everyone, Wolfe had enchanted the Moss family. He took up a lot of room at their table. I forgot how large he was. Thankfully he had forgone his emerald military jacket. The warm jacket he had been wearing when he appeared with Jonas was hanging up on the Moss' coat pegs, the fur around the cuffs and collar proclaiming Wolfe's wealth. His shirt and waistcoat were finely made, his boats, his trousers. He looked powerful and rich, his white-gold hilted sword propped against the wall. Just being near him made me feel safe. I thought of L's words of wisdom in the woods and longed to reach out and brush his hair off his face, stroke his arm, anything to feel the heat and life of him under my fingertips. But he refused to look at me. I watched him talk animatedly with Jonas. From what I'd gathered, Wolfe clearly knew the Moss'. How?

L stared at me. Her eyes demanded me to question Wolfe about it but I was frightened any conversation might start an argument. She kicked me under the table and I muffled a cry of pain. I glared at her and exhaled, turning to Wolfe.

"So, Captain, when did you arrive?"

The sound of my voice made Wolfe tense and he glanced sharply at me. "Apparently a few hours after you and Miss Moss left for the Pool. Sarah and Jonas convinced me you were in safe hands and that it would better if I stayed with them to await your return." That last word he emphasized with an edge and his eyes suddenly turned dark with pure, undiluted fury. I tensed. I had expected him to be mad, but this… He looked ready to explode. "Jonas told me how L and he found you. Where they found you. With whom. In what state."

The breath whooshed out of my body. I hadn't ever wanted Wolfe to know about the Mountain Man. I looked away and scraped at my plate. "I see."

"Rogan…"

"Later, Wol- Captain."

Just as I had not wanted to, Wolfe and I had created tension at the table. I shifted uncomfortably.

"So, Captain Wolfe," L suddenly piped up. "How be ye findin' Rogan?"

Yes, I thought, glancing over at him. How had he found me at the Moss'?

Wolfe shrugged. "I'm a Glava as well, Miss Moss. If my emotions are strong enough I have a heightened sense of intuition."

L threw me a look. I had told her about Wolfe being Glava but had not mentioned this ability. I shrugged back at her. I hadn't *known* about that ability. And ability that only came to the fore when he was upset, or worried, or angry, or all three. I'd done that to him.

I sighed and refused to look at him. Wolfe was powerful. Extremely powerful. He could move things with his mind, call upon the elements, and he had some psychic talent as well. I had never heard of the like. Perhaps that's why he hadn't trusted me enough to tell me. I chanced a glower at him but Wolfe caught it. The glare he threw back said "Don't be mad at me for not trusting you. You who didn't trust me and got yourself almost raped in the Alvernian Mountains."

I grimaced and turned from him. L threw me a sympathetic smirk.

Chapter Twenty Eight

The sun bit into the morning chill and I breathed in the crispness of a summer morning in the Alvernian Mountains, feeling far more exuberant than I had in weeks. I had the plant, I was no longer alone, and I was heading back to Silvera to save Haydyn.

Sarah, Jonas and Jnr stood on the porch of their home while L helped me on with my pack. I could feel Wolfe waiting impatiently behind me at the end of the garden path, having already thanked the Moss' for their hospitality and made his goodbyes. Jnr was not amused to see Wolfe's sudden departure and was blaming me. He refused to say goodbye to me.

"Right," L said briskly, handing over the hunting knife.

I shook my head. "I can't take anything more from you." I was already wearing her clothes and carrying their food. They had so little and yet they gave so generously.

L gave me one of her characteristic scowls. "Ye be refusin' to let me escort ye down the mountain, so ye be takin' the damn knife."

I hid my smile. Last night, L had made quite a stink when I told her she was staying with her family, that I would be alright now that I had Wolfe with me. She'd given Wolfe, in his fine clothing, with his nice hair and skin, a dubious look. Wolfe had good-naturedly let her pick at his 'obvious uselessness' as she called it. I felt an ache in my chest as L had gone on and on, pretending to be put out. She was worried about me.

I took the knife and held her gaze. "You and your family must come to Silvera to see me, L. I'll arrange it." I nodded hopefully, looking past her to Sarah and Jonas. They smiled at the idea so I took that to mean yes.

"Ye isn't meaning that," L sniffed, kicking dirt on the path self-consciously, not looking me in the eyes. "Ye'll go back to yer fancy world and forget all about me and mine."

"L." I grinned, grabbing her arms. "L, you're just about the most unforgettable person I've ever met. And if you don't come to see me in Silvera, then I'm going to crawl all the way back up this mountain to you."

She reddened a little but she looked pleased. "Well no need to be gettin' all melodramatic on me," she drawled, waving me off.

I laughed, feeling that pang again. I felt as if I'd known her forever, and I was sorry to leave her and her family up here in these forsaken hills. I'd be back for them though. I was going to make sure they never had to worry about anything again. Ignoring L's gruffness I tugged her into a hug and was surprised by how tight she held me. After a moment she patted me on the back and pulled me away. Both our eyes were bright.

"Ye be careful," she warned and then peered around me to Wolfe. She threw him her famous scowl. "Ye be watchin' o'er this one, Captain Wolfe."

"I promise, Miss Moss."

"Miss Moss," L muttered under her breath and then threw me a look. "Ye ever heard the likes." Still muttering under her breath like an old woman, L turned on her heel to join her family on the porch. Wolfe and I waved one last time and then I walked away with him in a mixture of reluctance and anticipation.

We'd been walking an hour and still Wolfe hadn't said a word to me. The tension between us was thick and uncomfortable— even my teeth ached with it. I concentrated on watching where I was going, thankful to Sarah who had healed all my new blisters again. I'd probably have a few by the time we got off the mountains but maybe not so many. My feet were already feeling harder and stronger. That morning as I'd pulled on L's trousers and shirt, I realized how much weight I'd lost since I'd left Silvera. My calves and thighs had slimmed with muscle, my stomach flatter from eating sparingly and walking the hills. Still, despite our similar heights, L was wiry and I was still curvy. She wore her trousers tight, and on me they were indecent. I'd forgotten all about propriety up in the mountains without anyone from home to see me. But now that Wolfe was around, I was suddenly painfully aware of how revealing these clothes were. I had put my borrowed coat on over the top of the trousers and shirt before Wolfe had seen them. I wouldn't be removing it.

The silence continued between us, Wolfe keeping a careful distance, enough for me to know he wasn't speaking to me, but not enough so he couldn't keep an eye on me. I kept waiting for his explosion of indignation and anger, and when it didn't come I was strangely hurt.

The tension only grew thicker as the afternoon wore on and we found ourselves at the outskirts of Shadow Hill. Before I could warn Wolfe, he turned to me with a finger to his lips, hushing me. He knew about Shadow Hill. Either the Moss' had warned him, or he may have already met Brint in Hope o' Hill and Brint had warned him. We moved on the outskirts of the town with stealth and quiet, the voices in the distance making my heart pound. I grew unbearably warm under my coat. It was with a sigh of relief when we made it past the Hill without incident, and carried on at a quicker pace down the mountain. Again, we were making good time at this speed.

An hour or so later I heard the trickle of the stream in the distance and something about the wood seemed familiar. I shivered. We were close to where I'd been taken by the Mountain Man. Without explaining, I picked up my feet, almost running to get away from the spot, my skin crawled, and my neck prickled. I felt as if his shadow was watching me, taunting me. I shuddered in revulsion and began to run. The sounds of Wolfe's running footsteps grew louder and closer, but I couldn't stop.

Abruptly, I was forced to a halt, Wolfe's hand catching my arm and dragging me around to face him. His features were fierce with anger, the golden striations in his blue eyes prominent with passion. "What the hell were you thinking?!" He yelled, not caring if his voice carried now that we were miles from Shadow Hill.

I struggled to get out of his grip. "I just felt like running."

"Not that Rogan," he bit out, his jaw clenched. He looked close to violence. I struggled harder to get away from him, but he only pulled me closer. "I'm talking about you running off from Arrana, alone without an escort. I'm talking about you lying to me and making a fool of me, and of nearly getting yourself raped and killed!"

Like always his overbearing attitude caused my knee jerk reaction— to dispute him. "Nearly. *Nearly*, alright. I managed well enough without you, Wolfe."

"Well enough? Jonas told me how he found you, Rogan, and he spared me no details!"

"Will you stop yelling? Are you trying to get us into bother?" I hissed, glancing around to make sure we were still alone.

"Stop trying to wriggle your way out of discussing it."

Using all my strength, I tugged out of Wolfe's grasp, my own face now red with frustration and anger. "Did you ever stop to consider I might not be ready to discuss it?"

Wolfe's expression changed instantly. He slumped, his eyes grew anxious. "Rogan..."

I shook my head.

He nodded, his lips pinched tight. "Fine. But what about my first question? You ran away, Rogan. From me. You knew I would come after you and as far as you knew I had no way of knowing which way you went. I could have got lost up here, Rogan."

Guilt gnawed at me, and I shook my head in denial. "No. I didn't... I thought if you did chance into the mountains you would bring an escort. I thought you'd bring Chaeron, or a few of the men. I didn't think you would be foolish enough to come all the way into the Mountains after me alone."

"You're lying," he hissed in my face, causing me to flinch. "You knew I'd come after you, Rogan, you had to have known that."

I clenched my own jaw trying to stop the tears that choked me. Hanging my head, I didn't say anything in return. Was he right? Had I known Wolfe loved me enough to do that? I knew what kind of man he was. Because of my fear of being alone with him, a fear of my own damn feelings, had I selfishly put him in danger? I didn't know. I had no response. There was nothing I could say.

All this time I'd fretted that his parentage meant perhaps he didn't deserve me. But really... I didn't deserve him.

"I don't know what I was thinking. I just knew I had to get this plant. For Haydyn."

"And still she lies," he whispered bitterly.

We didn't speak after that.

***

The journey downhill cut the time in half. By late night Wolfe and I broke out of the trees and into Hill o' Hope.

I chanced a glance at Wolfe. "You came through here too?"

He nodded, not looking at me. "I stayed with a man called Brint Lokam. He told me he'd sheltered a young woman with him who was looking for the Pool of Phaedra."

My mouth fell open. "He knew I was a girl?"

Wolfe rolled his eyes but not directly at me. I harrumphed. I'd so thought my disguise had worked. Had all of Hill o' Hope known I was a girl? My cheeks flamed with embarrassment. We crossed through the quiet hill, noise, cheer and light spilling out of Hope Tavern. Wolfe didn't stop. He was heading for the Lokam's shack. I shook my head in wonder at the thought of Brint. He'd been such a gentleman to me. No wonder he'd seemed so concerned about letting me go into the mountains alone. He knew I was a girl!

The door to the shack opened before we even reached it and the tall figure of Brint came out. He squinted in the dark, holding up a lantern, and then grinned when he recognized us. "Well, hullo there."

I waved and followed Wolfe up to the door.

"Brint." Wolfe held out his hand to shake. Brint took it heartily, grinning at us both. "Could we perhaps trespass upon your hospitality one more evening, Mr. Lokam?"

"No needin' to be askin'." He shook us off gruffly and grinned wider at me as I passed. Brint must have seen the look on my face because he said, "Ye wasn't thinkin' ol' Brint was bein' fooled by the boy's outfit o yers? No one was but wee Tera. She be mighty embarrassed when she be told she flirted with a girl."

Wolfe raised an eyebrow questioningly as I blushed but I refused to tell him about the night at Hope Tavern. Not that I was sure he'd appreciate me speaking to him anyway.

Anna was happy to offer us some food and ale, and they put down blankets by the fire for us to sleep on. Wolfe was so mad at me he slept at the kitchen table.

***

I didn't think I had ever been happier to be on flat ground in my life. I celebrated my last step off the Alvernian Mountains by rushing into the arms of Lieutenant Chaeron, who, unlike Wolfe, was happy to see me. I ignored Wolfe's grunt as he strode past us. Chaeron squeezed me hard and I pulled back. Half The Guard filled the narrow trade road leading away from the mountains. They all pretended to be indifferent to my clothing and the fact that I was informally hugging Chaeron, treating him as a friend. But he *was* a friend. And I was thankful to see him again.

"Another hour and be damned Wolfe's orders, I was coming up to get you both. I am delighted to see you are well, Miss Rogan," Chaeron smiled wearily at me. It didn't seem as if he'd slept much since I had left.

"You too, Chaeron. I got the plant!" I whispered excitedly.

He smiled in relief and then lifted his gaze to Wolfe, who was taking off the winter coat and replacing it with his emerald jacket. We both watched as he mounted his horse, not looking back at me.

"He's not speaking with me," I told Chaeron forlornly.

"You frightened him, Miss Rogan. Give him time."

I nodded, but I didn't think even time would fix the situation between me and Wolfe. Chaeron had no idea what I'd gone through up in that mountain. For that to have happened to me surely made Wolfe sick with impotence. He was a man who believed in protecting others. And I hadn't let him protect me. I hadn't trusted him.

With another woeful look at the man who had so surprisingly complicated my life, I turned and mounted the horse Chaeron had waiting for me.

"Don't you wish to remove that coat, Miss Rogan?" Chaeron enquired as he pulled up beside me.

"Don't you dare." Wolfe was suddenly in front of us, his eyes blazing. "It's indecent what you're wearing, Rogan. You will not take that off in front of my men."

"Indecent?" Chaeron's brow furrowed.

"You saw?" I blushed, aghast.

"At the Moss'." He nodded. "Before you put the jacket on." A strange look entered his eyes and I could have sworn a flush rose on the crest of his cheeks. He shifted on his horse and then glared at me. "Keep it on." And then he headed off, leading the way for me and Chaeron to move through the men (who all nodded their relieved greetings at me) so we were in front of the entourage.

"Indecent?" Chaeron asked again.

I shrugged, throwing him a sheepish look. "I'm wearing trousers. They leave little to the imagination."

"Ah." Chaeron shifted his gaze to Wolfe who began to gallop off ahead of us. His mouth broke into a wide, knowing grin. "I think you'll be fine, Miss Rogan. You and Wolfe both."

It was cold and black as tar outside by the time we entered Arrana and were allowed entrance into the Vojvoda's home. I still had the coat on, and after a day of blazing heat in the valley, my clothes were sticking to me. I needed a warm bath, badly.

As soon as I was inside Chaeron took care of everything. I was taken to the room I had been given before and I watched impatiently as the servants filled a tin tub with hot water, leaving rose scented soap out for me. After the last maid had laid out one of my dresses for me, I shooed them out and began taking off L's now dirty clothing. Sinking into the tub was like sinking into my own piece of haven. I breathed a sigh of relief, not really able to comprehend that I had succeeded in retrieving the plant, and that I was off those forsaken mountains.

I felt as if I'd spent months up there.

I broke into hysterical sobs.

My chest ached with the harsh racking, my throat closing and unclosing as I struggled to draw breath, tears burning my cheeks as they rolled down one after the other as quickly as rainfall. I hugged my body, trying to blot out the memory of the Mountain Man, assuring myself my body was mine, and mine alone, and that he'd never get near me again.

"My Lady?" a voice asked softly, followed by a tapping on the door.

I swiped at my tears and shuddered in air. "I'm fine," I called out, my voice quavering. "I'm alright."

"Are ye sure, My Lady?"

"Yes. Thank you."

I waited for the sounds of fading footsteps and then reached for the soap, scrubbing the bar over my body and lathering it into my hair. I couldn't think about the bad things that had happened to me in Alvernia. I had to think of the good. Like Brint. And L. Especially L. Had I really only known her a matter of days? I smiled through my tears, thinking of gruff L who had saved my life and burrowed her way into my much guarded heart. Haydyn would love L. I couldn't wait for them to meet. I couldn't wait to repay the Moss' for all of their help.

Once I had calmed myself and gotten most of the poisonous memories out of my system for the night, I changed into my dress. It felt strange swishing about my ankles. Encumbering. I frowned at it and kicked out with my legs. I missed trousers. Sighing, I plaited my hair back and frowned at the way the dress lifted from my waist. My clothes no longer fit well.

The Vojvoda Andrei Rada and his son the Markiz awaited me with Wolfe in the dark, masculine dining room.

"There she is," Vojvoda Andrei called out, approaching me with a fatherly smile. He took my hands and I found it difficult to smile politely back at him. "Lady Rogan, what a scare you gave us running off to tour Alvernia alone."

I grimaced at our lie. I grimaced at the way the Vojvoda looked down on me condescendingly, in his gated home and isolated city. Where was he for the people of the Mountains? All my anger and frustration over everything that had happened suddenly seethed to the surface. If I'd known this was going to be my reaction at seeing him again I would never have come down for dinner. I struggled to maintain calm.

"Well." He shrugged, seeming nonplussed by my silence. "I'm very glad the good Captain caught up with you to keep you safe. How did you find my rough lands?"

I thought of L and her forthright honesty. Of the Moss' kindness and sincerity. Of Brint Lokam and the people of Hill o' Hope's generosity.

"Like everywhere else in Phaedra, Your Grace. Populated with good people and bad people... and poorly governed." I straightened my shoulders, jutting out my chin defiantly. "If you'll excuse me."

And leaving all three of the men with their jaws hanging to the floor, I spun on my heel and left them to it.

Chapter Twenty Nine

The days ahead were filled with a mixture of anticipation and a sickening coldness. I barely ate a thing as we galloped through Daeronia, stopping to pick up the two soldiers in the mining village, who now greeted us happily, offering us bread and shelter. But we didn't stay long. If our pace had been grueling before, now it was frantic. I knew The Guard was curious, that they all suspected something more was going on, especially since they'd seen me come out of the mountains. They wondered what an earth had possessed me to go up them. But I didn't want to panic anyone, especially when we were so close to saving Haydyn. I'd rather they'd think I'd gone light in the mind than know the truth. The times I did sleep, I twisted and turned with the nightmares. I dreamt of arriving in Silvera only to find we were too late and Haydyn was gone. I dreamt the Mountain Man was still alive and chased me into the empty palace, no one there to protect me from his deranged lust. And I dreamt of Wolfe. Always he stood on the Silver Cliffs, his eyes begging me to save him. I'd make a move towards him and feel a tug on my hand. I'd turn to find Haydyn, shaking her head at me, my parents and little brother behind her, mirroring her expression. When I looked back at Wolfe, he'd glare at me, hatred filling his eyes. And then he'd leap, leap right over the cliffs into the crashing water.

I didn't need to be a scholar to interpret the dream.

We reached Caera in record time, not stopping enough to make time for incidents. I was exhausted by the time Vojvodkyna Winter welcomed us into our home. Taking in my bedraggled state, even she was kind to me. As she ushered me to the guest suite herself, ordering a bath and food tray for me, I forgot to be jealous of her. I even came to the conclusion, that as before, I may have judged her too harshly.

The next morning as the maid's giggled in the hallway all my good feelings toward Winter flew out the window. It was easy in a household as large as Winter's for the gossip to reach my ears. Wolfe had been seen leaving Winter's bedroom early that morning. I stumbled when I heard the gossip, the pain of that knowledge hitting me in the chest with the force of a sledgehammer. I turned on my heel, no longer hungry for breakfast, or able to stand the sight of Wolfe and Winter together. I could barely draw breath. My whole body ached with the grief. With the betrayal.

But he wasn't mine to betray me.

Sniffling back silly tears that were best not wasted on him, I pulled on my travelling cloak and clutched the pack with the Somna Plant inside. It was time to leave.

**

Chaeron and the others seemed confused. Before Caera, Wolfe had been the one not talking to *me*. Now every time he passed me an icy blast would burst out of me, my looks so quelling they made everyone flinch. Wolfe caught my looks and frowned, his eyes asking Chaeron if he knew what had upset me. With no answer, he grew even more indignant. I imagined the Lieutenant and The Guard were just as exhausted with Wolfe's attitude and my own, as much as they were of the journey.

We crossed into Raphizya, stopping in Ryl to stay with Matai's cousins again. This time I met Mr. Zanst, who welcomed us into his home just as warmly as his wife had. From his dark good looks to his charming stoicism, he reminded me much of Matai… and I longed for home. Mrs. Zanst was so worried for me I felt terrible for deceiving her, for having been foolish enough to be kidnapped by the Iavii in Ryl. She asked me if I had been treated badly, and I assured her that Wolfe had come to my rescue and kept me safe.

After a wonderfully civilized and pleasantly refreshing evening with the Zansts The Guard and I set off for Peza. It rained the entire journey, and I wasn't sure if it was because my body had hardened with its recent experiences but I escaped the cold that seemed to be sweeping through The Guard. Mayhap because of their position distant from The Guard, Wolfe and Lieutenant Chaeron managed to get by unscathed also. Still, I was glad to reach Grof Krill Rada's home. I'd never heard supposedly strapping and capable men complain so much about a little cold.

I wasn't the only one happy to see me in Peza. Grof Krill came bounding out of his mansion with Strider, the wolfhound, at his side. Strider seemed to remember me and my generosity at the dinner table and licked my hand when I reached out to pet him. Grof Krill was grinning at me so brightly I was taken aback. We hadn't exactly left on the best of terms.

"My Lord." I bobbed a curtsey.

"You are a vision, Lady Rogan." His grin grew even brighter if that was possible. There was no flirtatiousness in his tone, nothing seedy. He seemed genuinely *happy* to see me.

I was completely bemused. "Thank you, My Lord."

Seeming to catch my confused look, Groff Krill laughed. "Come, I want you to meet someone."

As I took his arm and followed him inside, forgetting Wolfe and Chaeron at my back, a suspicion grew.

No. It couldn't be. Could it?

The door was swept open by the butler, my heart pounding in my chest, praying my suspicion was correct.

As soon as we stepped inside I saw her. I broke out into a choked laugh. "Ariana?"

The pretty young woman came forward at a hurry, her gray eyes brimming with happiness. "Is this her, Krill?"

"This is she." He spun me around, gripping me by my upper arms. "How can I ever repay you for writing that letter, Lady Rogan?"

Ariana joined us, pulling me into a hug, joyful tears filling her eyes as she told me all about receiving the letter; how she couldn't believe the Handmaiden of Phaedra had written to her, and how she so wanted to believe me about Krill's love for her that she'd left her life behind and took a chance on what I had confided.

Grof Krill and Ariana married three days after her arrival in Peza. She was now Grofka Ariana.

Exhausted and incredibly elated that I'd done one good thing on this quest of mine, I felt tears well up in my eyes.

"Lady Rogan, are you alright?" Grof Krill asked anxiously, seeing my dark eyes shine.

"I'm fine," I whispered hoarsely. "I'm just delighted for you and... so very tired."

"Oh." Ariana looked aghast. "Here we've been monopolizing your time when you must be so weary from your journey. How ill-mannered of us."

"No, no," I rushed to assure her. "I am so pleased to meet you, Ariana, and I am so happy I had a hand in bringing you and Grof Krill together. It's just been such a long trip."

I was struggling now to keep my tears in check.

With a perceptiveness that bothered me, Grof Krill straightened his spine in alert. "Nothing untoward has happened to you, Lady Rogan?"

"No, no. Please… I just need to rest."

"Krill, stop pestering the poor girl," Ariana admonished gently. She took my arm. "Come, I shall show you to your room."

Ariana left me in the suite I'd stayed in during my last visit and rang the servants to send for a supper tray. With one last grateful hug, she swept from the room and I flopped down on the bed. I was glad the Grof had gotten his happily ever after. At least someone in my life had.

The food arrived, and delicious though it was, I barely tasted it as I shoveled it down. I kept seeing Winter at the door to her mansion, waving her handkerchief at Wolfe with that knowing, intimate look in her eyes.

I slid back on the bed and rested my head against a fluffy gold brocade pillow, willing the nightmares away tonight. I'd give anything for a restful, dreamless sleep.

My eyes were just closing when I heard the handle on the door turn, someone entering without knocking. I bolted upright at the impudence, my heart spluttering when the intruder revealed himself.

Wolfe.

He closed the door behind, turning the key in the lock.

I glared at him as he leaned back against the door, his eyes washing over me, his expression inscrutable.

"Grof Krill and Grofka Ariana are so sickeningly happy I had to get away from them." He smirked.

I was surprised by his even tone. There was no ice in his eyes. No growl in his words.

"Get out," I snapped, feeling the hurt roll over and over me again in crashing waves.

Wolfe's expression hardened. "No." He shook his head and pushed away from the door, striding towards me. I felt my pulse race at that familiar languid walk. "I'm weary of fighting with you. I keep waiting for you to come to your senses… but then I realized something today."

I continued glowering. "What was that?"

He stopped in front of me so I had to crane my neck back to meet his eyes. "You never just come to your senses, Rogan. You have to have them shaken into you." He reached out to touch my cheek and I jerked back, ignoring his wounded look as he dropped his hand. "I love you, Rogan."

All the pain and anger I felt brimmed over in my eyes. "Then why did you bed Winter when we were in Caera?" I choked back a cry.

Wolfe looked stunned. He hurried to sit beside me, and attempted to reach for my hands to pull me to him, but I wouldn't let him. "Rogan, I never bedded Winter. I never touched her. I shared a room with Chaeron that night. You can ask him. You know he won't lie to you."

I glanced up at him sharply, my heart pounding. "What?"

"I was nowhere near her. The last time we were in Caera I told Winter there would never be anything between us again because… because… because I love you. I'm in love with *you*."

I trembled, hope desperately clambering its way back inside of me. I tried to shake it back out. I was so confused. "The servants were gossiping about you leaving her bedroom in the morning."

Wolfe sighed in exasperation. "Winter likes to use her servants for her little games. She wants me back, Rogan. She's trying to put up a wall between us."

"You refused to converse with me anyway. There was already a wall."

He slid a hand down my cheek and around my neck, forcing me to look at him. I shivered at his gentle touch. "I was terrified, Rogan. Every time I think about what could have happened… what did happen… I—"

"Wolfe, don't," I urged, shushing him. I reached for his hand on the bedspread and slowly threaded my fingers through his. For a moment we gazed at our hands so entangled together. His skin felt warm and rough against mine. Safe.

"I don't want a wall between us ever again," Wolfe whispered.

I looked up to find his eyes on my face. There was pain there I had never seen before, and I know it was fear that I would turn from him. I knew… because I knew him.

I *knew* him.

Slowly, my breath hitching and falling, I leaned across the space between us and pressed my lips to his. Wolfe sat tense, unmoving as I kissed him softly, almost as if he were afraid to touch me.

I pulled back.

I knew him. "He didn't hurt me, Wolfe. He didn't... rape me."

Wolfe swallowed, his eyes glistening. "Promise?"

"Promise."

Tentatively, he lifted our clasped hands off the bed and kissed my knuckles.

"Are you going to seduce me, Wolfe, or am I going to have to seduce you?" I grinned a little shyly.

Wolfe's eyes darkened as his lips curved into that wicked smile. "I'm happy with either scenario."

In the end... we seduced each other.

I had never been shy. Mindful of the proprieties, yes, but not shy. And with Wolfe I felt all my inhibitions melt out of existence, no longer caring I was younger and inexperienced in comparison to the women he had been with previously. His declaration of love made me bold. Certain. I kissed his throat, loving the vibration of his groan against my lips. I leaned back and gazed up into his eyes. I realized something wonderful.

He knew me.

Gazes locked, we slowly undressed one another, leisurely, deliciously, savoring our connection...

…When I was naked under him, I felt no fear, just want. I stroked my hands over his strong chest, felt the brush of his thighs against my own and trembled with the want.

And consequences be damned, for once I was taking what *I* wanted.

Wolfe gazed down at me with such love I almost cried. I noted the spark of uncertainty in his eyes and deliberately brushed my hand over the scar on his lower abdomen that represented so much of the strife between us. With my eyes I told him I didn't care about any of that anymore. I had finally put the past where it belonged.

I wrapped my legs around his waist and Wolfe groaned, making me gasp at the feel of him nudging against me. He'd kissed every inch of my body, shown me things I had never dreamt of, made me blush from the top of my head to the tip of my toes, but this was different. This was irreversible.

"Wolfe!" I gasped, as he pushed inside me, a flinch of pain making me stiffen.

He stopped moving, a bead of sweat rolling down his forehead with the effort. "Did I hurt you? Are you alright?" he asked frantically.

I tried to smooth my expression to ease his anxiety. And then something changed. The pain was dissipating. I shifted under him and my eyes widened at the pleasurable rush that burst throughout me. "Mm," I bit my lip. "No, I'm alright. Don't stop."

Wolfe began to move again and I cried out, this time in amazement. I tightened my hold on him, swearing I would find a way to never let go.

Chapter Thirty

I had never known I could feel this close and connected to anyone. We lay together after our lovemaking, his arm around me, my head on his chest. His heart thumped under my ear, not quite steady.

Despite what I had sworn to myself as he loved me, I felt reality creep in quickly. My plan had never been to marry. The reason? If I were honest with myself it was because I was trying to keep the people in my life that I cared about to a minimum. That way there was less heartbreak when they were taken from me. I didn't want to love someone as much as I loved Wolfe and have to deal with the pain of losing him, or have children and fear losing them too. I'd wanted romance, passion, but not love. And I loved Wolfe. My earlier excuses that I couldn't be with Wolfe because of who his father was no longer seemed to stand. L, in all her pragmatism, had knocked that wall down so I couldn't hide behind it anymore. But I had other reasons not to be with Wolfe. I did! I had never planned on being pulled into the bonds that would make me a society wife and take me away from Haydyn. She needed me. Now more than ever she needed me. Perhaps I could have Wolfe for a little while. Without marriage. We could be happy with that… I tried to convince myself.

For now, as we lay together, I wouldn't say anything to break the spell.

I shivered at the goosebumps spreading up my arm in the wake of his fingertips stroking my skin. "This is nice," I whispered.

"Mm," Wolfe murmured and pressed a kiss to my temple. I snuggled deeper against him.

"Thank you for coming after me into the mountains, Wolfe. I should have said that before."

I felt him smile against me head. "You're welcome."

"So… you have psychic abilities now?"

He chuckled. "How long have you been waiting to pester me with questions about that?"

"Since the night at the Moss'."

He huffed. "I didn't say anything because I don't want people to fear me."

"Because you're this astonishingly, inconceivable, all powerful mage?"

"Yes."

I snickered this time and shook my head. "No one would be afraid of you, Wolfe. You're too kind to people for them to fear you."

"I can be fearsome if I want to be."

I hid my smile. "I know."

"I can be plenty fearsome."

"Oh I know."

"I can—"

Afraid he'd want to prove how fearsome he could be, I said, "You know I've discovered something interesting on this quest of ours."

Wolfe grunted at having been interrupted. "What's that?"

I drew away from him to lean up on my elbow and meet his gaze. "Mage, Wolfe. Quite a few of them."

Wolfe frowned. "Well, there have been some…"

I shook my head impatiently. "For a world whose mage are apparently dying out, I find it strange to have come across over a handful of mage since leaving Silvera. I mean, it seems like too much of a coincidence."

"Meaning?"

"There are mage out there. Lots of them. I'd bet Haydyn's Somna Plant on that."

Wolfe raised his eyebrows. "Perhaps you're right. If so then…"

I sighed. "It has to be taken into consideration with everything else."

"Everything else?"

Lying back down in his arms, I went on to tell Wolfe about all I had discovered, what I thought of the people of Phaedra and the way we governed.

"What's the use in the evocation if we don't solidify its properties with good government? There are places in Phaedra, Alvernia for one, where good people are lumped in with the bad, and nothing is done to help them."

"You know my feelings on the subject. I agree that people are people no matter their situation or location, good or bad, it's all to do with the person. And there are certain people I intend to see punished for their crimes, such as Markiz Solom and those damn Iavii. But the bad people will stop being bad when the evocation strengthens again. When Haydyn is well."

I growled in frustration. "Not in Alvernia. Haydyn's evocation begins to wane, and people like L and her family are the ones who suffer for that, having to live side by side with uncivilized, foul people who need laws and consequences. What if the evocation is wrong, Wolfe? Do you really think it gives us peace and freedom? Or is it just the pretense of it?"

His chest rose and fell beneath my ear with deep exhalation. "That's a philosophical question that not only needs time to mull over but… can really only be posed to one person."

"Haydyn."

"Yes. Haydyn." Wolfe kissed me lightly on the lips and slid out of bed.

I took delicious enjoyment watching him dress. I bit my lip. It was all just as Haydyn promised it would be. "Where are you going?"

Wolfe grinned back at me as he buttoned his shirt, and then leaned over to kiss me deeply. I moaned at the taste of him and wrapped my arms around him, trying to pull him back down. If he left the room… my heart beat unsteadily in panic.

Laughing against my mouth, Wolfe pulled away, his eyes telling me it was with great reluctance that he did so. "I have to leave before someone finds me here."

I dropped my arms at that. That was true. We couldn't be caught together. I bit my lip. That was something I'd have to think about if we did begin an affair.

I nodded numbly, wrapping my arms around my drawn up knees so I wouldn't touch him again.

"You are so beautiful," he told me hoarsely, his eyes running over me, making my skin blush. I smiled shyly back at him. With a heavy sigh, Wolfe picked up his jacket and strode to the door. Just as he was about to disappear out of it, he turned back to me.

"We'll work it out all, Rogan," he promised, his expression tender. "After Haydyn is well and good, we'll get married, and then we can take all the time we need convincing Haydyn of what's right."

Wolfe was gone before I could respond, my heart thumping hard in my chest. I groaned and flopped back on my pillow. Damn it. I'd have to tell him.

I was not looking forward to that. Not one little bit.

Chapter Thirty One

Ariana was quite possibly the sweetest person I had ever met, even more so than Haydyn which was quite a feat. In contrast to L, it was almost shocking to sit and converse with Ariana: one so gruff and straightforward, the other so gentle and affable. Despite the effaceable impact L and the Moss' had made on my life, I found it soothing to sit at a beautiful breakfast table, with refined people, and eat sumptuous food. I almost snorted, thinking of all the times I'd argued with Wolfe for calling me Lady Rogan instead of Miss. He'd be happy to know in the end he was right. I'd been raised a lady since I was a girl and that had left more of a mark on me than I'd come to realize. It was time to accept who I was.

We ate companionably, just Ariana and I as Grof Krill had business to attend to. He still hadn't returned by the time I was readying to leave, so I told Ariana to thank him for his hospitality and to tell him that I looked forward to seeing them both at the ball during the Autumn Season.

"I cannot wait to meet again, Lady Rogan," Ariana hugged me quickly, informally, "It's been such a pleasure. I do wish you could stay longer."

I thought of the pack that was being tied to Midnight as we spoke. The pack with the Somna Plant. Haydyn was waiting. We were so close now. I smiled softly. "We will see each other soon." Catching sight of Wolfe out of the corner of my eye as he mounted his horse, my body woke up. Tingles shot out of my nerve endings and my heart began to race like a galloping horse. My stomach fluttered with nerves. I needed to tell him. Mind you, I narrowed my eyes in thought, it wasn't as if he'd actually *asked* me to marry him. He'd just *told* me. With another farewell to Ariana, I lifted my skirts and tried to act casually as I strode over to Wolfe. I touched his leg, and he glanced down, his mouth widening into the warmest smile he'd ever bestowed on me. I was struck dumb for a moment.

"Lady Rogan?"

For once I didn't argue with the title. "Wolfe," I responded in a low voice, glancing around to make sure no one was close enough to overhear. "Marriage?" I asked, raising my eyebrow indignantly.

He exhaled heavily, sensing my tone. Wolfe dismounted and towered over me, standing far too close to me than propriety allowed. "We made love, Rogan," he hissed in my ear, "I took your virginity. We *have* to marry."

I flinched back. "No." I told him stubbornly, crossing my arms over my chest and glaring into his face. All the reasons I had for not marrying him flew out the window. The only one prickling my pride was... well... he hadn't *asked* me!

In his usual exasperation, Wolfe rolled his eyes, scraping a hand through his thick hair. "Rogan, don't do this." He glanced around, catching Chaeron's eye (who quickly looked away, whistling under his breath as if he hadn't been trying to eavesdrop). "We'll discuss this later." He eyed me sternly.

I harrumphed. "There's nothing to discuss. I'm not marrying you."

And like the society girl I tried to tell myself I was nothing like, I flounced away in a dramatic air of petulance and mounted Midnight without looking at Wolfe again. I kept seeing that smile he'd given me when I'd first approached him. It made me want to throw all my silly reasons out the window. I was such a befuddled mess. With no one to confide in without Haydyn, it seemed I was incapable of processing my emotions, sorting out the truths from the excuses. I smiled wearily at the Lieutenant as we set off through Raphizya.

Once Haydyn was administered the cure I could think about my feelings for Wolfe. Talk them over with her. I just needed time.

***

Wolfe wasn't as convinced. He clipped orders at me like I was one of his men and snapped at me when I dared to wander away from The Guard when we took our lunch break. My whole body felt wrecked with the tension between us, and my chest ached every time I saw that damnable hurt flickering in his eyes.

When we crossed the border into Sabithia and began making our way through Lumberland, I found my head thumping from overuse.

Despite my resolve to put aside my worries over Wolfe until we returned to Silvera, all the questions kept creeping back, mixed in with my anxiety over reaching Haydyn. I was still no closer to an answer when we came upon the village of WoodMill again. Wolfe sidled his horse next to Midnight.

"Lieutenant Chaeron, perhaps you can speak with Mr. Dena again about accommodation for Lady Rogan."

Chaeron grinned at Wolfe's pointed dismissal and trotted off ahead of The Guard, dismounting as Jac Dena came out of his factory to greet him. I felt tense as ever, my body longing to lean across the distance between Wolfe and I.

"Rogan," Wolfe said so softly I had to look at him.

Expecting to see pain and panic in his features I was surprised to see angry determination. I knew that look. Wolfe was ready to do anything to get what he wanted. I jerked back a little from him. "What?" I asked warily.

"Not marrying me… that means some time in the future you'll marry someone else. I'll marry someone else."

"I have no intention of marrying anyone, Wolfe. That's what I was trying to explain earlier."

He nodded, as if he was actually listening to what I was telling him. "But I'll marry, Rogan. I must, for the title. And I want a family. Could you stand to watch me marry someone else, Rogan?" His voice deepened. "Because I will."

Now I was the one panicking. A deep, ragged cut splicing my chest open. I thought how painful it had been when I'd suspected he'd bedded Winter. If he married, I'd have to go through that pain every single day. "Why are you doing this?" I trembled. "It's unkind."

Wolfe searched my face for a long moment and then he nodded. "You're right. I apologize. I just wanted to prepare you for the future."

Snapping his stallion's reins, Wolfe took off to meet up with Chaeron and Dena, leaving me on Midnight, hyperventilating at the thought of Wolfe with someone else. Mayhap he'd marry Winter.

I struggled to draw breath.

***

The Dena's were on their best behavior after their sons, Leon and Jac Jnr's, performances last time. It barely registered with me as I pushed my food around my plate, not able to eat under the heavy emotional weight I carried. It didn't help that Wolfe hadn't taken his eyes off me the entire meal. The Dena's had been surprised and happy to have Wolfe at the table this time rather than Chaeron, but I would have given anything for Chaeron's easy company, and was thankful when dinner was over and enough time had passed for it to be polite to retire to my room.

This time I slept in the extra bedroom by myself. Or tried to sleep. I sat huddled on the bed, my brain refusing to shut down as I went over and over Wolfe's warning.

What would Haydyn say? I worried my lip.

I shook my head, snorting out loud. Haydyn was a romantic. I knew exactly what she'd say. She'd tell me to throw off all my concerns. I held one palm out. On the one hand there was the pain I'd experience when I inevitably lost Wolfe. I held my right palm out. On the other, there was the pain I'd experience at having to watch him live his life with another woman, and watch him with the children he'd have down the years that wouldn't be mine.

"This is it, Rogan," I whispered at myself angrily. "You've managed to overcome the fact that he's the son of the man who killed your family but you can't overcome your own fears?" I was a coward. How could I be a coward after all I'd gone through? Yes, I had made mistakes. Yes, there had been moments during this entire rescue mission that I'd fumbled and hated myself for it. But I retrieved the plant. I escaped ruthless gypsies, dirty rookery thugs, a perverted mountain man, and saved L's life to boot. I'd even brought two star-crossed lovers together. I had faced a great deal in my life. How could I not find the courage to do the simplest thing of all…

… love Wolfe?

I loved Wolfe.

I *loved* Wolfe…

… *it be as simple as that*, I heard L's smirking, know-it-all voice in my head.

At the sound of the door handle rattling, I froze. When it rattled again I slid one leg out of the bed, thinking of the hunting knife I still carried in my pack. Just as my foot touched the cold wooden floor, the door opened and shut quickly, a familiar shadowed figure leaning against it.

"Wolfe?" I whispered, half relieved, half stunned.

The floorboards creaked as he tip-toed over to the bed, sliding in next to me without a by your leave.

"*Wolfe!*" I tried to act outraged but inside my heart was hammering, my body already tingling with anticipation.

His eyes sparkled in the light from the moon outside the window and he grinned at me, playfully yanking me under him. My cry of surprise was swallowed by his mouth.

Oh well, I thought. Hadn't I already decided? I smiled against his lips and kissed him back. When he took a breath, I eased a hand down his face, afraid to stop touching him. "What made you think I'd be amenable to you sneaking into my room?"

Wolfe shrugged, still grinning wickedly down at me. "I thought perhaps I'd finally gotten through to you. And... I don't know." He frowned now. "Something told me you wanted me here."

My lips parted in shocked realization. "Your magic? Can you read my mind now?"

He laughed against my cheek, shaking his head, his words whispering seductively against my ear, "No. Intuition again." He nibbled my earlobe and I shivered. "I gather, my intuition assumed correct. You want me here?"

I gasped under him as he deliberately tried to seduce an answer from me. With a growl of indignation I pushed his head back. "What do you think?" I replied huskily, pushing him onto his back, straddling him. "I'm not throwing you out am I."

***

Wolfe looked guilty as he leaned over me after our lovemaking. I frowned up at him and reached out to smooth his furrowed brow. "What?"

He exhaled slowly. "You might be carrying my child, Rogan. You *have* to marry me now."

I took more pleasure than I should have at the way he almost closed his eyes, his features wincing, waiting for the coming hysterics. But before Wolfe had even come into my room—intent on seducing me to his will, the scoundrel— I had decided I was going to marry him. I wanted a life with him, even at the risk of losing everything we would build together. I wasn't a coward. I could doubt myself and the choices I had made in this life, but deep down, I had always prided myself on the fact that I wasn't a weak-willed society girl. I wasn't a coward. Not yesterday. Not today. And definitely not tomorrow.

I nodded somberly up at Wolfe, teasing him. "I guess it does."

His eyes widened. "You mean it?"

I nodded, chuckling now. "Yes."

"You'll marry me?"

"Yes."

He cried out happily, pulling me into arms and I laughed, trying to shush him before he woke the Dena's and really created a scandal. "I don't care." He kissed me, his hand resting over my chest so my heart thumped against his palm. "You're mine now. I'm allowed to be here."

Wolfe relaxed into sleep easily now that I had agreed to marry him. My heart was still beating so hard, my brain still buzzing with all the things I now had to explain to Haydyn when she woke, that I watched over him, not able to close my eyes. Before the sun rose, I woke Wolfe and he reluctantly got out of bed and began dressing. He kissed me one more time, and then another time, and another... until eventually I laughed and pushed him towards the door. Just as he was about to leave I realized I hadn't told him something.

"Wolfe," I called out quietly.

He turned back expectantly.

I smiled, feeling a weight lift off my shoulders. "I love you."

At my quietly spoken declaration, Wolfe's eyes closed, relief softening his features, his whole face growing younger before my very eyes. I suddenly remembered he was only twenty one. A tension I hadn't even known was there visibly melted out of his body. Wolfe opened his eyes again and they were light with deep emotion. "I love you too. Have done ever since you punched Niall Tromskin on the nose for pushing Valena in the courtyard and making her cry."

My jaw dropped at the revelation. "I was fourteen!"

With one last warm chuckle Wolfe nodded and quickly left.

Chapter Thirty Two

With our love declared and our betrothal decided, Wolfe and I both galloped towards Silvera with renewed determination. There was nothing else worrying us now but the ever growing need to wake Haydyn up. I think Chaeron knew something had happened between me and Wolfe. To be fair I think the entire Guard knew, considering we stared at one another with loopy smiles on our faces.

Now all I wanted was for Haydyn to be well. If I saved her, and somehow managed to banish my nightmares of the Mountain Man, everything would be almost perfect.

I was glad when Wolfe found ways to stay the night with me. He was furious I was still having nightmares, and I feared at first it would cause a disagreement again, but instead he soothed me back to sleep with his presence. The nightmares didn't go away. I wasn't sure they would for a while, but at least when I woke up I wasn't alone. Wolfe snuck into my room at Mag's Inn in Sabith Town, and as he tiptoed in, his eyes so happy and mischievous he looked more boy than man, I wondered if we'd ever grow weary of one another. I also wondered about his other women but was too afraid to bring up the subject for fear of what it would do to my self-esteem. Wolfe had only ever had liaisons with beautiful women. Then again... he thought I was beautiful, and who was I to argue with that?

"You know," Wolfe mused as he pressed kisses over my stomach. "I think I'm starting to miss you arguing with me."

I huffed, grinning. "That can be easily remedied, Captain."

I felt him grin against my skin. "Mmm. I imagine it could." He looked up abruptly, frowning. "One thing I keep wondering about…"

"Mmm?"

"You've stopped objecting to being called Lady Rogan."

I nodded, stroking my fingers through his hair as he crawled up my body. He braced himself above me. "Perhaps I came to the conclusion that I am a lady, despite circumstances of birth."

"Finally." He rolled his eyes mockingly.

I laughed. "Just because you came to this realization before I did—"

"That's not why I insisted on calling you Lady Rogan," Wolfe interrupted.

I frowned. "Then why?"

Instead of answering he kissed me, his tongue stroking deep into my mouth, tangling with mine, trapping me in whatever spell he had me under. "I insisted on it," he breathed raggedly. "Because one day I knew you were going to be my wife, and I wanted you accustomed to being called Lady Rogan."

"You're lying," I replied breathlessly. "How could you possibly know I'd ever come to terms with everything between us?"

"I didn't have to know." Those aquamarine eyes blazed down at me, all masculine arrogance and determination. "I always get what I want, Rogan. Always."

"And what about what I want?"

Wolfe pressed a soft, tender kiss to my lips, the arrogance giving way to deep sincerity. "I'll always give you what you want, Rogan. Always."

***

We arrived in Silvera with a fierce burst of renewed energy. I galloped by Wolfe's side, Chaeron and the men at our backs as we tore through the city, through the marketplace, and out passed the palace to the cliffs. We ignored the cries of surprise and shock as we forced people from our paths. The Silverians watched in anxiety as we raced past them, their eyes troubled by our haste. The palace servants were even more surprised as Wolfe and I hurtled by them, having instructed Chaeron to stop with the Guard in the Palace Courtyard. We took off down a side entrance to the palace, out onto the rough trail that led us onto the Cliffside. Our horses, sensing our urgency, kept their footing and made the half hour journey to the Land's End Cottage in twenty, both of our horses' coats thick with sweat, and our own clothes were plastered to our skin.

I dismounted so fast I nearly fell, ignoring Wolfe calling out to me as I thrust the door to the cottage open, startling Rowan who stood in the hallway, a tray of sandwiches in her hands.

"Lady Rogan!" she gasped, her eyes alight with relief. "You've returned."

"Where is she?" I demanded, not giving to pleasantries.

"Upstairs." Rowan jerked the tray towards the narrow stairwell. "Valena is with—"

"Rogan!" Raj appeared in the doorway to the sitting room just as Wolfe appeared at my back. The healer hurried towards me. "You have it?"

I held up the pack. "I have it."

My heart was pounding hard as we hurried up the stairwell to the large bedroom Haydyn loved. It was the view. She loved a view. The wide window looked out over the Silver Sea, like a master painting created by nature. I hugged Valena as she threw herself at me, my hands stroking her hair affectionately, while my eyes drank in the sight of Haydyn.

I felt a raw choking burn in my throat at how pale and slight she looked lying on the bed, her moon-colored hair spread out on the pillow. "Oh haven," I choked. "She looks—"

"You're in time, Lady Rogan," Raj reassured me, removing the blue plant from the pack. He breathed a sigh of relief and then turned to us all. "I hate to ask it of you but I need time alone with the Princezna to do this. I'll require Valena's help of course."

I didn't want to leave. I felt that old stubbornness take hold of my legs, gluing them to the ground. It was only when Wolfe's arm came around me and was joined by another man's hand on my lower back that I realized Matai was there. I hadn't even seen him. I let them lead me out.

"Matai," I mumbled as I was taken downstairs in a daze. I was exhausted, like my body could just float up into the air and drift away on the wind.

In the sitting room Matai enveloped me in a tight hug. "Thank you, Rogan," he whispered in my ear, hoarsely, grief and worry and heartache soaking every word. "Thank you so much."

I gave him a watery smile and let Wolfe draw me into his arms. My head rested on his shoulder as we waited.

"We're betrothed." I heard Wolfe tell Matai. Clearly Matai was shocked by how intimate Wolfe and I were with one another.

"What?" Matai choked. "Dear haven, has the world gone topsy turvy?"

"Actually, yes," I replied, turning my head on Wolfe's chest to stare at Matai belligerently. "You should see it out there, Lord Matai. What a mess."

"It's not that bad," Wolfe insisted, rubbing his hand up and down my back.

I sniffed. "It's not that good, either."

Matai lowered himself into a chair. He looked exhausted. "Tell me all that happened."

And so that's what we did, to pass the horribly anxious wait we had while Raj hurried to save Haydyn's life.

***

I put it down to Haydyn's love for the dramatic that instead of Raj coming down to tell us she was cured, that a tousled blonde head peeped around the doorframe of the sitting room, followed by a stunning face suddenly blooming with color.

"HAYDYN!" I screeched like a little girl, pulling from Wolfe's embrace and rushing to meet my best friend, who squealed and crossed the room to meet me. As we shook in each other's arms, tears and snot mingling in our hysteria, no one would have guessed that the Princezna of Phaedra had only hours before been moments from death.

I pulled back, barely able to see her through my tears. "Look at you! Should you be out of bed?"

"Not really," Raj opined from the doorway, his eyebrows drawn together in consternation.

Haydyn shrugged, grinning widely. "I don't care. My body hurts from not being used but I feel so awake! I've been sleeping forever, Rogan, don't make me go back to bed."

I laughed and pulled her tight, afraid to ever let go of her again. "Don't ever do anything like that to me again."

She huffed against my shoulder. "It's not like I could help it. Oh, Rogan." She pulled back now, her eyes brimming with love. "How can I ever thank you for what you did for me? Raj explained everything. How you went all the way to Alvernia, into the mountains, for the cure. Rogan…"

I shrugged back at her. "You would have done it for me."

"In a heartbeat."

"Well it took a little longer than that but—"

"Can I perhaps…?" Matai suddenly appeared at our side, his eyes fixed to Haydyn as if he couldn't believe she was real.

Reluctantly I stood back and let the two lovers embrace. I raised an eyebrow at Wolfe when they kissed in front of Raj. Raj, for one didn't look surprised by the kiss.

"Ah… happily ever after." Valena sighed dreamily from the doorway.

Chapter Thirty Three

If I could have wished for anything in this life then I would have wished for Valena's words that day to be true. But unfortunately, life just doesn't always work out that way.

Haydyn and I had much to catch up on once we got back to the palace. The sight of Haydyn killed all the rumors and gossip that had spread across Sabithia and even into the neighboring provinces. Calm swam through the provinces like the tide flowing in at night. With the evocation stronger than ever, word began to reach the palace that Markiz Solom Rada had begun working on ridding Vasterya of the rookery as well as his little army he'd been building. It was too late, however. The Guard had been sent out to arrest the Markiz. He would be tried before the court of the Rada for treachery. Jarvis was furious, and left little doubt in my mind that the Markiz would be dismissed from the Rada and imprisoned.

I received a letter from Kir asking after me and confirming the rumors of Vasterya, and the worry in Pharya over the Markiz' arrest. He promised to keep me informed, my own little spy, while we dealt with the Markiz. As we wrote back and forth I was glad for his friendship again. He was unsurprised to learn of my betrothal to Wolfe, having discerned Wolfe's feelings for me during our time in the rookery. I grimaced at that. I really had been blind.

The Iavii were surprised, now that they were caught in the trap of the evocation, to find themselves agreeing to settle in a few acres of land on the northern border of Javinia. As for Tiger, Bird, Vrik and a few others, they were imprisoned in the palace jail for murder, theft and kidnapping. No one questioned it now that the Dyzvati reigned supreme again.

For her part, Haydyn was so busy over the next few weeks that we never found a moment to really talk. She was mostly in discussions with Ava and Jarvis. Although I hadn't gone into the details, I'd told Haydyn enough of what occurred on my quest for her to have questions and want answers. Moreover, I knew Jarvis was interested in conducting some kind of census to discover just how many mage were being born every year. The thought of magic truly returning to our world was sweeping Silvera with excitement.

In all that excitement it was easy for me and Haydyn to keep missing opportunities to really talk. Wolfe kept pushing me to just grab her and make her sit and listen to me, since my worrying was making him worry.

Finally, I took hold of my moment, leaving Jarek (who *was* surprised at my betrothal to Wolfe— a little skeptical even, but nonetheless happy for me, proving I was right when I suspected I was nothing but a mere flirtation to him) in the stables and hurrying to catch Haydyn as she left a meeting with Ava and Jarvis. I urged Haydyn to postpone a meeting with a dignitary from Alvernia to discuss the Autumn ball and 'close' relations with the Markiz Andrei

and the Princezna. Seeing how troubled I was, Haydyn agreed and
we headed to her suite, my palms sweating and my heart racing with
all I had to discuss.

Once we were seated, Haydyn took my hand in hers, her eyes
bright with remorse. "I haven't spent nearly enough time with you,
Rogan, and after all you've done—"

"Haydyn, don't—"

"We haven't even had time to discuss your betrothal to Captain
Wolfe. Wolfe, Rogan! You've barely given me any answers to how
that really came about. And none of that fluff about realizing how
you felt about one another." She grinned, her eyes bright. "I want the
luscious details."

So I told her. But not just about Wolfe. I told her everything that
had happened to me. She already knew some of it. About the Iavii
and the rookery. But this time I didn't leave out any details. I told
her about Alvernia. About the good people of Hill o' Hope. About
the Mountain Man. About L and the Moss family.

When I drew quiet, Haydyn promptly burst into tears. Guilt
crashed through me at having assailed her with such heavy
information all at once. I reached for her hand but she drew away.
"Don't. How can you even touch me after all you've been through
because of me? That man, Rogan… what he did to you…" She
shook her head, her eyes so full of anguish.

"Haydyn," I said sternly, easing down beside her and hugging her
close. "I didn't tell you to make you feel guilty. Nothing happened to
me that couldn't be dealt with. But I came to question things…

important things… about Phaedra. About the way we run things. For that, I need you."

She still looked pale and uneasy, guilt flickering in and out of her clear gaze. "Things? What things?"

I pulled back. "Didn't you hear what I told you? There are issues in your provinces, Haydyn, the evocation cannot fix."

Haydyn shook her head now. "Of course it can. The evocation stops anyone from doing anything that would hurt the peace in Phaedra."

I felt frustration prickle. "But what if something happened again to the evocation? We'd be left with a world that isn't properly governed."

"But that's what I'm trying to do." Haydyn stood up now. "I heard all this the first time around, Rogan. I understood. Believe me. The provinces have been left in the hands of the Rada who have relied upon the evocation for everything. Laws need to be instituted to protect people like that kind family you met in the mountains. And they will be. It will just take time." She drew breath. "In fact… I've decided to move the palace to Vasterya. I was just discussing it with Jarvis and Ava."

"What?" I asked, my mouth gaping open in shock.

"The province is central. From there my power will be absolute. It will even reach Alvernia. What happened to you need never happen to anyone again. But as I say, this will all take time. Patience, Rogan." She smiled.

For a moment I was taken aback by how determined and self-possessed Haydyn was. Then again, I had witnessed a change in her these last few weeks. She was taking charge with remarkable aplomb. The Sleeping Disease had changed her as much as I.

Still… I needed her to *understand*. "Perhaps once you've set up proper government, you might think about easing Phaedra out of the evocation?" I waited nervously for the answer.

Haydyn guffawed. "Are you jesting, Rogan?"

I frowned. "No."

"Why would I take away the evocation? It's my purpose in life."

"Your purpose in life is to reign over your people and take care of them. Make decisions that will better their lives. Not control them."

The edge in my voice was intentional but Haydyn heard it and flinched. "Control them?"

I sighed. I was doing this all wrong. "Not control them. That's not what I meant. I meant…" I searched the room, looking for the words. They landed on Haydyn's bed, where I'd kissed her temple weeks before, promising I'd wake her up. "We're all asleep under the evocation. We're not free to be truly ourselves. You more than anyone must understand the imprisonment of sleep, Haydyn. We're not prepared for what will happen when we wake up. We never will be unless we stop relying on the evocation."

Something happened to her as she stood before me. I saw her shoulders flick back, her spine lengthening as her chin jutted out. Her eyes were still kind, still loving, but they were determined. They were her own. "In sleep we don't get the choice between dreams and nightmares. With my evocation, Phaedra sleeps peacefully. Without it… it could be a waking nightmare. And why should we worry about there being no evocation. That's not going to happen. I won't let it. You won't."

"I wouldn't want anything to happen to you ever. And you're right— I will do anything to make sure nothing ever happens to you again. But surely we should prepare for the worst when we're talking about securing your people's futures."

"I am securing my people's futures. I will marry. I will have children. I will teach those children to use the evocation. After everything you've gone through, how can you tell me the evocation isn't worth it?"

I could feel myself losing my grip on this discussion, so I said the one thing I thought may penetrate, "It's dangerous to rely on this, Haydyn. You can't guarantee your children will be born with the evocation."

Haydyn flinched. "The Dyzvati reign has not been broken in all these centuries. I doubt it's going to end with me. But since you insist on being a pessimist, I'll remind you that the contingency plan, as you suggest, is to enforce the evocation with proper legislation and closer involvement in each of the provinces."

She was sure. There was no wavering self-doubt. This was a new Haydyn. She'd grown up. Finally.

I gave her a bittersweet smile. "I'm not going to convince you otherwise?"

My best friend shook her head firmly and then laughed softly at my expression, her eyes pleading with me to understand. "You wanted me to wake up, Rogan, and take control of my land. Well this is what I see now that I'm awake."

I sighed heavily. Haydyn was right of course. All these years all I had ever wanted was her to be the Princezna I knew she could be. I had just never realized that when she did, we'd see things differently from one another. Governing Phaedra, making the decisions for our people, had never been my journey. My journey had been saving the person who was destined for that… and in saving her, I saved myself.

I thought of Wolfe, the beginning of my new family, and it immediately made me think of Matai. "And Matai?" I asked, almost dreading her reply.

Sadness slid into Haydyn's features easily, a bright sheen casting over her eyes. "An alliance with Alvernia would be advantageous for everyone. It's difficult enough sticking my nose in on the Rada's business, but as the wife of the son of the Rada of Alvernia, it would be in my rights to do what I could for the land and its people. I could bring so much to your friend L and her family's life. But… if I marry Matai, a man of lower rank, then people will see it as a weakness. They'll know I married for love. They might think me frail and too feminine to rule them. I cannot afford to be seen as weak right now."

I felt a flush of anger, not only on Matai's behalf, but because I was terrified Haydyn would make the wrong choice and spend her life miserable because of it. I knew what it was to love now, and I didn't want her throwing that away. "I told you," I argued, "You have all the power. They're not going to object to anything you do."

Haydyn sat down slowly, leaning over to take my hand in hers, her eyes begging me to understand. "I need time to think on it. I'm still holding the ball. I'll make my decision then."

I remembered Wolfe's warning to me when I refused to marry him. "Matai won't wait forever, Haydyn."

She pulled back from me again, hurt in her beautiful and kind gaze. "You were the one who told me to make my own decisions. Now you're angry because you don't agree with them!"

I closed my eyes, my shoulders slumping in exasperation. Again... she was right. I glanced up at her through my lashes and nodded. "You are correct." I tried to shrug off my misgivings. Haydyn wasn't a little girl anymore. I had to let her make her own choices and believe she could cope with the consequences when they came. "I am glad you're making your own decisions. Our opinions may differ but... all that matters," I took her hand again, "is I have faith in you. I went to the ends of the world because of that faith. I'm not going to give up on it now."

She grinned back at me, relief thrumming visibly through her.

I squelched my fear at her glad smile. I'd just have to take every day as it came and hope the decisions she made were the kind that ended in her own happily ever after.

Epilogue

Although Haydyn's happily ever after was uncertain, I knew I was as close to mine as I would ever be as I sat beside Wolfe on the cliffs outside Land's End Cottage. After weeks of travelling, I wanted nothing more than a little bit of haven out here on the cliffs, away from everyone else. The quiet was wonderful. Back at the palace, Haydyn was arranging my wedding to Wolfe. It was to take place the first day of the Autumn Season and she was turning it into a lavish affair that made my head spin and my ears bleed. Wolfe had finally come to my rescue and absconded with me to the cliffs.

I sighed contentedly, snuggling into his side, loving the drizzle of sea spray that caught on the wind and kissed my cheeks. I knew I would have to deal with all the trappings that came with being a Vikomtesa: the large wedding, and getting to know the dowager Vikomtesa. Wolfe's mother was a bird of a woman, twittering at me nervously— her eyes asking how on earth the two of us had come to fall in love. She was gentle and kind but hated confrontation. I could see how easy it must have been for Syracen to hurt and abuse her. We were a different breed of woman, but for Wolfe's sake I would try to be a good daughter to her, try to befriend her— even if that meant discussing dress fittings, menus, and sheet music. I'd have plenty of time in which to get to know her better, as Wolfe had agreed to move into the new palace in Vasterya so I could still be close to Haydyn, but only under the condition that we didn't leave his mother behind in Silvera.

One bright spot in my busy social schedule was L. The two messengers I'd sent into the Alvernian Mountains (two of The Guard well equipped to deal with the harsh hills) had returned two days ago from their visit with the Moss family with a message from L. They had agreed to come to the wedding and spend a month of the fall with me here in Silvera. I couldn't believe it. I'd thought it would take blackmail to get L off that mountain of hers. I couldn't wait for Haydyn to meet her. I wouldn't push L to meet anyone else in society if she didn't want to. I knew what their reaction to her rough speech and unladylike ways would be, and she was too good a person to be subjected to that. But, deep down, I secretly hoped that after travelling through the provinces (in style—I was sending a carriage for them that would meet them at the bottom of the mountains) L and her family may come to like my world, and perhaps think of making a new life in Vasterya with me and Wolfe and Haydyn. I smiled inwardly. It was a bit of a fairytale, I knew. But I could hope. And if L and her family did decide to return to the Alvernian Mountains, then I'd make sure they were sent supplies every month, and perhaps have a larger home constructed for them. Wolfe had already told me to rein in my plans for the Moss' in case I overwhelmed them. But I wanted to overwhelm them. They'd saved my life.

"When does the Princezna plan to move us to Vasterya?" Wolfe asked quietly, stroking my back.

I shivered at his touch, still amazed that he had this effect on me. "As soon as the rookery is depleted and rebuilt as a civilized town. And she has architects overhauling one of the mansions in Pharya for her arrival. She'll no doubt live in the fanciest mansion we've ever seen until palace construction is completed."

"She seems strong," Wolfe assured me softly, as if he heard the concern that was in my heart, in my words. "In control. She appears to know what she's about."

"She is," I agreed quietly. She'd surprised me over and over these last weeks. "She really wants to make a difference after everything I told her."

Wolfe made a huffing noise. "Still annoyed she didn't take your advice?"

I slapped at him half-heartedly. And then after a minute I shook my head, leaning back on my palms, my fingers digging into the rich grass below us. I smiled into Wolfe's eyes, feeling lighter, lighter than I'd felt since lazy summer days by a brook in Vasterya. "No."

He exhaled heavily, reaching up to brush the hair off my face. "I'm glad. You set out to wake the Princezna up… and that's exactly what you did."

I grinned, proud and happy, reminding myself that this surreal feeling of contentment was actually real. Months ago I would never have imagined loving Wolfe, and how in doing so I was finally putting the past behind me, finally learning that by accepting my future I wasn't turning my back on my family's memory. Moreover, I'd changed. I'd grown up. Never would I have imagined becoming friends with Alvernian Mountain people, or thought I'd have the strength to accept what could and couldn't be changed, or finally come to terms with who I was as a person, and who life had shaped me to be.

"Better yet..."

"What?" Wolfe murmured, seeing the somewhat smug look in my eye.

"…I woke up too."

The End

ABOUT THE AUTHOR

New York Times and USA Today bestselling author, Samantha Young, is a 26 year old writer from Stirlingshire, Scotland. After graduating from the university of Edinburgh, Samantha returned to Stirlingshire where she happily spends her days writing about people she's keen for others to meet, and worlds she's dying for them to visit. Having written over ten young adult urban fantasy novels, Samantha took the big plunge into adult contemporary romance with her novel 'On Dublin Street'. 'On Dublin Street' is a #1 National Bestseller and has been re-published by NAL(Penguin US).

For more info on Samantha's adult fiction visit
http://www.ondublinstreet.com

For info on her young adult fiction visit www.samanthayoungbooks.com

53652029R00224

Made in the USA
Columbia, SC
18 March 2019